THE MAGNIFICENT MAGGIE

THE MAGNIFICENT MAGGIE

ROD MCFAIN

Mikalena Press

Cover Design by Danna Mathias Steele

2024 Mikalena Press

Published in the United States
By Mikalena Press

Paperback ISBN 979-8-98651-33-0-0

Printed in the United States of America

With Much Appreciation to my dear friends—Zelda and Clara

But Most of All—For Linda

Prologue

From the time she could walk, Maggie O'Sullivan was a trial, a challenge. She seemed predestined to live an untamed life. At twenty-two, she married well. In the following decades, she drew the public's zeal, and the tabloids couldn't get enough of her.

Her twinkling eyes exposed her curiosity and mischievous nature, her most striking peculiarity. Her heart-shaped face was sprinkled with freckles across her nose when she squinted in the sunlight. That was something she hated. Framed in curly bobbed hair, her countenance was radiant, even without a hint of makeup. When close to her, she had the scent of vanilla, or Channel #5, soothing and enjoyable.

A warm orange evening sky gave way to a night glowing in city lights. Lights so bright they blinded many of those flocking to Hollywood. The neon Marquee outside Grauman's Egyptian Theater flamboyantly ballyhooed The Wind Starring—Maggie Elliott.

An Arabian guard in full costume, including helmet and curved sword, paraded back and forth across the top of the tiled roof. A red carpet stretched from the door to the street.

Tuxedo and evening-gowned Hollywood elite emerged

from long black limousines. Reporters scribbled down notes detailing who was with whom. Flashbulbs popped. Some celebrities ducked and scurried through the crowd. Others stopped to talk to the press and be touched by fans.

With the opening of each car door, the throng of admirers chanted Maggie, Maggie. Every time, they were disappointed.

The movie's producer and its Swedish director, Victor Seastrom, paced across the outdoor courtyard, went back inside, and hurried up to Sid Grauman's private boxes.

The producer was beside himself. "Where is she?"

"You don't think she'd be a no-show?" Seastrom asked.

"She couldn't be that bold."

At seven fifty-two, a red convertible Kissel pulled up. Out she stepped, wearing a glittering Cleopatra cap and a low-cut silver gown.

The adoring throng roared. "Maggie, Maggie, Maggie."

She smiled and blew kisses while her husband helped dart her through the crowd.

Maybe she'd sign autographs after the film. Perhaps not.

The Egyptian seated almost eighteen hundred patrons, all on one level. There were six large windows in the rear wall, two of which were private boxes for Sid Grauman's guests. On either side of the auditorium were Singer's Boxes, used for the elaborate prologues Grauman was famous for staging before movie screenings.

Over the screen glowed the centerpiece, a massive stylized sunburst. Above the plasterwork columns framing the screen sat two organ chambers concealed from view. From there, the organs would flood melody into the auditorium via the sunburst grille.

The Elliotts slipped up the back stairs to the private boxes, sliding into their seats as the first scene came on the screen. One row in front, the film's director turned around. "Where have you been?"

"Oh Victor, I've been at home, getting all dolled up," Maggie said in her best Swedish accent to mock him.

"You were supposed to make an entrance. Interact with the fans. You should have been mingling."

"I'll mingle afterward. After I know they liked me. Now, be quiet. I want to see if I soar."

Before the final reel ended, Maggie stood up and pulled C.J. to his feet. "Come on, Elliott. I want to be in the lobby when people start to come out. I'll have autographs to sign. Don't you think so?"

Hollywood's biggest stars fawned over Maggie and called her brilliant. They invited her to their private parties. Told her they must work together. Maggie loved it.

***

Laying the paper in his wife's lap, C.J. Elliott smiled. "Read this."

Los Angeles Sentinel—The Wind Movie Review

The film's first and most apparent advantage is the presence of Maggie Elliott. An opera star and jazz singer, Elliott comes to the silver screen for only the second time and is now, assuredly, one of the greatest actresses of our era. She is impulsive, impetuous, and exciting. Move over Davies, Pickford, and Anna May.

Despite her glorious eyes, Elliott excels at portraying a virtuous girl thrust into a harsh world. The Wind allows her to put a sophisticated spin on Letty Mason, a rather plain character.

Letty is innocent and good, but Maggie Elliott shows Letty has her share of flaws. At the film's beginning, she is taken in by the superficial. Letting the story float alongside haunting imagery without interference, this fine young actress perfectly interprets the narrative.

The imperfections, Maggie Elliott adds, balance Letty and make her far more interesting than the usual virginal heroine. It makes her eventual journey to the brink of madness much more tragic and engrossing. This is a real person being driven insane. Maggie Elliott excels in controlled hysteria. Her horror is heart-rending because it is completely believable. Go see The Wind and be enthralled by— The Magnificent Maggie.

"I told you they'd like you," C.J. said.

"That's what you said, alright. I was so hoping you were right. I think I'd have been wrecked if they hadn't."

Embracing her, C.J. kissed her forehead and both cheeks. "You have what you've wanted. Are you happy?"

"I'm blissful. Or, I will be as soon as you tell me one thing." Playfully, she bit his lower lip, then his ear lobe, before whispering. "Did you like me? I mean, honestly, like me?"

Her tanned face turned up, her arms thrown out as if she meant to fly—she gazed into her husband's eyes. With her hair disheveled and her large green eyes peeking from the round wire-rimmed glasses she wore for reading, but never in public, she was a woman completely unafraid, despite the question she asked. Most remarkable, something in her being made her more than beautiful. She was mesmerizing.

Before answering, he sat on the overstuffed couch and pulled her beside him. "Of course. You were wonderful."

"Are you lying?" she asked, mischievousness in her voice.

He was not. She was brilliant, magnificent. But she always had been in his mind and heart—*from their very beginning.*

I

Chapter One

Their Beginning 1920

The first time he laid eyes on Maggie O'Sulllivan, the opinionated, shrewd, stubborn, enticing, and sassy Gaelic girl became his muse—his fancy. And, oh, what a looker: tall and willowy, she had soft red hair, beguiling eyes as green as the emerald isle itself, a warm skin tone, and a hint of a Donegal lilt in her voice. Today, feeling bold, he decided to tell her. At least the first part.

"Your muse?" Pulling her collar up and her black beret down over newly cut locks, she laughed at him.

"Yes," C.J. responded conceitedly. "Doesn't a Mount Holyoke senior understand what that is?"

"Of course I do. But, I'm quite astounded an Amherst boy does," Maggie said while eyeing the book in her arm, *The Seas of God.*

Happy to take her bait, C.J. scowled at the novel. "Scandalous."

"Remember what they say about Holyoke and Smith girls," Maggie said, increasing the swiftness of her gait.

C.J. rushed to catch up with her.

"Elliott," she said, calling him as she always did by his last name, "you should head home before this starts to stick."

Stick? The snow was hardly flurries. Still, arguing with this girl was pointless. He argued himself mindless, trying to make her stop using his last name. After three years, he remained Elliott. Surrendering to her, he muttered something about, "Saturday then?"

"Yes. And don't you dare be late."

As he turned to leave, she grabbed the back of his coat. "Elliott, aren't you going to smooch me goodbye?" He leaned down to kiss her divine lips until she tilted her face and tapped her cheek.

***

Grace Brown, in Maggie's opinion, was the perfect college roommate. Friendly, sweet, neat, and tidy, Grace never tried to sneak a boy into their room. She came from a close-knit, moneyed family in Bar Harbor, Maine, but early in their relationship, Maggie learned money was unimportant to Grace.

"Fun with the beau?"

Maggie tossed her coat and beret on her bed. Something Grace would never do. "Lovely." She sighed. "He said I'm his muse. What do you think of that?"

"Well, I suppose you should be flattered. Being someone's inspiration is flattering."

"Perhaps," Maggie said. She batted her long, auburn

eyelashes, almost black with mascara. The blue and gray cardigan she wore to keep her warm in class was at least a size too big. "Still, a muse seems like a rather thankless endeavor with little reward."

Sitting in front of her mirror, she brushed her hands through her bushy hair, redder at this length. "My folks aren't going to like this bob."

"Why'd you do it?"

"Why not? It's not their hair." Maggie shook her head, disheveling red shocks in every direction. She loved her wild locks and gave them one more tussle before hanging up her coat and putting the beret in a drawer, for Grace's benefit.

She flopped on her back and picked up her novel. She held the book out at arm's length while starting to laugh. "Elliot called *The Seas of God* scandalous."

"He's right. Being written by a Holyoke alum doesn't make it respectable." Grace chuckled.

"I asked him if he's aware of what they say about Holyoke and Smith girls," Maggie said, naughtiness in her voice.

"You mean Smith girls to bed, Holyoke girls to wed?"

"Oh, child, they only say it that way at Holyoke." Maggie hopped up, laughing. "Time to eat. Let's go. I'm famished."

Leaving their room and heading down the stairs, Maggie remained chatty. "I'm going out with Elliott Saturday night. Want to do something together?"

"I wish," Grace said, "but Bill has something planned. I think he's going to invite me for Christmas."

"Christmas? Christmas is next week. Isn't it a little late to ask you now?"

Grace smiled at Maggie. "I think he's hoping so."

Grace asked Maggie about C.J.'s Christmas intentions as they sashayed into the dining room, a formal affair for a college dormitory, complete with white tablecloths for evening meals.

"No idea. None." Maggie said, sounding disinterested. "I think everyone in his family is dead. Except for his mother. But they're alienated."

Grace suggested Maggie take Elliott home with her.

"With me?" Maggie squealed. "Three days and nights on a train together? My mother would fairly croak. My father, oh my, he would send Elliott to the gates of perdition." Maggie leaned close, patting Grace's arm. "Truth be told, I'm hoping the weather gets much worse, and I won't be able to go. Tulsa be damned."

A girl with curly blonde hair, a student from England whom everyone called Curls, asked if she might join them.

"'Tis a private conversation; be away with yourself," Maggie replied in her best Irish brogue.

Curls rolled her eyes. "O'Sullivan, you Micks are such a pain in the arse." She sat down with two other girls, who laughed at Maggie's behavior.

After four years of Maggie's rapid mood swings, Grace immediately picked up on them. She took a bite of her ham salad sandwich and sighed.

"What's wrong?"

Maggie hid her deeply secret thoughts from everyone—except Grace. "Grace," she said, pausing, glancing around the room, and turning back to Grace. "Do you ever think about how much our lives are about to change? One more semester, and we'll be on our own."

"You need to wed C.J. ahead of prohibition kicking in," Grace said. "If you wait, you won't have any champagne at your wedding."

Maggie peered at Grace across the top of her teacup. Blowing on the orange pekoe before taking two sips and declaring it too hot.

"Marry Elliott? He hasn't asked me."

"He will."

Marriage. Now, there was a commitment. Maggie wanted marriage and family, a brood to replace her dreadful one.

***

C.J.'s roommate and best friend, a New Yorker named Sam Taylor, loved golf and Scotch. Not much of a golfer himself, C.J. abhorred Scotch. Despite those differences, they got along, indulging most of their free time discussing girls, women, as Sam called them.

He complained since C.J. started spending all his time with this Maggie O'Sullivan, he turned boring. He lectured C.J. about how courting a woman without bedding her wasted a young man's virility.

For C.J., the weekend took forever to arrive. Maggie took over his every thought. Studying became a challenge. Around six Saturday evening, he swung his midnight blue 1918 Jeffery Touring Car with black fenders and window curtains to the curb in front of Brigham Hall.

He rushed up the stairs three at a time and went through the white entry doors. He smiled at a girl sitting in the reception area and announced he was calling for Miss O'Sullivan. The young woman wearing red lipstick, too bright red, in C.J.'s opinion, picked up the telephone and rang the third floor.

"Tell Maggie O her beau is here, in a lavender suit and purple tie." She turned back to C.J., "You must be tough," she teased, flashing a seductive smile.

"Enough to wear lavender," he said, shooting her his best John Barrymore smirk. The girl laughed. He hoped at his charm, not attire.

"Elliott! Where on earth is your overcoat?" Maggie came bouncing down the dark wooden stairs cocooned in a fur-collared maroon wrap, elongating her silhouette. The coat with a below-the-waist belt hovered past mid-calf, showing a bit of her charcoal skirt and side-buttoned, cream-colored Victorian ankle boots. She topped everything off with a black and tan cloche hat with a burgundy flower.

He smiled and wolf-whistled. Maggie bounced into his arms, getting a quick whirl and a peck on the cheek.

"Very striking," the lip-sticked girl said, offering a little mock applause.

Maggie curtsied. "We're going bowling."

C.J. shook his head. "Steaks at Bull Edwards and the premiere of The Cinema Murder."

At the restaurant, he ordered oysters as appetizers without consulting Maggie. She chased hers with two swallows of his dark beer.

"I wonder if the ban on drinking will hurt oyster sales?" Maggie asked before sliding another out of its shell and into her mouth.

"Sam's acquainted with a fella in New York with a fourteen-year gin supply," he said, helping himself to the last oyster. "He says the man wants us as 'distributors.' There'd be a lot of money."

Maggie's Irish eyes were not smiling.

"So, you plan to become a bootlegger?"

Her ire baffled him.

"I don't believe I care for your roommate. I've been around bootleggers. Oklahoma has some dry counties."

In an awkward spot, his instinct told him he better change the topic—quick.

"I'm not going to be a bootlegger. Or a rum runner." His face flushing, he fiddled at the knot of his tie. "I was kidding."

"Bloody hell, you were."

Bloody hell? C.J. thought that an English term, not Irish.

"I was joking."

Maggie took a sip of her wine.

"This is bitter."

C.J. waved a waiter over and asked for a sweeter vintage. A time for discretion, not explanations, he sat in silence and stopped making eye contact. Dinner arrived right before the wine.

Maggie found the new selection pleasing and her meal delightful. C.J. assumed her content with his denial regarding rum-running and gin distribution because she dropped the matter. Dropping matters was not her usual way.

Snow was falling when they pulled up at the movie theater, so he let Maggie out at the front door and parked the car. Once inside, he brushed the moisture off his suit and wondered why he didn't wear an overcoat. "Last time I'll forego sensibility for vanity," he said to himself.

They bought chocolate-covered caramels and hot cider for treats before finding seats as the silent newsreel started.

When Marion Davies finally appeared on the screen in The Cinema Murder, Maggie laid her head on his shoulder.

"She's utterly shameful," Maggie said, snuggling up to him.

II

Chapter Two

The severe snowstorms Maggie hoped for never came, and she ended up on a train to Tulsa. Despite the promises railroad brochures made of dreamy sleeper cars, carpeted floors, and excellent meals, riding the rails bored Maggie. The holidays in Tulsa would bore her more.

Christmas day wouldn't be so bad. Family was bearable for one day, even uncles. But two weeks of Uncle Paddy and his horrible wife coming over, cousins pestering her to spend time with them, and high school classmates, always the ones she didn't like, dropping around would be too much.

Worse yet, Elliott announced his intentions to stay at Amherst for the entire holiday break. He'd leave for Christmas dinner with Sam's parents in New York and return to campus. At least a dozen girls were staying at Holyoke. No telling how many of them Elliott was acquainted with—or would be.

A gale blew her hat off when she stepped off the train. Her

brother chased the bucket hat down the platform. Before she said hello, Pop lifted her off the ground and hollered.

"Welcome home, Lassie."

Reluctantly, she hugged back. He'd change his tune soon enough.

Her mother smothered both her cheeks with kisses. Uncle Paddy planted an enormous kiss—right on her mouth.

After Tommy returned, she nudged his head down and whispered into his ear.

"If Paddy ever does that again, I'll be wanting you to break his bloody jaw. The manky old goat." The visit did not improve.

****

When Maggie's train pulled in, newspapers burst with coverage of the Palmer Raids.

3,000 ARRESTED IN NATIONWIDE ROUND-UP OF REDS

The Globe reported over fifty arrests in Boston and seven hundred in Massachusetts, with many women among the detainees.

C.J. rushed up. He was dashing in the herringbone news-boy cap she gave him for Christmas. "Oh, Elliott, I missed you." She threw her arms around his neck. "I've been so bored." They picked up her luggage, and he sped his touring car toward Mount Holyoke.

"What do you think of these Palmer raids?" Maggie asked before tossing the paper on the floorboard. Elliott was politically active, so she knew he'd be pleased she asked.

"Thirty-five cities. Biggest in US history," he said. "Cops

went in swinging nightsticks and blackjacks. Lots of heads cracked."

Maggie breathed on the window and drew a heart in the condensation. "I suppose anarchists and communists need their skulls busted for blowing things up."

For a moment, C.J. teetered on the edge of a total political rant. Then, noticing the heart Maggie had drawn, ranting seemed silly.

C.J. glanced at Maggie. "Are you hungry?"

"I'm famished. I'd kill for a bowl of clam chowder." Maggie threw her head back and arms out, hitting Elliott on the side of his face. "I'm *sooo* glad to be home."

"The Shack is the perfect place," he said. "It's a dive, but the chowder is wonderful, and they serve enormous bowls."

"A dive. I love dives! I hope this one is devilishly wicked."

Joe's Shack House was a dive. But not too wicked. They served clam chowder, nothing else, to ship and dock workers too worn out to be scandalous. The diner smelled of clams and beer. Maggie and Elliott found a corner table right after she told every single person how delightful she perceived their company. The chowder came with hard rolls. She ate three, washing them down with two lagers.

"You won't be able to drink a Pabst a week from now."

Maggie sarcastically laughed, raising her glass in a toast to the whole place. "To prohibition! Goodbye immorality, crime, and outrageous living." With a broad smile and two great gulps, she drained her glass. "Ahh, fill it again."

***

A few miles down the road, Maggie was sound asleep and drooling.

Her head tilted across the back of the seat and snoring, C.J. still found her adorable. Thirty minutes later, he stopped to knock snow and slush out of his windshield wipers for the third time. After he got back in the car, wet and cold, Maggie asked him how long the storm had been raging. "Around two hours. We're making terrible time."

"Where are we?"

"Massachusetts. I hope. Maybe Canada."

They hadn't yet made the town of Palmer. The traveling was slow. Slow enough to take another hour before they'd arrive at Holyoke.

After parking in front of Brigham Hall, C.J. slid out from behind the steering wheel and opened his arms for Maggie to squeeze into. He leaned down until they were face to face. He put his mouth on hers. For a long time, his lips and tongue explored hers. He stopped and pulled his face away. He could feel Maggie's heart beating faster. He slipped his hand under her coat, sweater, and blouse across her stomach.

"If you want me to stop, tell me."

Maggie said nothing. Her eyes closed as she sought his lips. He kissed her softly, cautiously, but she wanted more. She entangled her fingers in his hair, pulling him harder against her. His arms circled her. They became tangled together, still kissing.

"I love you," Maggie whispered. It wasn't the first time she said it. But it was the first time she said it as he touched her bare skin.

***

When he got back to his room, Sam asked him why he was so late. Was he implying something? C.J.'s face turned red with anger as Sam's implication hung in the air like an accusation. He leaned forward, poking a finger in Sam's direction. His eyes narrowing into fiery slits, he delivered every word deliberately through gritted teeth. "Stick your head outside that window," he seethed, emphasizing each syllable for maximum impact. "And while it's out there, consider being careful what you say." C.J. tossed his coat and cap into a chair before sitting at his desk. He picked up the newspaper and turned to the stocks section. "I'm going to be rich," he said.

"You already are."

"Well, I'm going to be richer." He folded and pitched the paper at the waste can. "Bucket," he said, holding both arms up. "I'm going down to the vending machine. You want anything?"

"Cracker Jacks."

No Cracker Jacks, so C.J. brought him peanuts, which Sam grumbled about, saying he wanted something sweet. "Go down yourself," C.J. said.

Too lazy to go, Sam ate the peanuts. He started talking about how, while in New York, he spoke to the man with gin, 14,000 gallons, or fourteen years' worth, one or the other. He said a job waited for them as delivery men making a lot of money.

"Not interested," C.J. said, flabbergasting his roommate. "Volstead, remember?"

Sam jumped to his feet. Back and forth, he paced. "When did you become so virtuous?"

C.J. didn't answer or bother looking at him. When Sam began yelling and swearing at him, he still ignored him. Once

Sam stopped ranting, he told him to "Go ahead, be a gin runner. Nobody is stopping you."

"Why are you carrying a torch for that suffragette?" Sam steamed into a renewed rant. "You're uxorious! And you're not married to her, you patsy."

"What's uxorious?"

Sam glared at him. "Henpecked, you damn moron."

"Why didn't you say that?"

With the entire conversation now pointless, he flopped on his bed and rolled the other way. Sam switched the light off.

Fifteen minutes later, irritated with his roommate's muttering, C.J. turned back over. "What are you mumbling about?"

"My New York acquaintance doesn't like being let down."

III

Chapter Three

C.J. didn't see Maggie again until the weekend. He got to South Hadley an hour before time to pick her up. He needed the time to meet with her roommate. Grace arrived late to the empty little ice cream shop, deserted because of the below-zero temperature outside with a biting wind. He handed her a small box. She glanced inside at Maggie's sapphire ring. The one she had given him to get the size right.

"Did everything work out?" she asked.

"Perfectly," he said. Self-satisfied, he flashed his dreamy smile.

"Let me see the one you picked out," she begged, leaning toward him.

He wagged his finger. "You have to hold your horses until after Maggie sees it." He hoped she wouldn't push him. He didn't trust his willpower. He couldn't wait for someone to ooh and ahh.

"You're a romantic one, you are." Grace scrunched her nose and winked at him. "They have hot cider. Want a quick sip before you pick up Maggie?"

"Absolutely, I love spicy cider."

"Spicy girls, too," Grace laughed.

C.J. asked her if she needed a ride back.

"Billy Boy is picking me up. He's taking me to the Amherst basketball game. He's not as passionate as you."

C.J. fidgeted and waited for Grace's boyfriend to arrive prior to rushing off to Maggie. "You don't have to wait," Grace said. "Go ahead, I'm fine."

As he started to leave, Grace chuckled. "I hope Maggie O says yes. You never can tell about her."

C.J. stopped—abruptly. He spun back toward Grace.

Grace's face lit up like one of those new neon signs. She entirely abandoned her body to merriment. Laughing, she put her arms around C.J. and her face against his. "I wish Maggie O could have seen the look on your face." She gave him a quick squeeze. "Oh, don't worry, my darling boy. She'll say yes."

The same girl sitting at the front desk the evening he wore the lavender suit sat there again, this time without the bright red lipstick.

"Where's your purple suit?"

"Lavender," he said.

She picked up the phone and rang the third floor. "Tell Maggie O her beau is here; he looks more respectable this time."

Maggie looked him up and down and up and down again. He loved her being so dramatic.

"Charcoal gray suit, white shirt, black tie. Boring." She stepped close to his face. "How do you like my eyes?"

She batted them theatrically to show off the dark kohl eyeliner and blue eye shadow.

"You look like a floozy."

"Excellent. Perfect. Take me someplace I can floozy."

He gazed at his girl. "God, help me," he said, flashing her a smile.

He excused himself at an exclusive, romantic restaurant, not a place for a lavender suit, leaving Maggie fumbling with her purse and sipping water as if dehydrated.

On his way back, he stepped into a shadowy corner to moon over Maggie. In a room full of beautiful women, none compared to Maggie O'Sullivan.

He liked everything about her: the way the string of pearls hung around her throat, the softness of her almost red hair, her beaded Cleopatra cap, the way she smiled at people when they passed by the table. Let Sam make fun of him. He was in love with the girl.

"I thought you abandoned me. Where were you?"

He grinned. In a sudden burst of honesty, he admitted hiding in a dark alcove, watching her. He relished his confession embarrassing her.

The tuxedo-clad waiter who said he would serve them asked if they'd like drinks, apologizing about the poor selection with the ban on liquor sales beginning in a couple of days. They each ordered a martini, C.J. asking for gin with two olives. "Well, cheers," he said as they tapped their glasses together.

"Last chance to ply me with alcohol."

His duck was perfect, but the only thing important to him was Maggie loving her lamb adorned with mint chimichurri.

A few minutes after they finished dinner, the waiter returned with a dish under a silver serving dome. "Your dessert, ma'am," he said, setting the plate in front of her. Beneath the top, Maggie found a little blue velvet box—the kind rings come in. Her mouth dropped. She covered her face. Tears were welling up in her eyes. Her breathing stopped. Her hands were trembling. It was all C.J. could do not to grab the box and open it. Maggie O'Sullivan was not the only one struggling to breathe. "You better look inside."

"Elliott!" She gasped. A two-carat marquise diamond, sitting in a split shank embedded with round diamonds, glittered up at her.

He came to her side and knelt on one knee.

"Miss O'Sullivan, Miss Maggie Kathryn O'Sullivan, will you marry me?"

He wasn't sure if she said yes or said anything. Either way, she had her arms around him and her tongue in his mouth. He took her tongue for affirmation.

He couldn't talk her into waiting in the doorway while he got the automobile. Not that he tried much. He embraced her at the car, and they swayed back and forth, unmindful of the wet snow falling. He squeezed and kissed her and asked her to pick a wedding date.

"Tonight," she said. Leaning close, she tugged his shirt free from his trousers and slid her hands over his bare back. "I want to marry you tonight. I want you to explore me, to know me as no one has ever known me."

Kissing the nape of his neck, she held him tighter. "How did you fall in love with me?

He separated from her enough to look into her eyes.

"How did I fall in love? With you? Drinking ginger ale and eating cheesecake in the middle of the night. Sharing a look or a moment and wanting a night together." He chuckled, not much, only a little. "You played the game well. Keeping my interest and your innocence. All with that same smile."

"Marry me tonight."

"We don't have a license."

Maggie giggled at his virtuousness—or his naïveté.

After getting in the car, he again took her into his arms. Holding her flooded him with emotions. He couldn't imagine making love to her. He loosened his embrace. She said she wanted to stare at the ring.

"Elliott, this is gorgeous."

"Not as beautiful as you." *How cliché.*

Maggie sensed his embarrassment. Her eyes brightened; her mouth widened into a grin.

"You are a silver-tongued devil." She laughed, giving him a quick kiss on the lips before a question burst into her mind. "How did you know my ring size?"

"Well..." he tried to think fast. He failed. The truth became his only option. "I didn't."

"So, just lucky?" She gave his tie a little tug.

"I might have had a little help," he said.

Maggie threw her arms around him and leaned forward until their noses touched. Another peck. "What kind of help? A co-conspirator?"

He couldn't keep from laughing a little. "Grace," he said.

"She snuck me your sapphire ring. I returned it this afternoon. We were very clandestine, he said with a wink and a smile."

Maggie bit her bottom lip. Then her eyes widened, and she smiled. It was that naughty little grin C.J. loved. Two more quick pecks on the lips before she insisted they go to the Amherst basketball game. She wanted to hunt down the co-conspirator and show her the *fruit of their deception.*

He put the car in gear. "Since we're engaged, are you going to stop calling me by my last name?"

"Of course not, don't be silly."

***

The fourth quarter was half over when they arrived. With Amherst way behind, finding Grace and her boyfriend in the shrinking by-the-minute crowd was easy. Grace went crazy at the sight of the ring. C.J. extended his hand to Grace's beau, "C.J. Elliott."

"Bill Byrd. I'm acquainted with Sam Taylor. We have a mutual friend in New York. Arnold Rothstein."

Maggie and Grace looked surprised—and not happy.

Amherst missed a shot, got their rebound, and tossed up a brick. Grace needed to powder her nose; Maggie, of course, went along. As soon as they left the gym, Grace stopped and took Maggie by the arm with complete shock on her face. "Damn. Arnold Rothstein?"

"I'll bet he's the one Elliott's roommate, Sam, has been talking to about bootlegging," Maggie said, her eyebrows drawn together and her lips pursed.

"What the hell have we gotten ourselves into?" Grace asked.

Grimacing, Maggie shook her head.

When the girls returned, C.J. did not hesitate to get Maggie alone. Settled in the car, he began explaining. "Maggie, I don't know Rothstein. I swear, I don't."

"He's the guy who wants Sam to deliver liquor. Don't lie." Maggie spat, hugging the door, not C.J.

"He's never told me the guy's name. But I suppose so," he conceded, touching Maggie's arm. At first, he thought she might pull away. Instead, she glared at him. Glared hard enough he removed his hand and scooted a little further away.

"Don't you get involved in something foolish."

Her face relaxed, and her voice softened. Sliding closer, she put her arms around his neck and her head on his shoulder.

"I think your roommate is heading for trouble. Don't let him take you with him."

"Nothing foolish. I promise. I rejected him. Turned him down flat."

"Tell me everything about your family. I've never been able to get much out of you. I know they're all dead, except your mother, but how did you get so rich? "

"No gangsters." He laughed, wanting to change the subject. "Not one racketeer or numbers runner." For emphasis, he crossed his heart.

"So, how did you get wealthy?"

"My dad died before my grandfather. Grandad had no other children or grandchildren. So, he left his fortune to me. I'm the only one still kicking."

She snugged her coat up and pulled the Laidlaw motor robe tight. "I want the entire story."

All was lost. It was a matter of where to start.

"Fine. Grandfather came from Pennsylvania. He began as a telegrapher, became a bond salesman, moved into railroads, banking, real estate, and the steel industry. I guess he had the Midas touch."

Maggie nodded. "Keep going."

"He was an abolitionist who supported Booker T. Washington." Maggie smiled. "His reputation suffered, along with men like Henry Clay Frick, Philander Chase Cox, and Andrew Carnegie because they belonged to the South Fork Fishing and Hunting Club."

He pulled a silver flask from his coat and started to remove the cap but didn't. "Some people blamed the members for the Johnstown Flood. When the court acquitted them, Grandfather sold his steel interests and moved to Boston. He became involved in shipbuilding before dying. He left his businesses and his money to me. That's it."

"What about your mother? Why are you so estranged?"

C.J. tried to stop it. But his mind went back in time.

The room was a dull white. Everything was white except his mother's washed-out, sickly green gown. The place was depressing.

Even in sad hospital rooms, mothers, including sick ones, should comfort scared sons, not tell them they want to die. She told him on a Wednesday. Wednesday, October 5, 1910. The day their relationship shattered. She meant nothing. He was alone, perhaps scarred forever.

"We don't speak. When I was twelve, she got ill. She said being dead would be better than her life. As far as I'm concerned, she is."

He tugged the motor robe over his lap and chest.

"How long was she unwell?"

"About sixteen days. In the hospital eleven."

Maggie's expression softened. "I know how traumatic it

is to be cared so little about by your mother." She paused, looked away, and back at her fiancé. "Show a little chivalry."

Later, when she kissed him goodnight, she whispered, "I love the ring and you."

He promised no gangsters.

IV

Chapter Four

Grace sat brushing her hair when Maggie swept in, throwing her arms around her and rejoicing over being engaged. Within moments, every resident from the third floor of Brigham Hall crowded into their room wide-eyed and swooning over the ring.

The Brit with the too-curly blonde locks brought a bottle of gin hiding in her closet. Each girl raised a glass in a toast.

"My, but you look flushed. Dear Maggie, what have you been doing?" one classmate from Alabama asked in her southern drawl while waving her hand in front of her face.

"Why spooning, of course," another girl laughed.

Another breathed heavily, sighing, "Oh, Elliott, Elliott."

Maggie batted her eyes, squinched her lips, and blew kisses. "A little of this, a little of that," she chirped, dropping a King Oliver record on the Victrola, and the party plunged into full swing. Until two girls from upstairs came down and told them to shut up.

Quiet again, Maggie wrote to her brother, telling him about her engagement.

Dear Tommy,

I've been naughty, not writing often enough. It's been over two months since I received your fine, long letter. I'll try to do better. Grace says to send you her love. She can't wait to see you at the wedding.

Yes, I have been asked. I even have the engagement diamond. It is grand. All the girls are jealous. I would describe it, but you wouldn't grasp what I was talking about. You don't know what a diamond-studded split shaft is, do you?

Elliot's proposal was magnificent. He had the ring delivered as dessert under a silver dome. He was so romantic, dropping to one knee. I grabbed him in both arms and kissed him. I believe I stuck my tongue halfway down his throat. I am such a vamp.

How can I make the days go faster until the wedding? I'm sure our father will burst when he finds out I want to be married in South Hadley. I'll make Elliott pick you as his best man or grooms-man, at the least. I can't wait to see you. It will be lovely. Must go to bed now. Yes, silly, alone.

Lovingly,

Mags

V

Chapter Five

Prohibition went into effect. Winter ended. Grace broke up with Billy Boy. C.J. argued with Sam over Arnold Rothstein, who was accused of fixing the 1919 World Series.

To Maggie's delight—and irritation—the Boston Fadette Orchestra accepted her as a cellist, leading to C.J.'s enduring a few extra lectures on women's rights. Otherwise, life remained ordinary.

To C.J.'s liking, Grace, the soon-to-be maid-of-honor, accompanied them to the station to meet Maggie's folks. C.J. never asked Maggie's father for her hand. He didn't think the man would berate him for his social failure in front of Grace.

Half of New England seemed to de-board before her parents. Maggie waved at them until her mother saw her. Her father struggled along with an oversized suitcase under each arm.

"Go help him," Grace said, jabbing C.J. in the ribs.

C. J. scurried across the platform, dodging passengers. Howard O'Sullivan was short and bald. He had a round red face with dead features and cold gray eyes.

"Mr. O'Sullivan? C.J. Elliott. Let me take those from you, sir."

"They're heavy. Mrs. O'Sullivan does not travel light. Where are the porters? We have porters in Tulsa."

The luggage was weighty enough C.J. regretted having parked two blocks from the depot. Leaving C.J. lugging both bags, Mr. O'Sullivan jogged ahead to grab his daughter. As always, he picked her up and gave her a spin. This time, he did not call her Lassie.

"I thought I told you to let your hair grow." And there it was. Nothing ever changed; her father still aimed to dictate her life.

"I like my curly bob. All types of bobs are most stylish," Maggie said.

Her mother, interceding, avoided a blowup. "Oh, leave the child alone. She's young."

Putting her hand on Grace's back, Maggie nudged her toward her parents. "This is Grace, my roommate and best friend."

"She doesn't have one of those butchered haircuts," Mr. O'Sullivan growled.

"Because a bob would call attention to my mouth. My mouth is so kissable it gets me in trouble," Grace said, giving Maggie's father a quick squeeze. Neither the comment nor the hug was well received by Mr. O'Sullivan. He disapproved of such boldness in a female.

C.J. set the bags on the ground next to Maggie.

Taking him by the hand, Maggie pulled him over in front of her mother. "Mother, this is Elliott, my fiancé."

"You are quite handsome," Mrs. O'Sullivan said, smiling and extending her hand.

"Elliott's the bee's knees." Maggie gave him a peck on the cheek. "And he's scholarly. He's going to be a novelist, write the Great American novel."

Her father interrupted. "Can we get on our way? We've had a long trip, and we're hungry. As well as anxious to settle into our hotel."

Maggie's expression soured. Nothing ever changed with her father. He was self-centered and would never be anything else. She turned away from him. She was done with the man.

C.J. picked up both suitcases. "The car is about two blocks away."

"I hope we can all fit with all this luggage," Mr. O'Sullivan said.

"We can put the bags in the rumble seat."

During the entire drive to the Franklin Café, Mr. O'Sullivan complained about South Hadley. He didn't like this, didn't like that. In the eatery, his complaining didn't stop. He would never understand why he allowed his daughter to go to school in such a place.

"Because Holyoke is one of the finest schools in the country," Grace said. "Our music program earned Maggie a chair in the Boston Women's Symphony." Oops, the cat was out of the bag. "If she accepts." Grace's face tightened as she glanced at Maggie. "Sorry," she whispered, squinting her eyes.

"I planned to tell you this afternoon," Maggie said to her father. "Well, you don't need to have a stroke," she added when his veins started bursting out of his neck. "I'm a New Englander."

To avert a public catastrophe, C.J. attempted to appeal to a father's pride. "Mr. O'Sullivan, Maggie being offered a chair in the Boston Women's Symphony is very prestigious. Boston Women's is America's premier women's symphony. "Maggie is an accomplished musician. You should be proud of her." Appealing to the man's ego didn't appear to be working

It was pointless trying to avoid the confrontation. Maggie decided to make it clear she wasn't backing down.

"I'm not going back to Oklahoma, Father. My place is here in New England."

"Your home, young lady, is with your family. In Tulsa."

"Howard, we can discuss this later," Maggie's mother said.

Much to Maggie's surprise, with lunch's arrival, her father let the matter drop—for the time being. Her mother raved about the scrumptious lunch; her father growled, "Numerous Tulsa restaurants are better." Maggie fidgeted with her fork and tightened her frowning lips. C.J. and everyone else kept quiet.

Weary of the uncomfortable silence, Maggie announced Grace, their class president, would give their valedictorian speech. "Grace is brilliant."

Mrs. O'Sullivan called Grace *Dear* and asked her about the topic of her graduation address.

"The Road of the Loving Heart. I'm wildly nervous," Grace said. "I'm sure Maggie has told you she'll be performing *The Vamp* on her cello."

Maggie shrugged.

Grace nearly swooned. She put her forearm to her forehead.

"Don't be modest. Jazz on the cello is innovative genius. No one else is playing an instrument during the ceremony."

"How many of your classmates have one of those haircuts?" Maggie's father asked, returning to the matter of her hair. Maggie's face wilted.

She sounded defeated. "None. I'm the only one." Pushing her slice of rich chocolate cake away, her motions slow and deliberate, she folded her green napkin with great care before tossing the thing over her dessert.

"You're the only one because no one wants to look so hideous," he spat out venomously. The cruelty in his words pierced through Maggie's heart, leaving her utterly crushed. Her father's face contorted with disgust as he glared at his wife and daughter.

Maggie slumped in her chair. A slight breeze from the open window at the end of their table drifted gray smoke from her father's cigarette into her eyes. At least she had an excuse to dab at her eyes.

C.J., more than familiar with unloving parents who cared nothing about their child's feelings, interceeded. *About time*, thought Grace.

"Who cares how many others bob their hair?" He was not asking a question; he was issuing a challenge.

Mr. O'Sullivan's spun toward C.J. Maggie's fiance did not budge. Not one bit. Maggie threw her arm across his chest, preventing him from standing.

"Stop." Glaring at her father, she was close to crying, her hand shaking against C.J.'s breast.

Howard O'Sullivan's glare shot back to Maggie. "I won't

be quiet. You will not be living in Boston, young lady. As for a marriage, the matter is undecided."

Maggie's sass, temper, and willpower erupted. Elliott vividly remembered the firey eyes the night Maggie glared at him about bootlegging. Those eyes flashing under her auburn hair were where her power lived.

"Undecided? Undecided?"

This was the high-spirited girl, the one C.J. loved.

Rising from her chair, Maggie's voice also elevated. "I'll marry whomever I please." She pointed her finger straight at her father. "Whoever, the hell I want." Before anyone responded, Maggie headed for the door.

C.J. stood and fumbled for his wallet. He tossed out fifteen dollars and mumbled about waiting outside.

Maggie, leaning on the front fender, shook with fury. "That man!"

C.J. held his hands up. "Don't glare at me."

"Now, do you understand why I don't want to be married in Tulsa?"

C.J. wrapped his arms around her. The embrace quieted her—a little.

"How will I put up with this for an entire week?"

After the O'Sullivans and Grace got to the car, an ugly argument between Maggie's parents intensified. Mrs. O'Sullivan, for once on her daughter's side, was still upset by something her husband must have said before they left the café, informed him Maggie was their only daughter. She followed with Maggie being an accomplished young woman, listing all her achievements: full music scholarship to a prestigious school, President of the Mount Holyoke Suffrage Society,

Phi Beta Kappa, Glee Club, and on and on. Mrs. O'Sullivan sought testimony from Grace as to Maggie's virtues.

"She's graduating a virgin." That shut everyone up...for a moment.

Even coming from Grace, the statement was a mighty shock to Maggie. It could not be drowned out. The only distraction was the cold, tingling numbness spreading across her forehead, her cheeks, and into her mouth. She couldn't speak because the muscles in her jaw were paralyzed. If she could talk, she wouldn't know what to say.

Unfortunately, her father could. "You are a vulgar young woman. I'd be ashamed if you were my daughter.

Unfazed, Grace tilted her head to the side and shrugged. "As would I."

"Maggie booked you a room at the College Inn," C.J. finally said, struggling not to laugh as he pulled away from the curb.

"It's a charming colonial house remodeled with new furniture," Grace said while losing her endeavor not to chuckle. Maggie's roommate didn't care one way or the other how Maggie's father would respond. She considered him nothing special. As far as she was concerned, being around the man was like standing in a freezing rain—in your underwear.

The Inn was lovely. C.J. tugged the luggage up the front steps to the second level and the O'Sullivan's room. Mr. O'Sullivan did not help. When he returned to the hallway, C.J. watched Maggie go into the room with her parents, where she gave her mother a brief embrace and glancing peck on the cheek. Her father received no hug or goodbye.

Maggie got in the car and scooted close to C.J. "My dear father is the east end of a westbound horse."

C.J. held his silence, but Grace agreed. He dropped the girls off at Brigham Hall. He had about two hours to drive to Amherst, shower, change clothes, find some prohibited booze, and go back to the Class of 1920 Mount Holyoke Graduation Party.

***

Like the dependable roommate, Sam had three quarts of alcohol, two vodkas, and one gin waiting for him. He also had a clay jug of what he called "moonshine, the authentic thing." C.J. pulled the cork and took a hefty swig. The clear, tasteless liquid lit his tongue ablaze, burned his throat, exploded in his belly, bloodshot his eyes, and set off a hacking fit.

"Best dilute the stuff before you pour the ladies any," Sam said, laughing.

Again, he asked Sam if he wanted to come, reminding him Curls, whom he had dated, would be there.

"I have something better planned for tonight," Sam said brashly.

Although curious, C.J. decided not to ask.

***

Grace taped the sign on the outside door, Class of 1920 Private Party. The English girl, Curls, pulled a bottle of Beefeater Gin from the light tan canvas bag she used for a purse.

A New Jersey classmate gasped. "Where do you keep getting the stuff?"

"From my merry old England, of course."

"She's trying to get us expelled two days before graduation," another howled.

With Maggie playing the piano, the entire group broke into song.

Curls took a long drink of her gin while putting her arm around Grace. "This is a lovely ditty. What is it?"

"Why, Curls, it's our class song," Grace laughed, offering her glass to be filled.

***

C.J. arrived with several other young men.

"Cassie," one of them said, referring to his Mount Holyoke girlfriend, "says there won't be any chaperones here tonight."

"I hope not," a fellow wearing a blue bowtie with orange polka-dots said. "I have two bottles of Kentucky Bourbon wrapped up in my coat."

"I brought Scotch," another said.

Prohibition was a raging success.

The way the girls were dressed shocked the boyfriends. They expected fancy evening dresses, strings of pearls, and feather boas. Instead, the class of 1920 all wore the Holyoke uniform: white blouses with blue sailor collars, pleated blue skirts, white knee socks, and black shoes.

Their conservative dress dimmed the expectations of most of the men—unnecessarily. Illegal booze flowed, and a jazz quartet kept everyone dancing. Four, sometimes tedious, sometimes tricky, and often fun years were concluding for the young women. Time to revel, and revel they did.

VI

Chapter Six

"Oh, what a headache," Grace moaned. "I don't think I can crawl out of my bed."

"Please don't yell," Maggie begged. "The world is much too loud." She pulled her pillow over her head. Except for a missing knee sock, Maggie remained dressed.

"I think some dog slept with his butt in my mouth."

"Who's here?" Maggie and Grace rolled over.

"What are you doing here?" Grace asked, trying to sit up and identify the third person.

Curls, minus her skirt, her bloomers twisted, had curled up halfway under Maggie's bed.

"I'm not sure. I don't think I could find my room."

"Well, don't make any noise," Maggie said. "I told you the world is horribly loud."

Two hours passed before Maggie and the other two girls stirred again.

Struggling to read the clock, Grace wobbled up. "Oh, Lord, twenty after twelve. I'm supposed to meet my parents at one."

Rubbing her burning eyes, Maggie struggled to focus. "Your nightgown is on backward,"

Grace kept pulling and tugging on the thing. "I'm all bound up."

"I think you also have your nightie over your clothes."

Grace had the gown over her head when she stumbled around, tripped over Curls, and tumbled over Maggie before landing on Curls. "Well, Hells Bells."

Maggie tried to stand. She stepped on something. "Ow. Ouch." she yelped, grabbing one foot and hopping on the other. Maggie lost her balance on the fourth, or fifth, or sixth hop. Down she went on Grace and Curls with her legs in a figure four. She picked up a blue jack. "What's this thing doing on the floor?"

Curls struggled into a sitting position and suffered a hiccupping fit. "We played, *hiccup*, jacks when we got home, *hiccup*, last night, don't you remember?"

Maggie and Grace both stared glass-eyed at her. Maggie flung the jack across the room. It bounced off a dresser and then her head.

Grace appeared dumbfounded. "Who won?"

"I don't think I can recall," Curls said.

"You're still drunk," Maggie said—right before she passed out again.

***

Grace's folks came out of the College Inn restaurant as C.J. took Maggie's in for a late lunch. Long friendly with Grace's parents, Ken and Barbara, he told them the same story about the girls being busy. The O'Sullivan's bought the tale, but Grace's dad, not so much. He ushered C.J. away, ostensibly to show him Grace's graduation present.

Once away from the others, Ken mentioned they went to Brigham Hall earlier and discovered Friday night had been some party. He asked C.J. if he thought the girls would be up and around by dinner.

"I hope so," he said. "If they're not, I'll have a hard time figuring out what I'm going to tell the O'Sullivans."

"We'll go back to their room. Barbara can try to start them moving."

A few minutes later, Barbara found Grace and Maggie sprawled out in their room, Grace conscious, more or less. Maggie lay sound asleep, with her mouth gaped open and snoring. Grace, glassy-eyed and pale, gawked at her mother. "I missed our lunch."

"It'll be lucky if you don't miss breakfast tomorrow," her mother said. "Almost three o'clock," she told her daughter while trying to pull her up. "Time to face the day."

"We've got to wake Maggie O up," she said. Grace burst into a silly fit. "She must face the music."

They found Curls draped over a toilet, retching her guts out. "I'm sick. Or, I'm dead. I'm not sure."

Grace's mother helped Curls. "You're not deceased, dear. Although, I suspect you wish you were."

"You're Grace's mum. So nice to see you."

"Thank you, Marian; nice to see you too.

Two hours later, Maggie's eyes remained red and puffy. She hadn't bothered with eyeliner, eyeshadow, or lipstick; her breath smacked of Listerine, but overall, she was presentable. She kissed C.J. on the cheek and thanked him for caring for her parents while she was busy with commencement planning.

"You appear tired," her mother said. "Hard Day?"

"Hectic day."

"Is there an Italian restaurant here?" Mr. O'Sullivan asked as they headed toward the door.

"Italian?" C.J. mulled over the question. "Maggie, what do you think of Asiago's?"

"Asiago's? Hmm," Maggie wanted to step on C.J.'s foot or kick him in the shin, Italian food, on her stomach. "I thought we might go for Italian after graduation tomorrow night." She pinched C.J. in the small of his back. "How about seafood? I'd like some salmon."

"Salmon?" Mrs. O'Sullivan's eyebrows bounced. "I didn't think you liked salmon."

Maggie didn't like salmon, but it was reputedly excellent for a hangover. "Occasionally, I crave fish," Maggie said, putting her arm around Elliott and squeezing him.

"She does," he said. "I believe salmon has grown on her."

"Fine. I hope they serve swordfish," Mr. O'Sullivan said. "I like swordfish."

Brewster's Seafood Restaurant served swordfish, but C.J. persuaded Mr. O'Sullivan to try lobster after assuring him tonight's meal and tomorrow night's at Asiago's would be his treat. Lobster was something new for Maggie's father. He liked it.

Fifteen, sixteen, twenty times during dinner, Maggie referred to C.J. as Elliott, exasperating her mother. "Maggie

Kathryn O'Sullivan! Are you going to keep calling this poor boy Elliott after you're married?"

"Well, I'm not going to call him Wilson."

VII

❦

Chapter Seven

Maggie woke up on Sunday to see the tremendous change in Grace.

"You're bobbed! How glorious!" She leaped out of bed and ran her hands through Grace's beautiful, short hair.

"I did it for your father's benefit. We'll show the old bear."

"You are splendid. I love your bob. I love you!" The roommates hugged and danced around the room. "Perhaps I must marry you instead of Elliott."

"Speaking of Elliott," Grace said, "he's called three times this morning. You better call him before you brush your teeth. By the way, your breath is like a salmon swimming in Listerine."

One of C.J.'s fraternity brothers said he left with Sam about an hour ago. Elliott's roommate was still a thorn in Maggie's side. Once she became Mrs. Elliott, she would deal with Sam—forever.

Maggie took ninety minutes to shower, put on eyeliner, eyeshadow, and arrange the bob right. Still in her red slip, she opened the door to phone Elliott again. Grace grabbed her arm. "Maggie, fathers are on the floor."

"Who cares? I'm sure they've seen females in slips before."

"They haven't seen you," Grace said. "Slip this on. What would C.J. think?"

"He'd think, Woo-hoo!" Nevertheless, she slipped on the robe. Elliot still wasn't at his frat house, but he left a message. He would pick her up at one o'clock. Maggie chose a washed-out yellow dress. Almost as pale as her complexion.

She staggered down to the dining hall for the dregs of coffee and any breakfast that might remain. The few girls she saw from the Class of 1920 were still sluggish and reminded one of anguished souls in Hell.

When Elliott drove up, he had the roof down on his touring car. Maggie told him it wouldn't do for her hair. They turned in the parking lot at the College Inn with the top up. Maggie's parents were in a chipper mood. "We'll drop Maggie off so she can fix up for graduation," C.J. said. "I'll take you for lunch, and if you would like, I'll take you on a quick spin around Amherst."

The afternoon's only uneasiness came when Mr. O'Sullivan asked him where he would work after graduating. C.J. danced, hinting at working as a journalist for the Boston Globe. He added the expectation of completing his first novel in about two months.

Sensing his answer didn't satisfy Mr. O'Sullivan, he mentioned, without details, his being heir to some family money.

Mrs. O'Sullivan pointed out his employment was not their business.

C.J. let out a soft sigh.

***

Professor Hammond nodded to the Dean and hit the first note of Pomp and Circumstance on the organ.

As the audience stood, Dean Purington led the procession of graduates into the auditorium. The Dean, the President of Mount Holyoke, another stern-looking woman, the class officers, speakers, and the cellist took their places.

A Holyoke Chaplain prayed before President Woolley welcomed all family and friends without smiling one time. After an assistant dean's twenty-minute, monotonous speech, Mrs. Dickenson from the music department introduced Maggie as the evening's musical interlude.

The instant Maggie pulled her bow across the strings of her cello, the tenor of the evening changed—lost its pomp. *The Vamp*...jazz...on a cello. Students started chanting: Maggie, Maggie, Maggie. President Woolley's face would have soured milk. Maggie grinned.

Dean Purington tottered to the podium to introduce the class valedictorian. "Miss O'Sullivan. That was..." That was where Dean Purington began to stammer. "It was...different."

"Thank you, Dean Purington." Maggie bowed and waved her mortarboard cap in a sweeping motion.

Grace Brown began by thanking everyone for their attendance. "I wish to speak to you about *The Road of the Loving Heart*." Pausing, she removed her mortarboard cap. "This silly thing keeps trying to fall off," she half-laughed, tossing it across the stage toward her seat.

"Now we have built our pathway through our shining college years. Joining always in our gladness, in our toil, and in our fears, this road is lined with memories. You will find them if you look, running through the words and pictures in here," Grace tapped on her heart, "forever, in our hearts."

Curls bent over and whispered to the girl beside her, "What the hell is she talking about?"

"And the time shall come when the sound of the bugle shall be heard in the land. And we as young maidens shall turn pale and take refuge in the mountains of knowledge."

Curls leaned over again. "She's making this bull up as she goes."

"And nuts, yea verily nuts, shall be found in the cocoa, even in the lower parts of the cocoa, and in the utter parts of the pitcher. And cereal, the cereal of truth shall we eat." Grace curtsied and took her seat.

Maggie and Grace's mother jumped to their feet, the first to burst into applause. The entire class celebrated the brilliance of Grace's speech. Or the audacity.

The only thing left was the presentation of the diplomas. Frances Abrams...Grace Elizabeth Brown...Maggie Kathryn O'Sullivan...Marian Voorhees, whose name brought loud cheers of "Curls."

Elliott and the O'Sullivans made their way through the crowd to Maggie. Grace, Curls, and two other girls stood with her. She grabbed Elliott around the neck, raised her feet off the ground, and hung on while he gave her a twirl. "I am a graduate." She squealed. Maggie freed Elliott, grabbing her mother. "Are you proud of me?"

As Maggie bantered with her parents, Grace seized Elliott,

demanding a graduation kiss. With a cautionary glance at her father, he obliged.

Mrs. O'Sullivan asked Grace about her plans. "I intend to be elected to the Senate, put my feet on a table, and smoke a cigar."

Maggie hugged her mother and Elliot. "I need to hang my robe in the cloakroom. I'll be right back, and we'll be off to Asiago's." Curls said goodbye; Grace ran off with her folks.

When Maggie returned, her father lost his ability to speak. His daughter, if he was still going to claim her, was no girl. Her loose-fitting, sleeveless, very red chiffon dress with a drop-waste and a v-neckline, a deep v-neckline, was meant to make that statement. Pearls, three long strings, swayed from her neck. Two diagonal panels crossed at the front of the skirt, making the sides slightly longer than the middle, the middle short of her knees. A bow below one hip, the back hem also hung lower than the front, the front hardly brushing her knees.

Stepping in front of Elliott, Maggie took his hands and batted her eyes at him. "What do you think of my attire...old sport?"

"Fabulous," C.J. said. "Yes, I rather like the color...And the cut of your jib," he added, in a voice too soft for Father O'Sullivan to catch.

VIII

Chapter Eight

Mount Holyoke allowed seniors to remain in their housing through Thursday. Maggie and Grace rented a room at the College Inn until after C.J. graduated Sunday. Something else, Mr. Howard O'Sullivan, left peeved over.

The Amherst graduation was staid. No cellist played *The Vamp*. The valedictorian did not mention cocoa nuts. Every graduate received a dark reddish-brown chestnut cane of the Derby Standard type, with a handle shaped in a delicate S-curve.

According to school lore, the canes represented a visual metaphor for a college education—to support graduates throughout their lives. Graduation caps sailing through the air were the only similarity to the Holyoke ceremony.

C.J.'s mother did not attend. Nor would she grace him with her presence at his Tulsa wedding, perhaps in Boston, but not Oklahoma.

The honeymoon location remained debated, with the nuptials only two weeks away. C.J. leaned toward a resort in the Rocky Mountains; Maggie wanted to hike the Grand Canyon. Since you can't put your arms around a beautiful view, make love with a mountain, can't be loved by the great divide, C.J., without his bride's knowledge, booked a suite at the EL Tovar Hotel along the rim of the Grand Canyon. All that mattered was Maggie getting what she desired.

* * *

Maggie and Grace boarded a train for Tulsa. "How does it feel to finally be caught," Grace asked.

"Caught? I'm the one who did the catching," Maggie said.

Grace unwrapped the dry roasted peanuts, rich caramel, and smooth nougat of a Baby Ruth candy bar, broke it in two, and offered half to Maggie. "Those things are always stale," Maggie said, waving the offer away.

Grace took one bite. "You're right. The damn thing is stale." She lowered the window and threw the bar out. "Are you sure that old bear who spawned you will let me stay in your house?"

"He will if he plans to attend my wedding. And he does...since he's paying for it."

"Well, I'll be happy to poison him if you want me to."

"It won't be necessary," Maggie said. "I can handle him for the four days we'll be there."

"I'll bet you can," Grace laughed.

As railroad miles clanked into the mid-west, the landscape grew more wearisome, a few rolling hills, a time along a muddy river, the almost hypnotizing allure of knee-high corn flying past the train window. Between uncomfortable naps,

Grace developed an insatiable interest in Maggie's thoughts on marriage. What do you think it will be like? Who's going to be the boss? You know one of you will be. What's Elliott's favorite meal? How many kids are you going to have? When?

Nothing can prepare the uninitiated to discuss the good and bad of marriage. Never married, Maggie was inexperienced, unskilled, and unversed to answer.

All of Grace's questions were accompanied by quizzical looks. The more inquiries and curious gazes, the more anxious Maggie became. She realized she didn't have any answers, none.

Distraught, Maggie needed a change in the conversation. "Let's go to the dinner car and get some lunch."

Grace requested fruit and cream. After scrutinizing the menu, Maggie ordered a Sardolive Sandwich, a mix of equal parts sardines, chopped olives, hard-boiled egg yolks seasoned with lemon juice, and salt. She also requested two glasses of champagne, to, of course, be denied—prohibition.

"Are you really going to eat that mess?" Grace asked, squinting her eyes and puckering her mouth.

Grace motioned for the waiter. "You better bring her gin instead of champaign." The humorless waiter shook his head and left.

Soon after devouring the sandwich, smacking her lips, and licking each finger, Maggie turned to her best friend. "I know this much about the life I'm going to have with Elliott. It's going to be grand, overwhelming."

***

C.J. and Sam were making the trip by car, picking up

Maggie's brother in St. Louis. Suitcases would travel in the rumble seat with the hope of sunny weather.

Sam gave C.J. a fancily wrapped box. "Arnie sent you a wedding present."

"Who's Arnie?"

"Arnold Rothstein."

C.J.'s demeanor changed drastically.

"What? He's a friendly fella," Sam said.

C.J. stepped back from his friend. "He's a damn gangster."

"He is not. He's a businessman, a flourishing one."

"Honest businessmen don't fix the World Series," C.J. said.

"Nothing but a rumor. A baseless one."

"Sure, the way the White Sox were baseless in the games. Maggie will never accept anything from him."

"Don't tell her who it's from."

"Not giving it to her," C.J. said, his words snapping. After a brief pause, he asked, "What is it?"

"If the gift is fine enough, you'll take it?" Sam asked.

There may have been truth in Sam's comment, more than C.J. cared to admit. A bit stung, he had to gather himself. "No, I won't give it to her. Doesn't matter what it is. We're not taking a present from Rothstein. It likely comes with expectations. We want no part of those."

"Suit yourself," Sam said, tossing the package in the back seat. "I'm not so picky. I'll keep it. If I don't like it, it's probably expensive, so if I don't like it, I'll sell it to somebody who wants it."

Flat tires, two of them in one day, put the trip off to an inauspicious start. They would sleep Tuesday night, their second night, in Indianapolis. Not bad, considering the tire delays. After picking up Tommy in St. Louis, they'd decide whether to drive to Tulsa or spend Wednesday night on the road and arrive on Thursday.

They arrived at Union Station in St. Louis about thirty minutes before Tommy's train. "He's a long, lanky guy," C.J. said, "he's a carrot top." His hair made him easy to find. The three tossed all the luggage in the rumble seat and headed to Tulsa. "How's the lawyering business?" C.J. asked.

"Somewhat exciting," Tom, the name everyone except his family called him, said. "I think The Bureau will assign me to Chicago, but I'm not sure."

"Do you arrest people?" Sam asked.

"No, I'm in the legal department, a federal prosecutor." Tom shifted around in the back, trying to stretch his long legs. "I enjoy jailing gangsters, tax cheats, bootleggers, and the like. Ku Klux Klanners constitute a significant target in some parts of the country. Hopefully, they won't give me Tulsa. I might have to put my Uncle Paddy away."

"He may be dead," C.J. chuckled. "Maggie said if he kisses her on the mouth again, she's gonna kill him. You wouldn't lock Maggie up, would you?"

"I'd like to meet the man to jail her, wouldn't be me," Tom assured his soon-to-be brother-in-law.

C.J. and Sam wore out. They discussed stopping for the night or driving into Tulsa. "It will be after midnight if we go all the way to Tulsa," Tom said. "If we stop in Joplin, Missouri, we'll be less than three hours away." With little sleep the last night, the idea appealed to everyone.

"Your sister says tornados are fond of Tulsa," C.J. chuckled. "And mosquitoes."

Tom kept squirming around, trying to find a comfortable position in a back seat too small for him. "Oh, our hometown is not as awful as Mags makes out. Tulsa is the world's oil capital, at least it claims to be. The population is booming, attracting people with money from Pennsylvania and New York, who are building some grand homes." Tom hesitated and laughed, "Tulsa might be the place for you, Sam. Why, we've got a skyscraper, eighteen floors high."

"That's not how Maggie describes Tulsa," C.J. said.

Laughing, Tom listed her opinions. "Cultureless hicks, hot, boring, smelly. I'm sure her list goes on."

"You didn't scratch the surface." C.J. grinned.

***

After an early start, the three pulled up in front of the O'Sullivan home before mid-morning. The house was a two-story stucco with a tile roof and a Spanish flair sitting back from the street. A red brick walk led to the porch. A heavy oak door inlaid with stained glass, was a bit imposing. It was much nicer and more prominent than Maggie described.

Maggie came outside wearing a white blouse, a man's black tie hanging loose around her neck, and wide-legged cream slacks. She beamed at C.J.—said nothing. She just smiled.

He ran to her and lifted her off her feet. "You are a pretty one, prettier than I remembered."

Tom, who would again be Tommy, leaned over and whispered to Sam, "I'll bet Pop is fit to be tied over those pants."

Mrs. O'Sullivan scampered down to hug Tommy and C.J. She extended her hand. "You must be Sam. Welcome to Tulsa."

Inside the house, a raised tile entry led to an open great

room with hardwood floors. The wood flooring continued through the house, except for the linoleum in the kitchen. The living room featured coordinated pieces, armchairs, a sofa, a reception seat, a straight-back rocker, a mahogany buffet, and two tabourets, stools, Tommy called them. Trendy wrought-iron bridge lamps provided lighting.

An oversized dining room included a massive dinner table with cut-cornered edges, five chairs, and a host chair covered with tapestry upholstery.

"Where's Pop?" Tommy asked.

"He's not here now," Mrs. O'Sullivan said.

Tommy nudged his sister. Maggie snuggled under his shoulder, whispering about how much she had missed him. Always happy to see Mags, Tommy gave her a quick peck on the side of her head.

"Has the old man seen those pants?"

Maggie laughed and swung her arm around her brother's shoulder. "Why do you think he's not here?"

Releasing Tommy, Maggie grabbed C.J. "Oh, how I have longed for you, old sport. After Saturday, no more being apart." She hugged him and, hoping no one was watching, patted his butt.

"I must show you the room I grew up in," she said, leading him toward the stairs.

The room was girly, pink with white woodwork. The Llamarada, her Mount Holyoke Yearbook, lay open on the bed. C.J. paged through to find Maggie's photo. Taken before she bobbed her hair, he commented on how different she looked.

Each senior picture had a quote from the student. Maggie's

said: *"I intend to sip cognac and lecture suffrage with the late Mr. Twain. We'll pass the hat."*

Thumbing through the book, he stopped at a page with a picture of the Crowning of the May Queen, a play Holyoke put on last fall. Grace had been the Queen, Maggie, the Witch, and Curls, the Jester.

"Your long, flowing red hair made you the perfect witch."

"The perfect witch!" Maggie jabbed, no, slugged him on the shoulder.

"Yes, a perfect old crone. Where's Grace?"

"With the bridesmaids. They're picking up their dresses." Maggie sat on the bed, patting the mattress for him to sit next to her. "I can't wait until being in a bedroom together is a nightly occurrence."

C.J. blushed as she knew he would.

***

After returning, Grace hugged Sam, tapped her finger on his lips, and said, "Don't be flirting with me."

"Gracie, how can I not flirt when you flash those come-hither eyes? I'm hoping for a double wedding."

"Keep dreaming, bucko." She planted a quick peck on his forehead. "Tommy here is the man of my dreams." Tommy's face turned as red as his hair.

Never successful with women, Tommy got redder when Grace blew him a kiss. "C.J., I want you to make Tommy your best man so he can escort me down the aisle instead of Sammy Boy here."

Sam clutched his chest, flopped on the sofa, moaning loudly.

"I want ice cream," Maggie proclaimed while grabbing

C.J.'s arm. "Strawberry. We have a superb soda fountain down-town." *Oh, dread,* she said something complimentary about Tulsa. "Well, passable by Tulsa standards."

IX

❦

Chapter Nine

At last, the wedding day arrived.

C.J. wore tails. His best man and groomsmen were in black tuxes with formal waistcoats. All sported wing-collared shirts, bow ties, and single button coats.

The Maid of Honor and bridesmaids entered in divine sleeveless mauve-pink dresses with square necklines and sweeping asymmetrical lace accents cascading to a dropped waist, embellished with a mesh rose.

The doors at the back of the sanctuary opened. The bride and her father were framed in soft, orangish light. Maggie glowed in an exquisite, daringly modern, yet classically beautiful gown delicately adorned in crystals, sequins, and glass beads. A plunging V neckline at the front and back made the dress a touch naughty in C.J.'s opinion, but he liked it.

The gown's flattering feminine silhouette gently flared from hip to floor, finishing with an intricately sequined scallop hem, adding to Maggie's eloquence. A pearl-beaded Juliet Cap veil with two layers of luxurious silk in differing lengths, framing her face, created a magical appearance.

The six-piece orchestra hit the first chord of the Wedding March. C.J. wanted to race to the back of the church, yelling, "I do, I do, she does," and sweep Maggie away to the honeymoon. Too gauche. Instead, he gasped, fixing his eyes on his bride as she walked toward him.

Her father gave C.J. Maggie's hand, pulling it back for an instant. A joke, a little tease. Or not.

The ceremony was charming, not ordinary. Music, every note selected by Maggie, included Grace accompanying the orchestra in a rousing rendition of *When My Baby Smiles at Me*, making Maggie's father shake his head. *That Old Irish Mother of Mine* made her mother cry.

At last, they exchanged simple gold wedding bands—almost. Her hand shaking, Maggie put C.J.'s ring on the wrong hand. Mortified by her error and chagrinned more about Elliott standing there and letting her do it, she attempted to remove it. *Stuck.* She squeezed his finger and tugged. Nope. She twisted and tugged. Not yet. Only one option left. She lifted his hand to her mouth and gave the finger a wet lick. Thank goodness.

Smiling, the preacher said, "I now pronounce you husband and wife." The guests applauded. C.J. kissed the bride. Running down the aisle, rice flying, he stopped. He kissed her again. This time, he leaned her over and really kissed her, with passion—and tongue.

At the reception, Maggie charmed their guests, danced with Tommy, and even her father. Tommy danced with Grace.

Sam half fell in love with one of the other bridesmaids. C.J. pointed out to Sam, "The girl is an Okie." They cut the cake, smeared frosting on each other's faces, and everyone toasted them with lemonade and sweet tea. The honeymooners escaped right after Grace whispered in C.J.'s ear. "Maggie walks around naked in the mornings."

***

At dinner one night during the honeymoon, Maggie brought up something bothering her.

"Elliott, have you given any thought to the little detail we've no place to live? No furniture, if we did?"

"Not much."

"My parents became rather fretful when I didn't leave an address to send my clothes."

"We have plenty to wear with us. We can buy more. There are a lot of stores in Boston and New York."

"I suppose we can sleep in the car," Maggie said, "and restaurants have restrooms. You're right; we'll be fine."

***

On the second day of their trip home, C.J. brought up the subject of a place to live. Revealing his love of the ocean, he suggested a bungalow in Boston, where they would stay during the orchestra season.

"You mean the Woman's Symphony season," Maggie said. "Have you forgotten? Women aren't allowed in real orchestras. Becoming more depressed as the countryside passed outside the train window, she reached for her new husband, the one at a loss about what to do or say.

"Elliott," she said, dabbing at a shameful tear and looking at him. "Do you think I should lose opportunities because I'm a female?" She didn't pause long enough for an answer. "Did you know thirty musicians left the Boston Symphony over not being unionized? I couldn't audition because I'm not a man. Worse, I can't vote because I'm a woman. It's not fair, not right."

"No, it is not," he whispered, taking Maggie by the hand.

Annoyance replaced the sorrow she'd been struggling with. "I'm a better musician than half the men in that orchestra. And I'm a lot damn smarter than most males who cast ballots."

He moved next to her and put his arm around her. "Yes, you are," he said, squeezing her to him. "Yes, you are." She lay with her head on his shoulder. They did not talk. They sat, C.J. holding her, Maggie breathing softly on his neck, defeated. C.J. would change that defeat when they made love.

***

In Boston, Maggie's mood lightened, her spirits brightened, hope bloomed inside her. Her cheerfulness was so intense it scared her. She thought she might die of joy. Everyone's heart pounded with happiness, and their souls started dancing when Maggie was around. She loved being a wife; cooking, cleaning, and doing laundry were times of fulfillment. One joyful afternoon they purchased a tiny bungalow with a sitting room, bedroom, kitchen, and bath, all small and furnished to Maggie's approval.

***

At breakfast one morning, C.J. asked Maggie if she liked Bar Harbor.

"In Maine?"

"Yes."

"I love it."

"You do remember Grace lives in Bar Harbor."

"I do."

"I like the ocean," he said off-handedly.

Maggie telephoned Grace, half-expecting another conspiracy afoot similar to the one for her ring size. There was no confederacy between Grace and Elliott, but Grace said she would call someone in real estate and arrange a meeting.

When the Elliotts, seasoned riders of the rails, arrived, Grace threw her arms around Maggie and asked about the honeymoon. "My wife is the only person in the world to go to the Grand Canyon but never see it."

"Why, sweet thing, I didn't want to leave our bed," Maggie said, batting her eyes at C.J., whose face burned like he'd lain in the sun for hours.

The exchange put a delighted expression on Grace's face. "My folks are dying to see you, Maggie O. I think my mother hopes you can instruct me on finding a man. Don't you dare. I'm thrilled flirting about."

＊＊＊

Grace's parents didn't mention her marital status, but they encouraged the newlyweds to find a Bar Harbor home. "Bar Harbor property makes a sound investment, more solid if the selection includes a shorefront," her father said.

The following morning, the Elliotts spoke with a home salesman on the phone. "I have a gorgeous residence to show you. It's a twenty-acre estate never lived in because the owners drowned in a sailing accident before moving in."

Walking up the driveway behind the realtor, C.J. leaned against Maggie. "I found out the bank has been stuck with this place for a year because of the property's price—and the drowning. I think someone in a position to make a cash offer might pick up a bargain, an expensive one, but a bargain."

C.J., while young, had soaked up his grandfather's tutelage. Still a month from being twenty-two, he already knew how to snooker fifty-two-year-old salt-and-pepper-haired business veterans.

"I can out-negotiate these folks," C.J. whispered to Maggie. "So, if we fall in love with the place, don't let the salesman know."

"The home's superior architectural pedigree of Redwood was a design of the renowned architect William Ralph Emerson. It has six bedrooms and sits within a peaceful walk of Bar Harbor," the realtor said.

It was all Maggie could do to hide her delight. "This is such a tranquil neighborhood. I adore how such beautiful homes are all on multiple-acre estates. I've always wanted a formal living and dining room with fireplaces. I've lost count of all the sitting rooms."

"Think about how we could entertain in that massive sunroom accessing the deck," C.J. said.

They loved how access came down a long, winding private drive with surrounding wooded areas providing additional privacy. Huge, elegant old-growth trees framed the residence with a sweeping lawn ending at the ocean bulkhead.

The realtor turned on the charm. "You won't find a property with more dramatic views of Frenchman Bay islands. And, the Bar Harbor Breakwater changes with the maritime activity, the weather, and gulls soaring in the sky."

Now was the time. "I plan to be a novelist. This would be a

wonderful place to write." Now the *but*. There must always be a *but*. "But Maggie is a classical musician and theatre-quality soprano. She's about to audition for the Metropolitan Opera, with almost certain acceptance because of her angelic voice. It may be better for us to live in New York."

The real estate agent called early the next morning and asked if the Elliotts would meet with him and the bank president.

C.J. smiled at Maggie. "We've got them. They're desperate."

At the meeting, C.J. fidgeted. He ebbed and flowed. Maybe yes, perhaps they should go to New York. Maggie was a helpless female. Decisions like this were too much for her. They must think.

Three hours later, although making sure to sound unsure, C.J. made a cash offer. His grandfather taught him bankers adore funds-in-hand offers.

Dinner at an outdoor café followed the house purchase. Maggie flashed him a mischievous, naughty grin. "It surprised me, Elliott dear, to hear I'm auditioning for an opera. At The Met, no less. Which opera am I auditioning for?"

"Zazà."

"Zazà? Hmm. When does this audition take place?"

"We'll need to ask Mrs. Dickenson from the Mount Holyoke Music Department. You remember Mrs. Dickenson, don't you?"

Maggie was full of questions. "What does Mrs. Dickenson have to do with this?"

"She called one day while you were shopping. It took some effort, but I finally got her to tell me why she was calling. She said she ran into a friend who is often a director at The Met.

This director is currently casting for an opera. Mrs. Dickenson believes you are enormously talented. She told the director he should let you audition. It seems he has agreed."

Elliott leaned close. He struggled to make eye contact. "You deserve more than being in a women's symphony. Not that there is anything wrong with the Boston Fadette Orchestra," he said. "You, however, are uncommon and rate more."

He tried to hide his emotion, but his chin quivered, his chest bounced, speech was difficult. Not only that, he couldn't find the words to express all the things he wanted to tell her.

"Anyway, Mrs. Dickenson said she'll arrange the audition; the rest will be up to you."

Maggie, seldom speechless, was speechless.

On the telephone that evening, Mrs. Dickenson gave Maggie the name she should contact at the Met to set up the details. She told Maggie to practice all the soprano parts from the opera. "I understand your love for the cello. But, child, do not underestimate the beauty of your voice. It is a gift to share with the world."

Maggie sang for the next five weeks, and C.J. wrote.

With Maggie so busy rehearsing, C.J. asked Grace to critique his novel. She agreed. Halfway through the manuscript, regret came calling.

Chapter Ten

Three days into four days of predicted rain, Maggie came rushing into their living room.

"Elliott, we must rush to Tennessee."

Whatever Maggie had on her mind was always a must.

C.J. had two choices: start packing a suitcase or poke a little fun at his red-haired Irish wife. A grand champion of fun, he peered over his newspaper. "Why on earth would we want to go to a place as hot and humid as Tennessee?"

Maggie leaped into his lap, crushing the Bar Harbor Times. "To sweat, of course. Perspiring cleans toxins out of our bodies. Our cooler temperatures fill us with them. You don't want to be filled with poisons, do you?"

"We can go upstairs and make each other sweat. No need to drive four or five days."

Maggie threw her head back, waved her arm. "No Tennessee, no sweating with me."

Perhaps he pushed her a little, leaned forward a little. Whatever happened—thud—Maggie ended up on the floor. Incredulity shot across her face, her mouth agape, her green eyes ablaze.

Speechless, wild-eyed, and bewildered, Maggie glared at her husband. "Cecil Jethro Elliott, did you dump me on my butt?"

C.J. slid off the couch on her. "Did you threaten to withhold your charms?"

A smile quivered over her lips and eyes. "No Tennessee, no fadoodling."

"Why Tennessee? Why not North Carolina? The weather is hot in Raleigh."

"You know why." Maggie rolled on top, giving him a quick kiss on the forehead.

C.J. laughed, stealing another smooch.

"Tennessee will be state number thirty-six to ratify the amendment," Maggie smiled, kissing him back. "Can we take Grace along?"

"Does she need to sweat out toxins, too?" C.J. asked before being punched.

At Maggie's insistence, they rushed to Grace's house. "Three's a crowd," Grace said.

"We must have a crowd. The other side will turn out in force. Every voice is going to matter."

"Are you all right with me going?" Grace asked C.J.

"Do you need to sweat the toxins out of your body, too?" Grace didn't get the joke but laughed at Maggie, backhanding C.J. across the chest.

***

All three headed for Nashville the following day, where the ultimate battle for women's voting rights would occur. The 19th Amendment lagged one state shy of ratification, having passed in thirty-five states. American women needed Tennessee's vote for the *Perfect Thirty-Six*.

Carrie Chapman Catt, the most famous suffragist after the deaths of Susan B. Anthony and Elizabeth Cady Stanton, was in Nashville, staying at the Hermitage Hotel, across from the State Capitol.

Oddly, Josephine Pearson, the leader of the anti-suffrage movement in Tennessee, was also in Nashville and at the same hotel. Maggie and Grace were euphoric when C.J. booked rooms at the Hermitage.

The crusade between the two sides would be bitter.

Maggie, C.J., and Grace marched for two long, hot weeks. They passed out pamphlets, pounded on doors, lobbied state congressmen in their offices, and made a few impromptu speeches. Maggie rented a cello and played ninety minutes every morning sitting outside the legislature. She sat next to a sign saying, "Women Can't Vote. They Can't Even Play in a Symphony."

Amendment opponents handed out red roses as their symbol, while the Amendment proponents used yellow ones.

A fever of anger flooded through Nashville, tempers increased.

Rumors ran rampant that neither side was sure they had enough votes.

August 18 came. The Senate approved the Amendment earlier. General Assembly members showed their colors by wearing roses on their lapels. Counting the number of red roses worn by the representatives, the Amendment would be defeated.

In front of packed galleries, voting began on a motion to table the amendment, meaning the amendment would not receive a vote. The vote tied 48 to 48. A second ballot on tabling tied again.

Realizing if the vote on the Amendment itself tied, it could not be ratified, House Speaker Seth Walker, opposing the Amendment, called for a vote—not on tabling, but on the Amendment. Maggie and Grace were sick to their stomachs.

Harry T. Burn of Niota, Tennessee, wore an anti-suffrage red rose pinned to his lapel, voting both times to table the Amendment. But, in his pocket, he carried a letter.

Dear Son,

Hurrah and vote suffrage! Don't forget to be a good boy and help Mrs. Catt put the "rat" in ratification. Ha! No more from Mama this time. With lots of love.

Your Mother

Speaker Walker called Burn's name. Quietly, he voiced his vote. It was hard to tell. At first, no one was sure how he voted, but the crowd became more excited as the word passed. At the end of the roll call, they announced the resolution carried 49 to 47.

Maggie threw her arms around C.J. and kissed him. She hugged Grace; Grace hugged C.J.

"Women have the vote!" Maggie shouted.

The celebration in Nashville lasted all night. What a fantastic time to be an American woman.

The clock ticked to four thirty-six a.m. as C.J. and Maggie opened the door to their room. He squeezed her and gave her a spin before stepping back and looking into her eyes. "I am so happy for you, Maggie. I'm not sure I can imagine how you must feel. I'm thrilled for you."

Maggie wrapped herself around him. She whispered thank you and held him—for a long time. "The hotel restaurant opens at five a.m.," Maggie said, breaking the silence of the embrace. "Let's eat breakfast and go to sleep."

The crowd was significant for so early. Almost all were ratification celebrators who had not yet found their way to bed. Maggie was reflective, in fact, subdued. Captivated by her face, C.J. asked what she was thinking. Some smiles are loud, some are quiet, some are playful, and some are peaceful. The one on Maggie's face was contented.

"This is no small thing," Maggie said. "We've changed the meaning of being a woman."

Around six o'clock, the Elliotts came meandering through the lobby and spotted Grace. Maggie's face lit up. "Not what you think, Gracie. No barneymugging." Grace turned beet red. "Well, there was," Maggie said, taking Grace by the arm. "But that was this morning. We've been sleeping since about eleven." Grace and Elliott both flushed crimson. Grace recovered first, saying she hoped to be so wicked one day.

On the streets, Nashville remained in a merry mood. Occasionally, an anti-suffragette would claim females voting would be the ruination of American families.

One anti, a female no less, made that comment too close to Maggie and Grace. They erupted. Maggie gave her a stiff lecture about how discriminatory and plain wrong things had been for women, notably cellists of the gender.

Grace unleashed an entire discourse, complete with

alliteration and two-part harmony. Somehow, she worked in finding nuts, yea, verily nuts, in the cocoa. Maggie beamed with pride over her former roommate.

Maggie turned and batted her green eyes at Elliott. Grabbing his lapels and pulling him close, she kissed his nose. "What did you think of that, old sport?"

"I don't understand how either of you got past twelve years old without being arrested." C.J. laughed before adding, "And institutionalized."

At dinner, C.J. asked the question. "Grace, what do you think of my novel?"

Grace sort of mumbled. "Your novel?"

"Yes, my novel."

Grace feigned the need for a drink of water. After swallowing, she didn't make eye contact with C.J.

"Why...I love your book," she said, not at all convincingly.

"Terrible, isn't it?" C.J. sounded so dejected.

"No!" Grace exclaimed, looking at Maggie for help.

Maggie came to her rescue. "Something inciting needs to happen."

"Dammit, I thought so."

Grace put not one but both hands on his arm and poured on a thick dose of empathy. "You are an excellent writer. Your prose is beautiful. Reading your descriptions is like being in a room full of sweet-smelling flowers."

His eyes proclaimed *you're feeding me horse crap.*

Grace began to stutter. "It's..."

"That not a damn thing happens," Maggie said, shrugging her shoulders. "For Heaven's sake, Elliott, your hero, this Alex fellow, comes back from the war and embarks on the most boring life in...in the entire history of living."

Grace agreed.

Highlighting her words with a grand and dramatic sweeping motion of her arm, Grace suggested starting the story during the fighting in the Argonne Forest. "Blow one of Alex's legs off. Both."

He shook his head and groaned.

"Give the poor guy something to overcome, something to battle."

Maggie wasn't sure about blowing his appendages off. "Or, let him keep his limbs, but make him a cop, catching anarchists. Better yet," she said, pointing her finger at C.J., "make him a criminal. A twentieth-century Robin Hood."

"No, not a Robin Hood," Grace countered, "a modern-day Vlad the Impaler. An irrefutable villain with no moral virtues. Who's brought to justice by a female!" Grace's face burst with glee.

"Glorious! There is your plot," Maggie said before biting his shoulder.

Later in the evening, after Maggie fell asleep, Alex began his transition, not to an impaler, but bit by a bat in the Argonne Forest, into a sensual vampire.

XI

Chapter Eleven

Two weeks after Maggie auditioned for the opera Zazà, not a peep. Silence always meant rejection. She was taking it hard. After three weeks, neither C.J. nor Grace could pull her from her sulking.

She and Grace were shopping when the call came. "The Met called," C.J. told her when she got home.

"Got around to telling me no?"

"Not exactly. They want you to audition a second time. Telephone this number and ask for Harry."

The conversation with Harry lasted twenty minutes. Maggie's emotions bounced between depressed and high, thrilled and scared. "Elliott, they want me to audition for Zazà."

"The lead?"

"Yes, they're giving me two weeks. I'm going to call Mrs. Dickenson."

Mrs. Dickenson knew. She said she didn't let Maggie know because she wanted the Met to call first. "I spoke to David Belasco, the director. David loves you; they all do, Maggie, dear." She went on and on about how beautiful they thought Maggie's voice was. She told Maggie about their only concern —an enormous one. "You are a newcomer. Never has a newcomer, someone with no experience, sang the lead."

Mrs. Dickenson informed Maggie she faced a fierce battle and must work tirelessly between now and her tryout. "Do you know what verismo is?"

"I do," Maggie said, "it's realism, truth, post-romantic, much like naturalism in literature."

"Excellent, that's excellent." Mrs. Dickenson explained how Director Belasco wants realism because the opera is not about the rich. "Remember, Zazà was born in the gutter, sings in low-class cafés and cabarets. She will fight dirty for what she desires."

"So, I should be a floozy."

"Yes, dear, you may pretend to be a floozy." Mrs. Dickenson placed an emphasis on "pretend." She had a little more advice. "Don't play jazz on your cello. She changed her mind about being a floozy but was clear about one thing—do fight dirty for what you want."

She told her young protégé to be coarse, within the limits of boundaries acceptable to opera audiences. "Become Zazà, unrefined, heartless in what you want and the lengths you'll go."

Maggie received mixed reviews—at best. They loved her singing and acting, but remained anxious about her lack of experience and fame. They instructed her to rehearse for three more days, come back, and audition with the male lead.

Maggie spent the time practicing lines and researching French music hall singers. At night, she made Elliott take her to dives and cheap clubs where less fortunate people went for entertainment. She studied how the female entertainers moved, danced, and painted their faces.

Before she paraded on for her last chance, she overheard the male lead saying, "This girl is nothing but a baby, barely off the teat."

Such a rude assessment would devastate most young women in her situation. Not Maggie Kathryn Elliott; she was not typical. She'd show that pompous ass.

Striding brazenly to the stage, she was no child. Wearing far too much makeup, especially rouge, and courtesy of the costume department, an orange dress with a plunging neckline, within minutes, she made anyone who heard the disparaging remark realize the actor would pale next to this beginner.

At the end of the audition, the orchestra conductor bowed to Maggie and saluted her with his baton. Everyone else sat silent.

Director Belasco waved two others over to him: the assistant director and a starch-collared woman Maggie believed to be an opera board member. Watching them whisper to each other, not one smiling, her thoughts were spoiled by a murky haze, turning her hopes into a dusky fog. She had been in many musical competitions, and frowning judges are never a good sign.

At last, David Belasco waved Maggie over. Standing and

extending his hand, he still did not smile. "Is it Miss Elliott or Mrs.?"

"Mrs., sir."

If eyes could frown, Belasco's did. "Unfortunate," he mumbled in a voice Maggie was not supposed to hear. He motioned for her to sit. It was all very formal. As if formality would ease the blow. "Would you prefer me to call you Maggie or Margaret?"

Over her four Mount Holyoke years with Curls, Maggie had mastered the British proficiency of keeping a stiff upper lip. Highbrows, though they might be—haughty directors, seasoned actors, board members with their noses in the air, it didn't matter. They would not intimidate her. Hell would freeze before they would delight in her disappointment.

"Maggie, please."

"Very well." Director Belasco sat down and leaned toward her, avoiding her eyes, another bad sign. The self-satisfied male lead smirked from across the stage—the smug ass.

Not casting her would be their loss. Maybe not today, perhaps not this year, but they would bemoan their error— someday.

"Maggie...can you make history?"

Describing the expression on Maggie's face would have been, well, impossible. Joy, astonishment, thrill, elation, rapture, all would have been inadequate descriptions. She threw her arms around Director Belasco. Appropriateness be damned.

The opera board member, if she was a board member, gleamed. "You will be the first, first-timer to play the title role at the Metropolitan."

Take that, you egotistic male lead.

After the audition, Maggie and C.J. rushed to Harold's Square for mutton at Keen's Chophouse. A waiter in a white dinner jacket brought them menus. C.J. told him they would like a cup of tea to toast Lillie Langtry.

"Do you know the Jersey Lily?"

"I dined with her in 1905," C.J. said.

"Then I'll bring English tea."

"Why would you tell someone you ate with Lily Langtry? And why would we want to toast her?"

"She was the first woman to be served here. Until then, this was strictly a gentleman's club. Don't you think we should toast her?"

"I think we must salute her."

While waiting for their mutton chops, Maggie described everything about her audition, including how the man playing Milio Dufresne wasn't happy about a newcomer cast in the title role. "Rough for him. My voice is far better," Maggie proclaimed.

C.J. laughed at her.

"Well, it is, and I'm much prettier."

He laughed again.

The waiter brought their dinner and a small pot of tea. He poured the brew into delicate china cups and asked if they needed anything else. C.J. said they should be fine.

Maggie sipped hers. Her eyes popped. Red-faced and coughing, she reached for her napkin. "Elliott...that's whiskey."

"A benefit of knowing Lily Langtry," he smiled.

XII

Chapter Twelve

Inside The Metropolitan Opera, a stagehand threw the switch. Maggie and C.J. stood outside the theater when the marquee burst to life.

Zazà

Starring

Maggie Elliott

Maggie Elliott, she was billed above the male lead. The Met preferred her to be Maggie Marino, an operatic-sounding Italian stage name. She refused. Her name was Elliott; that's what she'd be called. Maggie might be a newcomer, but she was not naïve. They wanted the public to believe she was single. She wouldn't have it. Nor would she be a phony Italian.

There was not an empty seat. Grace and her family, Sam Taylor, wearing a raccoon coat and escorting a flapper in a beaded headband and with a cynicism for tradition, came to

Maggie's premier. Sam also brought the pasty-skinned Arnold Rothstein.

***

Maggie waited for the curtain to open. She was to enter from the left. She takes a deep breath, lets it out, closes her eyes as the sound of a bassoon soares. Another deep breath before a sense analogous to a slow burn spreads through her body. *The music*, she tells herself, *the greatness of the music, will carry the night.* "Feel the music," she whispered to herself. "Let the music wash away your tension." The strings sweep upwards, the horns surge, and Maggie's Zaza flings herself into the audience's arms.

The scene is set at The Alcazar, a cafe in St. Etienne in the 1890s. Zaza flirts with friends at the cafe concert as she prepares to perform with her partner and former lover, Cascart.

C.J. watches Maggie, enthralled by her performance. Her acting is marvelous. Her voice, rich and warm, seizes the lush harmony. She captures Zazà's cabaret heart and the self-protective peasant spirit of a woman refusing to be either heroine or victim.

Maggie did not portray Zazà—she became the French Music-Hall singer. Headstrong and sure of herself, Maggie revealed Zazà, knowing precisely what she wanted and settling for no less. Alternating between moments of passion, intensity, and stretches of humor, Maggie conveyed a sense of frustrated desire and a scandalous lifestyle, all challenging the limits of women's freedom.

The New York Times, and every other newspaper's reviews raved with bravura.

Animated and charismatic, with a fiery and brazen personality,

Elliott commanded the attention of everyone. Eccentric and flamboyant with the strut of an elaborate Peacock, she filled the role with an unbridled amount of energy, with her beauty and physicality dominating the stage.

Eyes brimming with tears, conveying every psychological shift with an extraordinary blaze of excitement and talent, this newcomer was breathtaking. She lived rather than sang the music.

Charm, vivacious nonchalance, fervent passion, dejected self-pity, blazing anger, and stoic selflessness: Maggie Elliott was the chanteuse raised from the backstreets to the bright lights and a walking compilation of emotions.

Even with her sudden fame, Maggie's personality did not change, at least not much. She remained utterly magnetic, warm, and witty. Accomplished, although sometimes prickly, when talking with the press, she had only one slight fault. Sometimes she overindulged in gin.

Once, when asked how she felt about her success as Zazà, she described it as like Christmas Eve and receiving the gift you have wanted all your life. Asked the same question another time, after perhaps a few too many gins, she told the reporter he was over-fawning in his approach and that he "must be the king of hypocrisy in sincerity. You praise my performance but clearly would have considered Zazà herself a cheap drunken tramp. I believe you, a callow fool, and your publication unworthy of reading."

XIII

Chapter Thirteen

By May 1921, if viewed from C.J.'s perspective, life was fraught with frustration. Rewrite after rewrite, followed by writer's block, the manuscript became his master, then his tormenter. Maggie and Grace called Alex, the sensual vampire of the novel, a toothless mosquito.

Maggie outright spurned his old friend, Sam. She threatened to shoot him if he came around again.

For Maggie, 1921 was a fine year—until Tommy telephoned. "Have you heard what happened? In Greenwood?"

"No." She would have been better off if she never did.

Tommy, not given to emotion, was a wreck on the other end of the line. His voice cracked; he choked up. "They're calling it the Tulsa race massacre. Hundreds are dead; thousands are homeless. The town is in ashes."

Greenwood, the Black Wall Street obliterated, burned to cinders. Maggie couldn't imagine a loss so significant; it wasn't possible. Greenwood thrived as a home to prosperous business districts, the epicenter of Negro commerce and culture; such a community couldn't be in embers. Neither the newspapers nor the radio stations outside Tulsa reported a word.

"I'll bet The KKK is behind the violence," Tommy said.

Maggie couldn't conceive of the city in flames. "What started something so horrific?"

Having read police accounts and Bureau of Investigation reports, Tommy shared what details he knew, some he described as sketchy. "A black teenager named Dick Rowland entered an elevator at the Drexel Building. At some point, the white operator, a seventeen-year-old named Sarah Page, screamed. Rowland fled, only to be arrested the next morning. I've never heard of either one, have you?"

"No."

The *Tribune* ran headlines claiming Rowland sexually assaulted Page. At dark, angry whites gathered in front of the courthouse, demanding Sheriff McCullough hand him over. He refused, and his deputies barricaded the top floor to safeguard their prisoner.

Tommy's voice cracked. He took a deep breath. "About twenty-five armed blacks assembled to help protect Rowland. After the sheriff turned them away, rumors of a lynching started flying. Around seventy armed black men returned. Some fifteen hundred white men, many carrying firearms and clubs, met them."

Tommy told her with shots fired and chaos breaking out, the outnumbered blacks retreated to Greenwood. For several hours, groups of racist Tulsans—some deputized and given weapons by city officials—committed violent acts against negroes, including shooting an unarmed man in a movie theater.

False rumors of a large-scale insurrection among black Tulsans spread. Bogus reports claimed reinforcements from nearby towns and cities with bulging negro populations fueled the increasing hysteria. "That was when hell and destruction exploded," Tommy said.

Dawn broke, with thousands of white citizens pouring into the Greenwood District, looting and burning homes and businesses over thirty-five blocks. Hooded Ku Klux Klanners threatened firefighters with guns and forced them to leave. White rioters burned over twelve hundred and fifty houses. They looted two hundred and fifty others. Two newspapers, a school, a library, a hospital, churches, hotels, stores, and many other black-owned establishments were destroyed or damaged.

Tommy stopped talking, slipped into his own distressing world. Maggie listened to his heavy breathing, waiting for him to say something. He didn't.

"What's wrong?"

Tommy hesitated. "Uncle Paddy is up to his ass in this mess."

Maggie rubbed her hand over the smooth, dark table where the telephone sat. The morning air still had a chill. The breeze coming through an open window carried the salty smell of the ocean. She loved mornings like this. Tommy's call ruined this one.

She collapsed into the yellow mustard-striped chair by the phone. "What about our father?"

Tommy cleared his throat. "He may not be in as deep

as Paddy, but he's involved." Another lengthy pause. "Mags, I think our father was in on the looting and burning. They suspect Paddy of being a shooter."

"You mean he murdered people?"

"He's on the suspect list. I can't tell you what will happen. Tulsa and Oklahoma authorities are trying to squelch the whole thing."

Maggie felt drained of the necessary strengths that make one human. She crumpled into a bleak, withering, and deadened state. Life was ashy, motionless, and yet insolent enough to allow for a smothering torment. Her bearings were lost; all things were dark and depleted of emotion. The slippage into mindlessness was rapid. She possessed no will, everything was an effort, and nothing seemed worth the struggle.

An hour after asking her brother to call back when he knew more, she went hunting for Elliott, finding him on the shore, where the waves crept past him, soaking his shoes and pants. No need to ask what the problem was. Some publisher rejected the novel—again. Instead of telling him to move back, she sat next to him.

Sitting with his knees in his arms, he turned to her. "The sand is wet here."

"Well, silly, the tide is coming up here." The ocean rolled, a little colder than Maggie expected. "The tide's going out. It will stop hitting us in a little while." A few breakers later, the water stopped short of them. "Tommy called. They've had a race riot in Tulsa."

C.J. twisted toward her. She was staring straight ahead, expressionless.

"Greenwood's been destroyed," she said.

Before their wedding, C.J. knew little about Greenwood. He didn't know much now; Tulsa's most affluent coloreds live there, nothing else.

Maggie changed the subject. "Did someone turn your novel down?"

"Again."

"I'm sorry."

"Doesn't matter. One shining star in a family is enough."

Maggie's face clouded, turned white, then dark. "That was uncalled for."

C.J. got up, wishing he had better sense than to sit in the waves. The clingy, wet pants and soggy shoes made him miserable and annoyed with himself. He held out his hand and helped an unhappy Maggie to her feet.

***

Two days passed without hearing from Tommy. Newspaper and radio reports remained scant. The Boston Globe reported eighty-five dead, including nine whites.

When Tommy called, he gave her bad news. Per Tommy, the number dead was in the hundreds, as many as three hundred fifty.

He had talked with their mother; she wavered between denying and defending the family's involvement. She also let something slip. Their father had severe burns on his forearms but wouldn't say how he got them.

He told Maggie men claiming to be deputies shot and killed Dr. A.C. Jackson, a prominent black physician who'd been attracting the Mayo brothers' attention. Worse, retired Judge and Police Commissioner John Oliphant witnessed the act, calling it cold-blooded murder.

"He says seven or eight armed whites intercepted Dr. Jackson. Two of them shot him. He fell, and one of them shot him again. Judge Oliphant identified Paddy as one of the shooters."

Maggie's knees buckled. She leaned against the wall not to fall. Vomiting was a possibility. She heard Tommy asking if she was all right. "No. I think I may be sick." She called for C.J., handed him the phone, and slumped in the mustard-striped chair.

Tommy said they should have charged Paddy with murder, but they didn't. No one was indicted. Not one person. While remaining vague about their father's involvement in the riot, Tommy claimed the lack of arrests was corrupt, a cowardly whitewash.

Tommy doubted charges would ever come against Pop or Uncle Paddy. Sarah Page and Dick Rowland, if those were their actual names, both disappeared. Prosecutors dropped the charges against Rowland. Whatever his real name was, Rowland vanished among several reports saying Tulsa Sheriff Willard McCullough took him to Kansas City.

Embarrassment and shame plummeted Maggie into a profound depression. It was all C.J. and Grace could do to prevent her from leaving Zazà. Had the opera not been on hiatus, they would have failed. With the O'Sullivans disgraced, 1921 turned sour, a time of discontent.

A womanizing president, illegal liquor, shady oil tycoons, corrupt politicians, and sacks of bribery money plagued the nation. A frustrated writer and heart-sick actress/musician plagued the household.

XIV

Chapter Fourteen

Now a minion of Arnold Rothstein, Sam Taylor raked in cash, every red-cent illicit. His frequent visits infuriated Maggie. He tried to sneak C.J. away from the house this time, but Maggie saw them leave. She assumed to hatch some scheme using C.J.'s finances.

It was worse. Sam drove C.J. to a swanky Bar Harbor restaurant, where he introduced him to Arnold Rothstein.

The man was well-tailored, well-mannered, and had the quiet look of respectability. He didn't look old, not quite middle-aged, but not young, either.

Standing, Rothstein extended his hand. His handshake was solid and firm. Pointing to a chair, he told C.J. to sit. "Order some lunch," he said, handing C.J. a menu. "Sam speaks highly of you. He says you are extremely bright and capable of going a long way."

He took a slow drink of water, keeping his eyes on C.J.

"My desire is to build a business empire. A conglomerate, if you will, based on diverse interests. I need youthful, fresh minds."

C.J., sitting with his elbow on the table and his hand curled in front of his lips, stared at Rothstein. He leaned back in his chair. "I hope you'll forgive my saying this, Mr. Rothstein, but aren't your businesses slightly illegal? Gambling, numbers running, alcohol, and drug trafficking?"

Rothstein smiled good-naturedly—in fact, long-sufferingly. It was one of those sham grins, almost a smirk of inherent superiority. Then it vanished.

"You impress me with your forthrightness. But, my dear boy, you have been misinformed."

Raising and lowering his eyes, C.J. was skeptical.

Unperturbed, Rothstein smiled again, an arrogant and somewhat sleazy smile. The kind you get from people who don't care what anyone thinks.

As he told C.J. to call him, Arnie took his time removing a cigar from the breast pocket of his pinstriped suit. "My father," he began, speaking at an irritatingly slow pace, "was a true American success story. Working in New York City's Garment District and steering clear of shady dealings," he added, smugness in his voice, "became a successful businessman. That's the type of man I'm endeavoring to be."

C.J. turned down the offer of a cigar.

Rothstein put it back in his coat pocket. "I can say, in all honesty, I've been able to make friends with high-placed politicians and businessmen. That is always helpful in business." Rothstein droned on about his success, about his connections in elevated places. He was unreserved in touting his many diverse multinational accomplishments. C.J. assumed multinational meant bootlegging Canadian booze.

Details flowed about how his businesses needed bright young managers and directors. Go-getters with entrepreneurial and sales skills were always valuable. Financial backing from endowed investors looking for significant returns was always welcome.

With lunch's arrival, the conversation changed to lighter topics. How did C.J. like living in Maine? Did he follow politics? How did he like being married to such a talented wife?

After lunch, C.J. took a deep breath and told Rothstein although the offer was tempting, with everything he was involved in and considering the time his wife's career demanded, he would have to decline.

A gracious Arnie understood his decision. As they shook hands to leave, he asked C.J. to take a little more time to consider his choice. Or, perhaps, to contemplate only investing.

***

A week later, Sam surprised his old roommate while walking along the shore during a mid-July visit. "Arnie is ingenious. They're calling him The Brain."

C.J. stopped, picked a flat rock, and skipped the stone out in the surf. "He doesn't strike me as bright; he strikes me as crooked."

Sam poked his finger into C.J.'s chest. "He's formidable. He has money, women, fine houses, and power. Power is the important thing, not being smart. Arnie's both." Sam took one step back. "An intelligent man can grab his share. I think I'm smart enough to seize some."

Sam tapped a pack of cigarettes on the palm of his hand,

offered one to C.J., and flicked the flame of a silver lighter when C.J. refused. He took a drag on the cigarette, sucking smoke deep into his lungs before exhaling through his nose. He flipped a small sand crab away with the toe of his shoe.

"Arnie thinks I have potential. He's setting me up with an area, Queens, and part of Manhattan. He says he'll finance me, Charlie, and Meyer. Teach us the business." Sam tossed a piece of driftwood out in the water. "The Brain wants you to change your mind about joining his organization. In fact, he insists on it."

Patience was at the heart of C.J.'s nature. He had an unhappy youth, which had made him tolerant. But his composure had its limits. "I'm not having anything to do with Rothstein, and you'll end up getting yourself murdered."

"Not likely. We'll be too connected."

"Why tell me all this?"

"To bring you in as a financial partner, use your investment to expand into gambling, prostitution. We'll be rich and efficacious men."

"I thought Arnie's dealings were all legitimate."

Sam ignored the comment.

C.J. glared at his former roommate. "You've lost your mind. I doubt you know what efficacious means."

Sam's demeanor changed. "Don't act self-righteous with me. Your wife's relations are up to their necks in that Tulsa situation. Hell, they've got blood all over their hands."

That was true, according to Tommy. C.J. hurt for Maggie, but he was used to family estrangement. Maggie, with his help, would survive the pain.

Sam put his hand on C.J., not in a friendly way. He took a

fistful of C.J.'s shirt. "Don't be a damn fool. People don't turn down Arnold Rothstein. Not if they know what's good for them. He's offering you money and power. Me, Charlie, and Meyer prove what he can do for people he likes."

Elliot slapped Sam's hand away. "I've never heard of your Charlie and Meyer."

"Charlie's a WOP. He's part of Arnie's muscle. Meyer's a Jew. He knows money. Until now, the Italians, the Jews, and the Irish have been working alone. Hell, they've been warring with each other. Arnie's uniting everybody into one organization. With Arnie's influence...we'll take over."

"Not with me."

Sam's eyes narrowed; the corners of his mouth turned down. He let C.J. walk away—this time.

XV

Chapter Fifteen

For three weeks, C.J. kept the Sam problem from Maggie, but with the meetings continuing to haunt him, he confided in Tommy.

When Tommy called him back, C.J. and Maggie were in Boston, where Maggie was playing in the Fadette Orchestra. "The two fellas you asked about are Meyer Lansky and Charlie Luciano. At least, I think they are. They call Luciano Lucky. They're rough, Five Point Gang boys. They show up in Rothstein's file and have extensive files of their own. I didn't unearth anything regarding Sam."

"Do you mean he isn't involved in any crime?"

"No. Sam hasn't caught anybody's attention yet. He will, though."

C.J. took a deep breath and exhaled slowly.

***

Another month passed without C.J. confiding in Maggie

about Sam. During that time, Sam became more persistent in his requests for financial backing. The appeals stopped being asks and bordered on threats.

Maggie did not take it well when she found out. Quite by accident, she and Grace saw Sam drive through Bar Harbor. She confronted C.J., then called Tommy. Finding out Tommy knew infuriated her. Taking her anger out on C.J., the first major fight of the marriage ensued. She locked him out of the bedroom for four nights.

The Bureau of Investigation made a personal call on Sam. Something which did not sit well. One Sunday afternoon, C.J. received a visit from Sam and his two friends, Meyer and Charlie. They insisted on a stroll along the shore and accused him of *dropping a dime* on them.

Charlie got mouthy, and C.J. split his lip. Sam stepped into the middle when his old friend asked Meyer if he wanted smacked in the mouth, too. Sam mumbled something about coming to talk business, not to get into a fight.

"Nobody blames you, but you've got to call Maggie's brother off. Let's keep walking."

"As long as your goons walk in front of us," C.J. said while jerking Lansky and Luciano's coats open to see if they were armed. Only the Italian was. C.J. yanked the revolver out of a shoulder holster and heaved it into the bay as far as he could.

Sam pushed Luciano back and motioned for his two associates to step ahead. Charlie was still holding a handkerchief to his lip.

Sam got cocky while they walked. "Listen, C.J., we've been pals for years. I've your best interests at heart. We could make a lot of dough together."

C.J. shook his head and gazed across the harbor, but didn't respond.

"You'd have no risk. You provide front money. We give you close to triple in return."

"Where's all this income come from?"

"Booze. Some gambling, narcotics. Hell, there's even the numbers racket."

C.J. stopped and turned to his old friend. "You went to Amherst. Why are you involved in something like this? You could be making substantial income legitimately."

"Not this kind of income. And, I only work a few hours a week."

"You'll end up dead, and that's forever."

Sam blocked C.J. "I won't be the one taking the big sleep." He raised his head toward the Elliott home. "Stage doors get pretty dark at night. Little clubs are darker."

That was it. C.J. grabbed Sam by the lapels. His hot breath made Sam's eyes widen. "Was that a threat? Are you threatening Maggie? You listen to me. I'm the one with the finances; I can buy plenty of muscle and protection. You remember that before you threaten my wife. Point it out to your friend Arnie. Now take your mouthy talk and those two dopes and get the hell out of here," C.J. screamed while pushing his old roommate hard enough to land him on his hind end in the wet sand.

C.J.'s call to Tommy was short. The next day, Arnold Rothstein took an extended tour of an exceedingly unpleasant New York jail.

A few days later, a sympathy card reading *My Deepest Regrets Over Samuel* arrived. It was signed—Arnie.

XVI

❦

Chapter Sixteen

Hollow, a shadowy stairway to nowhere, that was January through March 1922, according to Maggie. Oklahoma newspaper articles and law enforcement investigations publically unmasked her father and Uncle Paddy as racists. How she loathed her father, no, more than that, she abhorred the man with such high morals he denounced his daughter over bobbed hair and pants, the one who put scars across her lower back because she was too willful. Now, he was exposed as a long-time racketeer. Good, maybe he goes to jail.

Nothing in her childhood had been true. Nothing except the cruelty. The root of a massive and deplorable social ill, self-righteous hypocrisy came a little closer to home.

Her mother never stood up for her when she was beaten, never intervened, or questioned what type of abuse Maggie suffered. She stuck by Maggie's father and uncle, unwilling to forego her lifestyle. They moved to Los Angeles, where society overlooked crimes—if you were rich. Maggie didn't have their address. She didn't want it.

Rejection bit Alex, C.J.'s romantic vampire, four more times. The last time Maggie saw the manuscript, the pages were bobbing away in the high tide. C.J. stopped working. He spent his time brooding in Bar Harbor or reveling in the New York party scene, something open to them because of Maggie's musical success.

Like other flappers, Maggie shortened her skirts and danced in dark speakeasies. She and her cello soloed at The Met, and she sang in Clubs to audiences of a different social level. She auditioned for an opera. She was offered a secondary part, not the lead. She rejected it. Her mood spiraled.

Her husband's writer's block intensified his drinking of illegal booze. Her family issues pushed her into a bleak hole.

She tried to overcome her personal demons with work, singing five nights a week and partying with C.J. the other two.

She belted jazz at The Cotton Club to predominately white listeners, including her imbibing husband. Sore throats became the price for her fun. Some mornings she was so hoarse she couldn't speak. Who cared? Clubs aren't open in the mornings.

By evening, Maggie was always ready to sing again. When not at the Cotton Club, she favored Chumley's or New York's reigning queen of nightlife, Mary Louise Cecilia's Texas Guinan 300 Club, a place for a notoriously good time. That's where she was on a cold Friday night when they were back in New York.

To the delight of those tippling the bar's illegal liquor

while forty fan dancers flew from the stage to dance in the aisles, Texas Guinan herself came on to announce Maggie.

"Hello Suckers! Come on in, leave your wallet on the bar, and give this little lady a great big hand! The wonderful Maggie Elliott."

With her arms and hips swinging, Maggie danced and hummed across the stage. The audience swung into action as some started dancing and applauding one of their favorite singers. This spurred the musicians to turn to the patrons, with the saxophonist using his mobility to move into the crowd as he played. Applause animated the artists.

At first, the jazz group concentrated on their individual instruments as they slowly introduced the performance. Then it changed as the beats soared. In minutes, the interaction between performers and the spectators increased. The saxophonist blended into the revelers. Maggie moved up next to the drummer and pretended to smack the symbol.

Flappers, sailors, actors, and bohemians heading for nowhere ate and drank as long as the entertainment lasted. Always until the wee hours.

Despite C.J. telling her not to leave alone, Maggie always exited through a stairwell leading into an alley closer to where her parked car was watched over by the club's security force.

The stairwell reeked of moldy wood and rat droppings. From kitchen windows came the smell of spoiled cabbage and pork. The cheap, stuffy apartments across the alley stank of stale dust, the bedrooms of greasy sheets and urine-soaked featherbeds. It was far different from the Metropolitan Opera. People staggered past, reeking of whiskey. The stink came from both sides of the alley, from the ground to the roof. The stench of sulfur rose from the chimneys.

On damp nights like this, the entire area was immersed in a vileness unimaginable to someone living in Bar Harbor. Yet, the thrill of an audience drew her back.

As she pranced through the little passageway, swirls of cold air whirled dust and debris into corkscrews of eye-irritating dirt. There was no color in anything except some window panes a block away.

Suddenly, from nowhere, a short black mustachioed man blocked her way. Immediately over his shoulder, another shadowy man tossed away a cigarette. Down at the street corner, another leaned on a brand-new Studebaker. That one's unbuttoned coat whipped fitfully in the wind.

The mustached man moved to the side. The larger man behind him clutched Maggie's elbow. When he spoke, his breath stank of rotten teeth. "You're a real looker, doll. You don't look like you're from this neighborhood." He stepped forward and pressed against Maggie. "I'll bet you're a singer at Texas Guinan's place. Is that right, honey?'

"Let me go."

"Go where? With me? Want a good time with me?"

The answer was no. With all the force she could muster, Maggie slammed her knee into the man's groin.

"Ugh." The old boy fell hard, landing in a fetal position.

She started to run but was grabbed by the mustached man, who dragged her down the alley to the man leaning on the Studebaker.

He put his massive hand around her chin. "That was a bit unkind." In a rough motion, he jerked Maggie's face up and bent his forehead against hers. "You listen, little missy. Your jellybean hubby has been making some poor business decisions. You should tell him to reconsider some things."

He took his hand away and got in the driver's seat. The mustachioed man tipped his derby hat and got in the other side. They drove away with him waving goodbye.

Maggie ran for her car. Fumbling through her purse for her key, Maggie turned her head to look back, to gain some sense of whether the man she kneed was anywhere to be seen. She saw two figures running toward her through a patch of moonlight sliding between the dark buildings. Her heart leaped to her throat. As she found her key, only to scuffle with getting it into the door lock, the two figures, a young man and woman squealing and laughing, ran by.

Relieved, she fired the engine and screeched away. As far as she knew, the man she disabled was still lying in the alley.

***

C.J. had his head in his hands, but his emotions were apparent even with his face obscured.

"What are you so mad about?" Maggie demanded, heated herself. "Because I was threatened or because I won't stop performing?"

C.J. stood. His anger drained. "In the last month, two women were beaten in the neighborhood you were in. One died. She had a wire wrapped around her throat so tight it almost cut her head off. "

"So?"

"Do you care?" There was no response. "Does it worry you at all?"

"I don't think about it."

Shoulders slumping, C.J. seemed to wilt. "Well, I do."

"What do you want?"

"I want you to feel what I feel. The worry, the fear some-one will hurt you. The trembling I feel when you ignore real threats. The sickness I'd feel if I lost you. Those people don't kid about hurting people."

Unaffected, Maggie didn't bother to look at her husband. "I'm not going to quit singing in clubs. Besides, it's your damn fault I was threatened. You fix it."

"My fault? I told Rothstein no. And you lied to me. You said you were singing in Manhattan. Then you went to Texas Guinan's. If you hadn't lied, I'd have gone with you to protect you."

"Fine, come along next time. I'm not going to stop. Not until I have what I want."

XVII

Chapter Seventeen

"Our lives aren't what I thought they'd be," Maggie said one day while feeling sorry for herself. Looking out their bay window, her mood was as dark as the charcoal sky rolling over the harbor, promising a squall.

"Don't worry. Tomorrow is another day," C.J. said in an unusual burst of optimism. "And like every day, no matter how special or how ordinary, we'll have to live it out."

"Save your Occam's Razor speech, old sport. Today is not the day for it."

The expected storm came softly at first, then the rain built to a steady drumming on the windows and the roof. Waves in the bay increased in tempo. The gales crescendoed as an opera might. Even after progressing into a torrential downpour, it pounded in overtures and interludes.

Within an hour, all sense of form and path was lost. The sea raged. Its gales screamed under dark, menacing clouds.

***

"Undress and put this on."

"This? This thing'll barely cover my front, and none of my backside."

"Dr. Allen needs to examine you."

"Examine my throat. Nothing else." Maggie pitched the tiny gown at the nurse. "He'll see all he needs when I open my mouth."

"Wearing this is a requirement."

"Fine, you wear it. Or tell him to."

Maggie did not remove her clothes. The doctor removed the tongue depressor and tossed the stick in a trash basket. He felt Maggie's throat, right under her jaw, pushing hard enough to make her cough. "What did you say you do?"

"You're a forgetful one. I sing."

"Where? How often?"

"Opera. I also sing jazz in clubs."

"Well, young lady, your vocal cords are raw. Keep this up, and you won't sing anywhere." He poked down her throat again, none too gently, and swabbed it with a terrible-tasting paste before scribbling out a prescription.

Maggie's shoulders sagged. Pale and tired, she struggled to raise her head. Her thoughts enclosed in a black box; she felt like a sailboat trying to sail with its sails furled.

"How long will it take me to get well? Will I get well?"

"If you rest your voice and follow these instructions, about a month."

***

Trudging home, the day was as grey as the ashes in a dying fire. Week-old frozen slush crunched beneath her feet.

The shop windows were frosted over, the people she passed were chilled and unfriendly. The bay lie empty, vast, and unmoving."

It began to snow—again. Maggie watched sleepy flakes, large and white, falling in the streetlights. She pulled her coat closed, holding it with her red, wet, cold fingers.

She slipped on the ice, caught herself on one hand, losing her grip on the long sleeve cover-up embellished with sequins. The wrap coat wasn't too thick or thin. The lady clerk said it was an elegant cover-up and a wonderful option for modern ladies. She said the lack of buttons made it a versatile piece without being restrictive.

"Why would anyone make a coat with no buttons," Maggie growled, trying to keep it closed in the now-biting wind. "And why would any idiot buy it?"

When she entered their living room, her eyes were puffy and red-rimmed. Pale tracks ran down her face, leaving dis-colored blotches in her makeup and her humor.

Maggie tossed her coat on the couch, slumped into the overstuffed chair.

"What did the Doc say?"

Maggie studied C.J. Her eyes scrutinized him. She was undecided about answering. He sat next to her and took her hand.

"He said my vocal cords are raw." She said nothing else.

"What do we do?"

She used her feet to flip her shoes off. Her red knee socks had a hole over one toe. She pulled that one off and pitched it across the room toward a waste can. She missed by two yards. "We don't sing for a month. We rest and drink lots of water, juices, hot tea, and honey. I—I mean, we—don't talk too much and avoid coffee and alcohol."

"So, if you do those things, your throat will heal, and you can sing again?"

"As long as I don't smoke and stay away from anything in the air I'm allergic to."

***

Would their future be like this? In the absence of vocalizing, Maggie composed music, but not jazz. Her creations were nothing like jazz. She wrote of small towns and big cities. Sad and happy at the same time, her words and sounds made life slow down. She said she wanted it to be the people's voice when their voices weren't loud enough. C.J. called her a storyteller who would someday bless the world.

Still, melancholy filled the grand house in Bar Harbor. A rejected novelist and dejected musician are not pleasant company.

***

In the early spring, C.J. and Maggie packed their dreams, aspirations, cellos, and three-piece suits and boarded a ship to France. They sought escape from dead former roommates, not-so-veiled threats from crime heads, estranged families, and rejection letters.

C.J. said he was looking for somewhere. Not something, somewhere. A place to find success, a life, a place to watch Maggie's cinnamon hair turn grey.

The second day out, the Elliotts stood on the top deck, leaning over the railing, marveling at the dolphins swimming along the bow. C.J. held his newsboy cap, the Christmas present from almost three years ago, tightly in his fist. Otherwise, it would be blown across the ocean.

Another couple, about their age, approached them. "I'm sorry to interrupt," the woman said. "But are you Maggie Elliott?"

"I am," Maggie said, surprised at being asked."

"You were Zazà at the Met. How glorious."

C.J. beamed. "Yes. She was wonderful. After playing Zazà, she was in Floriani's Wife on Broadway."

"For its entire sixteen-performance run," Maggie laughed.

The man smiled and extended his hand. "Scott Fitzgerald. This is my wife Zelda and our daughter Scottie."

C.J. stammered. "Scott Fitzgerald? F. Scott Fitzgerald?"

"I often try to deny those scandalous accusations, but I'm afraid so."

"He disowns nothing," Zelda Fitzgerald said. "He flaunts it."

C.J. took his hand. "C.J. Elliott."

"It's sometimes best to ignore Zelda," Fitzgerald said." She likes to be a bit theatrical. Usually, to mortify me."

Zelda stuck her tongue out at her husband, something Scottie Fitzgerald mocked.

Maggie twisted into C.J. "Elliott is also a writer. He's dreadfully talented."

"No, I'm a failed one. I suspect it's time to accept the truth and give up."

Fitzgerald leaned against the rail and slapped C.J. on the shoulder. "Find a quiet room and start over. Adroit writers are in demand."

"I've tried. Publishers have been, let's say, unimpressed.

Unimpressed enough, I sent my last manuscript floating off the Maine coast in Frenchman's Bay."

"Scott rips his to shreds," Zelda said. "Learn to ignore rejection. Perseverance is the key."

Maggie jabbed C.J.'s arm. "What did I tell you?"

The Fitzgerald's daughter tugged on her father's slacks. "Stop," her father said. She did not.

Maggie picked her up and asked her if she liked sailing. "No."

Zelda took the little girl. "This is my beautiful little fool. She's probably hungry. We should give her some lunch."

"Would you like to join us?" Scott asked.

To C.J.'s disappointment, Maggie declined the invitation.

They were out of American waters and out of the reach of The Volstead Act. Since they were also long past Maggie's drinking ban because of her throat, C.J. wanted to drop by one of the bars for a cognac.

After their cognacs, they spent the next few hours touring the ship's numerous lounges, smoking rooms, a palm court, formal dining room, two swimming pools, a gallery of informal dining decorated in art déco, private dining areas, a promenade on the B deck, isolated verandahs. A writing room made the vessel an extraordinary place for C.J. After the tour, they tried out one of the pools, swimming laps for almost an hour.

C.J. turned the key to their stateroom. Maggie flopped on the bed and sighed before rolling toward her husband. "Have you written anything since drowning Alex?"

C.J. didn't respond.

Sitting up and giving Elliott a crooked smile, she shook her head. "Answer me. Have you?"

"A little, not much."

"Let me read what you've done."

C.J. pointed at his suitcase, gave a half-hearted groan.

Hidden among his slacks, Maggie found a light brown leather portfolio. Comfortable on the edge of the bed, Maggie opened the small gold clasp and pulled out three pages.

Living Life

C.J. Elliott

Poets and philosophers claim life passes in seasons. If true, I'm in the summer of my life. The spring has ended. My rocking horses and peddle cars gather dust in some attic. Marriage and responsibilities lurk, wanting to replace yesterday's careless, carefree days. Ill-equipped for this phase, what lies ahead excites me, but I know already—life can deceive you.

I'm now turning the page to the hopes and dreams stage of life, the time of planting, accomplishment, and sowing for a harvest.

My name is Reid Johns. Being honest, this new chapter of life scares me. I'm not a lover of people. I'm more a collector of memories. I wonder if that's a poor way to live? I tell myself recollections will keep people close enough to have whenever they're needed, no matter how far I travel.

My road has stretched from Boston to San Fransisco. But, I've traveled it companionless. Not because I had to, but more by choice. At least, that's what I hope.

Walking under a summer sky or along a beach, I've often asked God for another day. I trust God. But He's the only one. So far, I've gotten that day. Time to spend alone or hopefully fall in love.

What if love never comes? What if my summer is brief? No

fall colors are guaranteed, no smell of burning leaves. Many never reach the winter of life, never walk through the hoarfrost, or feel the icy winds. Fate denies them the Currier and Ives paintings of their own lives.

"This is excellent." Maggie reread his new effort, smiled again at C.J. "This is tender, enticing, beautiful." She read the pages a third time before squeezing them to her chest. "You should, no; you must show this to Scott Fitzgerald."

"Three pages is hardly a novel."

"Don't you dare criticize yourself. Your prose seizes the reader." Maggie sat on C.J.'s lap, kissing his eyebrows before laying her head on his shoulder. Contentment, missing for some time, might be returning.

***

The formal dining room, with its crystal ceiling diffusing the light, bouncing shy colors all over the room, and available only with a reservation, was the bee's knees, according to Maggie. An aging Maître de escorted them to the adjoining lounge and offered complimentary wine.

Sitting in a dim corner with Zelda, Scott Fitzgerald waved Maggie and C.J. over. Scott motioned for the waiter to bring him a second Gin Rickey while Zelda nursed her Bees Knees cocktail. The Elliotts, planning on Oysters Rockefeller, ordered Riesling.

"You must join us for dinner," Zelda said, plucking the two cherries from her husband's fresh drink. "No more of these for you until after you eat. I'll not have you zozzled in front of our new pals."

A handsome young man in white-tie formal attire led

them to a table in the middle of the dining room. "Will this spot do?"

"It's perfect. Magnificent." Maggie's face beamed. Zelda grabbed Maggie, hugging her tight. "We're going to be outlandish friends, you and I."

Fitzgerald ordered his third Rickey. C.J. asked for a gin martini with two olives.

The dinner conversation, pleasant and light, skirted around celebrity. Fitzgerald, the writer, was in awe of Maggie, the musical performer. Both, but especially Maggie, still worried about their success enduring.

Zelda took the last swallow of her fourth Bees Knees and suggested they must embrace their illustrious accomplishments. "I'm jealous of each of you. I have been raised to be a delightful decoration for some lucky man, to be nothing on my own. I am cursed with brains and talent, but also bad judgment, all in equal proportions. That's why I wish Scottie to be a beautiful little fool."

Well, wonderful. Maggie would never let the statement regarding females with brains pass. Ignoring the opening would be impossible for her. With Maggie switching from Chardonnay to Gin, there would be no stopping her.

Maggie's speech was beginning to slur. But not her mind. "Oh Zelda, dear, such is the plague of a female. I'm an exceptional cellist. I dare say brilliant. I should be in the Boston Symphony, probably first chair. Except God gave me the wrong plumbing system. What the hell does not standing to pee have to do with being a musician?" She unintentionally caught a glimpse of her husband's reaction. "Don't look like someone is strangling you."

Zelda's original comment drew her husband into the conversation. "How are you cursed with poor judgment? Are you calling me a poor judgment?"

Affection poured out as Zelda's eyes brightened, and she patted Scott's cheek. "Oh, Goofo, we are bad judgment. Nothing can survive us, my sweet."

The waiter delivered dessert, pineapple upside-down cake, the new rage in desserts, as Scott deftly changed the subject. "Tell me about your writing."

In describing his first manuscript, his only one to date, C.J. emphasized his effort didn't start as a vampire novel. Friends encouraged him to make his protagonist a romantic bloodsucker. He said some publishers didn't respond at all. Those who did offered little encouragement.

"One publisher thanked me for my submission but said they seldom published horror novels. When they did, they liked them to be readable ones."

Fitzgerald smiled, almost laughed. "St. Vincent Millay said, 'to meet F. Scott Fitzgerald is to think of a stupid old woman with whom someone left a diamond; she is extremely proud of the diamond and shows it to everyone who comes by, and all are surprised such an ignorant old woman should possess so valuable a jewel.'"

Zelda shrugged, winked at her husband. "Who cares? Edna is nothing but a whore."

* * *

For the rest of the evening, Fitzgerald encouraged C.J. to write, even offering to read some of his work. Bound for their cabins, Zelda pulled Maggie away from the men. "Be careful, Maggie, don't let his writing become his mistress."

XVIII

Chapter Eighteen

C.J. woke invigorated, eager to share his tale with F. Scott Fitzgerald. "Are you ready for breakfast? At one of the smaller cafés?"

"Stop pacing and fetch my purse."

Maggie had tea and brioche with orange marmalade while C.J. drank coffee and smiled—a lot. After eating, they wandered out on the upper deck, where Maggie reclined in a lounge chair. She brushed a breadcrumb off her cream-colored trousers. Weary of sailing, Maggie contemplated being lost in the ocean, eaten by sharks. "The view is getting boring."

"We've only three more days."

"Three and a half, old sport."

C.J. finished reviewing his pages, his magnum opus, for the fourth or fifth time since finishing his third cup of coffee. "Do you think Fitzgerald will read this?" Nerves out of control, C.J. stood, sat, crossed, and uncrossed his legs.

"He said he would," Maggie said.,

C.J. kept fidgeting, running his fingers across the title page. Maggie grabbed the few pages. "Enough."

C.J. twitched—all over.

"Stop. I'm going to leap the railing if you don't." World-weary, she ambled toward the rail, put both hands on the top, and bounced a little before shooting a quirky smile at her husband. "I'm going to practice my cello. The ship's talent show is tonight. I must win. Why don't you wander around and find Scott and Zelda?"

***

C.J. found the Fitzgeralds playing shuffleboard. "Who's winning?"

"Scottie," Zelda said, chasing her daughter down the court to retrieve the puck she was escaping with. "She's too quick for us."

"We may as well give up," Scott said. "Shuffle boarding with a toddler is hopeless."

Scott pointed at the leather file in C.J.'s hand. "Your novel?"

They occupied one of the many little deck bars, and after ordering drinks, Scott, pen in hand, perused the now seven pages, occasionally stopping to scratch out a brief note.

Scott handed the work to Zelda, asking for her opinion without consulting C.J. She read his words twice.

"You've a captivating, sensitive style," Zelda said.

After promising he and Maggie would meet them for dinner and the talent show in the premier dining room, C.J. hurried back to their stateroom to give Maggie the encouraging news about his novel. On the way, he stopped to buy a bottle of gin.

Maggie rejoiced with him but nixed drinking until later. Sobriety was a must if she was to win the contest. As for Elliott, she wanted her husband to be clearheaded when he listened. If he was tipsy, he might yell something uncalled for. There'd be time for imbibing after the contest.

***

Wearing a sequined navy-blue trumpet-tailed gown, Maggie dropped her cello backstage and joined C.J., the Fitzgeralds, and their daughter in the dining room. Ever the southern belle, Zelda was nursing her second mint julep.

The conversation bounced from one topic to another, with Scott and Zelda bickering about everything. Witty and rebellious in her own right, Maggie was tame and modest matched against Zelda, now arguing with Scott about their parties.

To bristle his wife, Scott wagged his cigarette at Zelda before taking a long swallow of his gin. "Irredeemable. You are incorrigible and irredeemable whenever the Bankheads are around."

"I've done nothing to need redeeming. Tallulah is the one who, to all the boys' delight, runs naked through our bashes, not me." Zelda mocked Scott by pointing her cigarette at him. Her candy box face glowed under the crystal lighting. She glanced at C.J. and blew him a kiss, and another, from her little bow mouth.

Unreserved in front of the others, she started blowing kisses to other men; wrinkling her nose, she aimed them at her husband. "Scott, you're awfully silly. In the first place, I didn't kiss any boy goodbye. And in the second place, nobody was left in the first place."

She held her mint julep up, indicating to the waiter her

need for a new one. "If I did have an honest, or dishonest, desire to kiss one or two people, I might—but I couldn't ever want to—my mouth belongs to you."

Maddeningly, she kept talking.

"Suppose I did—don't you know it'd be just absolutely nothing. Why can't you understand nothing means anything except your darling self?" Another sip of the julep. "Maggie, don't you agree?"

Maggie sat up straight. "With every word."

Zelda patted Scott's arm. "Don't sulk, dear. Sulking is unbecoming." She turned back to Maggie. "C.J., er, Elliott, you must read Scott's new work, *The Beautiful and the Damned.*" Zelda hopped into C.J.'s lap. "I find it so interesting that it seems to me on one page, I recognized a portion of an old diary of mine, which mysteriously disappeared shortly after my marriage, along with scraps of letters, which, though somewhat edited, sound to me vaguely familiar. Mr. Fitzgerald—I believe that is how he pronounces his name—believes that plagiarism begins at home."

Scott, his face hardened, turned away from Zelda and toward Maggie. "What will you be doing for the talent show tonight?"

Maggie considered his question. He looked defeated by Zelda's comment. But it was the kind of defeat that might turn to anger. Maggie decided answering might avoid a Fitzgerald fight. "Playing the cello. Do you like the cello?" she asked, batting her eyes and pretending to flirt.

"Why, I guess I'm not sure." Scott's eyes focused back on Zelda and, in a snarky voice, asked, "Zelda, do I like the cello?"

In her stunning navy blue, Maggie came on stage following

a middle-aged woman who sang a terrible, pitchy version of Camptown Races.

For three flawless minutes, she mesmerized the audience with Maria Theresia von Paradis' Sicilienne. At the perfect time, she stopped, nodded to the crowded house, winked at Elliott, gave her cello a spin, and broke into The Charleston.

Jaws dropped, couples stared at each other, a few laughed, right before they all danced. The judges didn't bother to meet.

Chapter Nineteen

"Elliot, don't ever let me do that again."

"Do what?"

"Try to go drink for drink with Zelda Fitzgerald." Maggie rubbed her eyes and the back of her neck, threw her cover off, and put her feet on the floor. "Well, at least I can find the floor."

C.J. poured and offered Maggie a glass of orange juice before holding up four new pages of writing and declaring he was on a roll.

After Maggie dressed, they headed to one of the more petite cafés for lunch, Maggie's head pounding with every step. The sunny day added to her distress. She asked the garçon for their darkest corner and slumped into a chair, laying her head on the table and shooing the waiter away.

Elliott ordered a ham sandwich and Bromo Seltzer for Maggie.

"Let's go for a swim. I think floating around in the water will make me better."

The warm pool did relieve Maggie's aches. Re-energized, they strolled the decks and wandered through various little shops. Maggie bought a boa and beaded skull cap with tassels.

Four dance floors would be open for the last night afloat, two for ballroom dancing, and two with jazz bands. The Elliotts decided to enter the dance contest.

They spent the rest of the afternoon in their cabin practicing for the Charleston Contest. A contest Maggie planned to win. The lack of space in their stateroom resulted in Elliott knocking a lamp over, and over, and over. A backflip, the absolute winning move, had to be abandoned—Elliott was hopeless.

Halfway through the evening, the couples, wearing numbers on their backs, took the floor for the Charleston. The supreme flapper, Maggie, smiled, batted her lavish eyelashes at her partner, and gave her long string of pearls a quick spin. "The flip is back in."

Elliott wanted to object, but a bell rang, and the contest was underway. By pre-arrangement, judges would tap pairs on the shoulder, eliminating them. Those remaining when the band stopped were given two minutes to catch their breath before starting again.

Maggie's legs drew wolf whistles with every backflip over Elliott's back. Only five couples made the fourth round. An emcee held up three trophies and announced this would be the final round. The music started. The last note faded; three remained, including couple number fourteen, the Elliotts.

In tails and white tie, the emcee stepped to the center of

the dance floor with a four-inch bronze medal and called for applause for all the contestants. "Yowzah, yowzah, yowzah! Our third-place winners are...Couple fourteen."

Maggie bowed with a sweeping wave of her hand. She grabbed Elliott by the hand. "Come on, silly, we've won a medal." Maggie kissed the cheeks of the two remaining couples and wished them glorious luck.

XX

Chapter Twenty

France

Paris, at last. Weeks of hotel living didn't bother Maggie. She loved the commotion, but the cramped room frazzled C.J. At his insistence, they found and moved into an art déco decorated bungalow painted pale yellow. Sparsely furnished, everything except a thirty-one-inch-tall statue of a Russian Borzoi standing in one corner had sharp edges and acute angles, an interior design sophisticated but straightforward.

Maggie sent their address to Tommy, Grace, and Curls in Surrey, England, telling Curls they must cross the channel, swimming if necessary. Anxiety reigned as she waited for responses, in particular from Tommy.

The Fitzgeralds, often lit and fighting, became frequent visitors. Elliot told Maggie they needed more friends. Maggie claimed she didn't need friends, only crowds, an audience, nothing more.

Six weeks passed, then Tommy's letter came, bringing annoying news. The O'Sullivans were again under inquiry, not regarding the Tulsa Riots, but by the Los Angeles office of the Bureau of Investigation. According to Tommy, Paddy's arrest was imminent. He didn't speculate about their father's status.

"Read this." Maggie dropped Tommy's correspondence on Elliott's typewriter before sinking into their red, straight-backed couch. The correspondence filled four disheartening pages. C.J. laid it on his desk, walked over to a window, and, for a short time, watched a dreary drizzle fall. Tired of the depressing rain, he sat next to Maggie and patted her knee. Neither spoke for a long time.

"I didn't so much hate Tulsa. I didn't like being an O'Sullivan."

C.J. gave Maggie's cheek an ill-received light kiss.

Maggie, her eyes appearing wet and glassy, turned her face away. Elliott had seen her cry in excitement and happiness, once because she was mad but never in sorrow. She exhaled dramatically and stared back toward C.J. She was not crying. "Pop would make these buying hops every month, but there were never any new shipments corresponding with the trips."

Maggie nestled her face into the nap of Elliott's neck. "Do you remember how angry I got when I thought Sam was going to involve you in bootlegging? Oklahoma had dry counties. I suspected my old man of transporting whiskey and shine. Liquor in dry counties was illegal. He made us criminals."

"You're not a criminal," C.J. said.

"No, just the spawn of one," Maggie growled. "I loathe family."

That was a problem. Elliott thought he was her family; she was his.

XXI

Chapter Twenty-One

The Fitzgeralds, sober and getting along, dropped by early the following evening to ask Maggie and C.J. to go with them to Zelli's. An invitation Maggie was thrilled to accept.

Opening at midnight, Zelli's Royal Box was a huge underground hall on two floors. Cluttered with tables, the central area featured a bandstand, a stage, a dance floor, and ornate pillars. At one end was an arched alcove with mirrored walls. The entrance led to a balcony overlooking the dancing and bar. Seated in the royal boxes along the terrace, they could peer at all the festivities below. Telephones in the boxes allowed patrons to talk to each other.

Joe Zelli himself delivered a bottle of champagne. "Welcome back, Mr. and Mrs. Fitzgerald."

Scott introduced the Elliotts, emphasizing Maggie had starred as Zazà at the Metropolitan Opera, played cello in the

Boston Women's Symphony, and sang jazz in New York clubs. "C.J.," Fitzgerald said, "is an aspiring writer."

Happy, congenial, good-natured, and chubby, Zelli welcomed them. "I'm Italian by nationality, French by persuasion, and American by adoption," he laughed while opening and popping the sparkling wine. "You've picked a wonderful evening to come. Cole Porter is going to sit in at the piano a little later. He always enjoys meeting Americans." Zelli instructed one of his waiters to take excellent care of this table, wished them a delightful time, and hurried off to mingle with his clientele.

"The party here lasts all night," Zelda said. "They don't have to close because they sell the liquor by the bottle instead of the glass. At dawn, they'll serve us breakfast. It'll be undercooked, burnt, or greasy, but breakfast nevertheless."

A little Italian man carrying an art pad and pencils stopped by. "I'm Zito, the resident caricaturist." For the next thirty minutes, he sketched the Elliotts and Fitzgeralds, exaggerating Maggie's eyes and Zelda's little bow-shaped mouth. Zelda wanted to purchase the drawing but was told he drew them to hang on the club walls. Zelda acted disappointed, but in truth, she was thrilled about being immortalized in the gallery of sketches.

Scott claimed to see an acquaintance on the lower floor and excused himself to say hello. He worked his way through the crowd, putting one hand on Cole Porter's shoulder, extending his other hand. "F. Scott Fitzgerald."

"Of course, I recognize you from newspaper photos. I've also read *This Side of Paradise*, your brilliant novel."

"Joe Zelli told us you're playing tonight."

"Yes, at two in the morning. Can you imagine such a time? By the way, did you know we have some mutual acquaintances? The Murphys."

"Gerald and Sara. They are on the Riviera. Zelda and I are going down Monday to be with them." Despite being a gin man, Scott accepted the vodka offer and took a long drink. "Do you have time to come up and meet Zelda and our friends, Maggie and C.J. Elliott? Maggie played Zazà at the Met."

"Scott has Cole Porter with him." Zelda gasped before gulping the gin left in her glass.

Terrified, Maggie ran her hands through her bobbed hair. She was about to be introduced to Cole Porter.

"Cole, this is my wife, Zelda."

"America's first flapper. You're as stunning as rumored." Porter kissed Zelda's hand and set his gaze on Maggie. "Zazà, in person, I read your marvelous reviews. I would have died to attend your performance. Unfortunately, we were in Paris the entire run."

Scott introduced C.J. as an aspiring novelist, showing enormous potential. Zelda threw her arm around Maggie, raved about her beautiful voice, and told Porter he must have Maggie sing when he went up to play. Maggie blushed and said she couldn't possibly share his spotlight. Cole laughed and insisted Maggie perform with him.

Cole Porter paused four songs into his set, telling the audience he had a musical treat for them. "Straight from the finest clubs in New York City and the Metropolitan Opera, where she dazzled audiences as Zazà...Maggie Elliott!"

Wearing a huge smile, Maggie bounded to the stage to

face a doubtful and suddenly dead silent crowd. Surprised and self-conscious, Maggie froze—but not for long. Talented performers don't freeze. She waved at the crowd, half of them drunk or well on the way to being. She did an exaggerated shrug of her shoulders. "I bet you're all wondering, who the hell is she?" She laughed when the drummer gave her a rim shot.

Cole and the small jazz group backing him pounded out The Charleston. Maggie spread her wings with her palms parallel to the floor. Now swaying with the rhythm, she stepped out on her left foot, moved her right foot forward, and tapped it twice in front of her left, stepping back on her right foot, back on her left, tapping twice behind the right. With arms swinging back and forth, she added twisting movements, balancing on the balls of her feet while her jazzy knees jumped in and out from under her short fringe-covered black dress.

Once she started, she couldn't stop. She Charleston'd back and forth, legs flying. Without a break, the band switched from the Charleston to Ain't We Got Fun.

Maggie flung her head back, bounced to the mike, and burst into divine song.

Every morning, every evening...

Ain't we got fun

In one night, Maggie became a huge hit. A zealous Joe Zelli booked her weekly into his club. Zelda made him push the start date back because she and Scott were pinching the Elliotts for two weeks.

XXII

Chapter Twenty-Two

By train, the Elliotts and Fitzgeralds pulled into the sleepy town of Hyères, where they were to lease a house owned by Scott's friend, Edith Wharton. Finding it distressingly dreary and overrun with condescending British pensioners, and not being ones to stay distressed, they soon relocated to the Villa Marie, a charming property on a pine-shaded hillside in Saint-Raphaël.

When Scott found the lovely villa, he sped back to Hyères, thrilled about the little red village built close to the sea, with gay red-roofed houses and an air of repressed carnival about it.

For much-needed distractions, the four would take a jaunt in their little blue one-doored Renault Torpedo down the coastal road past the spectacular red rocks of the Esterel and the Gulf of Napoule's turquoise shallows to the Cap d'Antibes to visit the Fitzgeralds' friends, Sara and Gerald Murphy.

Here, the shore of the Mediterranean was a magnet for mythic personalities caught between cravings for glitz and elegance. With natural charm and unnatural overindulgence, it was a place to, without judgment, dive deep into the quest for happiness, meaning, the satisfaction of the decadent allure of extravagance, folly, and hedonism. All while escaping, for the most part, any chastisement over scandalous behavior.

Until this year, the stretch of coastline, starting in Toulon in the west and continuing through Nice to Menton on the Italian border, was trendy in the cold months. The area was a destination for wealthy Europeans looking for a mild climate to escape the winter. Riviera winters were also drawing wealthy Americans, many of them celebrities. Before this year, no one would have imagined going in the summer. Suppose one got suntanned? Utterly ill-bred!

Now, summer business was growing because Sara and Gerald Murphy had turned lying on the beach and soaking up the sun into an enticing social activity. The Riviera was becoming a year-round resort. Regular visitors included John Dos Passos and Coco Channel. The age was a time of excess. Writers wrote, painters painted, and drinkers drank.

Soon, in a cove on the Cap d' Antibes, to be nearer the Murphys, the Elliotts and Fitzgeralds unpacked their bags again, this time at the Villa Saint-Louis. They planned a time with days lived in the water and nights celebrated with champagne, indulgence, and fragrant decadence.

Like Scott and Zelda, Gerald and Sara found the Elliotts enrapturing. Maggie burst with vitality, desire, and intelligence irresistible to everyone. C.J., more subdued than his flapper wife, was harder to know, making him mysterious, especially to Zelda Fitzgerald. Within a short time, the Murphys introduced Maggie and C.J. to Archibald MacLeish and the painter Pablo Picasso.

In love with the Riviera, Maggie swam in the Mediterranean, lay under beach umbrellas when the sun got too hot, and wandered the white sands in espadrilles. With Zelda and the Murphys, she drank pitchers full of gin and partied late into the night. C.J. and Scott Fitzgerald wrote their novels during the day and joined in the partying at night.

Maggie fretted, but not much, about not hearing from Tommy. Like her new pals, she was too busy partying to concern herself with sticky family matters in the States.

For Maggie, the French Riviera was the perfect place to forget, rejoice, hide, have a fling, escape restraint, and be free. For C.J., Southern France already threatened to destroy his imaginings of a stable life.

While Maggie and Zelda made spectacles of themselves, C.J. and Scott became closer friends. On the other hand, Zelda was too flirty, making C.J. anxious. Worse, she tempted him, and Maggie didn't care.

When he mentioned returning to their bungalow in Paris, Maggie refused, claiming she was enjoying herself too extensively to leave.

"Elliott, it's beautiful here. We have no pressures on us; you're writing every day. Why would you want to go anywhere else?"

"We came to France because you said I was binge drinking. Now you're drinking more than I am."

Maggie did not react well. She did not like her behavior questioned by her father, and she didn't like being criticized by her husband. She said as much—emphatically—while throwing a cup at him.

Not wanting to fight, C.J. retreated from the argument. He also backed away from the constant partying with the Fitzgeralds and the Murphys, dining more with the reserved Archibald MacLeish than Maggie.

Mrs. Elliott ignored her husband's absences. Zelda Fitzgerald did not. Zelda started skipping golfing dates with Maggie and Sara Murphy and stopped swimming with them. She did drop in on C.J.—time and again—to check on him. Either Maggie didn't know or didn't care.

In a long letter to Grace, Maggie extolled the Riviera, rambling about trendy little shops and exotic food, baking herself scandalously tan on the beaches. Maggie described the extraordinary people she was now friends with, glowing over each. *"Oh, Grace, they're all baddies, at least all of them with any umph in their veins; the girls as much as the boys, maybe more than the boys. I love them all—except Pablo Picasso, a misogynist with repulsive political views."*

The Murphy's parties were one thing Maggie insisted she and C.J. do together. To Sara Murphy's extreme distress, Zelda enjoyed reckless diving from the cliffs behind the Murphy Villa. Often, she dove from as high as thirty or forty feet, requiring precision timing with the waves crashing below. The same waves Maggie, to exasperate C.J., occasionally skinny dipped in.

Among the tiny minority of Americans who turned their back on economic growth to take advantage of French art and American expatriate literature were Arthur and Elizabeth

Musgrove, Art and Liz. The Musgroves embodied the extravagance of the bohemian lifestyle.

Art's constant boasting annoyed Maggie. "I came to France during the war. We danced with death across the countryside, sometimes skirting the front. Being in the hell of battle numbed my nerves. The fighting filled all of us with silent pain."

The combat stories didn't bother C.J. He'd tuck them away for possible use in a novel. But the man's bragging about how he won his wife's affection was too much—too much for Maggie.

"My family hated her, but I diligently chased Elizabeth. I didn't care that she was a married woman continually beaten by an alcoholic spouse. In the beginning, she shunned my advances. I doubled my efforts, even threatening suicide. Elizabeth gave in, divorcing her always-intoxicated but wealthy husband. A week after the wedding, we headed for France."

Despite Maggie not liking Art, the Elliotts, Fitzgeralds, Murphys, and Musgroves became almost inseparable. The Riviera already had its fair share of unique personalities. But these four couples were more than a match.

In the mornings, they would squeeze into bathing suits, grab bottles of gin and wine, and head for the coastline. To battle the boredom of the sun and water, Art smoked heavily and drank more. Each day, he grew odder, painting his toenails and fingernails and betting excessive money on boat races. The rest of the time, he enjoyed chasing the uninhibited women of France's southern coast while his wife drank.

The Musgroves put considerable time and energy into everything they did, whether choosing wine, organizing extravagant parties and masked balls, or dreaming up wild dares to entertain their friends. C.J., however, began to find the Musgroves unsound. On a whim, they could set off with no destination in mind. Not even Zelda Fitzgerald was as erratic. A sudden craving was enough to justify leaving for Venice or Spain. The Musgroves soon developed a pronounced fondness for opium and marijuana. In short, they were terrible influences.

It is rarely easy to enjoy a stable life during domestic pandemonium. Despite C.J.'s cautionary words about their destructive behavior, or because of his concerns, Maggie now found herself drawn to the excitement and unpredictability Art and Liz brought into their lives. As they immersed themselves deeper into this unconventional circle of friends, Maggie's cravings for adventure and escape began to surface.

By mid-august, long past the two weeks, the Elliotts were supposed to spend on the Riviera, Zelda was openly flirting with C.J., her eyes sparkling mischievously. She brazenly fawned on C.J. She kissed him hello, goodbye, and as a reward for making her laugh. Instead of objecting, Maggie laughed about it, embarrassing C.J. To his shock, Maggie drew closer to Zelda, proving Zelda's prediction was correct. They became outlandish friends.

Scurrilous rumors hinted at how wild they could behave. Notoriety blurred their fun-loving personalities with some tales shading promiscuity.

A newspaper story about how friendly the Riviera could be mentioned Maggie and Zelda as very popular among partiers. The article proclaimed Maggie pretty, impudent, superbly assured, and worldly-wise. It called her husband hardworking, kind-hearted, and unpretentious. The coverage did not receive C.J.'s appreciation.

It got worse when a man claiming to be a French movie producer approached the Elliotts in a café and swooned over Maggie. "You have both innocence and the ability to project sexuality without coyness or calculation." He told her she was worthy of being cast in his movies. He said his next film would be about a woman who had never been in love. She believed if she ever did love a man, she could not be faithful to him. "She's a character that can never be trusted beyond a closed door," he said.

C.J. made it clear his wife was not interested. In their hotel room, Maggie, quite blitzed, erupted.

"Who the hell are you to decide what I am or am not interested in?"

"I'm your husband. And I'm tired of your behavior."

Fists clenched, arms flailing, Maggie charged, hitting him in the face, shoulders, and chest. C.J.'s face flushed red with frustration. His jaw tightened, and he struggled to restrain her.

"What is wrong with you?"

As Maggie thrashed and fought, C.J. managed to over-power her momentarily and pin her down. During their struggle, Maggie's anger subsided, and tears streamed down her face. She gasped between sobs, "You're ruining everything! I trusted you! You knew I wanted to be a star." Her words hinted at a more profound betrayal or disappointment fuel-ing her intense reaction, although C.J. had no idea what the issues were.

A tense silence hung in the air as both tried to collect

themselves. Emotions exhausted, they agreed to spend the night with Maggie in the bedroom and C.J. on the couch. A brief separation might benefit Maggie's mental well-being and C.J.'s physical health.

At breakfast, a repentant Maggie claimed not to know what had happened to her.

****

The Murphys' parties, not the Musgroves', were one of the few things everyone, including C.J., continued to enjoy. Almost everyone's drinking got worse. After two or three drinks, Scott often became obnoxious. One drunken night, he threw two of Sara's antique crystal wine glasses off the cliffs behind their patio, getting himself banned from their home for two weeks, leaving Zelda to merrily attend without her husband.

Without Scott, and sometimes minus C.J., Maggie and Zelda's notorious, alcohol-fuelled antics increased to the point they were on par with the misbehavior of Hollywood starlets at their most wanton. On a mutual dare, after way too much drink, Maggie joined Zelda in disrupting another of the Murphys' galas by jumping while holding hands off thirty-foot-high rocks into the pitch-black Mediterranean. Slogging out of the sea, Maggie yelled, "Take me back to that damn canyon. I'll show it some hiking."

Another night, Zelda stripped off her lace panties and tossed them to her hosts, encouraging an impromptu skinny dip in the pool with other inebriated guests gaily participating. On a more sobering occasion, Zelda downed a fist full of sleeping pills and then had to be forced around the hotel's grounds by Maggie and C.J. until morning.

Despite that scare, both Maggie's and Zelda's antics grew more frequent. They threw elaborate dress galas on the beach, lasting all day and all night. When not whooping it up, they lay in the sun or swam, now and then naked.

They became self-destructive, recklessly driving cars down winding roads, flirting with gigolos, and arguing with waiters and hotel staff.

After Zelda gave up on C.J. playing along with her silly affections, she spent more idle afternoons basking in the sun, which was what she was doing when she met a young French aviator. Her short-lived affair, if there was one, strained their marriage. Affair or not, Zelda threatened to leave Scott for the aviator.

Scott locked an ensemble of musicians in a room, refusing to let them out until they'd played long enough to stop Zelda from leaving. "Blame it on the dazzling landscape: the Riviera is a seductive place," said Zelda after reconciling. "The blare of the blue and those white palaces shimmering under the heat accentuates things."

As for the boys, Scott drank too much, and C.J. moped over his novel. Neither succeeded in curbing their wives' conduct. They all but gave up, meaning Zelda continued running amuck. Maggie suffered broad mood swings between manic and detached.

Indifference reigned one afternoon when C.J. came in later than was expected. "Don't bother trying to justify yourself. And don't expect any dinner."

"Scott and I rented a boat and sailed down the coast. We had trouble getting back. The wind wasn't cooperative."

"Not to mention, neither of you can sail."

"That might be true," C.J. said. He strode past Maggie to a cabinet where they kept snacks. "We're out of cookies."

"Tough."

"Yes, it is. I'm hungry."

"Again, tough."

A minute later, while still searching for something to eat, he ran across a party invitation from the Murphys. "Why didn't you tell me about this?"

"No reason. I didn't feel like telling you."

"Do you want to go?" he asked.

"Who cares? Gerald banned the Fitzgeralds again. Sara got mad about Zelda getting too drunk and falling down the stairs." Maggie's mouth twitched. "I'm going to hate myself for giving in, but do you want to go out and find someplace to eat?"

He smiled, then laughed. "Yes. I can say without exaggerating. I am starved."

"Fine. I'm ordering something expensive."

They decided to walk. Not far away, they found a lovely little café, dimly lit, quiet, romantic, and high-priced. The charming little restaurant turned them away because they had no reservation.

Further down the street and around a corner, they sat at a little sidewalk café. The place had a limited menu and a meager choice of wines. Still bothered by the comment about not trying to justify himself, and against his better judgment, he resolved to respond.

"By the way, you have a lot of damn nerve telling me not to try justifying my behavior. You're the one who needs to adjust your behavior."

Nothing. No response, no reaction at all. No reply. Maggie just stared out into the French night.

"Fine. Ignore everything."

"I saw a doctor today. I am not with child. I'm beginning to wonder if I ever will be."

The more time Maggie spent with Scottie Fitzgerald, the more she thought about a baby. "I think I might want a child. Although I don't know why. That four-year-old demon of the Fitzgeralds is incorrigible half the time."

"I could have told you you weren't pregnant. You're willow thin."

"The bright side," Maggie said, "is not too many actresses have offspring."

Rumors abounded about starlets, both opera and film, regarding children. Sometimes, young ingenues disappeared for a time during which their relatives, unbeknownst to neighbors and friends, had babies. More than one ingenue's mother gave birth late in life.

If Maggie were honest with herself, children would be inconvenient and not conducive to her chosen life. She longed to be a musician, a singer, and, in time, a film actress. She had never given any thought to kids...until recently.

"Be happy about one thing," Maggie said, half-smiling, "at least you're not the reason I've been upset."

***

At Zelda's insistence, the Elliotts and Fitzgeralds made their way to Italy, to Riomaggiore.

The rugged, cliffed coastline was breathtaking but hot. Climbing up the ridges overlooking the sea, Riomaggiore, the southernmost hamlet of the Cinque Terre, had stone houses with colored façades, yellow, red, green, and mauve, with slate roofs. They booked rooms in one of the charming hotels in the center of the quaint town.

On the second evening in the picturesque little village, they hiked along the trail Via dell' Amore—Lovers' lane. The path, its magical atmosphere excavated through hard rock and winding along the rock face overhanging the water, enchanted everyone except Maggie.

Delighting in Maggie's re-ignited distress about heights, Zelda teased without compromise—but kindly.

The four friends took about a half-hour to hike to Manarola, another beautiful village. The vibrant houses of Manarola almost tumbled down to its small harbor.

In the square at the top of the town, they explored Piazza Papa Innocenzo IV. Afterward, Maggie and Zelda headed toward the sea, discovering an old waterwheel and narrow, flower-filled, cobblestoned streets and alleys, where they would learn firsthand how unrestricted and insane the time was.

Two men, both Italian, came walking through the crowded tables. As they got to Maggie and Zelda, they stopped.

"You two look like a couple of gigolos," Zelda said with a smile, implying possible approval.

"We're tour guides," the taller, darker man replied before winking at Zelda.

"You two fit the label of the American flapper to a T," the other man said.

"A tour of what?" Maggie asked.

"The most stimulating sites in Riomaggiore," the one slightly more handsome said.

"And how long do your tours last?" Maggie asked, raising her eyebrows.

The taller man put his hands on the table and leaned over. He had a long face and rather large brown eyes. His appearance reminded Zelda a bit of a horse. Not that she had anything against horses.

"That is to our benefactors' discretion."

"No more than two hours," Maggie said, rising, to Zelda's astonishment but also to her approval.

As he extended his hand to her, the shorter man eyed her lengthy, slim figure as she eased her way through the crowded terrace and toward the ocean.

The "guida turisticas" assumed all American women had an attraction for them. That was apparent from their casual demeanors, their strutting down the beach, occasionally bumping against Maggie or Zelda.

"Did you ladies know Manarola is one of the most beautiful and romantic spots on the Italian Riviera? Have you tasted our Focaccia? It's best with cheese. Have you sipped any of our delicious wines? Have you observed our gorgeous sunsets...with someone who knows how to appreciate them?" Yada, Yada, Yada.

It surprised Maggie when Zelda immediately agreed when they were asked to have a look at the villa one of the men lived in. Once there, the four sampled cognac. Not good cognac, not even decent. Eventually, one of them, the one who didn't look like a horse, attempted to kiss Maggie. "You're barkin' up the wrong tree, Fido."

Zelda seemed disappointed over the comment. She shrugged her shoulders when Horse Face slid his hand up and down her bare forearm. "Sorry, Man O War, when my pal says no, her no goes for me too. You boys are out of luck. We're good girls, teases, maybe, but moral, upright young ladies."

"Does this routine work on Italian or French lasses?" Maggie asked, exaggerating her Irish lilt.

Not long after, Maggie and Zelda were walking, alone, back toward the old waterwheel. "If that's the best these beach Valantinos can muster, Italian lotharios are a vigorous disappointment," Zelda said, pretending to stick a finger down her throat.

While Maggie and Zelda had been busy tantalizing and rejecting suitors, at Scott's insistence, C.J. and Scott had visited The Church of San Lorenzo, the most often frequented monument in the tiny town. The gothic-styled chapel was of considerable architectural importance. The detached bell tower historically had defensive sighting functions. Neither thought the walk was worth the effort.

After hurrying down to the harbor at dusk, they met Maggie and Zelda, both looking tousled, for something to eat. "What were you two up to this afternoon," C.J. asked.

"We tried to get involved in some appallingly scandalous behavior," Maggie said. "We were utter failures."

Menus at every café featured fish and crabs. Anchovies in Liguria served marinated and lightly sauteed were on most menus and sold as street food, Fritti Misti—tasty paper cones stuffed with fried seafood. C.J. found them delicious, the other three not so scrumptious.

Maggie started a conversation with a group of locals. She loved soaking up local culture. Fascism, a movement born in

Italy after the First World War, was transforming Italy into a new civilization.

The locals said Mussolini's appointment as prime minister in 1922 did not result in the immediate institution of authoritarian rule. But autocracy soon followed, using force when required. Fascists employed Blackshirt squad violence to reduce the influence of parliamentary opposition and grasp power.

They told dreadful stories of police benefiting from enhanced powers, which made them less accountable for their brutal actions. Italians being monitored more frequently than in the past could easily fall victim to spies and informers—to the extent most grew careful about what they said in public.

Mussolini wanted women to return to their traditionally subservient positions as wives and mothers. Females became limited in their employment opportunities and social events. The fascists worked to abolish female impulses for emancipation.

Maggie first went on a tear about women's rights. Next, she announced they must immediately leave Italy. She didn't care how picturesque the villages and coastlines were. No self-respecting suffragette who had fought hard for equality would stay in such a repressive and backward place. Italy be dammed.

By the end of September, to C.J.'s relief, Maggie grew tired of the parties and wanted more time alone with C.J. They disappeared back to Paris.

XXIII

Chapter Twenty-Three

A foot of mail with multiple letters from Grace, Tommy, and Curls waited when they returned to their Left Bank Montparnasse bungalow. Maggie pushed her round glasses back up her nose every time they threatened to slip off. Curl's notes, including an offer to visit, were the happiest.

Grace talked about missing her best friends, wishing they would come home. There were hints about a new boyfriend, but she was secretive and vague about his identity.

Correspondence from Tommy mentioned Paddy had been arrested but released on bail. The charges related to transporting alcohol.

Glum, for some unknown reason, Maggie moped for the rest of the afternoon and refused to go to dinner. In response, C.J. isolated himself to their sitting room to work on his now one-hundred-page novel. At dusk, petulant and moody,

Maggie flopped into the only comfortable chair in the room Elliott used for writing.

"Elliott," she paused to ensure his attention, "what happened to the boy who wore a lavender suit? The one who loved fun and had such a romantic soul?"

No answer. After a long silence, C.J. pushed his typewriter to the back of the small desk.

"What are you talking about?"

"What happened to you?"

His ears turned red. His bottom lip quivered. "Nothing." Now he was biting his lower lip, proof something was wrong.

"Fine. If you don't want to discuss it, we won't. We won't talk about anything." Maggie stomped out of the room.

C.J. pulled the typewriter back to the front of the desk and started to type. Soon, he was pounding the keys. He stopped, drew a deep breath, and headed to the living room to find Maggie reclining on the red art déco couch, her arm across her eyes. C.J. marched over and stared down at her. Then he yelled at her.

"You want to know what happened?"

Startled by his yelling, Maggie sprang to a sitting position. Crimson-faced and trembling, C.J. repeated his question—louder. His answer followed. "This happened; you told me you were better off without family." The color drained from Elliott's face. He stopped shaking. "I thought I was your family." Elliott walked out.

* * *

A dismal rain was falling as C.J. hailed a cab. A dark veil hung over the city of lights. Most people find rainy days dreary and cheerless. C.J., in general, discovered a shadowy sort of well-being in the tapestry of black clouds and rain. But not this afternoon. The air was heavy, and the dampness suffocating.

C.J. quickened his pace as the taxi swung to the curb. "Sank Roo Doe Noo."

Harry's Bar—a dark mahogany bar polished by drunken elbows, full of faded American College pennants, drew bohemians, writers, and artists of many nationalities. Two of the Elliotts' recent acquaintances, a Toronto newspaper correspondent named Hemmingway, and his wife, Hadley, sat at the far end of the bar.

He joined them, ordering a Bloody Mary, an invention of Harry's bartender.

"Alone tonight?" Hadley asked.

"All alone."

Ernest raised his shot glass. "To those missing in action."

After drinking his whiskey straight, Hemingway ordered another round of scotch and a Sidecar, a blend of brandy, lemon juice, triple sec, and sugar for Hadley.

"Ever been to a bullfight?"

"Never," C.J. said, finishing his second Bloody Mary.

"We're going to the Pamplona Festival in July with several friends. Join us. The celebration's bullfights are the best." Hemingway lit Hadley's cigarette and one for himself.

C.J. declined his offer.

"Nothing is more invigorating than a fine bullfight. The animalistic bawling, the stink of the bull's sweat and blood, Matador's cape's sailing and snapping in the scorching breezes, I love it all." Another shot of whiskey. Tapping on C.J.'s hand, extremely drunk, Hemingway garbled his words. "We can run with the bulls. Elude their charging horns and hoofs beating the cobblestone."

Running with angry thousand-pound animals awakened an excitement in C.J. A third Bloody Mary had him shake Hemingway's hand in a pact to trifle with peril.

Two of Hemmingway's friends, both inebriated, staggered past on their way downstairs to listen to a piano player now pounding out jazz. Fresh drinks in hand, C.J. and the Hemingways followed.

***

The Dingo Bar was the fourth place Maggie searched for Elliott. Irritated, she stopped another taxi. "5 Rue Daunou." Her husband would be on his own unless she found him at Harry's.

A new keyboardist rushed the tempo of *Shine On Harvest Moon* as Maggie came down the stairs to find Elliott sitting in the back, still drinking Bloody Marys. "This is the fourth place I've been to, looking for you."

Maggie looked at the tiny watch hanging on a chain around her neck. It was after nine. "Hello, dumbass," she said, squinting through the shadows at Hemingway.

Near incoherent, Ernest glanced up, glassy-eyed and scowling, his speech slurred. "Well, little lady, you should have come here first."

Maggie grabbed Elliott's drink and flung the vodka and tomato juice in Hemmingway's face.

He jumped as the tabasco-loaded concoction set his eyes on fire. At first, Hemingway got angry; then, he started to laugh. Hadley told him the bath served him right.

All but falling out of his seat, Hemingway threw his arm

around C.J. and gave Maggie a drunken smile. "Cecil and I are going to run with the bulls. In July. This July." How he found out C.J.'s real name was anyone's guess.

"You're drunk, Ernest," Maggie said, her words clipped.

"He schertinly is," Hadley said, tapping her glass smartly on the table.

Hemingway took his hand off C.J.'s shoulder and wilted into his chair. "Mrs. Elliott, you should have come earlier. You could be inebriated with us." He pounded the table for emphasis. "Too late now. You are too far behind."

Maggie shook her head and eyeballed Elliott. "Are you ready?"

"For what?"

"To go."

"Go where?"

It was pointless. Maggie turned and darted up the stairs. Minutes later, she was back with a white lady, another of Harry's specialties. She raised her glass to Elliott. "Here's to you—Cecil."

XXIV

Chapter Twenty-Four

Despite Maggie's banging around the house and kitchen all morning, C.J. had not uttered a sound. Enough was enough.

"How long are you going to shun me?"

C.J. barely glanced at her. "No one is shunning anyone." He folded the newspaper and laid it on the floor. "I think I'll go for an extended walk."

"Am I invited, or do you plan to go alone?"

"You don't need my permission." C.J. started to the bedroom for his wallet.

Maggie blocked his path.

"Can I get past?"

Instead of letting him by, Maggie gave him a hard shove. "Fine, old sport; if you want to have it out, let's have it out."

He did not hesitate. "You make me feel like a decoration: nothing but an adornment to make you shine. I'm nothing. Just a refinement like that dog," he said, motioning at the

Borzoi statue standing in the corner. "Something to make you look noble."

Maggie backed away. Then stepped forward, again pushing on his chest. Her index finger pointing up, her eyebrows rose. "So, let me get this right. I fell in love with a decoration. I married someone who is going to shatter under the slightest pressure. Well, who's the fool here?"

Bright red a minute ago, C.J.'s face turned ashen. "It isn't being an ornament that hurts. You said you loathed family. Well, I want a family. I thought you were mine."

That was a shock. Maggie struggled to keep standing. She thought Elliott was mad because she had torn into him when the movie he forbade her from doing while they were on The Riviera was released.

Aggravated about not being in it, she forced him to take her when it was on the screen in Paris. It was a dark, dark film that, if she was honest, she'd have been embarrassed to be in. But that didn't matter. She didn't like Elliott deciding for her, even though the role of a woman seduced and dispatched to a reformatory run by a lesbian and then winding up in a brothel wouldn't have enhanced her standing as a performer.

Finding out why Elliott was upset, the fight in her gave way to guilt and remorse. Maggie reached out to touch C.J.'s arm. He recoiled in anger and stormed into the bedroom, leaving Maggie alone with her regrets and a deepening sense of despair.

For a long time, Maggie didn't move. Then, numb, emotionless, and disheartened, she drifted toward the bedroom where Elliott lay on the unmade bed.

"I'm sorry for saying that. I was sorry that day. When I

saw the sadness I brought to your face, it broke my heart. It devastates me for you to think my love is counterfeit."

Breaking down more, Maggie confessed to feeling trapped in a solitude darker than anything—short of death. The melancholy stretched beyond her reach and grasp. Near tears, she reached for him. "I have the horrible misfortune of being a female. It pushes me into incalculable distress. I am bursting with God-given talent for which there is no release."

Like a disciple, she swore her love for her dear Elliott, assuring him she would not wander through the rest of their lives in selfish sadness. Yet, he pulled away when she tried to wrap both arms around his neck and place her head on his shoulder.

Confusion and hurt filled her heart. She couldn't understand why he kept his distance, especially when she only desired to hold him tightly.

Did that awful statement about loathing family ruin things forever? Was he scared of commitment? Did he not feel the same intensity of love she did? Or perhaps deeper wounds from his past made it difficult for him to fully trust and let someone in.

Afraid, *truly* afraid, she had lost him, she reached for him again. "I am your family. I can't lose you. Don't move away."

She squeezed him. She wanted there to be no doubt she was his.

A mix of hesitation and longing filled Elliott's eyes. He took in her words, feeling the weight of her love and desperation. After a deep breath, he slowly allowed her arms to envelop him in an embrace, speaking magnitudes about their connection. At that moment, they would both realize their bond was unbreakable and worth fighting for.

After lovemaking, Maggie ran her fingers through his hair, raised on one elbow. "Do you really want to go to Pamplona? Act like an idiot by running from a herd of snot-slinging bulls?"

He snuggled close to her, flashed his trusty John Barrymore smile. "It sounded exhilarating...when I was drunk. Sober, I think Ernest is insane."

"Well, thank heavens. I don't want you gored by some silly bull." She rolled over him and scampered naked toward the shower. She turned back to him, laughing. "Sharp horns might destroy your manhood."

C.J.'s old feelings about his wife came slowly back. It was peculiar. Again, she was the girl who was fun, feisty, and self-confident—things that kept their relationship exciting. Besides, she was easy to look at, with long fine legs, a slim waist, curly red hair, and eyes that tantalize, laugh, and sparkle all at the same time."

They would talk, or at least Maggie would, for another hour before hailing a taxi for Château de Bagatelle, where they had attended the opening Olympic polo match between The United States and France.

The Château was charming. Endless English gardens burnished with roses of every shade showcased the lawn spreading out before the Château. The unassumingly small, dusty rose pink-hued castle was almost feminine in its architecture. Beautiful blue peacocks roamed freely, showing off their breathtaking plumage. The Château looked more like a museum glowing in the French sun than a palace.

In a two-piece sports costume of French jersey, Maggie looked as springy as the Paris day. The ankle-length frock, pleated at the front of the skirt and trimmed with a flat tie at the neckline, was of white and red in a geometric design. A two-button red jacket was lined in the same material as the frock. A wide-brimmed picture hat with the brim drooping down framed her face. Elliott, carrying a bottle of rosé wine and two stemmed glasses, wore a yellow shirt and sharply creased white trousers.

XXV

Chapter Twenty-Five

The next morning, a letter arrived from Tommy. He wrote about two University of Chicago students, Nathan Leopold and Richard Loeb, being arrested for the murder of a fourteen-year-old boy. Tommy called the case the trial of the century.

C.J. pointed out that in only 1924, this was the third trial of the century in America after the trials of Harry Thaw, and Sacco and Vanzetti. The fourth, if you counted Fatty Arbuckle's acquittal.

Tommy revealed the Bureau pinched Uncle Paddy for the second time, although he is again out on bail. Police also hauled their dear father in for questioning, twice. Somehow, their father had avoided arrest—so far.

His correspondence went on with a brief update regarding Sam.

Mags, in case you are interested, Sam is still missing. I'm relatively sure he is dead. Arnold Rothstein remains under heavy Bureau scrutiny. He may blame C.J., but I don't know.

He finished his letter, confident about his position with the bureau. He said his superiors appeared to trust him and did not fault him for his family's criminal involvements. Tommy didn't say so, not straight out, but Maggie believed he insinuated he provided helpful evidence about his family. A PostScript said their mother telephoned after they moved back to Tulsa. She claimed California was a little too hot.

Maggie wrote back she cared nothing about her parents' doings and had lost concern over Rothstein. She sent letters to Grace and Curls, inviting Curls to come to Paris for the Olympics.

Elliott wanted to go out to eat, suggesting Café du Dôme or La Closerie des Lilas. Maggie chose Café du Dôme because Hemingway and Ezra Pound, two men she didn't like, frequented La Closerie.

"After dinner," Maggie said, "we should drop by the Royal Box and ask Joe Zelli if he will still let me sing." Light rain began to patter against the windows. "I want to play my cello until we go out. I haven't touched it for three days. Not that practicing matters much. Female classical musicians face more discrimination here than in America."

"Since you're going to practice, I think I'll stop by a bookshop Hemingway keeps telling me to visit."

***

C.J. hailed a taxi. "12 rue de l'Odéon."

"The bookstore," the driver said as they pulled away. "Are you a writer? All the American writers flock to Sylvia's. She is most helpful to them. She published Joyce's Ulysses when no one else would."

The ride lasted only a few minutes, to C.J.'s relief. During the short trip, they experienced near misses with two other vehicles and bumped a yellow dog, which ran off yapping, but, as much as could be determined, unhurt. The cab jumped the curb when the driver slammed the brakes in front of their destination.

"Tell Sylvia, Remy says hello," the cabbie said as C.J. slid out the door.

Shakespeare and Company, narrow aisled, crammed with books, and dimly lit, smelled new and old at the same time. A faint, musty scent mixed with the aroma of coffee and chocolate hung in the shop like a subtle perfume. The quaint store was a place of literary perfection. Elliott was in bliss, lost in his scholarly dreams.

"Everything in this area is sold or reserved." The voice floated from behind.

"I didn't notice the poster."

"You should be more observant."

"I'll make a note."

The woman, dark-eyed with sharp features, stepped closer. "It's been a while since a Massachusetts inflection has blessed me."

"You have a fine ear," C.J. said.

"I'm an observer."

"Is this your shop?"

"Sylvia Beach," she said, extending her hand. "I'll bet you're C.J. Elliott."

Perplexed, his brows wrinkled.

"Oh, don't be so surprised; Ernest talks too much. You don't ever want to trust him with a secret."

Unsure of what to say, C.J. complimented the woman on her impressive store.

"Aspiring writers like my little shop," his hostess said, taking him by the arm and leading him toward a wooden table painted green.

A steeping metal coffee pot sat atop a sizeable stove in the back of the store. Mugs of all sizes and colors, yellow, blue, red, and brown, surrounded the pot. Not one of them matched another.

"You novelists and playwrights can be a bit of a nuisance. Poets are the worst. Nevertheless, I let you all mill around. One never knows who you'll turn out to be."

Sylvia poured him a full-bodied cup of coffee, almost too robust. When he coughed, she told him he'd become accustomed to it—everyone does.

"Hemingway says your wife is beautiful, a witchy woman." Sylvia laughed at his reaction. "Think absolutely nothing of what he mutters. He refers to Hadley as a bitchy woman and calls me worse. Ernest thinks all women should swoon over him. When they don't, his brain shrinks."

An ambitious Parisian writer, unfamiliar to C.J., dropped off a manuscript for Sylvia's review and hurried off for a book reading at the French bookstore across the street. Remy, the cabbie, who C.J. forgot to mention, stuck his head in the door and asked if he needed a ride home. Sylvia reminded the taxi driver of two books overdue to her lending library.

C.J. thanked Sylvia for her hospitality, purchased a copy of Sinclair Lewis' *Babbitt*, and promised to return soon.

***

"You're going to love Shakespeare and Company," C.J. said, flopping on the couch next to Maggie. "Every American writer in Paris frequents the place. Sylvia Beach, the owner, is cordial and can introduce us to everyone. She calls us Americans, expatriates."

"I'm not sure I enjoy being called an expatriate," Maggie said.

"It only means a person residing somewhere other than their native country."

"I know what the term means, but I still don't like the sound of it." She stood, said she was hungry, and went to change into an appropriate dinner dress, one of her flapper dresses. "In case Joe Zelli offers me a chance to sing."

Café du Dôme was splendid—and void of Hemingway and Pound. Only two tables away sat Ida Rubinstein and Maurice Ravel.

"Who?" C.J. asked.

Maggie's eyes popped in disbelief. "Who? Have you no culture? Rubinstein, the opera star, Ravel, the composer." Maggie beelined for the artists' table, dropping her unused white napkin on the closest empty chair.

Ravel's reaction to her interruption was frosty, but Rubinstein was gracious.

"I apologize for my brazenness, but I believe we have a mutual friend...David Belasco."

"Of course. How do you know David?"

"I was in his production of Zazà at the Met."

"How marvelous," Rubenstein said, "what part did you play?"

Maggie began blushing. A silly embarrassment rushed through her. "I was—uh—I was Zazà."

Ravel's jaw dropped. "Zazà? At The Metropolitan?"

Rubenstein leaped to her feet and threw her arms around Maggie. "I understood David cast a newcomer. I also heard you were magnificent." Ida let her out of the bear hug and pointed at C.J. "Is he your husband or your lover? Either way," she said before Maggie answered, "you must bring him over."

Pulling him by the hand, Maggie dragged C.J. along.

"Miss Rubinstein, Mr. Ravel, this is my husband, Elliott."

Ida took Elliott's hand. "Such a pleasure to meet you, young man. Although, I wish she called you her lover. Lovers are always available for stealing."

"Please join us," Ravel said. After everyone sat, Ravel apologized for not knowing the lady's name.

"Maggie Elliott."

"That makes you Elliott Elliott. How humorous," Ida said.

"It's C.J. She always calls me by my last name."

"How clever." Ida again took his hand in both of hers. "And what does C.J. stand for?"

He flushed. "Cecil Jethro."

"Oh my. Why did your mother hate you so?"

The red in his face deepened. "I don't think she feels anything at all for me."

"You must completely ignore her. And always go by Elliott," Ida said, raising and kissing his hand.

Ida spent the night laughing and flirtatious. The meticulously tailored Maurice Ravel came across as secretive, repressed, and shunned the prospect of a new friendship.

At home, the Elliotts would express different views when

discussing the experience. After wrestling off Ida Rubinstein, C.J. called the entire time traumatic and regretted not getting to Zelli's Royal Box. Maggie found the evening delightful.

XXVI

Chapter Twenty-Six

Ten days later, the letter from Curls arrived. She and her husband would love to visit. Her husband's coming along surprised C.J. He fussed and fretted all afternoon.

"Did you think she's going to leave him home? She married him. I doubt if she's ashamed of him."

"How do I act around him? I'll bet he's a bowler hat-wearing, stiff-upper-lipped proper Englishman who sips tea with his pinky finger in the air."

"Elliott, he'll be no such thing. He's with Curls, for heaven's sake. He's likely lost any hat he ever owned and guzzles Beef-eater Gin right from the bottle." Still laughing, Maggie closed the door and began playing her cello.

He poured himself a cup of coffee, sat down at his type-writer, and rolled in a sheet of clean paper. The novel, around half completed, told the story of one man, Dr. Reid Johns.

To C.J.'s frustration, he felt somehow his characters

usurped his control. Once their god, he was reduced to little more than an observer, a witness recording their lives.

His protagonist, Dr. Reid Johns, a social scientist teaching at an Ivy League University, regretted numerous of his life choices. At the top of John's regrets was his support of Woodrow Wilson's 1912 presidential candidacy.

"I was duped." Dr. Johns would say. "Wilson proved to be a devastating disappointment. It turned out I voted for a racist and supporter of Jim Crow. Wilson led the United States into the Great War with no American interests at stake."

Johns also thought the US President's policies endangered the world of another conflict. Still worse for C.J.'s main character, he was unsure of his love for the woman he married.

Now tapping the keys, his work was cut out for him if he planned to save his hero from emotional destruction. His more significant challenge would be keeping his own life out of the novel.

"Elliott," Maggie said as she rummaged around their tiny kitchen for a snack. "I'm bored. Aren't you hopelessly bored?"

"Three-thirty," Elliott said, glancing at his wristwatch. "If we hurry, I can take you to Shakespeare and Company. Later, we can grab a quick dinner and go to the Royal Box."

＊＊＊

An American short story writer was finishing a reading of his work to a small, somewhat disinterested crowd. He received only brief, polite applause. As the author moved through the store, Ernest Hemingway, whom Maggie despised, put his arm around him and whispered something in his ear. The young man did not like what he said.

Smiling, Sylvia Beach waved the Elliotts over. "This must be Mrs. Elliott. I'm Sylvia."

"Call me Maggie, please. You have a delightful shop."

Before Sylvia responded, Hemingway interrupted them. "Sylvia, what do you think of my friends?"

"I think they are grand. Perfect representatives of the lost generation."

"Lost generation?" Maggie asked.

Hemingway laughed and wrapped his arms around C.J. and Maggie. "Gertrude Stein calls people our age The Lost Generation."

Maggie pushed Hemingway's paw away. "I'm not lost." She gave him a nasty look. "You sure disprove the importance of being Ernest."

Sylvia took Maggie by the arm. "Let me show you through my bookshop. I don't want Ernest to tarnish you." Away from the others, Sylvia whispered to Maggie, "Ernest isn't such a ghastly person. Not once you are used to him."

She asked Maggie about being a musician. Sylvia said opportunities for females don't exist if they want to pursue classical music. "Jazz clubs are friendly to female singers if you're open to performing in nightspots."

"Opportunity is where you find it." Maggie shrugged her shoulders. "I suppose singing in dives isn't proper, but propriety has never stopped me. At least not yet."

***

"I like Shakespeare and Company. I like Sylvia," Maggie said as she and C.J. headed off for a quick meal before grabbing a cab for the Royal Box.

A sandwich board on the sidewalk in front of Zelli's

identified Cole Porter as the evening's entertainment. Inside, the Elliotts had to exhale to move through the perfumed and boisterous, predominantly American crowd.

"Why so crowded this evening?" Elliott asked a passing waiter.

"A rumor claims George Gershwin is joining Cole tonight. Damn lie's been flying around for a week. I don't know who started the nonsense." He stepped closer. "Zelli, probably. We'll run out of booze at this rate."

A table was too much to hope for, but the Elliotts found stools at the bar. "Gin martini and a French 75."

"Well, what a wonderful surprise." Cole Porter's saxophone player touched Maggie's shoulders and leaned over to kiss her cheeks. "Does Cole know you're here?"

"No. But I need to say hello."

"He's in a little room in the back, eating a bite before playing. Come on. He'll love to see you." The saxophonist grabbed Maggie by the hand and led her through the drunken revelers, with C.J. struggling to keep up.

Cole threw his arms open. "Maggie, where on earth have you been hiding?"

"The Fitzgeralds kidnapped us, whisked us off to the Riviera."

"You must sing with us tonight."

"I can't. I didn't dress to perform."

What a lie. Maggie cherry-picked the eye-catching gold coral knee-length gown with a V-neck, sheer mesh sleeves, blinking beads, and sequins to astound an audience.

Minutes later, she bounced to the microphone, winked at the crowd, and burst into *Ain't We Got Fun, It Had To Be You* and three more jazz-age hits. Maggie Elliott was where she loved being.

Planted on both feet, a testy Joe Zelli met Maggie as she left the stage. "You," he said, waving his stubby finger in Maggie's face, "were supposed to sing here once a week. We made a deal. I don't like being put in a lurch."

Maggie was stuck. "Well..."

"Well, what?"

Maggie squirmed, touched her fingers to her mouth, and swayed back and forth. "Well, you knew we were going to the Riviera with the Fitzgeralds."

"For two weeks," Zelli yelled.

Without making eye contact, overwhelmed by insecurity, a timid and fainthearted Maggie contrived her move. Placing her hand along Zelli's face, pouty-eyed, in a waiflike voice, she played her hand.

"Oh, Joe, we tried to escape. But Zelda demanded we stay. Have you ever defied Zelda Fitzgerald? Contesting her wishes is utterly impossible. Ask Cole Porter. He'll tell you— it's hopeless."

She had him.

Or maybe not.

"Don't try to con a con artist."

Pale and wide-eyed, Maggie stepped back, two steps back. A soft touch of the cheek always worked, never failed, until now.

Self-satisfied, Zelli smiled. "You can perform here. Thursday nights from one 'til two...as long as you draw a crowd."

Befuddled, Maggie weaved through the throng and sat next to Elliott. "I've been had." She took a swallow of Elliott's martini. "Zelli says I can sing here on Thursday nights—for one hour—for tips."

XXVII

Chapter Twenty-Seven

Incomes for writers writing novels with no guarantee of publication and singers singing for tips didn't add up too much. Thankfully, wages didn't matter. The shipping company Elliott inherited rolled in income. A smaller steel firm was also a gold mine. C.J. drew substantial salaries from both, primarily for letting the executives run the companies. While he invested cautiously, he and Maggie lived well off his investments.

Still, Maggie wanted to contribute to their finances, and C.J. remained determined to succeed as a writer. None of their friends in Montparnasse's artistic left bank neighborhood—popular for its cheap rents, creative fervor, and abundant cafes were aware of the Elliotts' wealth.

"Curls is going to think the weather here is wonderful coming from England's rainy skies and gales ."

C.J. laughed about Maggie needing to look out the window

because it was pouring. He checked his wristwatch. "Speaking of Curls, we better head to the train station. We don't want them to arrive and not find us."

Even on wet days like this one, Paris was marvelous in June. Années Folles, the crazy years, the roaring twenties.

"I can't wait to introduce Curls to our Parisian life," Maggie said on their way out the door. "She's a senior editor at The London Magazine, the first woman in the position. She'll find great material here."

"Gare de Lyon," C.J. said to the taxi driver.

As they crossed the Seine to the right bank, C.J. again worried about meeting Curl's husband.

"Stop being so silly. He's not an Earl or Lord. He might, however, be a descendent of Jack the Ripper."

"Another reason to put them in a hotel," C.J. said.

"Remember," Maggie said, "their last name is Yates. And she probably goes by Marian, not Curls."

"What's her husband's name?"

"Owen. And don't forget it."

The architecture of the train station, Gare de Lyon, particularly the clock tower, was impressive. "We're to meet them under the Maignan mural in the restaurant," she said, talking so fast he struggled to follow her speech. "We're not allowed in the de-boarding area. They don't arrive for twenty minutes, so we've plenty of time."

Far too excited to sit still, Maggie fidgeted, sat, paced. "Watch for them." She punched him in the shoulder. "I want to see them before they see us."

He didn't understand why it made any difference. But perhaps it did. Nothing in life is certain, accurate, or reliable.

Before they noticed her, Curls rushed toward them.

The Elliotts struggled to their feet, needing to hold each other up.

"I guess you're surprised," Curls said.

Sam Taylor extended his hand, only to have it hang in the air. "We thought you were dead," C.J. said, mumbled, really.

"That explains why you never wrote."

Maggie started to snap back but held her tongue. Curls stepped forward and embraced Maggie. Not one to be subtle, Maggie stiffened. "Why didn't you tell us?"

"Because, my breathtaking friend, I wanted to surprise you."

"We can explain," Sam, or Owen, or whatever the hell his name now was, said.

"You better hope so," C.J. said, grabbing Curls' suitcase and striding toward the ornate door.

Dark clouds blocked the sun. The left front window of the taxi wouldn't roll up, allowing the pounding rain to drench C.J. The friends, more like strangers at the moment, endured a ride as distressing and cruel as they came.

After fumbling with the keys, C.J. unlocked the door and squish-squashed straight to the bedroom to rid himself of his soggy cream-colored suit. Maggie waved her arm at a room next to the kitchen. "There's your room if you want to change into dry clothes."

The tan knickers and burgundy socks Curls changed into would have drawn raves from Maggie—if she wasn't so angry. Rather than speak, Maggie strode to their liquor cabinet and came back with a bottle of Beefeater Gin.

Tension sucked the humid air out of the room. Sweat

dripping from C.J.'s brow drew a small swarm of irritating gnats to his face. He gave Sam an unfriendly jab in the chest. "Do you know why we came to France?" He didn't wait for an answer. "Did you tell Arnold Rothstein we turned him into the Bureau of Investigation?"

"No to both questions," Sam said. "When Rothstein found out Tommy worked for The Bureau, he decided I was spying on him and ordered a hit on me. The guy he paid liked me. He told me to get out of the country and never come back. Rothstein thinks he put my feet in concrete and dumped me in New York Harbor. He'll kill my friend and me if he finds out I'm alive. No one told me about you two living in France until I ran into Curls in London."

"Does Rothstein want us dead?"

Sam shrugged. "Why would he? He figured you'd supply him with business funding. If you objected, he planned to scare you into it." Sam flipped his lighter, meaning to light a cigarette. Maggie snatched it away.

Intimidated by Maggie's assault, Sam shrunk and fumbled trying to stuff the cigarette back in the pack after Maggie threw it at him. "I doubt he wants to kill you. He'd be more likely to keep increasing pressure on you. But hell, you're out of his reach. I suspect he's forgotten about you."

C.J. poured a shot of gin, offering none to the others. Glaring at Sam, he bit off his words. "The last time I saw you, you accused me of ratting you out to the bureau. You threatened not only me, you threatened Maggie. Remember how those dark stage doors might be dangerous?"

Maggie turned toward Curls. "You should have warned us he was with you," Maggie said, trembling in anger.

The sweltering heat and crashing thunder shredding Curls' nerves were evident on her face. She looked close to vomiting. "Sometimes, I sort through old pictures from Mount Holyoke. I grin at how happy we were." Curls reached for her old friend. "Maggie O, I didn't know about this."

With disharmony high, Sam poured himself a drink. "I only told Curls about me—about my problems." His gaze danced between Maggie and C.J. without focusing on either. "Maggie hadn't written Curls anything about me or Rothstein, so I didn't tell her. I only confessed my troubles."

Sam pleaded with his former pal. "I'm sorry. All you said to me about Rothstein is true. I was a sap. I balled everything up. I'm still a sap for thinking you might welcome me. I'll understand if you want us or want me to leave."

Obvious to everyone, C.J. wanted to say goodbye, at least to Sam. But Maggie told them she and Elliott needed to talk. An umbrella stood in a floor vase next to the Borzoi. "Keep an eye on those two," Maggie said to the marble dog as she grabbed the umbrella. "We may be a while," she said as they slipped through the door. "Stay put."

As they headed to the street, Maggie smiled, hearing Curls yelling at Sam. "Bloody Hell..."

Arm in arm, the Elliotts ambled through the rain. Living in Paris among cathedrals and arches, towers, and cafés filled with artists and writers, being without responsibilities should have made life wonderful. And it did—most of the time.

With the showers ending, they ended up at Shakespeare and Company. Maggie sipped tea with Sylvia and Hadley while C.J. drank coffee with Hemingway. "Don't let Tatie talk you into going to the fight tonight," Hadley said, turning toward C.J. "Boxing is a dreadful bloody spectacle."

"Tatie can't talk me into anything. We have houseguests."

"Houseguests?" Sylvia asked. "Why aren't you entertaining them?"

"We're trying to decide whether to keep them or throw them out," Maggie said.

"Uninvited guests?"

"Not exactly. Specifically, we invited one of them."

"How utterly complicated," Hadley said.

"We invited my old college mate from London and her husband. The husband turns out to be an awful surprise."

Changing the subject, Hemingway said they were meeting Ezra Pound at Harry's Bar before the boxing match. He asked the Elliotts if they cared to come along. Maggie declined for both of them. Miffed, Hemingway reminded them he and Hadley were leaving the next day for Pamplona. "You'll regret not coming," he said.

With a wave of his beret, Hemingway departed. After watching them leave, Maggie glanced at C.J. "Never wear a beret."

For thirty minutes, Sylvia turned the conversation to C.J.'s manuscript. "You're writing," she said, "is excellent. If you would accept one small suggestion," she didn't wait for an answer, "change your title from Living Life to Life. Short, pointed titles are better."

She poured herself another cup of tea. Maggie and C.J. declined her offer.

"How's your manuscript progressing? We need to set you up some readings."

"Did Elliott tell you F. Scott Fitzgerald thinks the novel is dazzling?" Maggie asked.

Some people, when surprised, stare dumbfounded. Others burst with delight—Sylvia Beach burst.

She leaned hard against the back of her chair, her mouth agape. "You know F. Scott Fitzgerald? He's read your writing?"

"We're rather close friends. Scott started reading Elliott's manuscript while we sailed over from New York. We spent most of the winter with them on the Riviera." No one plays an audience like Maggie. "You would love Zelda. She's more charming than Scott."

Almost drooling, Sylvia muttered about how the Elliotts must let her introduce them to Maggie's fellow Irishman, James Joyce, and they must present her to Fitzgerald at the earliest opportunity. Everyone agreed.

Shocked by the lateness of the afternoon, Elliott said they needed to deal with the ugly situation awaiting them.

Rather than going to their bungalow, they headed, at Elliott's insistence, to Café de Flore, where Maggie succumbed to guilt about abandoning Curls. Elliott asked if she wanted to go home instead of eating. Maggie waved for the garçon.

After an enjoyable boeuf bourguignon, a dry martini for Elliott, and two sidecars for Maggie, they decided to keep Curls and her now undead husband.

***

When told they could stay, Curls was relieved; Sam was dubious. In their years rooming together, C.J. seldom changed his mind about things.

Sunny mornings after an all-night rain in Paris meant glistening drops dancing on leaves and flower petals, children splashing in puddles. Summer days open like a letter from a lover, warm and bathed in lustrous light.

Unable to resist the sunshine, Maggie and Curls rushed off to shop. C.J. intended a less pleasant morning for Sam.

"Are we in danger from Arnold Rothstein?"

"No, I told you that last night."

"I'm having trouble believing you. Especially since Tommy thinks we might be." Sam took a cigarette pack out of his pocket. "Not inside," C.J. said.

Frustrated, Sam put the pack back. "Tommy doesn't know everything."

C.J. shook his head. His frown grew more severe.

"I conveyed to Arnie you'd be a deep source of financing. Money was his interest in you. When you refused, he didn't like it. He ordered me to turn up the pressure. Make a few threats to scare you." Sam sank deeper into the couch. "Rothstein is no fool. They call him The Brain, after all. He dug into your background and Maggie's."

C.J. sat up straighter. His face turned dark. "And?"

"And he found Tommy. He didn't like his career choice." Now pacing back and forth, Sam said he needed a drink.

"At nine-thirty in the morning?" C.J. asked.

"I'm sorry. I'm nervous talking about people who want to kill me." On the couch, Sam talked a lot about Rothstein being upset about Tommy's position with the Bureau of Investigation. "He started snooping into the lives of the other O'Sullivans. They're not who you think they are."

He said both Maggie's father and Uncle Paddy dabbled in bootlegging. Not so much as moonshiners but as rum runners. They supplied liquor to the dry counties. Scattered, sparsely populated areas in Oklahoma didn't interest Rothstein. Not enough money was involved. Howard O'Sullivan's other side business fascinated him.

"Maggie's Pop is a fence—a mover of stolen merchandise—mostly art and artifacts. A furniture store is the perfect cover. He displays paintings and other works in the showroom while conducting clandestine searches for buyers on the sly. Staying anonymous, Rothstein started using O'Sullivan to move hot items. He considers Howard reliable, but not Paddy: too reckless, a drunk, and too loosed-lipped."

C.J. listened to Sam's story. "Why does Tommy still believe Rothstein is a threat to us?"

"I told you," Sam said. "Tommy doesn't know much. If you left America because Tommy said Rothstein was after you, you made a trip for nothing."

"If he's not concerned about Tommy or me causing him trouble, why did he put a hit out on you?"

"Because you damn fool, he blamed me for putting him in a vulnerable position. If Maggie's old man hadn't turned out to be a crook, Arnie wouldn't have had any leverage over you or Tommy. Now he does. He's not afraid of you talking."

"Is he pressuring Tommy to back off?"

Frustrated, Sam shook his head. "Do I need to draw you a picture? I keep telling you Tommy knows next to nothing. He suspects his dear father is a bootlegger, nothing else. Rothstein no longer cares what you might tell the bureau because he's not doing anything to you. You have nothing to tell. You don't have any complaints. I'm the one who got him involved with you or tried to. Now I'm dead. Figure things out."

No one said much for an hour, a little idle talk about

when the girls would come home, a check of the paper for the schedule of Olympic events. Elliott tossed together a light lunch and gave Sam a once-over with his eyes.

"So, is the bleached blond hair and mustache some disguise?"

"Yes," Sam said, not joking. "And you need to call me Owen Yates."

It was rude, but C.J. laughed. Owen didn't.

* * *

Right after noon, a taxi driver helped carry in the fruits of the ladies' shopping. Most of the packages were Curls'.

"We want you to take us to the Eiffel Tower," Maggie said, shooting a crooked frown at Elliott. "By the time we ride up, I'll decide what to do about your former roommate." She twirled and gave Sam's face a hard pinch. "To push, or not to push? That is the question."

Curls patted Sam's other cheek. "Never turn your back on an ireful Mick."

"Remember, it will be the proper Englishman, Owen Yates, who'll you be pushing. A man you should have nothing against," Sam said.

Maggie squinted her eyes and bit her lip. "Don't forget what Curls said."

A fantastic structure, the yellow tower rose three hundred-fifty meters, a thousand feet into the sky. Glamorous crowds packed the grounds. Moulin Rouge dancers pranced and sometimes climbed on the tower legs; lazy sunbathers soaked up the Paris sun. At the pinnacle, sightseers took turns peering through the telescopes.

The top—the idea of going to the pinnacle petrified

Maggie. But after her disgrace at the Grand Canyon, she must conquer her fear of heights. And she wanted to conquer that fear without the aid of gin or the urging of Zelda Fitzgerald. To the delight of a few, the sympathy of others, Maggie squealed when the lift jerked into motion. She yelped and grabbed C.J. when it creaked. The car bounced twice. "Damn you, Elliott."

Visitors switched cars on an intermediate landing to go up to the top. Elliott decided waiting for the next car was a perfect time to explain how these lifts were a mechanism unrivaled anywhere in the world. "They are neither elevators, in the traditional sense, nor cable cars. Powered by hydraulics with water reservoirs installed on each floor, they don't belong to any elevator category."

Maggie, a little green, embraced Elliott. "Sweetheart, old sport...shut up."

Even Maggie, once she opened her eyes, found the view breathtaking—literally.

A young woman in a guide uniform gave a brief speech about the structure in French and English. "During the great war," she said, "the Eiffel Tower intercepted enemy radio communications, relayed zeppelin alerts, and was used to dispatch emergency troop reinforcements. She took particular gratification over messages from the tower leading to the arrest of the Germans' spy, Mata Hari.

No one would have been happier to go down to the ground than Maggie. Instead, they stopped to eat on the first floor, still a hundred-eighty feet above the ground. With four different cafés to choose from, they selected the Russian one because no one was familiar with Russian food.

Thankful for the little things, like tables in the restaurant's center, a long way from the best views, Maggie ordered a Vodka, a double. She leaned over to Elliott, "The caviar and Pozharsky better be exceptional."

In the middle of their dessert, C.J. wanted Maggie to bring her cake and look over the edge.

"Preposterous, old sport. You wanted to push me off the Grand Canyon and now off this tower."

"Come on. There's a chest-high railing all the way around. You couldn't possibly fall."

Grudgingly, Maggie picked up her pineapple upside-down cake and shuffled off to the railing with C.J. half-pulling her by the arm.

Holding her cake over the railing, she leaned over and looked down. "Oh, Lord." Her hand shook. The gooey yellow cake slid off the saucer and plummeted to the ground. Splat.

XXVIII

Chapter Twenty-Eight

Notre Dame, The Paris Opera, The Arc de Triomphe, and The Louvre all made their list of places to visit.

Before anyone woke, Maggie started a letter to her brother.

Tommy,

Paris is fine. At least in many ways. We are meeting creative people. So far, they include Cole Porter, Ida Rubinstein, and the composer Maurice Ravel. Elliott is thrilled about being friends with F. Scott Fitzgerald and his wife. Zelda is, well, let's say, high-spirited. I hold grand admiration for her.

The letter rambled on about nothing important. It sounded pointless. So, Maggie decided to be candid.

There are a few things I need to—no, must tell you. Honestly, not everything is so splendid. Sometimes, I am exceedingly lonely. Daytime is the worst. Elliott spends every day writing or consorting with other literary types at a little bookstore. The place is his second home.

Beyond my frequent loneliness, I need to share something else. I am trusting you to secrecy. Do not betray me. Please do not...

The letter detailed all the slimy details about Sam Taylor and what she learned about her family, her awful family. Once she finished, she stuffed the note into a drawer. Mailing such notions required more thought.

Curls peeked her head outside her door. "I'm only half-dressed. Is Elliott up?"

"No. He's snoring like an old boar."

In only a chemise and knickers, Curls bounced out the door. "Are any nearby cafés open?"

"Yes, but not for one attired so casually."

"Will stockings suffice?"

It was grand having Curls back. "Along with a pair of shoes," Maggie said.

"Grab your purse," Curls said, "We're going to find a place to eat."

Curls came right back out, wearing stockings and ankle boots with a linen dress hung over her shoulder. Not to be out outlandished, Maggie stripped to her camisole and bloomers.

Several stared, a few laughed, but no one said anything as they walked to the nearest café. The café hostess, a young woman in her teens, commented about the hot morning. Disappointed by the lack of uproar, they slipped into the restroom and came out fully dressed.

"Zelda Fitzgerald would have loved that," Maggie said.

"Apparently, we were invisible," Curls said. "How disappointing."

***

"Where were you two?" Elliott asked, somewhat indignant about waking up to Maggie's absence.

"At breakfast, Old Sport. If you're going to sleep so late, you'll miss many of life's little melodramas."

"Where's Owen?" Curls asked.

"He went looking for you two," Elliott said.

"Brilliant," Curls said, "he'll be lost for hours."

Curls and Sam dated back in their university years, but the Elliotts weren't aware they'd been serious about each other. When C.J. asked Curls about the relationship, she kissed his forehead.

"Dear boy, my fancy was always for you. But you were taken, forcing me to settle for less." Curls smiled, sighed, and crumpled onto the red couch. "Heavens, a blind man could see you two want more scandalous tidbits about us."

For over an hour, Curls described her marriage to Elliott's former roommate in painstaking detail. Their reunion was intentional on Sam's part. For Curls, the courtship was frivolous—at first. Fun, nothing more until Sam bared his soul.

He told Curls everything pertaining to his lapses in judgment, everything about Arnold Rothstein and the gangster's ordering his execution. He brought all the details forth, except the Elliotts' name. That little surprise remained hidden until they reached the Paris train station.

Trying to hide things made no sense to Elliott or Maggie. Not to Curls either, which made explaining more difficult.

"His secret set off a major spat the night we arrived," Curls said. "Owen claimed if he told me before we came, I would have told you. He thought you would refuse to let us come."

"Damn right," C.J. said.

"You could have come," Maggie said, "alone."

With some success, Curls argued for Sam's forgiveness. While not entirely forgiven, he would receive a second chance. In Maggie's opinion, a fourth or fifth.

XXIX

Chapter Twenty-Nine

The sandwich board outside Zelli's announced Maggie Elliott as the featured entertainer.

"Well, look who showed up." A surly, intoxicated Joe Zelli met the Elliotts, Curls, and Sam at the door. "You're lucky you did."

"Who's he?" Curls asked, mortified.

"The owner," Maggie said. "He's quite charming, unless he's stumbling drunk."

Curls rolled her eyes. "He's a pig."

"He's mad at me. I'll win him back."

A waiter came over to lead them to a box. "Don't pay much attention to Joe. Eugene Bullard quit this afternoon. Joe's furious. He's been drinking heavily since the middle of the morning."

A black jazz band from America backed the once wildly popular Mistinguett, now a spiraling French singer with an unbearable raspy voice. "At least she'll be easy to follow," Maggie said. "If there's anyone here after she finishes."

"She was admired in all Europe," Curls said. "Now, the newspapers claim she has a severe alcohol problem."

Elliott got his hand slapped when he tried to pull Maggie's wine glass away. "Be careful, Old Sport."

A well-meaning emcee rambled monotonously about their next entertainer's impressive background, including starring at the Metropolitan Opera in New York. On and on, he blathered over her sharing the stage, right here at this venue with the fabulous Cole Porter.

To the delight of the rowdy horde, Maggie marched across the footlights. "Enough," she said, grabbing the microphone while giving the startled host a hip bump and pushing him away. After a curtsy and a wink at the crowd, Maggie turned to the musicians and asked for *It Had to Be You*.

If anyone deserved the spotlight, Maggie did. The ease and musicality of her singing, her perfect diction, and range enchanted the audience. More than anything, her infectious gaiety and pleasure in performing made her bewitching.

Her lyrics rose out, commanding and compelling. Maggie's musical connection with the band was entrancing. She circled around, moving in swift, liquid waves echoing the quicksilver moods of a mysterious femme fatale.

Pulling her skirt up, never showing too much, but more than C.J. favored, she seduced the audience without giving up her aura of innocence.

"Don't stop singing," screamed a wiry man with squinty eyes and a streak of gray running through his hair. "I want to sing with you," he declared as he tried to climb on the stage, a futile effort impeded by Maggie swatting him on the head with her mic stand.

"How about a little Bessie Smith?" an unaffected Maggie asked as she broke into A Good Man is Hard to Find, following it with Nobody Knows You When You're Down and Out. A high-kicking jazz baby and a white-haired gentleman in a tuxedo caused dancers to part or risk being kicked as the outrageous couple black-bottomed around the crowded floor.

Almost melted, and her Joe Zelli allotted time shrinking, Maggie cast a smile to her husband, "How was that?" she mouthed. After one more song, an across-the-boards bow, a broad smile, and three thank you dears, Maggie scampered from the stage while the revelers screamed for more.

Intentionally avoiding Joe Zelli, she led C.J., Curls, and Sam straight out the door. "Let old Joe sweat over whether I'll be back," she laughed.

In the morning paper, a reviewer at Zelli's covering Mistinguett referred to the once admired singer as off-key and sounding like a Parisian street hawker. Instead, he dedicated most of his review to newcomer Maggie Elliott.

Last night, a young American enamored a raucous community at Joe Zelli's Royal Box. Her singing was enchanting, her pitch was impeccable. Her effortless rhythm swayed from one beat to the next. There was no mistaking the sheer joyfulness of Maggie Elliott's performance, nor the remarkably relaxed quality of her voice as she sang for a screaming throng. The moment she burst into Ain't We Got Fun, her finale, she became the toast of Paris. Monsieur Zelli, give this girl more than thirty minutes.

XXX

Chapter Thirty

Saying goodbye to Curls and Sam proved awkward. In a letter later in the morning, Maggie cautioned Curls about Sam, calling him untrustworthy.

By mid-afternoon, C.J. grew tired of writing. "I'm going to Shakespeare and Company. Do you want to come along?"

Irritated about him leaving the house, Maggie declined, claiming she wanted to work on her vocal exercises. A lie. Making the deception worse, her refusal wounded Elliott, putting him into a pout. Despite their feelings, neither gave in. She wouldn't go. Elliott wouldn't stay home.

Alone, Maggie made a weak effort to sing, but lacked inspiration. The boredom, so prevalent before Curls' visit, threatened to return. Coffee increased her anxiety. Boredom and anxiety—what a combination.

She tried playing her cello, straightening up around the house, and composing a note to Grace. Nothing helped. For a while, she rambled about, muttering to herself about being so wretched. It had been some time since she read any of Elliott's novel. Perhaps a peek would occupy her mind, relieve the nagging guilt.

Wadded-up papers lay scattered about the floor. A piece of paper rolled into the typewriter, save one incomplete sentence, remained empty. Scrawled ripped-up notes filled two wastebaskets. A blackboard with a half-erased plot arc stood in the corner. Partially opened desk drawers overflowed with pages Elliott spurned.

The manuscript, always tucked in Elliott's leather portfolio, was gone. He must have taken it with him for Sylvia Beach's review.

One specific page peeking from an open drawer caught Maggie's eye: poetry. A scribbled poem dated the week before they sailed for France.

Paris is my new target,
and the need for a missing smile.
I've explored the shores
on this side of the sea
until my shoes are worn thin.
The smiles that answer my own
have become more a mockery
than a smile at all.
One more minute now
to look another time
over my shoulder
in case love
is desperately chasing after me.
No one is there.

The colors and the light permeating the room were too bright. The quiet screamed so loud it hurt. Maggie couldn't breathe, only gasp. She started shaking; her legs were trembling. She had to grab something to stay on her feet. Instead, she sank to the floor and drew into a ball, wanting to be small. She failed Elliott. He wanted—needed, more.

She needed a friend, someone to talk to. In anguish, she had no one, not Grace, Tommy, or Zelda.

Maggie put the metrical composition back and checked the room to ensure everything remained as she found it. Tears crept down her face, again. Questions, so many of them, battered her mind. Why didn't Elliott love her? When did he stop? Was it her fault? Was she misinterpreting his words?

"Nothing is simple in Paris," Hemingway told her that. He said, "Nothing is simple here, not poverty, sudden money, right and wrong, not the moonlight, or the breathing of someone who lay beside you in the moonlight."

Maggie didn't like the boor; she borderline despised him, but the braggart might be correct about Paris. The city was confounding and coming between her and Elliott.

Something must change. Part of the something, Maggie believed, meant changing Elliott's friends. Right or wrong about Hemingway, Maggie decided to keep her husband away from him—and far from the contemptible fascist Ezra Pound.

***

"I have a copy of Ulysses to loan you," Sylvia Beach hollered from the back when C.J. came in, announced by the tinkling bell hanging over the door. The obscene, blue-covered tome was in his hand, placed by the woman bold enough to publish what others wanted no involvement with. Thick, heavy, and banned in America to prevent harboring impure and lustful thoughts, C.J. wondered why she gave the unsolicited tome to him.

To feign interest, he leafed through the pages, almost dropping the ponderous volume. "How kind, Sylvia. I'll read this quickly and return it to you."

Hemingway sat in the back, drinking coffee. Thank heavens Maggie didn't come along.

"How was Pamplona?"

"You Elliotts should have come with us. Nothing is more invigorating than running with the bulls. Death, with its hot breath, is snorting at your heels. The whole experience is like a beautiful nightmare."

The chair across the table from Hemingway squeaked in protest as C.J. sat. "We enjoyed the Olympics. And no blood was shed."

"Oh, the shedding of blood," Hemingway said, mockery dripping from each word. "Tatie was concerned about the beasts dying. Now she realizes dying is the inevitable outcome of life—the pinnacle of the drama."

Contrary to Maggie's total disdain for the man, C.J. rather liked Hemingway. At least in measured doses. "The pinnacle? Pinnacles shouldn't be foregone conclusions."

"I enjoy sparring with you," Hemingway said, taking a small flask out of his pants pocket and pouring bourbon into his coffee. "We should spar in the ring. Do you box?"

"Once or twice at Amherst."

"Excellent. I've been trying to teach Ezra Pound, but he's a slow learner. He's not much of a challenge. Men need challenges to maintain their manhood."

Boxing Hemingway wasn't something he would tell Maggie about. He'd learned better after the disastrous bootlegging catastrophe. Sparring wasn't a wise idea, but C.J. was eager to box.

The bell over the door tinkled again. Hadley Hemingway strolled toward the back of the store. "Well, Mr. Elliott, did Tatie tell you how much you Elliotts missed not going to Spain with us?"

"He did. But I told him we found great pleasure in the Olympics. The Americans performed well."

"Time to go," Hadley said, turning her attention to her husband. "Gertrude asked us to dinner. You need to clean yourself up."

"C.J. and I are going to box a few rounds," Hemingway said. "Tomorrow or Thursday. You and Maggie should come. He'll provide a definite scuffle."

"I don't think I said yes," Elliott said. "But I believe I will agree."

XXXI

Chapter Thirty-One

The atmosphere in their bungalow was more like February in Massachusetts than late fall in Paris. The pain Maggie experienced reading Elliott's poetry turned into melancholy, irritation, and resentment, making her sullen.

She found a second poem, written while they vacationed at the Riviera.

If you meet someday,
a lonely person,
offer them love.
For they too, need understanding.
Perhaps they once knew love.
But it slipped away
in one fleeting moment
too short to clearly remember.
Now trying to forget
what can only be replaced,

they wander down the road alone.

Be kind,

smile,

offer them love.

Offer them love? What had she done? She gave him her love—willingly, all she had to give. Wasn't that enough? What did he want?

Brrrrr. Hostility filled the house. When C.J. walked in, Maggie left the room, stomped out, slamming the bedroom door behind her.

Oh well, C.J. always accepted life with this redhead would be exciting. But damn, what a stunner. Knocking on the door and asking what was wrong was not an option. Not a smart one anyway. The better choice would be to wait out the squall. Or at least for the eye of the hurricane.

C.J. sat down on the red art déco couch, an uncomfortable piece of furniture he was beginning to hate. At first, he leafed through Joyce's tome. Page one, line one—"*Stately, plump Buck Mulligan came from the stairhead, bearing a bowl of lather on which a mirror and a razor lay crossed.*"

The opening didn't compare to those of Twain or Dickens. Not with Fitzgerald's *The Beautiful and the Damned.*

Dinner time came and went without Maggie coming out. A few chapters into Joyce's novel and hungry, C.J. decided this sea of troubles flowed deeper than he thought. If he wanted to eat, evidently, he was on his own. C.J. hated cooking. Assembling meat and bread overwhelmed him. Too much of a chore.

While pouring himself some milk to go with the banquet he resented making, Maggie came waltzing into the kitchen in her nightgown, cold cream smeared all over her face. Not saying a word, she poured herself a half-glass of gin, spun on her heels, and went back to their bedroom, closing the door behind her.

C.J. had been scarred enough by his mother that he often wondered if there was anyone he couldn't live without. Or that he needed more than they needed him. Still, in those days alone, before Maggie, he did admit to himself he was searching for love. For someone to love for five minutes, five weeks, or until the love faded, as he thought it always would. When that happened, he would just leave. Prove he was as independent as he had ever been.

For him, looking for love was like walking down roads, not knowing where they would lead. Some led to smiles, others to situations far better forgotten. Then he met Maggie.

From Maggie, he learned love is simple. A warm embrace, a soft smile, or a quiet look. For the first time he could remember, he loved someone. She was the one thing he didn't want to lose.

After finishing his sandwich, C.J. washed his plate and headed to bed, only to find a locked door. He glanced at the rigid, disagreeable couch too short for a comfortable night's sleep. Any turbulence on the other side of the door beat sleeping another night on that obstinate sofa.

"Maggie, unlock the door." No response. "Come on, Maggie, I don't even know what I'm guilty of."

When the door opened, Maggie stood there, glass in hand. The gin, what was left, disappeared in one swig. "Turn off the light. And stay on your side."

The eye of the storm. There was a disaster waiting to happen.

The things that demolish love often cloak themselves as trivial. There is no declared war, no bombs or grenades. They're paper cuts or minuscule scratches that start to bleed. Whose job is it to put the toothpaste cap back on? Where the border lies on a plate of shared food.

One lover has a reason to be angry, the other is blissfully unaware of a problem.

Lying in bed, C.J. struggled in vain to figure out his dilemma.

Neither of the Elliotts slept much. One was mad. The other was afraid to sleep.

"Still agitated?" C. J. asked.

"Take me to breakfast. I'm not going to cook."

She wouldn't kill him in front of witnesses, so C.J. agreed. Halfway through her strawberry crêpes, Maggie announced she read some poetry and waited for a response. None came. "Are you listening to me?"

"You're reading poetry."

He was sharp. He didn't flush; his face didn't twitch. His eyes didn't dilate. He didn't pause from his eggs.

"Aren't you interested in whose?"

"I doubt if you're rushing through Ezra Pound."

They were about to leave the eye of the storm. Hundred and fifty miles an hour winds were building.

"Yours." She had his interest. His eyes showed that. Now, his face flushed.

"Mine?"

"Yours, old sport. And, I wouldn't say I liked them. Not much at all."

Denial wasn't an option. He composed them, which didn't allow too many options. "Which poems?"

"One you wrote right before we sailed for France. Another one from the Riviera."

Several of his fit her time periods. It would be helpful if she quoted one. Rather than guess, he stalled, took a bite of his Eggs Benedict, and a swallow of coffee. "What upset you about them?"

Maggie reached for her purse, yanked out two sheets of folded paper, and tossed them toward him. "What do you think?"

Avoiding eye contact, she gave him time to read. To her distress, her eyes grew hot, tears began welling up. Maggie hated crying. She considered blubbering a sign of frailty. For years, she'd been backhanded, whipped with a belt, and cuffed into surrender. She regarded tears as an indication of helplessness. Only weaklings cry.

She swung between anger and grief. "Why do you think I don't love you?" She hesitated, trying to gather her thoughts. "Or don't you love me?"

This was not a conversation for a café—or anywhere in public. "Let's talk at home."

C.J. waved a waitress over and asked for their check. He left the money and a generous tip before offering her his hand and leading her to the street.

As soon as they came through the door, he led her to the couch and eased down next to her. "Maggie, I love you.

The poetry is not about us. It's not about anyone. It's my imagination."

Neither said anything. They sat staring at each other, although Maggie's icy stare focused more through C.J. than at him.

C.J. was crushed. Maggie misinterpreted his poetry. Enough of the glaring. Standing, he started to walk away, unsure what he could say to lessen her fury.

"I don't believe you," Maggie said, sadness, pain, and resentment intertwined in her words.

For a moment, he froze; his heart stuttered while he tried to catch up to her words. His emotional defenses flew up. "Well, I'm at a loss," he said. Another extended silence. "No. That's not true. Not exactly. I feel like a runaway train is hurtling toward me."

"You betrayed me," Maggie said, her eyes flaming.

"I have not. That's absurd…even for you," he added, not intending to sound as cruel as he did. In his world, betrayal was an intentional choice, a resolution made in the mind and the heart. He had made no such decision.

"You betrayed me because you're resentful of my accomplishments."

"That's horsefeathers," he said.

"No, it's not. It's true."

"You're full of Irish bull, total crap." His neck burned, and the veins in his temples pulsated. "I've never betrayed you. I've never denied or resented anything you asked for. We honeymooned at the Grand Canyon because it was where you wanted to go. Even if you refused to look at it." C.J. almost laughed at that. But it wasn't a time to laugh. He had an argument to win. We drove to Nashville and marched for you to get to vote. I suggested living in Bar Harbor because your best friend was there. I never complained about bouncing to New York or Boston when I'd have preferred to write at home. I've been supportive of everything you've wanted to do. Hell, I've been your biggest fan."

"Fine. If you're not green-eyed, take me home to Bar Harbor, to New York, where I can thrive."

"No."

No? No can't be debated. He gave no reason to counter-argue and didn't set any conditions for going to America. He simply said no.

"What do you mean no?"

"We're not going. We are not leaving Paris."

Flying off the couch, that damn uncomfortable red torture rack, Maggie shot for the kitchen and the Beefeater Gin.

"Stay out of the booze," he said, grabbing the bottle from her. "What's wrong with you? It's ten-thirty in the morning."

"Nothing is wrong with me." Spinning on her heels, Maggie headed for the bedroom, locking the door before he got there.

The door didn't mute Maggie's swearing. Complete bedlam because she misinterpreted what, to his mind, were two trivial poems.

The door stayed locked all night. Maggie wouldn't even open it to throw a blanket at him. Much less a pillow. C.J. didn't sleep all night. By daybreak, he wanted to burn that Art Deco torture rack. The cuckoo clock, something else he hated, declared eight o'clock cuckoo, cuckoo. Eight times. Enough.

The door shook from C.J.'s pounding. "Wake up. We need to talk."

The door opened. Maggie, eyes blazing, was wearing her flannel nightgown, not the inviting sheer gown he liked. "Talk to yourself." The door slammed with a bang.

Stunned, he stepped back. "Fine. You'll starve if you stay in there forever."

It wasn't starving, which two hours later brought Maggie out. She dashed across the room, slamming the bathroom door. Water rushed from the faucet right before the glass crashed down on the porcelain sink, shattering.

"Bloody Hell."

"Are you all right?"

The door cracked. A bit ashy, Maggie held up her hand, revealing a badly bleeding cut running almost the length of her little finger. "Judge for yourself."

He reached behind her for a towel. "Let me wrap this around your hand." After leading her to the couch, he tried to wipe some blood away. "This may need stitches," he said before noticing how pale she was. "You're white. Are you going to faint?"

"I don't do well with people bleeding. Especially me."

C.J.'s attempt to pull her into his arms wasn't rejected, but it wasn't well received, either. "I'm sorry, Maggie. I'm sorry those poems hurt you. I was just trying to write poetry. They had nothing to do with you. I was just writing. I would never try to make you sad." He was defeated—and looked it. For an extended period, he was quiet. Maggie, her face emotionless, let the time weigh on him.

"I was trying to be sensitive," he eventually said. "I wanted to show independence at the same time. I guess they weren't perfect. It's hard to explain, but I live in a made-up world when I write."

Maggie relaxed a little—maybe—not much. It struck C.J. he once told this girl she was his muse. It would not be an opportune time for her to remember. Now, Maggie could feel a touch of nerves in the one holding her.

"I mean," C.J. searched for an explanation. "Sometimes things that have happened to me in my life slip into my words. Sometimes, I suppose a person might influence one of my characters. But only my prose, not my poetry. The poetry is all an illusion written on paper. It's not real."

He didn't think he was accomplishing much.

"If all that's true, why didn't you show them to me?"

Finally, a question he could answer.

"I was afraid to. They're sort of embarrassing. I'm not sure they are very manly."

She pushed him away, right before laughing at him.

"What?" Maggie gasped. Her green eyes were popping. C.J. had no clue whether they were popping mad or popping in amazement.

A terrible battle began to rage inside her. Should she stay angry, be livid with him, or laugh at this idiot? The damn poetry had stung her, hurt her. But this explanation, this outrageous excuse, was so bizarre it almost had to be true.

She kicked the dummy in the shin playfully, but it did make him hop. It appeared there was a shaky truce, a temporary cease-fire.

"Let's take you to the hospital and have your gash checked."

After eleven stitches and four madeleine cakes dusted

with powdered sugar, C.J. helped Maggie into the sunshine. Once in a cab home, Maggie leaned toward her husband. Her head dropped on his shoulder, but only for a moment. Just long enough for him to again say he was sorry. She asked to stop for something to eat.

C.J. suggested Closerie des Lilas. The café, with its warm and inviting atmosphere, was crowded inside and on the patio, still surrounded by faded end-of-the-season lilacs. The Elliotts sat on the terrace. Maggie's pain had been real, but the hurt was beginning to vanish. She was no longer filled with bitterness and distrust. A waiter served them each a café crème to sip while they reflected on the menu.

"See those two women?" C.J. asked, shifting his eyes to the left. Without being obvious, Maggie snuck a glance. "They're Gertrude Stein and Alice Toklas. They frequent Shakespeare and Company." He stifled a snicker. "Stein is a novelist and poet. She's the one who calls people our age a lost generation. Toklas is, uh..."

With a flick of her bandaged hand, Maggie waved off his explanation.

Later, during their lunch, C.J. leaned forward. "Maggie, the poetry is not about you. I told you it's not about anyone."

"No one?" Maggie reached into her purse, pulling out one poem. Her voice was subdued. "Paris is my new target, and the need for a missing smile." Her eyes rose, peering into his. "Whose target is Paris? Whose smile is missing? Are you going to say Paris isn't your target? The missing smile is not mine?"

C.J.'s head dropped.

"The smiles that answer my own have become more a

mockery than a smile at all." She looked up from the page, back at him. "Isn't it my smile that's a mockery?"

C.J. shook his head, defeated. "No. It's not your smile. Your smile has never been a mockery.

Maggie didn't seem as angry, but she did continue reading. "Somebody looks another time over their shoulder in case love is desperately chasing after them. That's not you? No one is there. I'm not the one missing?"

The waiter showing up with their check gave C.J. a little time to think.

"Yes, it's me," he said, "sort of. I'm expressing melancholy, anguish. I suppose the poems are about me but not you." For a moment, elbows on the table, he avoided eye contact. "You need to understand. Until you, I had no one. I love you. But I'm afraid. I live in fear of you leaving. The poetry is about my angsts, my self-doubt. I am not writing about you. I'm describing my fear."

His eyelids dropped. For a brief time, he seemed to be disappearing. His expression was empty. When he finally looked at Maggie, her gaze was softer. Was love returning to her eyes?

"You don't think I love you?" she asked, her voice faint.

His head swam. Maggie's love, being sure of her feelings, was the one thing capable of rescuing his soul. Answering was hard. It wasn't having her love but the unthinkable possibility of losing her. It was that awful recurring nightmare that had haunted him since her comment about not wanting family.

"Don't you think I love you?" she asked again. There may have been the slightest hint of mist in her eyes.

Head back in his hands, he wanted to scream for her to

quit asking. *Don't ask me. Assure me.* She didn't. She waited for an answer.

As much as the truth scared him, honesty loomed as his only option. She'd recognize anything else as a lie. He almost told her no one ever loved him, not unconditionally. That would make him sound so damn weak. "I think you love me now. But what if you stop?" That sounded weaker.

He looked so tortured. Maggie no longer wanted to fight. For all the ups and downs they had, for all that might come, she loved him. His carved-out cheekbones and seductive eyes would have made him irresistible even if she hadn't. But she did, especially what he was inside.

Maggie's hurt faded, taking her anger with it. For a time, not a lengthy time, she gazed at her Elliott. A wry smile tip-toed across her mouth. "You are forgiven. And I will never stop loving you." Humor, an absurd, splendid humor, lept into her voice. "This doll's bank won't close." Maggie jumped up and held out her hand. Let's run all the way home. Unless you want a petting party here."

Back at their bungalow and reassured, C.J., realizing he had never asked, something that now shamed him, asked Maggie why she wanted to go back to America. Her rambling lasted thirty minutes, centering on family issues and needing to talk to Tommy to find out how corrupt her father was. While she didn't say so, not straight out, she wondered if the musical and theatrical world remembered her. Any thought they forgot her terrified Maggie.

When asked, she admitted the appeal of fame: singer, cellist, or actress. Which didn't matter. She needed acknowledgment.

"What if they don't remember you?"

"I'll be wrecked."

C.J. leaned against the doorjamb. Maggie turned her gaze to him and gave him a smile spilling with love—nothing held back. No inhibitions, no restrictions. Her face showed her tender devotion.

"Paris offers lots of opportunities," he said.

"They're not the same."

"Why?"

Maggie moved toward him and shook her head, her bobbed hair shining in the light coming through the window. She stared into his ever-changing eyes. Before they left America, his eyes had been filled with defeat. On the Riviera, with loneliness. The distress in his eyes bothered her most. He brought the isolation on himself by rejecting their friends.

Zelda adored him, but her bold silliness embarrassed him. He spurned the Murphys because of their casual acceptance of everyone and everyone's behavior. Here in Paris, his eyes flooded with selfishness. At least in Maggie's view. Others saw confidence and success.

"Why are opportunities different here?" Maggie asked, sarcasm dripping from every word. "You don't know?"

"No."

Startled, Maggie's jaw dropped. Her head tilted. Her face twisted. "You can't possibly be serious." His demeanor astonished her. He was. "Elliott, there's New York City, Broadway, Hollywood. Nothing compares."

He mumbled something about the literary talent in Paris. The freedom of expression. "I don't want to argue again," he said.

Maggie put her arms around him. "We won't."

An awkward silence settled over the room. There was still a monster in the bungalow, hiding somewhere—under the coffee table, inside a closet, behind that damn art deco couch. An ogre was lurking.

He sat down and tried to write. Maggie piddled about the house. Neither accomplished much.

"Maggie," Elliott said, the coming compromise all over his face. "What if you make a visit home? Talk to Tommy, spend time with Grace, sing in a club or two, and come back."

She'd won. The win was shallow; she preferred going together but would take C.J.'s offer.

"You should probably pitch that plant while I'm gone. I don't think it's going to make it."

XXXII

Chapter Thirty-Two

Life alone made C.J. miserable. Depression, in the past, motivated him to write, but by himself, he was too distraught. Why did he agree to Maggie leaving? One week in, with seven to go, he plodded around unkempt, drinking, not sleeping, and spending too much time in the ruinous company of Ernest Hemingway and Ezra Pound.

Across the Atlantic, Maggie, not miserable at all, opened their sprawling Bar Harbor home for a huge party celebrating Grace's brand-new engagement. The last of their close-knit group from Mount Holyoke, perhaps of the graduating class, to walk the aisle, Grace proclaimed delaying her matrimony a grand decision. In a toast to her classmates, she declared she, Maggie O, and Curls as the most successful among the Class of 1920 in avoiding the burden of children.

In two days, Tommy would arrive. Concerns regarding her

family would be confirmed or refuted. Until his arrival, she would enjoy Grace and gush about Paris to Grace's parents.

On the first day home, Grace asked Maggie about Curls. The question put Maggie in a difficult situation. She couldn't deny seeing Curls, at least not in good conscience. She wanted to tell her best friend everything, but she made that idiotic promise. The one not to tell anyone about Sam. Maggie talked on and on about the Olympics, and how, if not for Curls injuring her knee, she'd have been on the Brit tennis team.

Grace didn't ask about Curl's marital status. *Thank God.*

Grace and her fiancé drove Maggie to New York to pick up Tommy.

"You've gained weight," Tommy said as Maggie squeezed him.

Maggie's eyes popped. She stepped away, studying her waist.

"You should be ashamed of yourself," Grace said, giving Tommy a playful kick in the shin.

"I confess, you're absolutely stunning as always," Tommy said, hugging his sister a second time.

After introducing Tommy to Grace's fiancé, a fella from money so old no one remembered how they got rich, Maggie suggested Keen's Chop House in Harold Square as an excellent place for dinner.

"I'm keen on Keen's," Grace said.

Once at The Chop House, while waiting to order mutton, Maggie motioned a waiter over. "We'd like to toast Lily Langtry."

The young man leaned over closer. "I'm sorry, but we can no longer celebrate Miss Langtry. Prohibition, you know." He lowered his voice. "But I can direct you to a rather nondescript building and provide you the code word."

Tommy cringed at the idea. He did work for the Bureau of Investigation. Maggie, always a loyal sister, came to his rescue. "Why on earth would I want to drink something likely brewed in a bathtub."

The fiancé, a quiet sort, offered to take them to a place where the liquor came from Canada. "Chumley's is a high-class speakeasy. The staff struck a deal with the police about raids. The coppers call first, then the employees empty people out the back door. The cops only enter through the front door. Their paths never cross."

Much to Tommy's relief, Grace, after wanting an explanation of how her future husband had such familiarity with speakeasies, nixed the idea, preferring to rent a hotel suite and play a rousing game of mahjong or bridge, whichever the others favored.

* * *

The drive from New York to Bar Harbor turned out tiring, too exhausting for any long conversation without a night's rest. Tommy slumbered like a baby. Maggie slept like a baby —with colic.

The following morning, Maggie rose early to fix Tommy a fancy breakfast: crème brûlée, French toast, bagels buttered with caviar, lobster scrambled eggs, and chocolate pancakes.

A cook can add dairy to tame the spice when she accidentally dumps in too much cayenne. But lobster, once those kings of all crustaceans have been forgotten, roasted a deep shade of black, once crème brûlée crisps to heaps of charred lacquer, there's no going back.

Without mentioning the smoke, or the stench, Tommy sat down to his bowl of cereal. The Kellogg's Krumbles, with all the valuable minerals hidden away in the bran and the rest of the grain, provided Tommy and Maggie with pep, vim, and vigor for making muscles, rebuilding bone, and restoring weary nerve cells.

Even in late fall and early winter, beautiful sailboats crowded the bay. Tommy spread out a couple of beach towels. Maggie rolled a small blanket over her thighs and knees. Tommy lay back, propping himself on his elbows.

"So, tell me about your work," Maggie said.

"The bureau brought in a new boss," Tommy said. "A guy named Hoover. He's a real zealot."

According to Tommy, a deep housecleaning was under-way, spurred in part by the Teapot Dome scandal. Incompetents and political hacks were getting the axe. Rigorous hiring criteria and interviews, including background checks, now weeded out poor candidates.

"With the investigations into current employees, I thought I might get the boot. I did a lot of explaining to persuade them I'm not involved with Pop and Paddy." Tommy smiled at his sister, may have laughed—a little. "So, where do I begin?" he asked. "With Rothstein or with our parents?

"Rothstein," Maggie said. "He's the easy discussion. But before you start, I need you to know something. And you can't speak about this to anyone, not even Grace. You can't tell your bosses, no one. Promise me." Her brother agreed. "I'm betraying Curls. Never, ever tell anyone." Unable to look Tommy in the eyes, staring at the bay, she told a shocked

Tommy the whole story of Sam Taylor being alive and well in England.

"The fella who let Sam go better be careful," Tommy said. "He'll disappear if he's smart. If Rothstein finds out, his life won't be worth a nickel."

At first, Tommy cautioned about believing Rothstein would have no interest in them. When Maggie pressed him, he conceded the man was probably no threat. They likely were no longer a concern to the gangster.

"Still, living in France is not a bad idea. No point in being easy to find."

The suggestion to stay in Paris didn't sit well with Maggie. The place suited Elliott. Other aspiring writers kept his life exciting. But Maggie wanted to conquer the American Stage, symphonies, and, in her wildest imagination, Hollywood.

"Well," Maggie said, ready to address the real issue, "What do you hear from our mother and father?"

Tommy's shoulders slumped. He sighed. "How mad they are at you."

"I guess we're even. I'm mad too," Maggie said.

"I suppose."

"It's all their fault," Maggie said, biting off her words. Her body tensed. "They're frauds. They lied to us about everything." Maggie turned around on the blanket to face Tommy. "What do you know about our father and mother?"

"What are you talking about?"

"How much are you aware of regarding our parents?" Maggie inhaled, let her breath out, and took another. She leaned toward her brother, looking broken but unapologetic. "They're crooks...or worse."

Tommy stiffened. He glanced away; Maggie presumed to avoid her question. "Some things. Most of them, I found out after the race massacre," Tommy said.

"I'll tell you what I know. To be truthful, I wrote all of this to you in a letter. But I lost my nerve and didn't mail it. I burned it. I didn't want Elliott to find it," Maggie said. "Their deceitfulness preceded Greenwood's burning. Our old man was never what he pretended to be. Everything we thought as kids was a lie."

First, Maggie talked about their father's involvement in bootlegging. Stolen merchandise being sold in the furniture store intensified Maggie's ire. Afterward, she went into a rant about how Arnold Rothstein got involved in the fencing—all because of Sam Taylor. Mostly, Tommy sat quiet and listened, but Maggie recognized surprise in his eyes when she spilled the beans about a Rothstein connection.

After Maggie pushed harder, he spoke about their father and Uncle Paddy's ties to oil field fraud, implying a conceivable association with William Hale, but probably not in murdering Osage people. He also suggested connections with corruption in the Tulsa police department. While not absolving Pop of violence or lynchings, he claimed those actions aligned better with Paddy's behavior.

When Maggie pressed him about their mother, he'd only say she was not stupid. That was enough for Maggie. She was done with her parents, like Elliott with his mother.

***

Grace and her fiancé came for dinner. Soon, Maggie pulled Grace away for a private conversation. Maggie had much to discuss. Everything she held back until before talking to Tommy. "I'm fed up with the way I'm living."

It was her life she was glum about. The never-ending façade, pretending to be joyful singing in saloons like Zelli's, putting up with misogynists like Hemingway, and the lack of friends with common interests had her searching for the bottom of gin bottles. How she missed Grace—and Zelda Fitzgerald. With them, Paris would be bearable.

"How can you be unhappy?" Grace asked. "You starred at the Metropolitan Opera. You bounce between this beautiful house, The Riviera, and Paris. You mingle with F. Scott Fitzgerald and Cole Porter. How can you possibly be dissatisfied with such excitement?"

The question gave Maggie pause. But not for long. "Like you said, I bounce. I never belong." Family secrets, scandals, and angsts of thwarted love poured out. Maggie described her life as turmoil.

Grace said Maggie's life sounded like a wonderful mix of intriguing characters, decadence, and fabulous clothes.

"Let's take a walk along the shore," Maggie said, opening the kitchen's back door.

"I do adore our Bah Hahbah," Grace said, gazing out at the harbor and sounding like the down east mariner she was at heart.

They sat at the tide's edge, absorbing the stunning winter coastal beauty, watching yachts and lobster boats bob around the bay. The ocean setting transformed from a glistening sunset to thick fog and mist as the old friends caught up.

"I wish you'd been here for the summertime," Grace said,

pulling her knees up to her chest and sighing. "The old-timers say everyone has nothing to do but are very busy doing it."

Like Grace, Maggie wished she had been home for the summer. It was a time when the world was green and blue. The breezes were warm and filled a person's senses. Summers in Bar Harbor drew the rich with their opulent ways. Gymkhanas with gorgeous horses and sailboat races added to the marvel of the beautiful weather.

The fall remained pleasant with a quieter atmosphere. The hardiest of the seasonal crowd often stayed for the Halloween Festivities and everything related to the harvest. A few hung around until Thanksgiving. Those who lived on the island year-round accepted the winters.

They did their best to endure the harsh months. Gathering for church socials, parties, and dances, they played parlor games in quaint cottages heated by wood and coal. On Friday and Saturday nights, they packed The Star Theatre, watching Clara Bow, Marion Davies, Ana May Wong, and Douglas Fairbanks.

"I love the harmony of the water," Maggie said. "The sea mesmerizes me, the way the boats are fading to silhouettes as the fog rolls in."

"I'm sorry about your family problems."

Maggie shook her head. Those things no longer mattered. She picked up a small crab before it burrowed away. Smaller than her thumb, she sat the tiny crustacean on her knee and brushed sand from its shell.

Her demeanor turning grave, Grace turned toward Maggie. "What did you mean by thwarted love? Are you and C.J. having difficulties?"

That was a difficult question to answer. At least if Maggie wanted to tell the truth.

"No," Maggie said in a less than convincing voice. The silhouettes of the boats disappeared into the dark. The tide moved them further up the beach before Maggie opened up.

"We're not having problems. We may be having...issues...sort of. The truth is hard to explain."

Maggie smiled at her former roommate. "You want to ask me some questions, don't you?"

"Well," Grace said, "I do have a few. But after four years with you, I know you'll tell me everything. All I have to do is wait."

Maggie laughed at Grace's accurate insight. "Paris is grand for Elliott. He has a passel of writers to spend time with. For me, the City of Lights is a lonely place."

One thing Maggie liked about Grace was her honesty. She always spoke her mind.

"Are you sure you're not being a bit selfish? My impression of Paris is it is unequaled in its glamor."

Maggie tossed her head back and ran a hand through her red hair. "Les Années Folles, the crazy years." Leaning back, she gazed into the darkness, now hiding the entire bay. "Do you think I am selfish? Or, too busy hating my family, pitying myself?"

"You might enjoy life a little more if you stopped believing in such utter nonsense."

"Nonsense?" Maggie whirled toward her friend. She leaned away, flabbergasted. "I may feel sorry for yours truly, but it isn't nonsense. I have reason to."

Grace wagged her finger at Maggie—vehemently. "Oh, no,

you don't. You're not getting away with crawling back into your slimy pond of self-pity. You're spouting rubbish, do you hear me? Rubbish. You're wallowing in your supposed misfortune like a fly in molasses."

Maggie stared at Grace with her mouth agape. Remorseless, Grace gave her head a quick nod. "So, stop it. This minute."

Eyes twinkling, the corners of her lips twitching, trying not to laugh, and failing, Maggie extended her hand to Grace. "I will. Right this minute. Shake on it. By the way, you looked preposterous, shaking your finger at me."

***

Three days later, after a fifty-mile drive, Maggie and Grace dropped Tommy off at the Bangor train station and headed the Elliotts' midnight blue Jeffery touring car toward New York City. They checked into the Plaza Hotel, where Maggie asked for the suite the Fitzgeralds stayed in. She wondered if there was any remaining damage.

The old and new, elegant and garish, Maggie loved New York. She wanted to experience it all on this short stay with Grace.

Coney Island's almost empty amusement park was still a grand starting place. Roller coasters, Ferris wheels, kewpie dolls with cotton candy, and hot dogs worked off by an invigorating wade in the wintry ocean. A room service meal and a deep night's sleep followed.

At the Cotton Club, a delighted, never-shy Maggie swooned when she found George Gershwin sitting in with a young black trumpet player. At her first opportunity, she rushed up to tell him she had starred at the Met, was friends with Cole Porter, and had sung with Cole at Zelli's bar in Paris. Impressed, or at least pretending to be, Gershwin asked her on stage.

He put an arm around her shoulder as they went up and recommended she do something from Broadway.

"How about Fascinating Rhythm?" Maggie asked.

Gershwin smiled broadly and kissed her hand. "You have fabulous taste."

Maggie wowed the audience the way she always had in this venue. She intoxicated men. She drove them crazy. Gershwin was enthralled with Maggie and invited her and Grace to a Lyndhurst Mansion gala the next night.

Extravagant parties require ritzy dresses. Extreme care must go into each selection. Helped out of the limousine, Maggie was decked out in a Coco Chanel dress, fox stole, long pearl necklace, and snakeskin shoes, all topped by a black turban. Grace also wore Chanel with a brimless hat.

Broadway musical actress Nancy Carroll, poet and party girl Edna St. Vincent Millay, whom Zelda Fitzgerald called a whore, and Maggie's old friend and Zazà director David Belasco attended. Wild red-hot mamma Clara Bow showed up in a short skirt with her stockings rolled down, honeybees painted on her knees, and wearing a silk scarf knotted flapper style behind her ear.

Carefree, reckless flappers flirted with everyone.

When Belasco introduced Clara to Maggie, Clara burst with passion. "You were Zazà at the Met. How I wanted to see that production, but I couldn't afford a ticket."

"That's terrible," Grace said. "You missed a wonderful performance."

Grace went on and on, humiliating Maggie with praise.

"Maggie never conforms. She is a total nonconformist. If she wants something, she gets it. Gets every little thing she desires. She holds the world in utter contempt. She lives boldly. In Maggie's brain, she is never wrong, not about anything." Grace paused. "She might be right."

Maggie gave Grace a push on the shoulder before telling Clara that Grace was astoundingly correct about her.

"You are right to live the way you want," Clara said. "I'm always criticized for my bohemian lifestyle, at least that's what they call it. They say I have dreadful manners," Clara fumed. "They yell at me to be dignified. But what are dignified people like? Snobs. Frightful snobs. I'm a curiosity in Hollywood. I'm a big freak because I'm myself!"

"I may be falling in love with you," Maggie said.

Drunk guests fell all over each other. Sex permeated the conversations. St. Vincent Millay, born of the desire to meet and misbehave with fellow writers and artists, sat between Maggie and Grace, finishing a bottle of wine and talking spiritedly.

Those paying court to Millay soon discovered she sang and had an extensive repertoire of the old risqué music-hall songs and obscene nursery rhymes she adored. Eight ditties into her routine, she turned green, utterly green. After Millay stopped retching, Maggie watched a waitress, supported by two waiters, being led downstairs sobbing. The lack of refinement of her idol Millay bitterly disillusioned the poor woman.

By the party's end, flappers and their jelly beans lie passed out all over the house. Zozzled and exhausted, Grace couldn't keep up with Maggie, who could have still reveled for hours.

***

"Close the curtains. I haven't been so dizzy since our graduation party," Grace said. "What time is it?"

"Eleven o'clock," Maggie said, "and raining like cats and dogs. So, you may as well stay in bed."

"I wonder who came up with such a phrase?" Grace asked. "It's so silly."

"Somebody in the Wilson administration," Maggie said.

Grace's forehead wrinkled. "Why on earth would you think that?"

"Why not? Can you prove otherwise?"

Grace, her eyes bloodshot, her face a shade of green, shook her head. "I wish you'd stopped me last night."

"You didn't want stopped."

"All the more reason you should have stopped me," Grace said. Before Maggie could answer, Grace pronounced the conversation too absurd to continue.

After a shower and four aspirin, Grace rebounded, ready to take on New York again.

They eased back by attending a matinee of Beau Brummel, starring John Barrymore and the striking Mary Astor. Watching the eight-year younger Aster on the screen depressed Maggie. That evening, they watched the ten years younger Peg Entwistle play Hedvig in Henrik Ibsen's The Wild Duck. Opportunity was passing her by.

XXXIII

Chapter Thirty-Three

A grouchy Maggie entered her last week in Bar Harbor. Personal achievement, for her, lay in America, not France. The cello was still her true calling. Her love for the instrument didn't matter; fame as a cellist was impossible. Symphonies remained closed to women on both sides of the Atlantic. In fact, in some ways, France was worse. New York had operas and Broadway, places where there were opportunities. On the other coast, America had Hollywood.

Too mad to enjoy her stroll, Maggie trudged down to their property's beach. She hurled stones in the bay and cussed Elliott for wanting to remain in Paris. To no avail, none.

The Elliotts' months-long absence from Bar Harbor was evident in how the back door creaked and the cobwebs Maggie still hadn't bothered to wipe off the kitchen counter.

The teapot landed with a clang against the bottom cupboard. Maggie swore, picked the pot up, and tossed in some loose tea. She filled it with water and turned the gas flame up. She blew some dust out of a cup instead of washing it. If a dusty teacup made her sick, who cared?

Looking through the Frigidaire they purchased before sailing for France, she found molded vegetables and spoiled milk. So much for dinner.

At last, the teakettle whistled. Like a fool, she grabbed the metal handle without an oven mitt. "Damn you, Elliott." It was all Elliott's failings. For another thirty minutes, Maggie slammed things around the house and swore at everything and everyone.

Her hand was not going to blister. Three of her fingers hurt, but not a great deal, a good thing since, in her sour disposition, she might have chopped them off.

Because Grace always improved her state of mind, Maggie stuck her round glasses on and drove over to her house, the one she would soon share with a new husband. A male pedestrian yelled at her for being a reckless driver. Others, including a couple of women, gawked as she whizzed by. While females could legally drive, not many did.

When Maggie pulled into the driveway, Grace was tossing mulch across a rose garden. She brushed the dirt off her pants and strolled toward the midnight blue touring car.

Maggie's mood was written all over her face.

"Well, what's wrong?" Grace asked.

"In one week—one week," she said, holding up her index finger, "I sail for France."

"We'll throw a going-away gala, build big bonfires, and go wild on the beach. We'll invite everyone," Grace said.

"I'm not in any emotional state for a party," Maggie said.

"Do you have any liquor hidden away?" she asked, walking past Grace to the house.

"Not a drop."

Maggie stopped and turned pensive. "Well, I thought you'd be a better hostess."

They started to the house, Maggie dragging along sluggish and indifferent. The house was modern, sunlit, much to Maggie's dismay. She needed dark corners, shadows, a place where things could be concealed. She wanted to hide in an old house, creeping in eerie atmosphere.

Maggie sat down on the new couch, another of those damn art deco affairs. Instead of welcoming woods and comfort—glitz, glamour, and geometric patterns filled the house. Gold accents, sculptural silhouettes, and sweeping collages, all big and bold, crowded every room. Frivolity and confidence permeated the house. To find something quiet and reserved, Maggie would have to go elsewhere.

"What am I going to do?"

"Go back to Paris...and your husband."

That's when Maggie's grand sulk began in earnest. Head down, she drew deep, brooding breaths followed by baleful moaning. She picked at non-existent lint on her mid-calf length skirt. The drama was ramping to its peak. Until Grace started laughing.

"Stop." Grace pushed on her friend's shoulder, laughed harder. "I thought you were a better actress." Forearm to her head, Grace threw her head back and swooned.

Maggie tried to appear shocked, astounded, and hurt—failing utterly at each. "Why the hell don't you have any alcohol?" Maggie asked, standing and walking toward a bay window facing Acadia Park.

"Come back over here and sit down. We need to talk."

With Maggie back next to her, Grace took her hand and played with the diamond ring she'd helped C.J. acquire. "What's wrong? I want the truth."

Maggie stared at the floor—said nothing.

"You aren't going to talk, are you?" Grace said.

"No."

"Too bad. You're going to listen." Grace kept playing with Maggie's ring. The lecture wasn't fresh. Over their years living together, Grace had delivered it before. "Your misery extends back to your adolescence, and you know it. You told me about the ugly rumors circulated the summer you were sixteen that, although unsuccessful, two members of Tulsa's high society tried to assault you."

Nothing. Then Maggie's heart thumped, no wrenched. Her mind refused to rehash what she was hearing.

"Your folks took rotten care of you. Your father was overbearing. Hell, he was abusive, and your mother did nothing to intercede." After a pause, Grace said, "Face it. And get over it."

As Grace talked, Maggie started to relive those menacing memories. Her past thundered back, painting pictures of selfish parents, unappreciative of their children's needs, in horrible black, deep green, and dark blood-red colors. She recalled how her musical talent was never praised. If anything, they discouraged her because she was female. The finest thing that ever happened to her was getting out of that house, escaping that biting belt, and going to Mount Holyoke.

"My youth, terrible or not, isn't my current problem."

"Then tell me what's wrong," Grace said again.

"Fine," Maggie hesitated, ground her teeth, and did her best Gloria Swanson tied to the railroad tracks damsel in distress imitation. "Guess what, Clara Bow and Louise Brooks," Maggie waited a moment before continuing, "Mary Astor and Ana May Wong have in common?"

"Well...they're movie stars," Grace said.

"All younger than me."

Wide-eyed, open-mouthed delight spurted from Grace's mouth. Her laugh was delicious. Even Maggie had to admit that despite being the one laughed at.

"Their age is what's bothering you. Unfathomable. You've lost your mind."

It was hopeless trying to be miserable with Grace happy, impossible.

Once she regained her composure, Grace lectured her dearest friend—briefly. "You need to; no, you must stop fretting over the future—or the past. Live in the present. Better yet, for the moment."

* * *

With Maggie in America, C.J. laughed little. He was drinking too much with the Hemingways and sparring with Ernest until he knocked Hemingway on the seat of his pants the second time. His buddy didn't enjoy losing.

His manuscript received encouraging comments from Sylvia Beach and Gertrude Stein, to whom Sylvia loaned the draft without his permission. He was deep into his writing and a bottle of merlot when Grace's wire arrived.

I put her on the ship. She needs a good spanking.

Thank heavens the solitude was about to end. Unless Maggie jumped overboard.

***

It was only 6:45 a.m., but someone was beating on the front door. C.J. pulled his pillow over his head. If he ignored the pounding, the uninvited guest would surely go away.

Minutes passed. Bang. Bang. Bang.

Stumbling around looking for his robe, C.J. roared at the door. "I'm coming." He picked up a table lamp in case he wanted to club the damn intruder, likely Hemingway. He unlocked the door and turned the knob.

The solid wood door, pushed from the other side, flew open. Whoever leaped on him jumped with enough force to knock him over backward. He was being smooched all over his face.

"We've missed you. Did you miss us?" Zelda had her legs straddling him and her hands pressing on his shoulders. She leaned down, her breath smelling of whiskey; she kissed him again. This time on the mouth and using her tongue. "Well, did you?"

Scott stepped over them and flopped down on the red Art Deco couch, laughing.

"Goofo and I got back this morning. We came here first thing," Zelda said, struggling to stand. She was wearing light blue knickers and pink and white argyle socks.

Once on her feet and stable—almost, she reached down to help C.J. up. "Where's Maggie?"

Too shocked to ask why they were here so early, C.J. answered. "On a ship coming back from America."

"Why was she back in the home of the free?" Scott asked from the couch, his words mushy.

"Doesn't matter," Zelda said. "How soon will she be here? We have so reverl," Zelda's eyes all but crossed. She worked her jaw back and forth, up and down, back and forth again. "We hab so much reveralizing to do."

"Reveling to do," Scott said, correcting her.

Zelda blew him a kiss. "Yes, that too." Zelda made a grand swooping motion with her arm. "Gin and wine to be drank." She paused. "Or is it drunk?" She weaved enough C.J. thought she might fall over. "Who cares? We'll empty a lot of bottles."

Zelda wobbled her way across the room and dropped next to her husband. "You didn't answer. Have you missed us?"

"Profoundly," C.J. said as he headed to the kitchen to brew coffee. Both Fitzgeralds were asleep when he came back.

Four hours passed before Zelda stirred. Her eyes bloodshot, she gave Scott a slight shake. "Goofo, Goofo, wake up." He kept snoring.

Zelda tottered toward C.J., "I think we might have been a bit tipsy when we arrived." She raised an empty gin bottle they had brought with them. "This was the drink that was drunk on that fateful hot evening, I mean last night. I maintain that if Goofo and I had just sat down and shared a couple of mint juleps, the drink a proper southern belle should drink, none of this sorry situation would have happened.

C.J. held out the pot of dark roast and a cup.

"With cream, please," Zelda said.

She blew on the coffee, took a sip, followed by a long drink. "Why did Mags go to America?"

At first, C.J. thought about avoiding the question. But,

despite her impassioned friendliness, he liked Zelda and trusted her for some perplexing reason. He started to talk.

"Some family issues needed her attention."

The corners of Zelda's tiny mouth turned up. She didn't believe him—at least not entirely.

Time to admit the truth. "And," C.J. paused, took in, and let out a deep breath. "I think she was growing discouraged by living in Paris. She's never happy anymore unless she's on a stage." C.J. stopped short of admitting his doubt about her love for him."

"Maggie's a vibrant gal," Zelda said. "I won't be surprised if she ends up a legend. She has the beauty and the talent." Zelda sat next to C.J. and, being quite casual, rubbed his knee. "Maggie is smart, shrewd, funny, and loves to party. She goes after what she wants and fancies herself the center of attention—just like me."

It wasn't the kiss that unsettled C.J. He was used to her kissing him, even kissing him with an open mouth. It wasn't her wandering hands, either. They'd wandered before. But that look in her eyes when she said "just like me," that lost, empty, lonely look. It was the look that scared him.

After a burst of giddy laughter, Zelda turned solemn, putting her hand along C.J.'s face. "Be careful, dear boy. Goofo and I were America's first couple: golden, carefree, creating our own mythology. You and Maggie remind me of us. Don't let glamor-filled days and gin-sopping nights linger too long. The lights dim without warning. You'll pay a high price for recklessness. You'll both take an awful beating."

XXXIV

Chapter Thirty-Four

Icy winds blew across Le Havre as Maggie docked. She grumbled and waved the baggage handler away for speaking French. Dragging two heavy bags, her eyes bounced all over the station, searching for C.J. *He couldn't be so bold as to not be here. He better not be.*

"Maggie," he was hurrying toward her. "You look fine," he said, putting his arms around her. "I thought you might never be back."

"You're thin," she said. "Have you been eating?"

Her demeanor made it clear she was still unhappy about being in France.

The ride to Paris didn't help. Maggie said little, almost nothing. C.J. retreated deeper into himself.

***

Still in love with Maggie's audacity, drive, and burning

self-confidence, a single-minded C.J. resolved to make things right at any cost—short of leaving Paris.

"I thought you might sell this couch, or burn the damn thing," Maggie said before tossing her coat on one end and plopping on the other. "What can we eat? The cupboards aren't empty, are they?"

"I shopped yesterday. Food was running a little low. You're aware I'm not one to cook."

Maggie stood and walked over to Elliott. She wrapped her arms around him, laying her head on his chest. "I'm tired. The seas were choppy, and the weather stayed miserable the whole trip." She slipped her arm through his. "Do you mind if we go out for dinner?"

About halfway through their meal, Maggie perked up. She teased C.J. about his new mustache and goatee, saying they must go. "I'll not sleep with a whiskbroom."

"Guess who's back."

Maggie didn't answer. She leaned across the table and gave the chin beard a slight tug. "This goes before you do any exploring of my body tonight." For the first time in too long, her voice was happy, her eyes sparkling. "I think I can daresay who's back," she said. "Scott and Zelda...I hope."

He smiled. "Your desire came true."

"Paris will be much better now. I adore Zelda." Maggie sat back, smiling and laughing. "How many times has she kissed you?"

This was the Maggie he loved. "Too many to count," he said, grasping her hands.

"My dearest wish is you smooched back."

"Maggie Kathryn Elliott...I did not."

With both stubborn, saving the relationship and their sanity would be no easy proposition. Devotion to each other would be their salvation—or their ruin. Maggie's talent and energy burned hot, C.J.'s intellect, patience, and literary character contrasted with her fire. She was a revolutionary. He was unadventurous. He wouldn't admit to being rather bland. He would deny his dull nature. Yet, he sought to domesticate her, transform her from Mabel Normand into Mary Pickford.

He laughed over Maggie hoping he kissed back. She expressed herself perfectly and freshly: no passé axioms, no striving for outcomes.

"Well, next time, kiss back. You mustn't hurt her feelings." Maggie paused, smiled, and winked. "Just don't be initiating the kissing."

"You know what we should do?" C.J. asked. "Let's wake up early and pound on the Fitzgerald's door before sunup."

Past daylight, beyond noon, Maggie and Elliott knocked on the Fitzgerald's front door. Zelda threw her arms around Maggie's neck. "Never go off again—without me."

Stepping back for a better view, Zelda raved about Maggie's attire. A short skirt and stockings rolled down left her knees, painted with flowers, exposed. "How fabulous. I must have mine done today." She lifted Maggie's skirt to mid-thigh. "Scott, aren't they ideal?"

To show them off, Maggie put one leg forward and then the other.

The champagne cork popped and flew across the room. Bubbles exploded from the bottle before Scott managed to start pouring.

For an hour, Maggie gushed about her trip to America.

"Grace and I met George Gershwin, Clara Bow, and," Maggie patted Zelda's hand, "Edna St. Vincent Millay."

"The whore," Zelda said.

"What's Clara Bow like?" Scott asked.

"Oh, Scott, I don't know what makes a female tempting, but she has it. She is gorgeous, and her personality is charismatic. I only whooped the town up with her one night, but I adore her."

Zelda jumped up and told Maggie to grab her coat. "I need a new dress, a short one. We must get my knees painted, or have you paint them. We'll rush back to the house as soon as we're done. I'll put on my Elizabeth Arden face, and we'll take our boys out and create grand mischief."

Five stores and almost two hours later, Zelda found the suitable garment, a black dropped waist, jaw-dropping one embellished with exquisite beads and sequins. Maggie also bought an outfit, a Cleopatra cap, and two long strings of pearls.

Next, they unearthed a knee painter. Zelda got a giant eyeball, an eye looking up, painted on one and a butterfly on the other. On the way home, they stopped at a sidewalk café for an earnest conversation.

Maggie confessed her resentment over Elliott refusing to go to America. "I don't understand how he can be so inconsiderate. Sometimes, I think I married a fiend, an absolute tyrant, a self-centered monster."

A young waitress asked what they'd like. "A cup of tea, something strong," Maggie said. "No, wait, make it a merlot. And some kind of Danish, preferably with frosting."

Back to the topic at hand, "Nevertheless," Maggie said,

"we're a couple. I suppose we're heading toward boom or bust. Together. We will celebrate our success and grapple with our failures. No matter what, we will always be us."

Zelda lit a cigarette and offered one to Maggie, who declined. "All I want," Zelda said, inhaling deeply on her mild as May, Marlboro cigarette of distinction, "is to stay young and irresponsible. My life is my own to live and be happy before I die in my own way to please myself." Lips puckered, she puffed several perfect smoke rings. "I do not suffer a single feeling of inferiority, or shyness, or doubt, and no moral principles."

Zelda paused to study the bluish circles on their way to extinction. "Of course, I don't get everything I want. I'd love to write a wonderful book. My individual sentences are often lovely, and I can create a mood and turn a clever phrase. But I'm told my works tend to be sketches, not full stories. I long to be an important writer, but I'm not. Oh well, doesn't matter. My soul prefers to dance."

* * *

Later, at The Dingo American Bar and Restaurant, a favorite gathering place for ex-pats, Maggie and Zelda gossiped. C.J. and Scott discussed writing over coq au vin while swigging gin.

Intellectuals and Paris luminaries Pound, Joyce, and Picasso frequented The Dingo, so it was no surprise to Maggie when Hemingway came in with Hadley on his arm. At a table for six, all was lost.

Three men with extraordinary genius, each battling his individual demons, shared their first drink. The first of many.

* * *

Back home, Maggie spread cream cheese across a bagel. "I like Hadley. But I loathe her husband."

C.J. stole a bite of her bagel.

Maggie stopped chewing. "Hemingway groveled over Scott? The oaf's behavior was loathsome."

C.J. took another bite.

"Ernest is nothing more than a leach, trying to slurp on the talent of others."

"He possesses some skill," C.J. said. "He let me read a bit of a story he's working on."

"What's his masterpiece about?" Maggie asked, irritated because her antagonist might be blessed with some creativity.

"The title is something about the sun rising. The tale is a love story. I guess. I believe his hero is impotent from a war injury."

Maggie rolled her eyes and blurted out something about the sun being the only thing rising. "Poor Hadley."

XXXV

Chapter Thirty-Five

"Good things come to those who wait," C.J. said.

"Elliott, Ida's note only says Ravel wants to lunch with us tomorrow. It might mean nothing."

C.J. mocked Maggie for being pessimistic. He should have taunted her harder. Ravel wanted far more than luncheon companions. He was sure of that.

Maurice Ravel sipped his wine and smiled at the Elliotts. "L'heure espagnole, my Opéra-bouffe is about to be presented by The Paris Opéra. Ida persuaded me to offer you the part of Concepción."

Maggie's jaw dropped. Not too much. She maintained her refinement.

Knowing he might embarrass Maggie, C.J. still gave in to his curiosity. "What is an Opéra bouffe?"

Ida Rubinstein's eyes twinkled. She winked at Maggie and lost her battle with a crooked little grin.

Ravel, without laughing, explained his one-act opera. "Opéras bouffes feature elements of comedy, satire, parody, and farce. Apart from the male lead, who sings sérénades and cavatinas with deliberately exaggerated melodies, the other rôles will give, I think, the impression of being spoken."

C.J. nodded his head despite still having no conception of cavatinas or exaggerated melodies.

"The opera builds over 21 scenes," Ravel said. "I will be involved in every aspect of the production. I want Maggie to play the role of the central character, the watchmaker's wife."

Ravel began a far too, at least for C.J., detailed description of his opera.

"After her husband leaves, Concepción takes advantage of his absence to plan meetings with gentleman friends." *Blah, Blah, Blah.*

Up too late trying to defend Hemingway to Maggie, C.J.'s eyelids trembled and fell shut until Maggie kicked him. Awake, he nodded and smiled, showing his intense interest in Ravel's endless recitation.

Ravel droned on.

Somebody conceals himself in another clock. Somebody enters the shop...

C.J. fidgeted in his chair, drawing a frown from Maggie. Below the table, he shifted his legs farther from her. C.J. stretched his eyes open in an effort not to doze off again.

On and on, Ravel blathered, "...To save face... purchase a clock...the singers also step out of character. . ." *Drone, drone, drone . . .*

Thank God. C.J. took a deep breath, nodded, and exhaled. "It sounds..."

Ida interrupted. "Exhausting." She sighed.

Home again, Maggie romped and Charleston'd around the room, sang at the top of her voice, and jumped into C.J.'s arms from ten feet away.

"I'm on stage again, old sport, on stage again." Joy bursting forth, she twirled across the room. She pirouetted, whirled, and gyrated with great energy. "Perhaps I was wrong. Perhaps Paris is remarkable. Yes, it absolutely is. I'm going to be a star. My blazing light will be a sight to behold. Kiss me, you fool. Smooch your blinding comet."

"Isn't this opera in French?" C.J. asked.

He was about to fall into deep, dark water. Maggie became uppity, "I took French. So, ferme le bouche et fais attention." Maggie burst into a French version of Ain't We Got Fun. She flung her arms wide. Whether she intended to smack him in the face, C.J. wasn't sure. Either way, it hurt.

XXXVI

Chapter Thirty-Six

With a lot of talking and some support from Sylvia Beach, C.J. and Scott convinced Maggie and Zelda to go to dinner at Gertrude Stein's house. The official invitation invited them to *"a salon, a gathering of talented thinkers, to advance modernism in literature"* at the home of Mrs. Stein and Mrs. Alice Toklas.

Maggie and Zelda laughed like hyenas at the idea of a salon. Maggie decided the Elliotts and Fitzgeralds would travel to the party in the same car to ensure she and Zelda could force the husbands to leave if the event became unbearable.

Had C.J. and Scott not forbidden them, both women would have worn pants to the affair. Maggie planned on wearing knickers.

Attendees included Sylvia Beach, Hemingway, Picasso, Sinclair Lewis, James Joyce, and Ezra Pound. All brought their wives—or mistresses. Man Ray came with his muse, the wicked Kiki de Montparnasse. Maggie still considered being a muse a thankless job. People would see a muse's face a thousand times, admire the work of an artist or sculptor, but they would not remember the muse's name. Kiki was the exception.

Over a delicious meal, something that irritated Maggie and Zelda; they had planned to hate it, Merlot flowed steadily into Zelda's glass. While they ate, Gertrude talked about how the salons began. She attributed the beginnings of the Saturday evening salons to her painter friend Matisse when people started visiting to view and gasp over her collection of his paintings. Matisse invited people. Those people brought people.

"They became a dreadful nuisance," Gertrude said.

Alice Toklas was the real hostess, at least for the wives and girlfriends. She shuffled the females, except Gertrude and Sylvia Beach, off to a separate room. The ladies, clearly second-class citizens, were too inept to contribute to Gertrude's intellectual exchanges with the writers and artists.

With Stein facilitating from a high-backed chair next to the stove in her cluttered studio, *This Side of Paradise* and *The Beautiful and the Damned* dominated the conversation. Stein, Hemingway, Lewis, and Ezra Pound gushed over Fitzgerald's writing. Especially Hemingway.

Gertrude declared Fitzgerald essentially created a new class in his debut novel. She claimed the relentless pessimism of his second release perfectly described the lost generation.

Pointing at C.J., Gertrude wagged her finger. "This young man," she said, "this amazing man is in the beginning stages of a delightful book. You all must force him to let you read his manuscript."

Both Sylvia Beach and Scott concurred. "He hooked me in the first paragraph," Scott said.

"The writing is shrewdly political," Stein said. "Mr. Elliott is subtle, sneaky," she chuckled, "in his witty criticism of that pompous American scoundrel Woodrow Wilson."

Fitzgerald poured himself some gin, took a long swallow. "What intrigues me about C.J.'s work is how he describes one person affected by government politics. Not the unwashed masses, one individual."

Always ready to rant about the carnage of the war, Pound, red-faced and shaking a fist, fumed about finance capitalism being to blame. Stein stood and lumbered across the room for her third piece of Alice's yellow sponge cake. "Ezra, dear, I like you. But you are not amusing."

* * *

The conversation in the living room, the room they had dismissed the females to, differed from the studio where the writers and artists shaped Modernism and plotted cultural change.

Stooped and self-effacing, Alice Toklas didn't so much sit in the overstuffed chair, she melted into it. She didn't lead the dialogue. She limited thought. No politics, no discussion of the arts. Alice, excruciatingly monotoned, kept the wives' and mistresses' conversations confined to what women should talk about—cooking, cleaning, reading, and, within restrictions, fashion.

Controlling Hadley Hemingway constantly challenged Alice. But the poor lady was over-matched by Zelda Fitzgerald. Hadley maintained some restraint. Not Zelda. With Zelda along, not Maggie.

Eyes shining, Maggie threw down the gauntlet. "Miss Toklas, do you ever consider getting drunk and bursting into the other room?"

Chapter Thirty-Seven

"Elliott, I'm bored. Paris can't have become this dull. Am I in a bad dream? One I can't wake up from?"

Astonished, Elliott was rapid in response. "What are you talking about? You've been cast as the lead in an opera. One composed by your hero, Ravel, no less."

That was true. But a bump she'd easily overcome. "Except we haven't begun to rehearse. That excitement, as wonderful as it will be, is in the future, weeks away. It's now, right now, that I'm utterly bored."

"Maybe it's your plight to be rebellious, witty...hopelessly bored. And self-indulgent."

Maggie's doubled-up fist crashed into his shoulder. She bared her teeth and growled. Laughing, she straddled him on the red couch. "You better be careful, old sport. I'll push you in the Seine."

C.J. turned contemplative. "What do you want, Maggie

dear?" He flipped Maggie off and bounced on top of her, pinning her shoulders. After giving her nose a quick peck, he gazed at her, his eyes smiling. "What do you desire? I'll give it to you." Another kiss, this one on her raspberry-tasting lips. "We have complete freedom to create our own lives with access to everything beautiful, exciting, and," he winked at her, "scandalous."

"I want," Maggie hesitated, laughing about what she was about to blurt out, "to be the center of attention. All the time, not periodically."

He howled, rolled to his side. "Magnificent." The pure honesty of her statement made it a masterpiece of freshness, imagination, and ingenuity.

"I want to jump up and down on the old-fashioned, horrible limits on women." Maggie leaped up, danced the black bottom, and pulled him up by his ears. "I must drink every drop of life, sing in jazz clubs, rub elbows with royalty and thieves, cavort with gigolos, paint my face, and be outrageous."

"Oh, my little chickadee..."

"Your little what?"

"My little chickadee," C.J. said, "you can do all those things here in Paris."

With a little peck on the cheek, Maggie threw her arms around his neck. "You best be right, old sport. Of course, with Zelda here, you may be."

"Call Scott and Zelda. Tell them to chase down a babysitter for Scottie and meet us at Zelli's. I'll dance with you and Zelda. But I'll only step on her feet."

With the place packed, Maggie took twenty minutes to find Joe Zelli and tell him, though Wednesday, not Thursday, she wanted to go on stage. With all of Paris loving her, Joe and the house jazz band delighted in letting her perform.

Two sips of C.J.'s white wine, and she was ready to sing, dance, and even stroke her cello—if she had brought the bulky instrument along.

As always, Joe's stable of hostesses and gigolos decorated the Royal Box. Thirty beautiful ladies, with one aim, selling as much alcohol as possible, earned their pay by taking a percentage of the price of every bottle they sold. Male counterparts, equally attractive and effective at their job, mirrored the girls.

The Fitzgeralds arrived prior to one o'clock and guzzled two gins each before Maggie sprang to the stage. Zelda started a chant of Maggie, Maggie. Smiling ear to ear, Maggie raised her hands to encourage the crowd. She was in her element.

Wine and gin flowed. The Russians in the audience swigged vodka. Joe Zelli beamed and slapped backs.

A drunk from Chicago yelled for something by Ida Cox. Maggie stopped dead.

"Who said that?"

"I did," a man struggling to stay on his feet said.

Stepping to the edge of the footlights, Maggie bent at the waist. She squinted at the man. "What's bum with you? I'm too happy to sing the blues." A quick toss of her head dismissed the well-oiled fella's request. "You're in the wrong place...pal."

With a rim shot, Maggie threw him a kiss and turned to the band. "A little Savoy Orpheans."

As soon as Maggie cut loose, everyone started doing The Charleston, followed by The Black Bottom. Zelda and Scott bumped their posteriors together, C.J. spun a party girl dancing next to him. Maggie was where she wanted to be—the center of attention.

Three frantic hours elapsed. "I'm exhausted," Zelda said, dissolving into a chair on Zelli's balcony.

"You mustn't think of stopping," Maggie said. "They'll serve breakfast in a little while, and refreshed by greasy sausage, you'll find your second wind."

"He won't," C.J. said, pointing at the sozzled and passed-out Scott crumpled over a table.

Zelda, taking a handful of Scott's hair, raised his head. "He doesn't hold his gin so well."

"Elliott," Maggie smiled at her husband. That you're-not-going-to-like-this-but-you'll-do-it-smile. "Would you take Scott home? Zelda and I want to go shopping." Without pointless complaining, he managed to half-drag Scott to the sidewalk and into a taxi.

After waving goodbye, Maggie and Zelda hurried off to find something better to eat than Zelli served.

* * *

Not long after the Fitzgeralds' return to Paris, Maggie glimpsed Art and Liz Musgrove. Before they left the Riviera, Zelda declared them off-limits. Something C.J. and Scott did not understand. It didn't matter. Their wives stood their ground. No partying with the Musgroves.

At dinner with Gerald and Sara Murphy, Maggie and a highly strung Zelda revealed, in strong terms, that the Musgroves were pariahs to them. Blacklisted. The Murphys would have to choose.

Of all the damn luck, Liz Musgrove sat alone in their

chosen café. She waved and motioned for Maggie and Zelda to join her. There was no couth way to decline.

Despite the early hour, she was tipsy on her third glass of port—and surly. She was wearing a shabby black coat, unusual for a wealthy American.

"Behold, the woman cheated on. Oh, the bastard has pulled the stunt before," she said, obviously drunk. "But this time, he did it so unskillfully. I should just kill him and be done with him. Wickedness is only interesting when it's hidden. Or at least the sinner tries to conceal it."

"But I love the nakedly wicked," Zelda said, sarcasm dripping in her voice. Or maybe not. "Those boldly scandalous."

Maggie laughed. Liz didn't. After looking off into space, she turned back and stared at her friends, her face pale. She looked ill. Her husband was a womanizer, a cheater.

When Art wasn't womanizing, he spent most of his days twenty miles from Paris, sun-worshipping. Daily perched on a knoll, he indulged in lengthy contemplation—of nothing. Except for philandering, literature was the only thing overshadowing his fascination with the sun, which he had tattooed on the soles of his feet.

While the Elliotts, Fitzgeralds, Hemingway, Pound, and Sylvia Beach viewed the Musgroves as affable maniacs and quite unhinged, they also saw them as enlightened readers. Given the socially redeeming qualities the Musgroves maintained, Maggie made an innocent comment about overlooking Art's indiscretions.

"So, you will forgive C.J.'s transgressions with me?" Liz asked hatefully.

An ordinary wife would slap the woman, but Maggie

could hardly force herself to breathe. She glanced around the café. What if she stomped out, went to some dress shop, never found out the truth?

How could a good spouse ignore such an accusation? How could she disregard such a slanderous statement about the man she loved and was making a life with? How indeed?

Wasn't it better to know if the marriage was on some treadmill to destruction? If it proved true, she couldn't live through that, not another family failure. She pushed those thoughts out of her mind, or at least to the back. She laid her hands flat on the table and leaned in. An oversized clock ticked loudly on the wall like a pounding heartbeat.

"You're a liar."

"Believe what you want. It doesn't matter to me," Liz said.

The loud slap echoed throughout the eatery, drowning out the clinking silverware and every conversation. Stunned at being slapped, Liz Musgrove was more astounded by who hit her. Not Maggie—Zelda.

Everyone there stared as Zelda poked a finger into the brunette's greying face. "Don't you ever come near the four of us again!" Zelda stopped in front of a middle-aged woman sipping vermouth. "You can read about this in F. Scott Fitzgerald's next novel."

XXXVIII

Chapter Thirty-Eight

Back home—alone—C.J. started to work on his novel but changed his mind. Instead, he scribbled out a poem. Not one for Maggie's eyes.

I'm not a lover of people
but a collector of memories.
They'll keep people close enough
to have whenever they're needed.
My road has stretched from Boston to Paris.
But I've traveled it alone.
Not because I had to,
but by choice.
Walking under a summer sky
or along a beach,
I often ask God for another day.
I trust God.
But He's the only one.

So far, I've always gotten another day.
To spend alone
or meeting tomorrow's friend.

It was a poem, something imagined, nothing more. Scott and Ezra would understand, and Sylvia would appreciate the sentiment. Even Ernest would comprehend the meaning. Zelda would adore the independent speaker. But Maggie, brighter than any of them, might burst. He best file the little ditty away. Perhaps slip the verse into his novel—innocuously.

Though never one to cook, his cooking always turned out to be a disaster; the lack of breakfast sent him to the kitchen to try his luck making an omelet. Soon, his eyes watered from the smoke and the stench of burned eggs filling the tiny kitchenette.

C.J. opened a window and plugged in the electric fan, a noisy damned contraption. Despite its infernal clicking, the noise was better than the fumes.

When someone knocked on the door, C.J. assumed Maggie had forgotten her key. He was wrong. A skinny man in a gray uniform handed him a cable—from America.

Another ninety minutes passed before Maggie came home. Walking there, she had decided, with Zelda's approval, Elliott would hear nothing about Elizabeth Musgrove's accusations. Whether she could stick to that, time would tell. She glanced at Elliott. "What's addling you?"

"This came a couple of hours ago."

Rothstein found out you were in NY. STAY IN FRANCE. Hope
our father is not a complete fool.
Tommy

"Do you think Pop would tell him where we are?" Maggie asked.

C.J. shrugged and shook his head. "I wouldn't think so." He poured Maggie a cup of coffee.

"Tommy doesn't think he would," Maggie said. She sighed and stepped toward C.J., once her safe place. Now, she wasn't so sure.

XXXIX

Chapter Thirty-Nine

Bookstores, the ones with shelves reaching the ceiling, lit by table lamps, and sunlight coming through front windows, are comforting places. Prose and poetry, well thought out by bright-minded intellectuals, each volume encased in leather or cloth bindings, offer astonishing paths of escape from life, whether the particular life be mundane, exciting, or menacing.

Maggie needed to elude life. Shakespeare and Company would be as good a place as any to try. Especially if Hemingway wasn't around.

C.J. engrossed himself in browsing. Sipping a Sylvia Beach prepared loganberry julep, served with raspberries and a sprig of mint, Maggie immersed herself in a borrowed copy of Edna Ferber's *So Big*, delighting in how its heroine found beauty everywhere, even in fields of cabbage. Arnold Rothstein was far away and not a concern.

Tomorrow, life would improve more. Rehearsals for Ravel's *L'heure espagnole* would begin.

***

Maggie's first rehearsal tickled her to the bone. First, the delightful clock noises of the opening could be heard from blocks away. And then the stage, which should have been a designer's dream, turned into a nightmare when the back wall collapsed, destroying Ravel's playful arrangements. The looks on the other cast members were precious. And the expression on Maurice Ravel's face...well, she couldn't wait to tell Elliott. Zelda! Zelda would just scream.

Later, after midnight, Joe Zelli stood in the spotlight of his Royal Box and excitingly announced his Thursday evening singer would soon star at the Paris Opera. Somehow, according to Joe, he deserved the credit.

With a quick hug of Joe, Maggie threw her arms wide and broke into *Hard Hearted Hanna, the Vamp of Savannah*. Elliott Fox Trotted with Zelda while F. Scott nursed gin and debated the advantages of living on the Left or Right Bank with anyone bold enough, or drunk enough, to take a position.

The rowdy crowd, almost all Royal Box regulars, chanted for *In Between Time*, now Maggie's signature song. Raising her skirt to flash the bees on her knees, the always amenable Maggie obliged.

"Well, hello, dear."

Maggie stopped, dead. Then turned as the music ceased. Up the stage steps, puffing a cigar, came the doyenne of cafe society, rival saloon performer Ada "Bricktop" Smith.

Born Ada Beatrice Queen Victoria Louise Virginia Smith, Bricktop knew as well as anyone it's about the company you keep. She ruled nightlife in Paris, teaching a 300-pound Aga Khan III to do the Charleston, getting Hoyningen-Huene to design the lighting for one of her Montmartre clubs, the one with black and white banquettes, red carpeting, and patent-leather curtains. Rumors had her scandalous newcomer, Josephine Baker's lover.

Maggie shrieked and bowed.

"Little girl, can you do the Charleston?" Bricktop asked, her voice booming.

"Yes," Maggie gushed.

When she demonstrated her dancing, Bricktop bellowed, "What legs! What gorgeous gams!"

Up in the balcony, a tanked French starlet was giving her boyfriend hell and pouring gin in his lap. Behind the band were several Negroes pushing and shoving five or six Russians trying to steal their table.

Bricktop hollered for the actress to shut up. After shutting the tart up, she pointed a finger at the Bolsheviks and told them to "Sit down and behave. This young lady is performing, and I plan to sing with her." The scamps obeyed. Immediately.

An hour later, perspiring profusely, Maggie and Bricktop joined C.J. and the Fitzgeralds. Scott wrapped his arms around Bricktop and gave her a peck on the cheek.

"My greatest claim to fame," Scott said, "I discovered Bricktop before Cole Porter could."

Maggie put her hand on Bricktop's forearm. "Tell me this, Miss Ada Beatrice Queen Victoria Louise Virginia Smith. Why does everyone call you Bricktop?"

The rotund woman laughed and patted her red hair. "Why do you think?"

The merriment lasted another two hours until Bricktop threw an arm over Maggie. "Don't burn yourself out, honey. You can't stay up 'til dawn every day."

The advice weighed on Maggie. But not much.

At breakfast with Scott and Zelda, Maggie talked about her frustration with Paris for the first time in front of anyone other than C.J., well, he and Grace.

Although still half-drunk, Scott put a hand on Maggie's shoulder and offered guidance. "For what my opinion is worth, darling Maggie, it's never too late, or in your case too early, to be whoever you want to be." Leaning forward glassy-eyed, his words were a bit slurred. "There's no time limit. No rules. We can be whatever we want to be."

"Oh, Goofo," Zelda said, "that's wonderful. I want to dance. Ballet."

XL

Chapter Forty

The differences between the Left and Right Banks annoyed Maggie. The Left Bank, artistic, bohemian, and literary, appealed to writers, artists, and students who flocked to the cheap housing. La Sorbonne and the university district spurned creativity.

But the left bank wouldn't be so desirable to Americans without Sylvia Beach and her Shakespeare and Company. While they wouldn't admit such a thing, many English-speaking ex-pats, including C.J., enjoyed the mother tongue they experienced at Sylvia's. Tripping over the French language became discomforting.

The Right Bank, populated by Paris' wealthier class, was home to France's finest museums, The Louvre, Musée de Art Moderne, and Musée de l'Orangerie. The fancier jazz clubs and entertainment also tended to be on the Right Bank.

Maggie grew jealous of the more elite homes on the right bank. At least she envied their size. More room was appealing.

One thing Maggie hated about Paris—French taxis. Last night, trying to hail one, rain soaked them. Enough.

"Elliott," she said, interrupting his writing, "we need a car."

"We have little income," C.J. said, looking up from his page.

Not much income? What a lie. The cheapskate.

"We pay nominal rent. Our expenses are petty." Maggie paused, considering what she was about to say. "I make money." Never shy, she said what she wanted to. Her words hung heavy. "And I'll bring in a lot when Ravel's opera opens."

Surprised, C.J. backed away. Shocks like that take a minute to wear off. Before he recovered, she stunned him again.

"Money is not a problem. That's what you've always told me. So why should we go without?"

Speechless for a moment, C.J. stared at her. "What are we lacking?"

He stood, stepped around the table, and moved toward her, causing her to step back.

"We do rather well. Remember our home in Bar Harbor and the appealing apartment in New York? And, if you haven't noticed, we live in Paris and do anything we want."

The color draining from her face; she turned away. Shaken, she stuttered as she tried to explain. "Of course, we have enough." She reached out to put her hands on C.J.'s chest. She was unsuccessful. He stepped out of reach.

She mumbled something about being sorry and left the room, leaving him to sit back down at his typewriter. C.J. and Maggie were battling demons ranging from self-doubt to affluence and the need for fame. They were losing.

The cupboard door, the one above the sink, squeaked when she opened it. The same way the damn thing always did. If she let her emotions go, she'd tear the cheap, flimsy thing off its hinges. She closed her eyes, shook her head, and sighed, trying to disregard her blunder. She failed.

Getting along with her husband was growing into a grueling task. The simplest things, things never mattering before, now caused arguments. Arguing was becoming a way of life. A habit she didn't like. After all, most of the fighting was her fault.

Unable to tolerate the maddening creaking again, she left the cupboard open. The toasted English muffin melted the butter she spread and burned her tongue. She muttered to herself. This Monday couldn't get any worse. In truth, the day could get worse. And did.

Whoever started pounding on the door didn't have the sense to stop and wait for someone to answer, let them in, or send them away. Maggie jerked the door open. The one knocking was no surprise. That damn Hemingway.

"Where's C.J.?" Full of himself, the ape pushed in without being asked. "C.J.," he yelled. "It's Ernest." He turned back toward Maggie and put an unwelcome hand on her shoulder. "You're flushed."

Before she replied, or slapped him, C.J. came out of his writing room. As he did, Hemingway patted the side of her face. A second later, perhaps less, he was jumping around the room on one leg, rubbing his throbbing shin.

"Why'd you kick me?" Ernest collapsed into a chair to rub his new bruise.

"For good measure," she said. "Do you want something to drink?"

"Whiskey. If you have any."

Maggie glanced at C.J., standing there with a bewildered look on his face. "What are you gawking at? I'm an amateur when it comes to kicking people. I think I did a right fair job." She went to the kitchen to pour him some. She would have added a little Ipecac had a bottle been handy.

"Here. Don't spill any."

"Thanks, I won't. You took half the skin off my shin."

"Pull your pants down. I don't want to be disgusted by your ugly leg."

****

C.J. couldn't argue about Maggie Elliott being a complicated woman. She was radiant, fascinating, and overflowing with curiosity. But her petulance was becoming a problem. She was getting touchy and sometimes cantankerous. Especially if someone had the gall to oppose her. Her wonderful attitude of not giving a damn changed after they got to Paris.

Nothing about C.J. was complex. His pleasures were modest: writing, informal dinners, lying on a beach, drinking with friends. He maintained an air of poise, self-assurance, and confidence in everything except, perhaps, himself.

He took Maggie as the center of his world. Unlike the love of his life, he accepted disappointments with the capability to change directions and move on.

After Maggie started changing, he tried to figure her out. What was missing in her life? Grace? New York? Tommy? Bar Harbor? He doubted it was Bar Harbor, although she claimed it to be if he pressed her.

The friendship between Maggie and Zelda also bothered him, at least to a degree. He, not a friend, should be the one making her happy.

While his liking Zelda softened the blow, he remained fretful about her influence over his wife. Zelda excited people. She grew up the belle of Montgomery. Like Maggie, she had beauty, talent, and the ability to make people do anything she wanted.

Unlike Maggie's questionable family, everyone admired the Sayres. All the Sayres. Well, except Zelda. Only the young admired her.

Scott once confided in C.J. how sometimes he wasn't sure if Zelda was real or a character he created. "She's cuckoo, crazy as a loon. But I'm devoted to her," Scott had said.

"I'm in love with Maggie," C.J. said in response. "But Maggie isn't cuckoo. Or crazy as a loon."

Hemingway asked for another whiskey. "Not a chance." Maggie turned her back and ignored him.

"Oh well, I didn't come here to drink," Hemingway said, sitting the glass next to him. "I want you and Fitzgerald to go to a boxing match with me Friday night. A couple of hard-hitting heavyweights are squaring off. Neither has any defensive skills. They'll beat the hell out of each other."

"And what are we wives supposed to do?"

"Anything you want. Come along if you want to."

"I don't want blood and sweat splattered all over me."

"The gore excites Hadley. But the three of you can go to a classy restaurant or the theatre. Cole Porter is going to sit in at Harry's Bar."

"Fine," Maggie said, giving C.J. a hostile glance. "Go ogle

two damn near-naked men trying to knock the other's head off. Zelda, Hadley, and I will go eat costly meals and listen to Cole while we drink expensive champagne. Then who can tell."

XLI

Chapter Forty-One

It was a brand-new Peugeot, a yellow one. Giving in was becoming a bad habit for C.J., at least, he said that when they picked up their car, which he said reminded him of a canary.

While reveling in her victory, Maggie admitted their shiny sports car resembled a torpedo with a radiator. Still, she rejoiced in driving their shiny toy home.

"Let's go to the Fitzgeralds. I need a drink," Maggie said, pushing him toward the car.

"You better let me drive," he said. "We don't want any pedestrians rundown."

Maggie refused to surrender the keys. "I'm as good a driver as you are. If you don't like riding with me, walk."

C.J., ever the good-natured one, tossed his arms up. "It's too far to walk. And besides, it looks like it might rain. I suppose the risk is worth staying dry." Smiling, he threw an arm around her while planting a kiss on her rouged cheek.

They laughed and sparred all the way to the Fitzgeralds, Maggie swatting C.J. across the chest every time he grabbed at the dashboard because she passed another car. "You could drive a taxi," he declared. "God help me."

***

Whenever they were with the Fitzgeralds, C.J. had to be on his toes, ready to ward off potential calamity. Maggie and Zelda were charming women, much alike and quite different. Maggie was classically beautiful, sophisticated, intelligent, witty, and opinionated. She was quick and ingenious, a female who would challenge any man's wits.

Zelda was childlike, often capricious, and wildly spirited. At ten, she called the fire department to rescue someone off the roof before crawling up there herself to be saved.

When Scott invited Maggie and Elliott in, the place was in bedlam. Still in pajamas, Scottie needed her face washed. Breakfast dishes piled in the sink, unmade beds, and unread scattered newspapers cluttering the living room added to the disarray. Ashtrays full of cigarette butts and empty liquor bottles lay all over. Maggie snuck a glimpse at her watch. Two in the afternoon.

Zelda was dressing with the bedroom door cracked open. She initiated a lively conversation. "Scott, tell them what we did last night."

Before Scott started, she began herself. "We went to Les Deux Magots and consumed sherry with Picasso and Olga. She is more fun than Pablo. We drank 'til we found the bottom of the bottles, as usual, and ended up dancing on the white tableclothed tables. I dazzled in the chef's hat." The story continued until Zelda came into the room, buttoning her dress.

Scottie tugged at her mother's skirt, whining about being hungry. "Scott, find this poor child something to eat. We can't have her perish in front of the Elliotts. We have enough trouble keeping friends."

"Let me fix her something," Maggie said, offering her hand to the toddler, which Scottie grabbed.

"Give her some meatloaf from the frig," Zelda said. "Make her a sandwich. And pour her a glass of milk if she wants one."

Scottie sat at the kitchen table and studied Maggie, fixing her lunch. "My momma and pop imbibe—a lot," she said, being as casual as if she were talking about puppies or going to a park. "They're always boozeled."

Astounded by the child's statement, Maggie stumbled over her words, trying to tell the child she was mistaken. "They don't drink too much. They're happy."

The smirk on Scottie's face screamed she knew better, but she was too involved in her meatloaf sandwich to chase the issue. "Mamma's meatloaf is always dry. Daddy says she cooks everything too long. He usually says too damn long."

"Do you want some ketchup?"

"No, I like mustard. But we're out. We're almost always out of things."

Zelda came into the kitchen for a half-empty bottle of red wine. "Is she pestering you?" she asked.

"Not at all," Maggie said. "She's a delight."

Zelda's mouth wrinkled, and she raised her cheek, causing her left eye to close. "If she's lucky, she'll be a beautiful little fool. I hope so."

Little about Zelda surprised Maggie. *But wow.* Saying you wanted your child to be a fool? *It might be better not to bother with children.* They appeared to be a vexation to both the Fitzgeralds and the Hemingways. Although not so much to Hadley.

With Scottie fed, Maggie went back into the cramped living room. Scott, Zelda, and C.J. were all on their second glasses of wine. "Take us to a movie, a funny one," Zelda said. Scott claimed French movies were boring and made no sense, even if one could read the French Intertitles. The last time they went to a movie, a picture of a woman wearing an enormous feathered hat appeared right before the movie started. Scott leaned over and asked Zelda, "What the hell does that say?"

"It says, Madame, how would you like to sit behind that hat you're wearing?"

"So, what do you want to do?" Zelda asked.

"Open another bottle of Riesling."

More drinking would mean they wouldn't go anywhere. Scott did not hold his liquor well. His alcohol consumption was becoming a problem. Every week, he went on two or three-day binges. Out on the town, he'd be tearing drunk by his fourth glass and not remember anything when they got home. Many nights, Mrs. Fitzgerald didn't behave any better, except Scott tended to be an unpleasant drunk. At least his mouth got hostile. When Zelda was well-oiled, she was almost always happy.

"I have a splendid idea," Zelda said. "Let's all go back to The Riviera. The Murphys must be bored without us."

"Terribly so," Scott said.

Maggie scoffed at the suggestion. "I can't go. I'm in an opera."

"How many more performances?" Zelda asked.

"Every Friday and Saturday for six weeks."

"Fabulous. We will leave in forty-two days." Life's little details seldom interfered with Zelda's plans.

While Maggie held her tongue, she wasn't going back to the Riviera. If she was going anywhere, it would be to America.

XLII

Chapter Forty-Two

L'heure Espagnole, Spanish Hours, or more accurately Spanish Time, filled the seats of the Paris Opera on opening night. It's challenging to get an opera like Ravel had written, right. If Maggie overplayed the bawdry, she risked coming across as tasteless. Understate the innuendo, and things become too tame.

Maggie, however, danced the balance between lewdness and sophistication, pirouetting on a razor's edge. Her Concepción tossed abundant double entendres directly to the audience.

Ravel's ravishing orchestration was sensual. Maggie, her voice bright and gleaming, lilted with a throwaway suggestiveness.

At the party after the premiere, and after several gins, Maggie patted Ravel's hand. "I must find my husband. I can't have him drinking in excess with my understudy."

When Maggie came to his rescue, C.J. was trapped in a corner by a French girl, no more than eighteen or nineteen, wearing far too much eyeshadow. Maggie whispered in the girl's ear and shooed her away.

"What did you tell her?" C.J. asked.

"About your venereal disease."

"What is wrong with you? She'll tell everybody what you said."

"Then don't be talking to dizzy girls."

Maggie moved off to a small group of musicians from the orchestra. A stuffy fella smoking a cigar sneered at her.

"Well, well, our little American star."

"It is, or I mean, I am," Maggie said, her tone tart. "And you blow the trombone—poorly."

A trumpet player struggled not to spit his drink. Glancing around at the others, Maggie's eyes settled on one. "Aren't you the cellist?" The still tuxedoed man nodded. "Do you have yours with you?"

"Yes. We may entertain after a while."

"Would you let me play it?" The musician stiffened and leaned away. "Oh, I'm quite remarkable. I attended Mount Holyoke in America on a music scholarship. I would have made the Boston Symphony. Except for my plumbing." Despite remaining reluctant, he couldn't deny such a beauty.

"You'll find my cello with the rest of the instruments. Please be careful."

Maggie opened the case and removed the cello. "How lovely." She scampered over and sat next to the piano. The instrument screeched the first time she drew the bow across the strings. Maggie laughed, winking at the sick-looking owner.

Bach. Tchaikovsky. A touch of The Capriccio, followed by a sliver of his 1812 Overture.

She could not resist. Not that she tried. Grace would have loved it. Zelda and Scott, special guests of the Elliotts, did. So did Ida Rubinstein. The Vamp. The partygoers burst into dancing, most of them into the black bottom.

A dark-haired, rather handsome man offered his hand to Maggie. "My name is George Gershwin. May I join you?"

Unflustered, Maggie stood, curtsied, and smiled ear to ear. Without missing a beat, Maggie asked, "What shall we play, Mr. Gershwin?"

"Do you know, *When You Want 'Em, You Can't Get 'Em, When You've Got 'Em, You Don't Want 'Em?*" Gershwin asked, stepping around to sit at the keyboard.

"Enough to follow you," Maggie said, smiling and thrilled with the opportunity.

Everyone was enraptured. Well, except, perhaps...possibly, Maurice Ravel. *Swanee* came next, with Maggie setting the cello aside to sing. For thirty minutes, Maggie and Gershwin sang and played.

When they finished, Ida Rubenstein rushed to Gershwin, flinging her arms around his neck. "George, I am elated you came. I wasn't sure you would after Maurice refused to instruct you."

"I've forgiven the old bird. Classical instruction would have destroyed my sense of rhythm, anyway. Besides, I couldn't avoid a party Maggie would be at."

"Have you met Maggie's husband? You must," Ida said without giving Gershwin time to answer. "The girl always calls her spouse by his last name. The poor boy."

Gershwin was a bit shy when introduced to C.J. He stumbled for something to say and tried to recover by asking C.J. what kind of work he did.

"I'm a novelist. Or I'm trying to be," he said.

Maggie, beaming, put her arm around C.J. "He's almost finished his novel. It is delicious." C.J. flushed. Maggie gave his cheek a quick kiss to relieve his embarrassment. Or increase it.

Now beet red, he mumbled, "Maggie is expressing her opinion. But her liking her husband's manuscript doesn't mean my prose is readable."

"Well," Maggie batted her blue shadowed and heavily mascaraed eyes at Elliott. "F. Scott Fitzgerald says it's brilliant. That means it is."

"If Fitzgerald thinks your work is intriguing, that's enough for me," Gershwin said.

"Would you like to meet Mr. Fitzgerald?" Maggie asked. "He's right there. I can introduce you this moment."

Maggie grabbed the jazz composer's arm and led him to the Fitzgeralds, with C.J. following.

"Scott, this is George Gershwin."

"I love your novels," Gershwin said, extending his hand. "Especially your first one."

"The boy used to be talented," Zelda said, intercepting the man's hand. "Now he's useless. Good for nothing...except getting zozzled."

"Pleased, Mr. Gershwin. You'll learn to put up with her if we become friends." Scott was struggling to stand and slurring his speech. "I write, and she shwims."

"And I dance," Zelda said, stumbling over her words.

"Zelda has an extraordinary talent for living," Scott said. "We lead a fantastical life. We create our own lives. Unfortunately, if one lingers too long in the myth, the light dims, and reality sets in. Life's promises begin to crumble, and recklessness, exciting though it may be, demands a high price. An exorbitant price."

Scott paused, finished his drink, and studied Maggie and C.J. "Be cautious, dear ones. You are walking the same path."

XLIII

Chapter Forty-Three

The following morning, Le Temps, Paris' most influential daily newspaper's headline, called Maggie BREATHTAKING, decreeing her singing as splendid and her acting funny yet touching. The entire opera is entertaining and well worth watching.

"Elliott," Maggie said as they sat to eat, "Do you think Scott is right? Are we on a reckless path?"

Not knowing how to answer, he bought time by getting some butter for his toast, which was already covered. "I don't know," he said, returning. There was no point in not being honest. "I haven't thought about our path. I guess everyone is on one. But I haven't thought much about ours."

"Do you think we should?" she asked.

Of all the possible delightful breakfast conversations, this wasn't one. Now he was trapped. Maggie's mind was on the subject, and there would be no escaping. He might as well get it over with.

"I'm not sure what road we're on," he said. "Are you?"

Twisting in her chair and playing with her French toast, a delight in no way French, Maggie took a moment to respond. "Not one to obscurity, I hope."

He chuckled. "What's wrong with obscurity?"

"I suppose nothing. Not for most."

He put his hand on her arm and smiled. Not much of a smile, if anything, more of a reassuring grin, innocent-looking. "But anonymity isn't for us. Right?"

"Nope. Not for us." Maggie got up and sat on his lap. "Not for us," she said, putting her arms around his neck. "Recognition is what we need," she said, making him laugh. "Lots and lots of admiration." Laughing herself, she smothered her handsome husband's face in kisses.

"And what if we don't acquire any?"

That got him a poke in the jaw. A gentle one.

"Oh, we will, old sport. I'm on my way to fame now."

More kissing, along with uncontrolled giggling, something recently out of character for the determined Maggie.

"And you're on the verge, on the threshold of distinction. I'll be a beloved star, and you'll be renowned." Maggie paused. "America will adore me as much as they love Clara Bow."

As loved as Clara Bow. The statement would have set off alarms if C.J. knew what the actress with such gorgeous eyes had told Maggie at the party in New York. Miss Bow despaired over having no childhood, declared she was being used up by Hollywood and was the victim of everyone else's expectations.

"I've worked like a dog. My nerves are shot, and I always want to cry," Clara had said. Sometime in the future, Maggie would realize she should have listened.

XLIV

Chapter Forty-Four

A long drive through the Paris countryside wasn't enough to push Scott's warning about recklessness out of Maggie's mind. After deeper thought, Maggie focused more on what Scott said. He called the path he and Zelda were on reckless. The key was to not be reckless. He advised avoiding drinking in excess, leaving parties early, not jumping in public fountains, or riding on the hoods of taxis. And be cautious about your spending."

Managing their finances was Scott and Zelda's biggest dilemma. Money was not an issue for the Elliotts. Regarding the drinking, they both handled their liquor better than the Fitzgeralds. It didn't take much alcohol to slam Scott. Zelda kept going until she passed out. Maggie and C.J., for the most part, held their booze. They had at least a modicum of self-control. Liquor was not a problem for them, or so she told herself.

Without intending to drive to the village of Barbizon,

they ended up there. After visiting Château de Fontainebleau, Barbizon proved to be a lovely place for a tasty meal, followed by a stroll. Concerns about following the Fitzgeralds' paths of recklessness diminished, replaced by a walk through picturesque stone houses, restored inns, and charming shops. Flowers painted on walls added to the village's distinctiveness.

French artists, including Théodore Rousseau and Jean-François Millet, were part of a movement born in this area of the wish to represent unspoiled nature.

They passed The Auberge Ganne, where penniless painters without money shared the same rooms. According to the locals, evenings in this modest inn always ended late, with everybody drunk. The lost generation Gertrude Stein constantly babbled about would have fit right in.

As they drifted along, Maggie slipped her arm through C.J.'s and leaned close. "Let's rent a room and spend the night."

The room was much less expensive than a comparable room in America. Most things in France were. Maggie flopped on the bed, crack. "Oops."

C.J. kneeled and peered under the double bed. "Yep. You cracked the slat."

"Well, it didn't take much to break it," Maggie said, scooting off the sagging mattress.

"What are you going to tell the host?" C.J. asked.

"Me? I think you should tell her. You're the man of the family."

"You're the one who broke it."

"Yes. But we would have destroyed this old, weak, slatted bed later tonight." On her hands and knees, Maggie lifted the faded green chenille bedspread for a peek. The slat was in two pieces. "Let's not tell her."

Elliott pulled up his cuff to check his wristwatch. "Ten after four. There's probably a lumber store in this town. I'll go buy a replacement."

"Get a heavier board," Maggie said. "One like this won't survive the night."

C.J. was gone for over an hour. He came back, sneaking up the back stairs with the new slats. "These will do the job," he said, leaning three two-by-fours against the wall.

"I'm hungry," Maggie said. "Let's go find someplace to eat. And for you to ply me with liquor. I've decided we should run down a reckless path."

After a whole bottle of Merlot, he struggled to lift the mattress and put in the new slats. He wrestled with the bed because Maggie kept attempting to help.

"Stop helping me."

"I'm not trying to be helpful. I'm teaching you to overcome hindrances."

"Well, you're failing."

"It's a work in progress." She stepped back. But not far enough. "The more I hinder, the more proficient you'll become. Soon, you'll be able to manage all kinds of tasks."

At last, C.J. got the mattress back in place. Stretching across it, he kicked off his tan and black saddle oxfords.

"Don't relax like we're finished. The sheets aren't on."

"I don't care. I'm too tired and too smashed to bother with them."

"I care." Maggie hopped on the bed and used her feet to

push him off the edge. She made the bed while he lay on the worn carpet, mumbling about the room spinning.

Before she knew it, Elliott was asleep and impossible to wake up. He always was when he drank too much wine. He was the only person she knew who did better on gin or hard liquor.

While he slept, she thumbed through an old agricultural magazine someone left in the room. Agricultural expertise was essential to keep people eating, but it made for dull reading.

Unable to read herself to sleep or count enough sheep, she gave a lot of thought to a cable she had dispatched to Grace a few days before they embarked on their countryside drive. In it, she sent Grace a detailed description of Liz Musgrove. She also revealed what that awful "bitch," a word the telegrapher refused to use, demanding Maggie change it to woman, had said regarding Elliott. The cable ended by asking if Grace thought it could be true.

At sunrise, Elliott was still on the floor. It was mid-morning when she could get him to stir.

XLV

Chapter Forty-Five

Grace's reply to Maggie's cable arrived three days after their Barbizon trip. It was only two words. ABSOLUTELY NOT!

As she shoved the reply in her pocket, C.J. grabbed her and swirled her about the room.

"I've typed *The End!*" He spun her again. "All done. What do you think?"

Whether because of Grace's cable or Elliott's announcement, she threw her arms over his neck and her legs around his waist. "Splendid. Let me read the masterpiece. Right now."

Having finished was one thing. Finishing was exciting and rewarding. Someone reading it was something else. Something terrifying. What if she didn't like this work he poured his heart into? Being demanding—and blunt, she might be ruthless, her criticism unbearable.

One couldn't discount the possibility she would tell him

to toss it in the Seine. Or throw all three hundred eighty-four pages in herself. The astronomical risk couldn't be avoided. If he said no, she would go into his writing room, lock the door, and read it anyway.

After giving him a wet kiss and a pat on the butt, she locked the door and began reading.

C.J. brewed some coffee, made a sandwich with stale bread, and sat down to wait. Tick tock, tick tock, cuckoo. That damn clock. An hour passed, two hours. Tick tock, tick tock, cuckoo.

He went into the bedroom. He might as well take a nap. Lying down didn't help. He couldn't fall asleep, which was for the best. Napping during the day would keep him up half the night.

In America, he would have turned on the radio. In Paris, what was the point? The stations were all French-speaking. Should he buy a station and convert the broadcasts to English? He'd use Fitzgerald and Hemingway as announcers and do a little announcing himself. He could air Maggie and Zelda on as a team. Females on the air would shock everyone, and those two would love shocking people. Maybe too much.

At the perfect time, right when he couldn't have taken waiting any longer, Maggie came out. Smiling ear to ear.

"The story is unbelievable. I've read almost one-third. Elliott, this is brilliant. I didn't want to put it down. You are a delightful writer, as talented as Scott. This might be your magnum opus. It's better than *The Age of Innocence*, more thought-provoking than Gibran, more politically clear-sighted than Hesse." Arms around her husband, Maggie smooched his forehead. "I am so proud of you."

At best, he had hoped she wouldn't hate it. For her to like it was more than he allowed himself to imagine. He wouldn't have dared dream of this reaction.

"You liked it? You're not being kind?"

"Everyone will. The writing is wonderful." If the tears Maggie was trying to blink away escaped and rolled down her cheeks, she'd blame the bright sunlight coming through the window. She held him, her face along his. Her breathing slowed as she melted into him.

"I love you" slipped across her lips for only him to hear. She kissed his cheek. Her mouth slid over his. Right then, she realized she didn't need New York, Hollywood, or fame; she only needed what she had. She had everything.

"Show this to Scott and ask him to send it to his publisher."

Lacking confidence, C.J. should have stiffened at her suggestion—he didn't. The opinions of others, approval, or rejection no longer mattered. He held all he needed in his arms.

***

The Fitzgeralds hadn't been around since Ravel's party. "They may be croaked in some alley, their drunken corpses rotting. Oh, I suppose not," Maggie said. "I guess they're still hung over."

The yellow Peugeot made life more convenient. Maggie did not miss obnoxious French taxi drivers nosing into their business. Nor did she yearn for the cabbie's reckless driving, a constant threat to man and beast.

When Zelda opened the door, the color, what color there was, drained from her face. She threw her arms around Maggie and then C.J., whom she kissed on the mouth—three times. "We didn't think you would ever come to visit us again," she said, dragging the Elliotts into the house.

Scottie charged at C.J., throwing herself around his legs. "Momma said you would never come back."

Zelda pulled Scottie away, telling her not to bother C.J. She turned and yelled toward their bedroom. "Goofo, race in here. Our best friends are here. They haven't deserted us."

Scott came in, glowing. "We thought we might have embarrassed you at Ravel's party. Sometimes, our behavior loses us our pals." Scott caught sight of the portfolio tucked under C.J.'s arm. "Your novel?"

Maggie beamed. "Scott, the novel is superb."

"Give it to me. I'll start reading immediately."

"Thank you, I'll appreciate your input," Elliott said. "There's no hurry."

"Nonsense. Beautiful prose is what I live for." Scott opened the folder and removed C.J.'s writing. "This is substantial. And heavy. I'm never patient enough to write this many words."

"It may need a lot of editing," C.J. said, his face flushing.

"Everyone's work needs some." Scott laughed. "Why do you think there are editors in the world? Damn their souls."

Zelda pulled the manuscript away from Scott. "You'll let me indulge, too, won't you? Goofo isn't the only scholarly Fitzgerald." Zelda reached over and pinched Scott's face. "Don't be pouty. I'm facetious, not cruel. You should learn the difference. Besides, you're the only boy I love."

"I'll go pour us all a glass of wine." Scott headed toward the kitchen.

"The poor thing must grow up," Zelda said, a touch of humor, or sarcasm, in her voice. It was hard to tell.

***

An agonizing week passed while C.J. waited for Fitzgerald's critique of his novel. The agony would have been worse had there not been Maggie's Thursday appearance at Zelli's and her Friday and Saturday night Opera Performance. Gershwin shared Zelli's stage with her, and he and Cole Porter attended the performance together. They said Maggie amazed them.

Finally, the Fitzgeralds drummed on the door. Like always, Zelda sprang on C.J. while Scott kissed Maggie's cheek—politely. "We brought champagne," Zelda squealed.

Scott handed C.J. his manuscript. The cork popped, disrupting the sudden silence hanging over the living room. Everyone, including the ceramic thirty-one-inch Russian borzoi standing in the corner, focused on Scott.

"The writing is outstanding," Scott said, his review short and sweet.

Not enough for Zelda. Granted, Zelda Fitzgerald was sometimes prone to hyperbole, but outstanding wasn't sufficient. She grabbed hold of C.J. again.

"Your book is genius. The beauty of your phrasing tears out the heart of the reader. I cried so much the pages are waterlogged." She flipped through the manuscript, stopping at a page she had dog-eared. "I'm crazy over this part here when your hero, Reid, who I may be in love with more than Goofo, writes the farewell note to Martha, his dreadful Italian mistress. I never liked her at all." Zelda began to read.

"Although I am sorry, I cannot continue. Too soon, you've tired of me. You wear someone else's name on your tongue and stumble when my touch brings you back. I know goodbye is near now. Too

soon for me, but overdue for you. Tomorrow I'll not call. Instead, I'll change my smile and search for someone new."

Zelda exhaled melodramatically. "I want to be bedded by Reid. Or, by you," she said, patting C.J.'s face. She jumped on Scott's lap. "Of course, I'm off the market because of Mr. Fitzgerald here. Doesn't that totally devastate you?"

Leaning around Zelda trying to see C.J., Scott, the one C.J. wanted to speak, at last, did. "My sweet baboo is right. The effort is genius." Shifting Zelda, who kept winking and blowing kisses at C.J., out of the way, he continued.

"Nowadays, almost every intolerable writer thinks he is a genius. Such ideas should frighten us into lusting for something honest about our work."

"Here's another line I love," Zelda interrupted, turning to another dog-eared page.

"Envision a cold New England morning."

"That line, while charming, is a problem," Scott said. "You have the narrator directing the reader on what to do. That is ill-advised."

"I like it," Zelda said. "Mr. Fussy Britches' approval or not."

Fitzgerald cautioned about the first chapter occasionally conveying an impression of condescension, which betrayed the sensitive nature portrayed throughout the remainder of the novel. "From the second chapter, I began to like the story. Fall in love, in truth."

Scott flipped through the manuscript, pointing out scenes he thought needed improvement—or deletion—most often because they were unimportant background.

The harshest criticism came when he accused C.J. of

writing too casually. "Stop playing with people's attention and emotions."

"By chapter thirty, you're on solid footing. But, C.J., I can't tell you the sense of disillusionment its occasional nonchalance gave me. My advice is to cut the work, not by mere trimming. Take out the weediest parts."

After two swallows of champagne, Scott read a couple more scenes. Those sequences are unsuccessful. They are too wordy, full of unnecessary anecdotes and jokes appealing to no one but you."

Maggie backed him up. "It's hard to hear, but he is right. Like musicians, you will need a thick skin if you want to write. The ones who judge our efforts are heartless."

Fitzgerald continued, pointing out snippets marring the whole narrative, along with what he considered glib, doggerel, or purposeless.

"Nevertheless," Scott said, "remember what I said first. The writing is outstanding. Make your revisions and give the manuscript back to me when you're finished. As soon as we finish the editing and you are ready, I'll send this to Perkins, my editor at Scribner. I'll include a solid recommendation for publishing."

Much to C.J.'s surprise, Maggie suggested taking the draft to Shakespeare and Company to show it to Sylvia Beach. An idea Zelda endorsed.

The damn luck when they arrived at the bookstore. Hemingway. Worse, he was with Ezra Pound. Hemingway started effusing praises over Fitzgerald. He wanted to take him to boxing matches, a long list of bars, and bullfights in Spain.

"I hate Spain," Zelda said, ending the conversation.

Sylvia skimmed the work. "I want to read this," she said, "The title itself is enticing."

"That's my only copy," C.J. said.

"You can't be serious."

"I am."

"Go straight home and start typing. Don't stop until you finish. When you do, bring me one. I have six girls who type for me. We'll divide the pages and make two sets."

***

The Elliotts and Fitzgeralds went to Les Deux Magots to drink dry sherry with a fine meal. As the discussion turned to writing and writers, to Maggie's mortification, Hemingway came up in their conversation. Scott called him talented.

"I enjoy Tolstoy and H.G. Wells, Lawrence, and Virginia Woolf. Joyce is too pompous," Maggie said, "but I detest Ernest Hemingway."

Maggie continued to disdain Hemingway, but Zelda had the last word. "Ernest is nothing but a pansy with a hairy chest."

XLVI

Chapter Forty-Six

Even worse than waiting for Maggie to finish the manuscript and for Scott to tell him what he thought of it, waiting to hear from Scott's editor was the most absolute misery C.J. had ever endured. Six weeks went by after Scott sent the manuscript. Seven and eight passed.

Maggie's run in L'heure espagnole ended. The cold months in Paris were reputed to be a magical experience—Christmas decorations, Valentine's Day treats, the chance of Courier and Ives snow scenes, and fewer crowds to fight. You weren't supposed to forget Paris in the winter.

But February dragged into March with no improvement in the weather. Icy roads trapped Parisians inside for days. Slick sidewalks broke the bones of unwary pedestrians. In the streets, cars slammed into each other and inattentive people. The Elliotts telephoned friends but rarely risked venturing outside.

A late ice and snow storm shut the city down for a week. On the fifth day, the sun came out, and with the sunshine, the Fitzgeralds.

Zelda held the nine-by-twelve envelope in front of her face. In the upper left corner was stamped, in blue ink, a burning antique, a Greco-Roman lamp, books, and a laurel wreath, the publisher's logo. Zelda handed the impressive-looking envelope to C.J. "This is yours to open."

It was addressed to Scott. For a moment, C.J. hesitated. When he did take it, he was almost hopelessly inept trying to unseal it. He had to stop, take a deep breath, and try again. The letter was short, three sentences.

You wanted to know the decision. We took it. A contract is en route.

C.J. was astounded—astonished—speechless. He looked at Maggie, viewing her as if she were a lioness seeking to steal his prize. He peered again at the correspondence. It was written on luxurious, elegant, pearl-colored textured paper. He caressed the single page as if it were something precious and fragile. He had yet to read the correspondence out loud.

"Well?" Maggie asked, trying to peek over his shoulder.

"They took it." His words came out in a shaky whisper. His brain refused to accept his good fortune.

"Of course, they did," Maggie said, taking the brief notice and reading the short message herself.

"Where shall we celebrate?" Zelda asked.

She never cared much about where, only that they party.

"The Royal Box?" C.J. asked.

"Perfect," Maggie said. "Joe will let me make our glorious announcement from the stage. The world must applaud you."

It surprised him how Maggie misconstrued his aspirations, the entire reason he suggested Zelli's Royal Box. If Maggie misjudged them, so did and so would everyone else, except, perhaps, Zelda. Crowds recognizing his triumph meant little to C.J. He didn't care about everyone knowing and certainly didn't need everybody caring.

The desire for the universe to treasure and appreciate, well, to adore, his work destroyed his first attempt to be a novelist. Concern about the reaction from the masses sent his sensual vampire floating off in the bay at Bar Harbor.

Without a doubt, the crowded Royal Box would make a superb venue for Maggie to announce his novel's coming publication, proclaiming her husband's achievement with all the zeal she could muster. Except, the audience at The Box would overwhelmingly—not care.

He wanted the novel to sell. Making money from it would be nice. To be praised would be grand. But what mattered most was a publisher finding his writing compelling. Fine enough to throw his Byzantine thoughts out to the public. To believe his effort was worthy of the reader's time.

C.J. wanted his efforts to provide a place for others to rest, to find peace amidst problems, an oasis in life's gales.

In truth, he longed for them to learn from his writing. What, he wasn't sure, but something. He had plowed through thousands of words, the twenty-six letters of the alphabet hundreds of thousands of times, linking them together in the perfect order.

C.J. had been a god. He created characters who believed in what he determined—until their beliefs changed while dealing with the disorder of their own realm and lives. Over time, his creations threw him away, ceased control of their existence, leaving the creator as nothing more than an observer. Although Fitzgerald called that notion nothing more than a writer feigning humility.

However it happens, a fictional character from a writer's mind becomes real, grows, prospers, or, from time to time, withers away. If done well, the bookworm follows along with everything in the story. By the last page, they have found something different in the world.

That's what C.J. Elliott wanted.

Maggie didn't understand. Nor should she have. She grasped music and theater. But as a performer, not as the conceiver. She did have bursts of songwriting. He hoped she would do more.

F. Scott Fitzgerald should have understood. He was a superb writer with more experience. His work was instantly recognizable. Filled with conflict: discipline vs. indulgence, love vs. passion, and money vs. refinement, his themes may have had a Jekyll and Hyde effect on the reader.

Fitzgerald set things in opposition, forcing his audience, on the one hand, to become emotionally absorbed while, on the other, being pushed back to an intellectual distance. By his last pages, the readers find something new. Often a dissatisfying world.

If any of the four did understand C.J.'s writing and what he wanted to express, it was Zelda. Mrs. Fitzgerald had a brilliant mind—even though always perched on the edge of insanity.

***

Undeterred by C.J.'s reluctance, Maggie announced the

novel's forthcoming publication to Zelli's half-drunken patrons. To her disappointment, the announcement of Elliott's upcoming release received only a polite round of applause. Not that Elliott cared.

As they drank gin and Scott cautioned C.J. about how hard the wait was while editors plowed through the work he had invested so much effort in, a drunk American woman approached them with a copy of Scott's, *The Beautiful and the Damned.*

"If you pease?"

"He's Mr. Fitzgerald," Scott said, pointing at C.J.

"You're F. Thcot Fitgeral?" the woman asked, trying and failing to focus on C.J. "In dat case, Mr. Fittergerald, would you biograph your book?"

"Of course, he will," Maggie said, taking the book and giving it to Zelda to pass to Elliott. "Who should I sign your new book to?"

"To Beth," the woman said, putting her hand on the table for balance.

Borrowing a pen from Scott, Elliott made the woman hand clapping happy.

Darling Beth,

You are beautiful. May you never be damned.

F. Scott Fitgarald

XLVII

Chapter Forty-Seven

A letter from Grace brought shocking news. She ditched her future husband—canceled their life together. Gave the fiancée the ankle boot. The engagement was kaput, but a wedding was still on the calendar. According to Grace, tall, dark, and semi-handsome was out. Tall, orange, and green eyes are in.

"What the Janey Mack?" Maggie stared at Elliott, her emerald eyes huge, praying mantis-like. "Bloody hell. Grace is marrying Tommy."

"What? I thought she was engaged."

"Now she's not. Well, she is...to my brother."

For once, something shocked Maggie. Her being astonished was a rare event. "Grace says she and Tommy hit it off at our wedding, and when she saw him while I was in America, she knew she was about to tie a knot that would do nothing but put a bigger one in her stomach."

"Let me see."

Grace said they were going to be married May twenty-third, but the Elliotts' presence would be required ten days earlier. The wedding will be smaller than planned, though still in Bar Harbor. The bridesmaid and best man were instructed to watch for more information in correspondence they should expect to receive from Tommy in the future. Said communication will arrive in a day or so.

Expectations in the Elliott bungalow called for Tommy's explanation to come the next day. Frustration came, not a letter. Maggie stomped, yelled, and waved her arms. Lucky for Tommy, she couldn't reach him. "You deceitful pig. You worthless bucket of pond slime." She did not refer to him as the cat's pajamas. More than once, she discussed blipping him off.

Wednesday, Tommy's correspondence came, again, astounding Maggie.

Paddy is dead. Police found him outside a crummy bar, shot in the back of the head, execution style.

Investigators had not arrested a suspect. Tommy doubted any would be.

Before you ask, I don't know if "The Brain" Rothstein is involved. Her brother said he had not spoken to their father about Paddy. *I don't communicate much with our parents,* he added. Not only did he not talk to them, they would not be at the wedding.

Since Maggie's childhood, literary families fascinated her. The idea large ones provided a refuge from a harsh world beguiled her. "I do think families are the most beautiful things in all the world," declared Little Women's Jo March.

Jo and the other March sisters were unacquainted with the O'Sullivans. The O'Sullivans' heritage must have once passed through a house of seven gables. Maggie was convinced of that.

After the notion her parents would not be invited settled on her, she decided to be happy about Tommy's decision.

"I hope Grace invites Curls," she said, her mind racing to all the fun they would have. The only thing that would make the reunion better would be Zelda. She would add fireworks. The whole state of Maine might explode.

"You'd want Sam around?" C.J asked.

"Of course. Think old sport. Someone might slip news of his presence to Arnold Rothstein. He might exterminate your pesty old roommate. Curls would be free to start with somebody new."

C. J. started to ignore the comment about Sam, but an awful thought burned through his brain. "You wouldn't leak word to Rothstein, would you?"

"Don't be silly. I'm not that awful. At least I don't think so," she added after a considerable pause.

"I think Scott and Zelda might be too broke to go to America," C.J. said.

"Broke? As successful as Scott is, they can't be poor!"

C.J. shrugged his shoulders. "I don't believe Scott manages money well."

Not having given any thought to their friends' financial management, their possible destitution surprised Maggie.

"I'm not sure they manage anything with much caution."

Maggie's impressions of their cohorts matched their public

image. She never thought of the Fitzgeralds as broke or near to broke.

After thinking about what C.J. said, Maggie changed her mind about asking them to travel with them. "I guess we shouldn't suggest they go. I don't want to embarrass or offend them."

With the Fitzgeralds out as traveling companions, Maggie's thoughts, to her dismay, wandered back to her parents not being invited to the wedding.

"Elliott, what do you think of Tommy not inviting our folks?"

"It's his decision."

Trying to continue the discussion was pointless. He wasn't going to engage, but she didn't blame him. She wouldn't have engaged if the situation had been reversed.

Paddy's shooting presented another issue, a peculiar one. How many families had the opportunity to discuss a snuffed relative? One thing she could count on, he wouldn't be kissing her on the mouth.

"Do you think Rothstein had him clipped?" She asked, cuddling next to him.

He slipped his arm around her and played with her hair. "I hope not."

Warm and comfortable in his embrace, Maggie snuggled deeper into his cashmere sweater. Sliding her hands inside his cardigan, she didn't care about discussing Paddy's demise anymore. Being dead is a permanent state.

If Arnold Rothstein was making money off the O'Sullivans, it was unlikely he ordered her uncle eradicated. Paddy probably bullied the wrong Tulsa thug and got payback.

Tulsa was far from Paris, and Maggie Elliott was much farther from the O'Sullivan clan. Let them fend for themselves. Maggie remembered that's how they said it in Oklahoma.

XLVIII

Chapter Forty-Eight

Every time Maggie crossed the Atlantic, she enjoyed the trip less. The deck chairs they lounged in on their initial European voyage held no allure. Why would they? The scenery never changed—except for the height of the waves.

Ship boredom affected C.J. as much as it did Maggie. That was almost unimaginable. The talent contests, fun on the first crossing, were no longer worth the effort. The Elliotts either slept in their stateroom or hung around one of the lounges, making idle talk with strangers.

Maggie did the majority of the talking. C.J. sat pretending to listen, but when asked a question, he apologized and asked for it to be repeated. Not even Maggie praising his writing engaged him.

Beefeater martinis with two olives, his new drink of choice, replaced any interest in his fellow cruisers. At dusk, he would explain he had to be up early and excuse himself. He hoped people understood. For the most part, they considered him rude.

"If we weren't arriving tomorrow, I think we might kill each other," she said on their last night at sea.

"I'm surprised the wedding hasn't improved your mood. After all, your best friend and brother are tying the knot."

"It's the rock and sway of this boat. The back-and-forth lulls my enthusiasm. I'll perk up on land, I think." She drifted toward the cabin door. "I'm going to stroll the deck." She wrapped a scarf around her hair, Clara Bow-style. "I hope I perk up. We have a reputation to live up to...or build."

* * *

Tommy and Grace met them in New York. Maggie, weary from the long and often rough trip, deboarded in a warm café-colored drop waist, A-line skirt. Even haggard, her tousled auburn bob, wildly smoky eyes, pencil-thin brows, and heart-shaped painted lips caught everyone's eyes. She embodied the quintessential spirit of the Roaring 20s. Haggard, pale, with a scruffy beard, C.J. dragged behind in a powder blue shirt, maroon tie, and light gray slacks.

"We reserved you a room at The Algonquin. The same place where we're staying." Grace said.

"In separate rooms," Tommy added.

"Hush," Grace said, slapping his shoulder. "You'll ruin their fantasy."

"I'm afraid they'll be over an hour getting our luggage to the dock," C.J. said.

"We'll eat lunch while we wait," Grace said, pulling Maggie off toward a small restaurant a half-block away.

The sidewalk bistro offered appetizers for their customers

awaiting their meals. In Tommy's opinion, munching on pimento stuffed celery did nothing but waste energy.

Grace described the wedding plans as they waited for their food. "We'll be married in the Episcopal Church. Tommy will wear tails, bridesmaids will be in pale green. I'm wearing a plaid dress and bright red shoes."

Two Waldorf salads, meatballs for Tommy, and Duchess potatoes accompanied by what C.J. called the most petite steak he had ever seen arrived moments before Tommy succumbed to starvation.

"What did our mother and father say when you told them they weren't invited?"

Tommy shrugged. "I didn't tell them."

"Good for you," C.J. said.

Grace, the only concerned person, asked Maggie about her mom and pop being left out.

It was irrelevant; who cared? The relationship was broken. At best, the likelihood of reunion or any reconciliation was vague. Her father was racist, dishonest, and had bullied her long enough.

As for her mother, Maggie felt deceived and betrayed. The last time, no, the only time her mother defended her was when her parents came to Mount Holyoke for her graduation. Thinking back, Maggie believed her dear mother had been worried about appearances in front of C.J. and Grace, not her daughter's feelings.

***

The phone number Clara Bow gave Maggie didn't work. Clara said she always had her line disconnected when she went to California. Maggie's slumped shoulders and bowed head revealed her disappointment.

"Elliott," Maggie said, sitting on a gray couch and motioning for him to sit beside her. "Do you ever miss having your mother in your life? Be honest."

"No."

That was honest. Not enlightening, but authentic. She wanted more, but C.J. never talked about his mother. Mama was out of his life. Whether she was alive was uncertain.

"Who were you trying to call?" C.J. asked, attempting to change the subject.

"Clara. But she must be in California."

"Clara who?"

"Clara Bow, silly. How many Claras do you think I know?"

"Clara Bow gave you her telephone number?"

"Well, of course." The astonishment on his face amused Maggie. "We floozies stay in touch."

The tap on the door rescued him. Jumping up, he rushed across the room as Maggie put her feet on the couch, chuckling. Grace proclaimed starvation and told her to change clothes so they could go to dinner.

The restaurant was crowded. "A thirty-minute wait?" Tommy asked, a frown furrowing his brow.

"The Roundtable is meeting," the maître d' said. "Gawkers always gather when they're here."

Maggie, Grace, and Tommy sipped cider punch while they waited. C.J. savored his ginger ale. A dark-eyed waiter brought them a bowl of peanuts, only to be shooed away by Maggie. "My friend is allergic to those. Are you trying to kill her?"

The young man swore he was not and hurried away, with Maggie following, whacking his backside.

Dorothy Parker and Robert Benchley were the first Roundtable writers to come out of the private room.

"Did you enjoy your meal, Mrs. Parker?" the maître d' asked.

"Wonderful. It always is, Max."

Grace handed her punch to Tommy, popped up, and took Dorothy by the arm.

"Dorothy, it is so thrilling to see you." The stare Dorothy Parker gave Grace would have spoiled The Algonquin cat's milk. Grace nudged the irritated writer toward Maggie. "Dorothy, surely you've met Maggie Elliott?"

Dorothy smiled. "I don't believe so," she said, nodding at Maggie. "Nor do I have any idea who she is or why I should have." She turned back to Grace, still smiling. "Young woman, if you don't release my arm, post haste, I shall slap you as you have never been slapped."

With Benchley by her side, Miss Dorothy Parker marched off.

"We know Clara Bow. And George Gershwin...and F. Scott Fitzgerald," Grace called to their backs.

XLIX

Chapter Forty-Nine

One expected early May temperatures in Bar Harbor to be on the cool side. Lower fifties were typical. This year, full-time residents were outside, planting vegetables and flowers, exploring the bay while basking in sixty-plus-degrees. Perfect weather for an outdoor ceremony.

In light of the groom being replaced, the event would be smaller but still a lavish affair. Clara Bow, Nancy Carroll, and David Belasco received invitations. Maggie suggested inviting Tallulah Bankhead. Grace said that woman was too wicked and immoral to attend her wedding.

Sailing close to the wind, the Brown family sloop cut through the seas with Grace at the tiller. Grace insisted on an afternoon sail because the sea breezes are at their strongest, providing the liveliest experience.

Not sparing the fair wind, Grace sailed past the Cranberry Islands, Bear Island Lighthouse, and Somes Sound Fjord toward East Bunker Ledge, where a colony of seals would be found sunbathing, swimming, and feeding.

Maggie, wearing a cream scarf like a pirate bandana and a black bathing suit because no store in Bar Harbor carried a flesh-colored one, sat on the bow, where the seafaring would be most rousing.

The wind, quite brisk, whipped across her face. In a moment of insanity, she hopped up and, with her feet apart, spread her arms.

"Sit down!" Grace screamed. "Do you want to be thrown overboard and drown?"

Maggie spun around and laughed at Grace. "I'm the queen of the sea. I'm immortal."

"You're not the queen of anything. You're crazy. Now plant your butt down."

If Elliott were writing a novel, a sudden wave would burst over the deck, washing the careless maiden away. This wasn't a C.J. Elliott story, and nothing so dramatic happened.

Maggie did, for a second, lose her balance. She dropped to her hands and knees and crawled to the stern, laughing the whole way.

"Behave yourself. I don't want to be eaten by a shark or swallowed by a whale because I'm trying to save you." Grace gave the tiller a jerk, tilting the boat to the right.

Maggie was unperturbed, but Tommy shrieked like a little girl. Grabbing for the side, he turned gray and then green. Grace jerked the tiller again. Another yelp.

"Is something wrong?" Tommy squealed, his knuckles white around the rail.

"Nothing is askew. I wanted to test our sloop's responsiveness in case I must dodge an octopus or something. This is my first time as captain. Father never lets me steer."

East Bunker Ledge was everything Grace promised. Seals swam along the sloop bobbing in the sea when Grace eased the sailboat to a near stop.

"I brought sardines. You can toss them to the seals," Grace said.

Some seals and a few porpoises came right up to the boat. Grace dropped their treats into their open mouths. She scratched a couple of them on the head. "Don't try this," she advised the others. "They can bite a finger off."

"Why don't they chomp yours off?"

"I've been around them all my life. You learn how to pick the most docile ones. But even lifelong Bar Harborites are bitten." Grace laughed. "Hand feeding is not an intelligent thing to do. Mother's brother got a hunk taken out of his hand."

An adjustment to the sail and the sloop was again in motion. Grace made a wide turn, causing Tommy to squeal in fear of being swept off into the open ocean, a concern Grace delighted over.

After continuing to Cranberry Island for a light dinner, a spectacular view of Mount Desert Island and the mountains of Acadia National Park highlighted the return trip. The evening breeze gradually mellowed as they sailed into the narrows, past Egg Rock Lighthouse, and back to Bar Harbor.

"There's Curls," Maggie said, pointing at the dock. The old roommates ran toward their British classmate, throwing their arms around her. C.J. sulked along behind.

"Where's Sam?" He asked, forgetting his old friend now called himself Owen.

"I left the bloody rotter in England. He better be out of my home when I go back."

Maggie and Grace grabbed Curls and rushed her off to their car. This was a conversation to be held in private. The girls sped away, leaving C.J. and Tommy to their own devices.

***

It didn't matter much, not to C.J. He wanted Tommy alone. He needed some answers. The walk to the Elliotts' house was short, twenty minutes.

Tommy's small talk along the way surprised C.J. "You've always intimidated me. A little."

"Why?" he asked, shocked.

"You're smart, self-confident, good-looking, rich, and yet hungry to succeed. Maggie and I come from a, well, let's say, somewhat successful family. But the Irish, Micks, Maggie would call us, were black sheep in Oklahoma, better than Indians or Jews, but still scorned. Maggie says your heritage can be traced back to the Mayflower on both sides. I've always wondered how an Irish Okie hooked you."

"With those emerald eyes. And that saucy disposition. C.J. said, laughing.

Walking the hill to the house winded Tommy. Too many cigarettes, C.J. assumed. He opened and closed every cupboard in the kitchen and searched two cabinets in the living room. He found no liquor. Good, he'd been drinking too much. Prohibition would benefit him.

After getting them a Coca-Cola, C.J. got straight to the subject. "What do you know about Paddy's murder?"

"Not a lot."

His answer was not going to suffice. It was beyond logic

authorities didn't maintain some idea or speculation about who was behind the killing. Without investigating, C.J. easily rambled off several reasonable suspects or reasons for his assassination. Revenge for his participation in the Tulsa Race Massacre, exploitation of Indians, crooked oil dealings, or, most importantly, Arnold Rothstein.

Tommy played with the ice in his drink, fidgeted with his watch, and stared out the window. He cleared his throat and mumbled something about being sunburned.

C.J. walked to the door leading to the deck and gazed out at the ocean with his cola in one hand, the other shoved in the pocket of his cream trousers. His short-sleeved white shirt was untucked, contradicting his inner turmoil.

"Maggie and I," he said, dragging out his words before turning toward his brother-in-law. "We need to know if Rothstein had Paddy killed."

Tommy swallowed the last of his Coke. "Do you have any more of this?"

"In the refrigerator."

Ice clinked. The soda fizzed as foam spilled over the tumbler. Tommy wiped up his small mess with a green dishtowel. One, two more long drinks. He refilled his glass and put the stopper back in the near-empty bottle.

That damn Sam Taylor, Tommy thought. He was the blaggard who brought Arnold Rothstein into their lives. This was all his fault.

Tommy sat on the rich brown leather living room couch. He inhaled, let the breath out, and peered at C.J. He shook his head. His eyes exposed how distraught he was by the pressure for an answer he didn't have.

C.J. handed him an ashtray for his fourth cigarette in an hour. "You must have some ideas about who shot him," C.J. said.

For the first time, Tommy locked his gaze on his interrogator. "Anything I'd say would be conjecture."

"Let's hear your suspicions."

"The bureau has investigated his killing, but not much. They're showing little interest. They think it was a local hit." After a deep drag, Tommy snuffed out his smoke. "The Tulsa police believe an outsider did him in. At least, so I'm told."

Still not enough. Not for C.J. He kept pushing, demanding Tommy to tell him who he, himself, no one else, thought fired the shot.

"What the hell do you want me to say? To pin Paddy's murder on Rothstein? Fine. There's no proof, but if you want it to be Rothstein, let's say it was." Tommy took out his cigarette pack. The thing was empty, and he wadded it up. "What's the difference who pulled the trigger?"

"What's the difference?" C.J.'s face heated up. He moved toward his brother-in-law, stopping only feet away. "Are you stupid? If he got hit in revenge for something he did in the race riot, cheating somebody in an oil scam, or stealing land from some Indian, it has nothing to do with Maggie and me. But if Rothstein is involved, it might."

C.J. talked about not being in any hurry to be killed and keeping Maggie and himself safe. Before he calmed down, he ranted about how he and Maggie should never have left France.

Unlike his sister, Tom, as he asked C.J. to call him, was not easy to excite and was slow to anger. Shrugging, he assured C.J. he understood their concerns.

Tom ran his fingers through his carrot-colored hair and made a long-winded speech regarding who dispatched Paddy. He emphasized if he didn't know who, he sure didn't know why. "His despicable cigarette and cheap perfume-smelling wife might have plugged him. Or paid someone to. Hell, I think 'Vile' might be her middle name."

Despite being unsure, C.J. accepted Tommy's account. He had no other choice. Maggie wouldn't put up with him holding her brother's head under the sea for extended periods.

***

At Grace's house, most of the conversation centered around Curls' estranged husband. She declared him a contemptible reprobate, claiming he would betray his mother. "The man has no soul."

Soul or not, Maggie considered him a threat. If he needed to, he would rat out his mother. She should have forced C.J. to cut off all association with his worthless roommate the day after graduation.

Curls tried to ease Maggie's distress. She and Sam had been void of contact with Rothstein and had no reason to believe he was looking for the Elliotts. The problems between her and Sam, er Owen, she corrected herself, had been over him being a poor husband and lousy provider. "And a crummy tennis player," she added.

After moving out to the veranda, Curls changed the subject to the Elliotts' life in Paris, a difficult thing for Maggie to discuss. "Elliott likes the city of lights. I'm willing to put up with it." That may or may not have been true. "I know it makes no sense, not to anyone but me, but I've grown bored with Paris."

"Oh, my silly friend," Curls laughed, "You aspire for life to be handed to you on a silver salver. It doesn't work that way."

"You're too uncompromising," Grace added. "All your decisions are made out of curiosity. Sometimes, it's poorly aimed."

Maggie's mouth opened, shut, opened again. "I've no idea what you are talking about."

"About the thing that kills cats," Curls said, eyes showing her delight.

"I mean, you are never wholly satisfied with what you have," Grace said. "Your associates include the most famous American expatriates, writers, artists, and art patrons. You revolve in the circles of McLeash, Lewis, Porter, Fitzgerald, Picasso, and Matisse. And you're bored?"

Maggie was aware not everyone got her. They didn't understand her, not her motivations, not her goals, and certainly not her sentiments.

Her friends were wrong. Her aspirations were not the result of curiosity. They were based on ambitions and targeted objectives. She knew what she wanted. To accomplish it, she did what professionals do—worked at her craft, played, sang, and practiced her acting every day. What she longed for was in America, not France.

Grace picked up her Amelia Earhart endorsed, toasted Lucky Strikes and tapped the pack on her palm three times. She and Curls each removed a cigarette. Maggie wrinkled her nose. "Neither Elliott nor I smoke. The taste spoils our kisses."

"Smoking helps me stay thin," Curls said. "If I didn't suck

on these things, I'd always be eating chocolate. I'd be a fat little pig."

Grace inhaled deeply and blew rings. Maggie unwrapped an Oh Henry Chocolate Bar, leaned toward Curls, and chewed pleasurably under her nose. "Mmm, Mmm, Mmm."

"Sometimes, Tommy sneaks in my window at night."

"How?"

"I leave it unlocked, silly." Pleasure beamed from Grace's eyes. "I was so virtuous. Your brother ruined me."

"I was ruined our first year at Holyoke," Curls said, her eyebrows bouncing.

L

Chapter Fifty

The wedding day weather was beautiful. Not that sunshine or rain mattered to Grace and Tommy. They skipped out on the outdoor reception. Clara Bow, filming The Plastic Age in Hollywood, and Nancy Carroll on stage in New York, sent expensive gifts. Nancy gifted an art deco statue, and Clara gave them silk sheets—and a scandalous note. Not getting to meet the stars devastated Tommy and C.J.

The Elliotts locked their Bar Harbor home early the next morning and headed for New York with Curls in tow.

"Drive fast," Curls urged. "We don't want to miss our boat."

Why not? Maggie wouldn't mind missing the ship, wouldn't care at all. She still preferred America to France. Maggie favored The Metropolitan Opera over the Paris Opera, New York Jazz clubs over Zelli's Royal Box, and Bar Harbor over The Riviera. Grace was a dearer friend than Zelda, although she did love Mrs. Fitzgerald. She was the one person who made France bearable.

Forty-five miles an hour, eating in the car, and only four rest stops. Elliott finished the drive in eleven hours. With time to spare, the girls scurried between the racks and the dressing rooms at Saks, the current talk of the town. Cousins Horace Saks and Bernard Gimbel had opened a shiny new store with an entire block of frontage on Fifth Avenue. Maggie and Curls would arrive in Europe a site to see.

***

For the first three days, the Atlantic raged, stayed rough and choppy. Fifteen to twenty-foot swells and wind gusts up to fifty miles per hour rolled the ship. Luckily, neither the Elliotts nor Curls were prone to seasickness.

Huddled in blankets, five covering Maggie, the Elliotts lounged in deck chairs, watching the orange sunset. At the end of the last summer, a glorious September provided the sunshine needed to produce some stunning French wines. Port enjoyed an extraordinary yield, with eighteen Port houses declaring the vintage some of the best. Maggie sat enjoying a glass of one.

Between sips, she shocked her husband, astonished, flabbergasted him, almost traumatized the man. "Are you growing tired of me?" Maggie stared at C.J. as he remained stunned. "I didn't expect an answer. Not an honest one."

Nothing exhibited the clash in the Elliotts' marriage as much as their different needs for recognition. Both wanted a reputation. But Maggie sought fame, celebrity, perhaps a touch of notoriety, like Marion Davies or Louise Brooks.

C.J. preferred something more refined, a quieter, more respectable acknowledgment. He desired to be esteemed.

"No, I'm not growing tired of you."

How could you come up with such a preposterous thought? He almost asked that. But he didn't. Instead, he grew quietly resentful. He adored Maggie. And he showed his adoration every day. He was sure he did.

I, C.J. Elliott, take you, Maggie O'Sullivan, to be my wife, to have and to hold, from this day forward, for better for worse, for richer, for poorer, in sickness and in health, to love and cherish always.

He made those vows. And he was faithful to them.

Maggie also made vows. And she had kept them. Well, a person might question the obey part. But C.J. had never much counted on obedience.

"Are you tired of me?" C.J. asked, vexed and staring straight ahead.

Maggie said no, but she wasn't telling the truth. The truth was hard to pin down. Maybe she no longer knew the truth. Maggie understood less and less about herself. For a long time now, she'd been unable to forgive people for their past. According to Liz Musgrove, C.J. had a past.

He glanced at Maggie. She looked peculiar, worn down. The corners of her mouth turned into a cowed frown. Without warning, an undeniable coolness settled between them, which he couldn't grasp.

She was often irritable. He was well aware of that. It was the why that eluded him.

Before her wedding to Tommy, Grace mentioned to him she noticed Maggie was emotionally frayed—inclined to sudden bursts of laughter and inappropriate emotional reactions.

"She is consumed with worrying about her talent," Grace said. "Worse, she focuses so much on fame, on people loving her. But not for herself, for her accomplishments. She worries me. Sometimes, she acts irrational."

Grace's observations bothered C.J. As she continued, his angst intensified.

"There's a raw magnetism oozing from Maggie," Grace said. "I suspect her reputation as a party girl is growing. She loves controversy, the spotlight, and the stage. That was true at Holyoke, and I'll bet it's grown."

Grace was right. And C.J. knew it.

"Maggie wears her soul for all to see. I don't know if she knows, but she does," Grace smiled. "She means to make every second count. The problem is that kind of lifestyle makes you a target. Being popular, the way Maggie wants to be, leads to jealousy. Gossip, lies, and disgrace usually aren't far away. Mags is an imaginative one, artistic, and inventive, but that can lead to madness."

The notion of a thin line between genius and madness was not new, not something Grace invented. The Roman writer Seneca insisted, "There is no great genius without a tincture of madness." C.J. had long considered Maggie to be a creative genius. Grace's confirmation troubled him more. Could she be on a path to madness?

Maggie would have lustfully disagreed with Grace. She believed she deserved to have her life seen in the same spirit she lived it—not as the creation of a madwoman, but as carefully pre-meditated and fashioned.

He hadn't told Grace, but except for the Fitzgeralds, Maggie attempted to avoid their Paris friends. When they were with them, her tension increased. More than with any-one, conflict boiled between Maggie and Hemingway.

Early on, Maggie and Hemingway shared a mutual dislike but remained polite—most of the time. Before leaving for Bar Harbor, Maggie had become hostile. As a result, when C.J. associated with Hemingway, he usually did so alone.

The strained relationships weren't limited to Hemingway and Paris companions. In America, Maggie held Tommy at arm's length. Now, C.J. felt he was being held at arm's length, at least that far. Their conversations were shallow. For agoniz-ing hours, they didn't as much as exchange glances. Antago-nism hung in the air, with no one acknowledging it.

Maggie turned in her deck chair. "According to Clara..."

More advice from Clara. The woman's counsel was get-ting stale.

"According to Clara, two kinds of girls attend every dance—those who prefer to dance—and those who prefer not to." She wavered, half-smiled, and continued. "Which am I?"

LI

Chapter Fifty-One

Thursday morning, there was a knock on the Elliotts' door. Without a doubt, the Fitzgeralds, at least Zelda, would be on the other side. Instead, two grim-looking French policemen stepped in without being invited.

"Do you speak French?" The heavier one asked.

"A little," Maggie said, stepping away from the intruders.

The thinner policeman, also shorter, explained their presence in English.

"If I am correct, you are acquainted with Arthur and Elizabeth Musgrove."

"Unfortunately," Maggie said. Probably an unfortunate thing to say.

"Sometime in the wee hours of yesterday morning, Mrs. Musgrove was shot. To death."

"Did he say Liz was murdered?" C.J. asked, coming from his writing room.

"She was found in the bedroom of her villa."

"Dead?" C.J. slumped into a chair.

"She looked dead to us. The pale green of her face was moving down her throat and into her chest. Her eyes were staring at the ceiling, but she never blinked. She was pretty stiff. I think that's called rigor mortise. I believe that happens to dead people. Isn't that right?" he asked, glancing at his partner. "We think it might be murder."

"We're just guessing based on the powder burns on her forehead and a bullet in her brain. That and all the gouging and slicing done to her belly. I'd say it is accurate to say she was butchered," the other police officer said.

A prolonged pause followed. C.J. mulled over the policemen's arrogant attitude and condescending mode of speech.

The color faded from his face, but he had not yet grasped the purpose of the visit.

Maggie took another step back. The skinny policeman said something in their native language to his partner, the one with more stripes on his sleeve.

"He says I'm acting guilty," Maggie said before reminding the patrolmen while she might not be fluent, she did understand considerable French.

One officer's shoulders slumped. The other one grinned, resulting in Maggie calling him a jackass.

The chair creaked as Maggie wilted into it, a blank stare on her face. C.J. stood, and with belligerence on the upsurge, he stepped toward les policiers. He wasn't so ignorant in French, either. He moved with such aggression and menacing glare, that both cops backed away.

"Are you accusing my wife of murder?" Screaming, he pushed one of the officers.

"We're here to ask you to come to speak to one of our superiors. Nothing more."

"Why do we need to speak to anybody?"

"You'll have to ask them," the larger cop said.

Red-faced, C.J. tried to regain his lost composure. His attempt was futile.

"Liz Musgrove may be dead. Maybe she was murdered, but we sure as hell don't know anything about it."

"Explain that to our supervisors."

***

Refusing to ride with the policemen, the Elliotts followed in their car, with Maggie swearing innocence the entire trip. The farther they drove, the more enraged she grew. "How can they dare accuse me of something so horrible? They're alleging I stabbed someone. They're calling me a butcher." By their arrival, Maggie was shaking, literally ill.

The chief inspector more resembled an overweight Italian than a Frenchman. That was natural, him being an Italian, one of many who preferred French politics to those of his own country.

He spoke English with a heavy Italian accent. He rolled every "r" and added "eh" to the end of every word. Another time, Maggie would have found his speech amusing, except for the situation. She was so weak, C.J. had to help her to a chair.

How the inspector said things might have been funny, but nothing was humorous about what he said. "Mr. Musgrove is accusing you of killing his wife. He claims you did her in because of the affair carried on by her and your husband."

"That's a damn lie." C.J. came out of his seat. The room, warm and stuffy to begin with, was now blistering hot. Leaning toward the inspector, CJ. tried to grab his lapel. Sweating profusely, the fat investigator slapped his hand away and yelled for him to sit.

"I'll not sit here while you accuse Maggie of murder or me of unfaithfulness. They're both lies."

"Down," the officer bellowed, pointing at the chair. "What you will allow or not allow is of no importance, eh."

C.J. screamed back. At first, he threatened the man. He called him a damn liar and several other things. Calming down while being held back, his anger cooled. It was replaced with sarcasm. Adding an "eh" to every word ending in a vowel. The constable did not appreciate the insult.

"If you will be quiet, I will explain. I do not believe the man."

A surprise to everyone, Maggie leaned over the arm of the chair and puked.

After the floor was cleaned up, C.J. quieted down—some. More inclined to thought than pure reaction, he began to grasp shutting up was to his and Maggie's advantage. He sat and mumbled some kind of apology while putting his arm around Maggie. An arm quickly knocked away. Perturbed, he backed away to regain his composure.

"First," the inspector said, "Someone bludgeoned the woman before they shot and stabbed her. We judge the assailant hit her with fists, not a weapon. I don't believe a woman would have been strong enough to leave the bruising we found. And," he said, pointing at Maggie's hands, "I suspect the assailant's hands would be showing swelling, probably contusions."

The chief inspector wiped his wet brow. "The husband's story is somewhat suspect." After everyone calmed down, he cast doubt on everything about Author Musgrove's version.

"Also, there is no evidence the killer forced the door open. I question whether Mrs. Musgrove would have invited in a woman who threw tea in her face days earlier." How did know that? Maggie hadn't even told Elliott. "Furthermore, she lay in the nude. I can't envision a woman opening her door naked. Why would any assailant take the time to undress their victim?"

Both C.J. and Maggie thought the reason was apparent.

"I would have been more concerned about escaping than stripping a woman. I don't care how attractive she was." Pausing, he smiled at C.J. "Wouldn't you?" He nodded in agreement to his own question. "Myself, I prefer my naked women alive. Paris offers more than ample opportunities to be with one."

One of the policemen who brought the Elliotts in laughed out loud. "Control yourself, Moreau," the inspector said in French, not realizing his employee was laughing about him thinking the woman was undressed after her murder. "I suspect there may have been some engagement before the crime."

"Unless you wear a monocle, Mrs. Elliott, I don't perceive you being a partaker."

Somewhat stunned by the remark, Maggie sat silent for a moment.

"Let me assure you, I do not."

"Do not what?"

"Wear a monocle."

"Maggie and I spent Thursday night at home. Together," C.J., the only one in the room at a loss about monocles, said.

"I've no doubt," the inspector said. "Still, a husband does not make the strongest alibi."

***

Several theories about Elizabeth Musgrove's death soon evolved. In the inspector's personal view, Mr. Musgrove did her in. Rumors ran rampant regarding the man being a womanizer. They linked him to affairs with numerous women—and a few men. Husbands like Musgrove often considered wives to be "*in their way.*"

Not only a cheater, Musgrove also proved to be an absolute oddball. Initially well-liked, people didn't take much time changing their minds about him. How a man with so many eccentricities gained such social status befuddled the chief inspector.

After the maid discovered her body, police made detailed notes about the bedroom being ransacked. A close search determined valuable jewels missing.

With the morning newspaper headlines asking, "Who Murdered the American Socialite?" detectives scrutinized Elizabeth's wealthy benefactors, the men other than her husband who kept her company, a line of thinking that might not bode well for C.J.

Two principal suspects garnered attention in the few hours after the murder, and Art accusing Maggie. A local gigolo named Jules Durand and, at the top, Arthur Musgrove. Stolen jewels created a motive for a gigolo. But for a married man having an affair, jewel theft was a way to mislead the police. Not eliminated, but far down the list remained a perhaps vindictive woman. Of course, in the inspector's own words, he couldn't ignore the old saying about scorned women.

LII

Chapter Fifty-Two

Insisting she wanted to be alone, Maggie pushed C.J. to leave. "I need to pout for a while, and I don't want you watching."

"Are you sure you're going to pout? Not plan how to eliminate Art Musgrove?"

"I'd have to shoot him. I doubt I could sneak close enough to poison him." Maggie shoved him out the door, asking him not to go drinking with Scott. She said she was dealing with sufficient problems without him drowning in booze.

Left Bank bungalows are ideal spaces for pouting. A pout doesn't require much room. A shabby décor is helpful, but posh furnishings can be ignored. The most important thing for a meaningful sulk is being alone. No place is more disheartening to be alone than a rented dwelling in a foreign city you don't want to be in.

Not one item, other than their clothes, in the temporary

domicile, belonged to the Elliotts. Not the bed, not the lamps, not even the soap. The pillows had cuddled other heads, some unwashed. Before they moved in, maids changed the sheets but not the mattresses. If Maggie searched hard enough, disgusting hairs would show up somewhere in the residence. Hairs from other people.

It didn't take long to initiate a perfect pout, a melancholy mope. Pouting differs from depression. A pout is easy to escape. Depression is something you can never flee. This mood was of her choosing. It was about what might happen, not what would. It was a "what if" pout.

What if the police arrested her? What if a court convicted her?

Maggie sipped a cup of tea, her mind adjusting to the darkness of that reality. Her life would be over. Never again would she drunkenly dive off cliffs with Zelda.

No more peeking out from off-stage, anticipating the roar of an audience. So much for putting on oodles of rouge and lipstick before striding on the boards in a low-cut dress to portray a low-class French club singer.

She remembered dressing in a black gown and playing in the Boston Women's Symphony. She'd played the last time there, too. There would be no Hollywood and no being the subject of scandal. After another sip of tea, she blinked away the tears.

The sulk wasn't enjoyable anymore. The things Maggie was pouting about might come true. Probably not, but they might.

Now it was time to leave the room. Time to find Elliott. Why did she shoo him off in the first place?

First stop, the Fitzgerald's suite. If he weren't there, he'd likely gone someplace with Scott, and Zelda would know where. Unless she didn't.

No answer. Back to the bungalow. The Murphys, now in Paris, were next on her list. Telephoning would be quicker. Two rings and Sarah answered.

"It's Maggie. Is Elliott at your house?"

"No. But Scott and Zelda are here. Being repentant, we let them back in. Not that their repentance will last long."

"Would you ask them if they've seen Elliott?"

"Hang on. They're on the patio."

Zelda picked up the phone. "Elliott didn't want to come with us. Not without you. Have you read the newspapers?" Zelda didn't wait for an answer. "Someone knocked off Liz Musgrove."

"I know more than the papers are writing. Come over tonight, and I'll tell you everything. Unless I'm in bracelets in the cooler. Don't say anything to the Murphys."

Before Zelda replied, Maggie hung up.

With no idea where to look for him, Maggie gave up on finding her husband and curled up on the bed. For the next hour, she contemplated buying a pet for company. A cocker spaniel. Growing up, their neighbors had one. The insufferable thing bit everybody, including the Tulsa sheriff.

When C.J. shook her awake, he interrupted the wonderful dream she was having. Her loyal mongrel, teeth bared, was protecting her from French constables and inspectors, tearing chunks out of their legs.

A minute or two passed while Maggie gained her wits. "The Fitzgeralds are coming over."

"What time?"

"Don't be silly, old sport. It does no good to give those two a time."

They showed up not long after seven-thirty. Zelda had to chase C.J. around the room twice to kiss him—on the mouth.

Triumphant, she landed on the red deco couch and flopped both feet on a chrome and glass coffee table. "Tell me the gooey details about Liz's assassination. Did they find her naked?"

Maggie finished pouring Scott a tumbler of merlot. An austere frown bent the corners of her mouth. "I don't have a lot of specifics. But that reprobate Art accused me of shooting her."

"Well, of course you did. The Jezebel was sleeping with your husband. The whore."

"I wouldn't have shot the witch. I'd have set her ablaze."

"Dazzling. Burning to death would be horrible." Before Maggie answered, Zelda changed the subject. "Forgive me for not telling you yesterday or a dozen days ago, but my news is more exciting than such an awful woman being bumped off. I've joined a little ballet company. I plan to become a prima ballerina," Zelda said as she glanced around the room, stopping her gaze on Scott and wrinkling her nose. "Everyone has been so drunk here lately. I must avoid the chaos enough to pursue my own ends, undisturbed."

The last thought made no sense to Maggie. Zelda could be like that. Maggie congratulated her friend. She intended to expound on the fantastic news, but Zelda didn't give her time.

"I couldn't like this ballet better—unless I composed it myself."

"You've written ballets?" C.J. asked.

"Only between her operas," Scott said.

"There is something else," Zelda said, pouring more wine. "We got ourselves two mutts."

"The hotel allows dogs?" C.J. asked.

"Who knows?" Zelda said, gulping the first swallow. "We haven't told them. Why should we?" Another drink. "One is blotchy, brown and white with long stiff whiskers. We call him Ezra Pound. We named the other Bouillabaisse, or Frank, or Larry. Doesn't matter. He won't come to any of them."

Tired of Zelda's pointless rambling, Scott suggested they drive to Italy for the weekend.

"That's over a hundred and fifty miles," Zelda said, "a four or five-hour trip."

"So?"

"Zelda," Maggie sniped, "You know I won't go back to that horrible place."

LIII

Chapter Fifty-Three

The newspaper headline on Tuesday morning read, *Husband of Murdered American Socialite, Slain.* The case made international headlines because of the Musgroves' vast wealth and the scandalous nature of their proclivities.

According to the story, the murder took place Sunday evening. Someone viciously slew Art Musgrove sometime during a violent storm that locked Parisians in place. No one discovered the body until late Monday when a friend couldn't get anyone to answer the door and called the authorities.

The police found a grizzly scene. After being brutally attacked, Arthur Musgrove lay on the floor in his blood. If the assault wasn't bad enough, the perpetrators tried to burn his remains. The burning failed, scorching only his hands, midsection, and a rectangular area of carpet.

The Chief Inspector asked George Payne, a constable with the London City Police since 1911, for assistance. Payne won a

Distinguished Conduct Medal for his actions during the Battle of Verdun in 1916. The Paris police seemed to think facing dogged German resistance under heavy sniper fire and single-handedly clearing several enemy positions was impressive.

A few friends had been at the Musgrove's home in the early evening on Friday. It was an unusual gathering in light of Musgrove's wife being murdered only a week earlier. When interviewed, the guests testified to having no idea who might have killed the man. Numerous theories, many of them ridiculous, about who was responsible for the Musgrove's deaths started to spread.

One theory proposed Art did his wife in, and the local gigolo Jules Durand, in an affair with Liz, offed Art in retaliation. One witness claimed to have seen Durand speeding away from the Musgrove house on Sunday night in a black car, not a yellow Peugeot. Durand's not owning an automobile cast some doubt on him being the killer.

Another theory maintained Musgrove, with the aid of American mobsters, was shipping wine into America. That allegation had varying accusations. One story indicated Musgrove's shipments kept coming up short.

A second gangster version had Arnold Rothstein, who the Musgroves formerly associated with, ordering Art's killing. Rothstein had earlier been in a sexual relationship with Liz. The rumored affair was one reason the Musgroves left America. According to this narrative, Art slew Liz and Rothstein ordered Art eliminated in revenge.

The rumors of Rothstein's involvement concerned the Elliotts. Scared Maggie.

There was also a rumor on the street about the Musgrove's

planning to smuggle millions into bank accounts in Brazil. Supposedly, the smuggling involved French, Italian, and Brazilian bankers. The Musgrove's role was to haul the money from France and Italy by ship to Brazil.

Elizabeth Musgrove was reputedly murdered to persuade her husband to accept a more minor cut. When he refused, they liquidated him and recruited another couple. Authorities gave little credence to something so complicated.

None of these theories stopped the police from showing up and knocking on the door of the Elliotts' bungalow.

"We thought you'd show up," C.J. said, stepping aside to let the chief inspector and the English constable in.

"I'll come straight to the point." George Payne, the copper from London, said. "Can you account for your whereabouts Sunday night?"

"Right here," Elliott said, knowing what the next question would be but deciding not to answer until asked. It was his way of exhibiting contempt over the visit.

"Alone?"

"No."

"Do you want to tell us who you were with?"

"I don't." C.J. sat back in his chair, looking indifferent. Defiant. "But I suppose I'll have to. We were with Scott and Zelda Fitzgerald. F. Scott Fitzgerald. The American novelist."

"Where do we find Mr. and Mrs. Fitzgerald? We'll need to speak with them."

Maggie stood and opened the door. "Saint James Albany Hotel. Unless they've been unceremoniously ejected. It can be a frequent occurrence because of their outrageous antics."

Saying the door slammed wouldn't have been wholly accurate. Actually, it would have.

"Pompous asses," Maggie said, sitting next to Elliott.

Elliott kissed Maggie's cheek before straddling her. "Wouldn't you love to be there when Zelda whizzes into them?"

***

When the inspectors knocked on the Fitzgerald's door, after climbing countless stairs, they were overcome by a bizarre-smelling goatskin Scott had hidden in their room. When they left, they found the elevator rigged with Zelda's belt, so it was perpetually waiting on their floor."

For weeks, accounts of the murders continued to be a source of fascination for newspapers. Despite the journalistic interest, with little evidence to support any premise of the crime, the prosecution did not file any charges. As a result, whispers of scandal, like the smell of the goatskin, would linger around the Elliotts.

LIV

Chapter Fifty-Four

Ida Rubenstein called just after midnight. "A new production is coming to Paris. La Traviata."

"La Traviata," Maggie gasped.

"This time, they're setting the opera in the decadent music hall scene of current-day Paris." According to Ida, audiences would experience this classic as never before. Lavish scenery, sumptuous costumes, and Verdi's iconic score would be transformed into 1924 Paris.

"Who would be better," Ida asked, "to portray the courtesan Violetta, consumed by love and a life-threatening illness? No one would be superior to the actress who so wonderfully brought Zazà, the French singer born in the gutter, singing in low-class cafés and cabarets to the stage of The Metropolitan in New York."

"You must rush to my apartment tomorrow," Ida said. "The director and producers are frothing for you to audition."

"Let's celebrate with the Fitzgeralds. We'll have a tremendous party."

"It's after midnight," C.J. pointed out.

"So what?"

C.J. changed Maggie's mind by suggesting he'd prefer lovemaking.

Maggie showered early and began to prepare herself to astonish everyone whose presence they would grace. She chose a wild, adventurous fashion risk, conveying her independent spirit.

After all, auditioning for a modernized La Traviata called for a bold, daring move. She wanted to have people staring and talking behind their hands. Covering her Henna-tinted red hair sat a sea foam and aqua cloche hat pulled down, the rim turned up and accented with a taffeta pleated band. Were cloche hats stylish in Paris? It didn't matter.

A swingy low-waisted cream silk sheath whisper of a dress festooned with pine and olive-colored wisteria stopped above her knees. Elegantly heeled and femininely decorated slouchy light green boots with Louis heels and tassels hanging from the top immediately drew everyone's eyes. Hauntingly beautiful, with flirtatious eyes and a beguiling smile, Maggie came across as untamed, yet demure and emotionally fragile.

Seated over a white marble floor with a vibrant mosaic, Ida raved about how Maggie must be cast. Her casting was a foregone conclusion for Mrs. Rubinstien.

***

While Maggie enticed the opera folks, C.J. went to the Fitzgeralds to relay the exciting news. At least the news was exciting to Maggie.

Zelda asked if there would be any dancers in the opera.

"I have no idea," C.J. said. "But I'll bet if there are, Maggie can land you an audition."

Scott could see C.J. wanted to change the subject. Zelda's endless discussions of how she aspired to dance were wearing on people.

"How is your new story coming along?" C.J. asked.

"The first draft is almost ready for the editor," Scott said. "When Zelda is around, the work is hard. She bothers me. When she's not around, it's hard to work. I worry about what mischief she might be getting into."

"Have you decided on a title?" C.J. asked as Scott and Zelda sipped gin martinis.

"I'm having a difficult time," Scott said. "I've been toying with Among Ash Heaps and Millionaires, Trimalchio, Trimalchio in West Egg, On the Road to West Egg"—*Zelda's eyes rolled*—"and The High Bouncing Lover. Perkins, my editor, will have input into the final decision."

"The Great Gatsby shall be the title," Zelda said before gobbling the olive from her martini and smacking her lips. "Be sensible. My choice is plain and simple, not like Trimalchio. No one would understand such a silly title." Zelda stepped over Scottie's game board and pinched her husband's cheek. "Stop being ridiculous. The novel is going to be titled The Great Gatsby."

Maggie met them for dinner, hoping Scott and Zelda would get along with each other throughout the evening. Doing so would take some willpower; for the most part, Zelda lacked will. A constant nightlife for the sweet indulgence of pleasure, wild partying, and living with a bright light always on the horizon weighs on anyone. It wears more on those who live on the edge of craziness, whether your name is Elliott, Fitzgerald, or Smith.

Paris, for Americans, was invented by arty expatriates with one goal—hedonism. Picasso painted it. Cole Porter serenaded about it, but no one celebrated Paris with the zeal of the Elliotts and Fitzgeralds. The sincerre and gin, the Seine, and Le Grand Ecart contributed to the madness.

One could get away with more in Paris than anywhere else, except perhaps the summer on The Riviera. It was the perfect place to romance the Jazz Age and throw glittering parties for the restless spirits celebrating their lives.

"I want to have a romp that will be renowned for a hundred years," Maggie declared.

"We must raise hell tomorrow night with all our friends," Zelda howled.

Early the next morning, after calling every friend they had in Paris to invite them to a party at the villa the Murphys were renting on the outskirts of the city, the foursome rushed to Gerald and Sara's, summoning them to their own gala.

That evening, the Murphys' house burst with uproarious people. Many, if not most, of the invitees had invited companions. No one knew everyone. A handful didn't know anyone. Some women, without reservation, enjoyed spooning with the boys they came with. Others, with few scruples, relished kissing men they'd never met.

On the patio, a group of strangers was playing charades. Partiers near the phonograph were dancing to a jazz record. Sara Murphy was trying to save her china. Gerald forced F. Scott to go to a nearby market for more food and alcohol.

Twenty or more people kept crowding around Maggie, entertained by her singing. A besotted Italian was performing magic and parlor tricks, twice sending fifty-two Bicycle Cards into the air.

C.J. leaned against the stone wall surrounding the terrace, watching the raucous affair he was partially responsible for. Zelda was whizzing about the room, acting like a bohemian, not giving a damn what the world thought of her.

A titanic splash soaked drunken guests when someone fell off the balcony into the pool. It was going to be a long night at the Murphy villa. This time, the Fitzgeralds and the Elliotts were both getting banned.

LV

Chapter Fifty-Five

Since being questioned about the Musgrove murders, guilt, though unjustified, lingered in Maggie's thoughts and behavior. Frequently, C.J. would find her muttering tearfully to herself. The most minor slight toward anyone sent her into rapid, fevered apologies. She made darting glances at people she perceived to have aggrieved.

Paranoia that others were passing judgment became her constant companion. Nervous fidgeting, squirming, and scattered gazes became commonplace. Insomnia left her pale and looking harried or haunted.

Her unfounded guilt nagged at her willpower and, when at its extreme, dictated her actions. Just under the surface, it gnawed at her character. She was innocent of murder but fretted she was a lousy wife and must be guilty of something.

Before La Traviata opened, C.J. traveled to the local police headquarters and asked to speak to the chief inspector. The sergeant at the desk was reluctant to let C.J. meet with the official and gave in only when C.J. created a finger-pointing scene.

"Maggie is going on stage at the Paris Opera, and I want to be sure there is no criminal suspicion hanging over our heads." That was all he needed the inspector to know. Maggie's uncalled-for guilt was something to be kept private.

Not interested in a conversation with an American expatriate, a chat interrupting his breakfast, the inspector, an expatriate himself, told C.J. to go wherever he wanted and do anything. He didn't believe they would ever solve the Musgrove murders.

"Everyone on the force," he said, believes Musgrove killed his wife. Who did in Musgrove? They had no real clues and had other crimes to worry about. As far as the Paris Police were concerned, the Musgroves were nothing but nouveau riche Americans who should have kept their peculiarities out of France.

"You and your pretty doll are not suspects. Go on your way."

Later, after C.J. told—exhaustively explained—the police no longer suspected her, had declared her innocent, and it was time to stop beating herself up, Maggie and C.J. stopped by Scott and Zelda's. They could hear their friends fighting. Zelda was screaming about not wanting to be respectable. "Respectable girls are not attractive. And attractive ones are not respectable."

The core of the argument entangled itself around Zelda's flirting. Since Zelda was the one doing all the yelling, her point of view was clear. She flirted because she found flirta-tion fun.

"Do you think we should knock?"

The question became moot when Scott stormed through their front door.

"I'm not going to be bored because I'm not boring," Zelda yelled at her husband's back.

Maggie shrugged her shoulders and shot a crooked smile at Scott. "Oops," she half-laughed. "Not an opportune time to drop by?"

Once Zelda spotted the Elliotts standing at the door, she blushed and shifted from one foot to the other. She stepped back and motioned for everyone, at least Maggie and C.J., to come in.

"Oh well, this is not the first time we've embarrassed our-selves in front of our friends. He's the cause of it all," she grumbled, pointing at Scott.

Disregarding Zelda's humiliation, Maggie mumbled about not being able to stay long.

Maggie patted Scottie's cheek, feeling sympathy for the child.

"Are they seeking any dancers for La Traviata?" Zelda asked again. For the five hundredth time, Maggie said sorry, but no.

To change the subject, C.J. asked Scott if he'd heard any-thing from Ernest. A chancy thing to do around Maggie.

"He sent me some chapters of what he's working on."

"What's it about?"

Zelda's eyes lit up. "Bullfighting, bull slinging, and bullshit."

Scott interrupted her. "Don't say things like that."

"Why shouldn't she?" Maggie asked.

"Lay off Hemingway," C.J. said, scowling at Maggie.

"Make me." Maggie's demeanor turned ice cold. "He's the east end of a westbound horse. He talks about Zelda and me, constantly criticizing us while he's trying to borrow money from you two dupes," she said, waving her hand at C.J. and Scott.

Zelda jumped back in. "He's as phony as a rubber check. And you both know it."

Deep into the Hemingway controversy, C.J. announced he and Maggie needed to leave. Maggie didn't admit it, but she was also relieved to depart their current company.

Maggie's aggravation over Hemingway chafed C.J. Her constant complaining about Hem, Tatie, that jackass, or whatever she felt like calling him drained her husband. Worse, it wasn't always Hemingway that set her off. One day, Maggie was breezy, bouncy, and sparkling. The next, sulky, cryptic, screaming about everything, including the other actors in the upcoming opera.

On those days, her eyes would turn spooky, the eyes of a predator lying in ambush, poised to destroy some unsuspecting prey.

On some stage, performing live was the only place she was always happy. Maggie was stunning and blessed with talent. Nevertheless, she would never go as far as she wanted without the remarkable harmony between her personality and the riotous times. That harmony made her frustrating to her husband.

The era she marched in step with was a marvelous time to be alive, a decade of prosperity, social and political change.

But, for all its glamor, the time was tricky for romance, love, marriage, and friendships. Even sanity was hard to maintain. Like the period, life with Maggie could be risky.

"I'm going out for a sandwich. Do you want something?" C.J. asked, standing and stretching.

"I'll go with you," Maggie said, surprising him.

Sitting at a small table, waiting for cucumber and cream cheese sandwiches, C.J. asked Maggie if she was looking forward to performing in another opera.

"Oh, Elliott, the stage is a part of who I am. The need for applause is in my bones and my blood. You should understand something so obvious." She leaned back in the short-backed metal chair, not much more than a stool. "Clara Bow, when we were partying together, told me I'm a natural Motion Pictures star. What do you think of that?"

An honest answer wouldn't go over. C.J. hated the thought of his wife in movies. The legitimate theatre irritated him enough. Hollywood would be worse with all its scandals, rumors, and casting couches.

It would be best to ignore her question, except Maggie wouldn't allow it. Respond or face a lecture on freedom and rights for women.

"The hours involved in making a movie are supposed to be brutal. Film doesn't appear, at least not to me, like a setting to show one's true talent. I mean, it's pantomime. Your beautiful voice, your skills as a musician, would vanish."

"So, you'd be opposed?"

"Don't they call the place the boulevard of broken dreams?"

Maggie shifted and gazed out the café window. Clack, clack, clack. She could hear the sound of a train blocks away. She disliked the rattle of the wheels on the track. The noise disturbed her thinking. She needed to contemplate her argument.

"Movie stars," she began, "live public lives, a dream existence heightened by being exotic yet remote. They're adored by the masses. They tease fans with decadence while somehow maintaining an illusion they observe the same moral code as their adoring admirers. That's what I dream of doing."

"A few salacious little rumors may make them alluring," C.J. said. "But, a series of vile scandals threaten to destroy that deceptive impression. Fatty Arbuckle may or may not have raped and murdered Virginia Rappe. Mary Pickford now struggles to reconcile her America's Sweetheart image with a divorce. Mabel Normand and Mary Miles Minter watched their careers ruined by being implicated in the murder of William Desmond Taylor. Matinee idol Wallace Reid died of morphine addiction. Is that what you want?'

The collective weight of these disgraces lent credibility to C.J.'s case Tinseltown was out of control and hedonistic. Therein might lie the best argument for C.J. to dissuade Maggie from Hollywood Boulevard, a place he wanted to dodge.

When they started back home, a twenty-block walk, a pouring rain drenched the Elliotts. Empty taxis sped by, more than one sending sheets of water spraying and waving over them. When one did stop, C.J. came near to blows with a beret-wearing French street mime who would have been no match for someone as athletic as Elliott.

An accident between a cab and a two-level bus blocked a bridge. "Damn Paris," Maggie muttered.

Letters from America, England, and Tulsa jammed their mailbox. Maggie almost tossed the ones from Oklahoma. Instead, she dropped them on the kitchen table to be dealt with later—or never.

Grace and Tommy wrote about marital bliss and a recent Bar Harbor scandal involving a shirt-tale relative of the Vanderbilts. The vice-president of one of the companies C.J.'s grandfather left him reported favorable, positive financial performance.

But a letter from Curls trumped all the other news. Sam, or Owen, if one preferred, was dead. This time, there was no doubt.

When Curls returned from Grace's wedding, one thing did surprise her: not finding a note or any indication of how to reach Sam on the off chance she might want to.

Three weeks after Curls' return, Sam floated up in the Thames, decayed and barely recognizable. He got hung up in brush, far downriver, in most of the investigators' opinions from where he went in. No water in his lungs meant he died before he went in. Curls wrote that British authorities are tying his death to some underworld corruption.

Because Curls did not think he had been involved in crime in London, she warned her American classmate that New York gangsters might be, and according to Scotland Yard, likely were. She urged the Elliotts to be cautious.

C.J. doubted they were in any peril. Maggie wasn't as sure and used the possible threat as another reason for returning to America. He refused, claiming they'd be in more danger in the States.

LVI

Chapter Fifty-Six

"Elliott, what do you think of my new opera?" Maggie asked.

"I think the music is brilliant," C.J. said.

Maggie sat next to Elliott and put her arms around him before giving him a wet kiss. "Does it bother you that in the opera's conclusion, happiness is but an illusion?"

"No. The ending doesn't concern me. Operas are just excellent expressions of imagination. Artistic creativity has little to do with real life."

His bored expression made it clear to Maggie that Elliott hoped she wouldn't ask him anymore about the ending. Or the beginning. Or the middle.

Who cared? The opportunity was too tempting to ignore. "What do you think about Alfredo proposing a toast celebrating true love, and Violetta responding in praise of free love?"

She had him, the poor boy. It was too easy. She should let him off the hook. She would—in time.

"Your Violetta reminds me of Zelda. Or Clara Bow, from what you've told me about Miss Bow."

"Well played. Outstanding, old sport. You win the round."

In the afternoon, an invitation came to a party. A costume ball at the home of Adrienne Monnier, the business and romantic partner of Sylvia Beach. Not well acquainted with Monnier, the invitation came as a surprise.

Assuming Monnier would invite Hemingway and Ezra Pound, Maggie did not want to go. She claimed she might survive Hemingway's presence with Zelda's help, but without Mrs. Fitzgerald, the event would kill her.

"Cole Porter and George Gershwin will be there," Elliott said, playing his trump card early.

"How do you know?"

"Sylvia called yesterday while you were at rehearsal."

The two composers being at the party was not a sufficient reason for Maggie to change her mind. But it was not a bad one. Besides, Maggie did like costume parties.

"If we go," Maggie turned toward C.J. and slipped her hands across his butt. "If we do go," she nibbled on his ear, "I want us to go as Anthony and Cleopatra. Are you game, old sport?"

It was hopeless to argue with her. Either go as Marc Anthony or miss the whole shebang.

The party was on a Wednesday night. Odd.

When Maggie brought their costumes home, Elliott's could not have been more embarrassing.

"You expect me to go out in public in this knee-length tunic? Why not have me go in my boxer shorts?"

After fifteen minutes of nagging from Maggie, he finally surrendered to trying the thing on. Worse than the tunic barely hanging past mid-thigh, the chest piece came with belts attached to the front, suede lappets dangling from the waist to just above his knees, and a ridiculous burgundy cape sewn to the shoulders, making the outfit not only silly-looking but miserably hot.

"I won't wear this. I refuse."

"Oh yes you will. I want to go as Cleopatra, and that makes you Anthony. So, stop whining. And keep that on while I change."

Unlike C.J., Maggie did not look ridiculous. As Cleopatra, Maggie was eye-catching in a V-neck and sleeveless design, accentuating her body's curves. The Egyptian gown, mainly gold on the upper body, with a metallic sheen, in contrast to the black skirt slit up the sides, all the way up both sides, would easily attract everyone's attention at first glance—at first eye-popping sight.

His face was almost purple. "You are not going out in public dressed like that. Not a chance."

"Wanna bet?"

***

The affair Monnier threw put the parties at Gerald and Sara Murphy's to shame. Those who came without costumes were denied entry or instructed to wear see-through harem pants from an old play at a Paris theatre.

In the sitting room stood a golden cage containing Pablo Picasso's wife, Olga, and Man Ray's muse, Kiki de

Montparnasse, dancing half-naked among a gaggle of singing concubines.

Two Invitees, costumed as Russian Wolfhounds, crawled around on all fours, barking and howling at other partygoers. A fire breather set the drapes aflame.

At last, the fire department showed up. They doused the curtains and revelers who wanted to run through the blasting hoses.

The whole affair was strange, full of unidentifiable guests expressing all their weirdness in one night. Pranks were being played, and money was donated to poor authors, painters, and countless charities.

Amidst all this, a select few took the chance to showcase their generosity in gifts to their hosts' bookstores. Everyone, well, at least most, enjoyed themselves. Best of all, Maggie had no confrontations with Hemingway. Cleopatra and a still angry Anthony did not go home until almost daylight.

LVII

Chapter Fifty-Seven

A bitter and hateful letter from her mother, correspondence from Tommy avoiding offering an opinion about Arnold Rothstein being involved in Sam's death, and not having Zelda, who'd been suffering from severe attacks of colitis, to create an uproar with weighed on Maggie. She wasn't sleeping and tended to sip a little too much gin.

C.J. was spending more time at Shakespeare and Company and, in Maggie's mind, not enough with her. It could be said when he was around, his nervousness about the coming release of his novel made him almost unbearable. Something had to change.

Two weeks into the run of La Traviata, C.J.'s book was released. *Life* was a rousing success. It flew up Publisher's Weekly's bestseller list, passing *The Plastic Age* and Edna Ferber's *So Big* for the number one spot. *Life* outsold Scott's

This Side of Paradise and *The Beautiful and the Damned* early sales.

In the dedication, C.J. thanked both Fitzgeralds for their advice and help. He mentioned Sylvia Beach's assistance and gave a nod to upcoming writer Ernest Hemingway for encouragement.

"Have you lost your mind? How can you thank that worthless, despicable, misogynistic pansy, Hemingway? I ought to divorce you. You jackass."

C.J. ignored her anger. More or less discounted it. Instead of responding, he sat staring at his novel, looking distressed.

Once Maggie decided she wasn't going to get a rise out of him, she tramped over and stood right in front of him.

"What are you pouting about?"

"I'm not pouting."

"You sure look like you are." She parked herself next to him. Leaned close.

He flipped through the pages of his book, closed it, and ran his fingers across its burgundy cloth cover. "This has passed Scott's last book in sales."

"You should be proud," Maggie said, running her hand through his hair.

"Do you think Scott will be upset? I don't want to lose their friendship. They may be crazy, but I like them."

"I don't think Scott's like that," Maggie said, giving her distraught husband a light kiss. "I know Zelda isn't."

"I hope you're right. I'm not exactly rolling in comrades these days. I'd hate to get so desperate as to ask Hemingway over."

The elbow to the ribs did hurt.

As it turned out, he'd agonized over nothing. A telegram, signed by both Scott and Zelda, arrived, praising the novel and pouring out their congratulations. They could not wait to celebrate with their best friends. *Maybe our only friends —Goofo, has again perturbed the Murphys,* Zelda added in parentheses.

Among the letters of praise from Grace and Tommy, Curls, and Grace's parents was a note from Clara Bow.

Maggie Dear,

Your husband's novel is all the rage. He is an absolute genius. Don't you let him off your hook.

Every producer in this town is awed. Tell Elliott if he sells the rights to Hollywood, he must do so only with the condition of my casting. Tell him to hold out until the sale makes him rich.

Your Dearest Devotee,

Clara

P.S. Make sure he demands some creative control.

The envelope also contained a lock of red hair clipped to a note saying, *For your boy.*

"Do you think they might turn *Life* into a movie?" C.J. asked after Maggie read him Bow's correspondence.

"Rumors claim Elinor Glyn's novel IT is being made into a film. The same rumors say they are going to cast Clara."

C.J. plopped on the couch. His eyes were sparkling, the corners of his mouth turned up. His face had a whimsical radiance.

"Don't get stars in your eyes yet," she said, flopping onto his lap.

"Do you have any idea what a writer is paid for the rights to a novel?"

"Not a clue."

"I don't either. A considerable amount, I'll bet."

They decided to ask Scott. He would know.

"I wonder if Clara Bow would really be interested in starring?" C.J. asked.

"Don't jump ahead of yourself, old sport. And what if I want to star?"

To celebrate, they went to dinner at a fancy and expensive restaurant on the West Bank. Escargots, steaks, and champagne. A suite at The Paris Ritz, where no need would go unmet, was rented not for a night or the weekend but for an entire week.

After a day of Maggie shopping, C.J. wanted to go to Harry's Bar. Rumor was Gershwin was going to be at the piano. Maggie locked the bedroom door and took a lengthy time getting ready. When she came out, she was wearing pumps, pearls, and a long-sleeved black dress belted to a low waist.

He stared at her. "Wow."

"They call it a little black dress," Maggie said, putting her arms around her beau and kissing his cheek. It's new from Coco Chanel. The design is so simple the fashion magazines are calling it The Ford."

"Doesn't remind me of a Ford," he said right before slipping his face into the nape of her neck. "You smell wonderful."

"CHANEL N°5," she whispered. "Coco says it is the essence of femininity."

LVIII

Chapter Fifty-Eight

By the time the spring of 1926 brought out the cherry blossoms and daffodils, Maggie was Paris' biggest star. After La Traviata, she starred as Káťa in Káťa Kabanová, but she was most loved for singing in the music halls.

No performer came close to her prominence until Josephine Baker tied a string of bananas around her waist and became an international sensation. Without even the banana skirt, Baker had made her Paris premiere with only a pink flamingo feather between her lips.

A black giant carried her upside down on his shoulders, with Josephine doing the splits. She stood stone still when he put her down, like a female ebony statue. The audience fell into complete silence.

Two weeks after Baker's first performance, Maggie strode to the front of Zelli's stage. "Thank you for coming to see me. I'm flattered by your applause. So much applause thrills me—

because I've never performed naked. And I won't be tonight. I haven't seen Miss Baker's act, but I understand she has added a fruit skirt to her attire."

By late fall, Maggie grew more cryptic and self-destructive. She claimed France was killing her. C.J. tried to cheer her. He argued they had been successful in France. His novel sold almost as many copies in France as in America. Well into his next book, he insisted his association with the writer pals he had at Shakespeare and Company improved his writing.

"And you are beloved here in Paris," he preached to Maggie. It didn't help.

Scott and Zelda felt obligated as friends to try reasoning with Maggie. No one had much success. She refused to let anyone close enough to encourage her, certainly not to criticize her.

Weary of her ranting, C.J. told her he was going to the Fitzgeralds. She curtly rebuffed his invitation to go along.

When he arrived, Scottie was sleeping, and Scott, according to Mrs. Fitzgerald, was off doing who knows what.

Confiding in Zelda, C.J. said, "Maggie is the most challenging person to deal with I've ever met. Here lately, the only time she has any interest in her appearance is when she's performing. The rest of the time, her hair is tousled. She's cut the back hideously short, but wild tufts always hang down over her forehead. Those piercing eyes of hers are always dark, and they'll burn right through you. What happened to my wife? The one who always wanted to be dressed to the nines?"

C.J. sipped a glass of the wine Zelda poured him before continuing. "She's barefoot the majority of the time and seldom changes out of a saggy pair of black slacks, with one of my shirts hanging from her shoulders. I don't know what's wrong with her."

"There's nothing wrong with her," Zelda said. "She wants you to take her home."

"So, I'll have no peace unless I do?"

"Not one minute."

Getting no help from Zelda, he headed for their bungalow but ended up at Shakespeare and Company instead. Hemingway was there, hiding from Hadley and wearing out his welcome. With Sylvia about to throw him out, he persuaded C.J. to go to Harry's Bar with him.

They ran into Man Ray drinking with a very drunk Scott Fitzgerald at Harry's. "Zelda's in a rage," Scott said, slurring his words. "I'm not wanted at home." He slung back a gin and raised his glass for another. "Do you suppose Maggie would let me come home with you?"

"That would be a bad idea," C.J. said after ordering his own gin.

"That wife of yours is crazy," Hemingway said to Scott before turning to C.J., "And yours doesn't follow far behind." After a brief hiccupping fit, Hemingway started talking again. "You two should go to Spain with Pauline and me."

"Who's Pauline?"

"A friend," Hemingway said, slurring his words.

"What about Hadley?"

"She won't be going," Hemingway snapped.

His speech almost to the point of being impossible to understand, Scott said, "Zelda hates Spain. How many times must I tell you that?"

"I'm not inviting your screwball wives," Hemmingway said, his tone nasty.

Fitzgerald was too drunk to object to Hemingway's statement, but C.J. wasn't. It didn't matter that Maggie was now irrational and a bit hard to get along with. He didn't need Ernest's opinion. And he told him so.

Taken aback, Hemingway upped the ante, tossing a couple more insults toward Maggie. "She's more malicious than Fitzgerald's wife."

C.J. ignored the flowing contempt. Maggie was right. The man was a blowhard. He might weave a captivating tale, but he lacked social skills. Arguing was pointless with someone so self-absorbed.

All three men, C.J., Scott, and Hemingway, had extraordinary talent, but each battled their respective demons.

"You know," C.J., the only one remotely sober, said, "We have many things in common. For one, we despise our mothers. Me because mine is selfish and uncaring, You two because yours were so damn domineering."

Scott, drunk to the point of struggling to stay in his chair, chimed in. "Our mates' differences make our relationship difficult. Hadley is a good sport, jolly, a hiker who enjoys the outdoors. She's a notable contrast to our stunning spouses. Maggie and Zelda are creative, love music and the theater, and bask in being outlandish."

"That's why our interactions with you, Ernest, turn less amicable every time we come together," C.J. said, now on his third gin. "You may be impressed with our prose, but you don't respect us as individuals. You blame our wives for interfering with your stupid need for male bonding. Maybe you are what Zelda says. Nothing but a fairy with a hairy chest."

"C.J. and I are generous with our talents. We want to help others. We are cautious about our writing because we are smart enough to suffer from self-doubts." Scott took a deep breath and slapped his hand on C.J.'s shoulder. "We both enjoy the glamorous lifestyle, although, in your case, Mr. Elliott, it is in part because Maggie loves it."

C.J. put a cap on the conversation. "You, Hemingway, are competitive, egotistic, demanding, and short-tempered. You are so set on testing your courage and moral values that you, foolish as you are, seek violence in sports and war. All things Mrs. Elliott and Mrs. Fitzgerald dislike."

As C.J. left Harry's, the meeting place of the lost generation of writers, he walked past bartender Harry MacElhone, mixing gin, Crème de menthe, Triple sec, and lemon juice into a White Lady for Olga Picasso.

C.J. loved the mahogany bar, wall panels, and brass rails the bar's founder, American jockey Tod Sloan, hauled from New York because he was so keen to recreate the atmosphere of a New York saloon.

No matter what time of day, Harry's Bar had the feel of early evening, a sense of privacy. If you were around at the right time, you might swing to Gershwin playing Rhapsody in Blue or experimenting with the beginning of An American in Paris.

It provided the perfect place for a writer to drink. All writers drank. Most of them too much. Though C.J. resolved to be done with Hemingway, he would never abandon Harry's.

***

When C.J. opened the bungalow door, the rich sounds of Maggie's cello greeted him. Quite the surprise. Maggie had almost abandoned her cello. More surprising, downright bewildering, was seeing Zelda flowing across the room in ballet's graceful balance and symmetry. Dressed for the part in a multilayered skirt, allowing her freedom of movement and creating an impression of lightness and flight, she danced with pleasing grace.

Maggie, noticing him, stopped playing, leaving Zelda in mid-pirouette. "She's rather talented, isn't she, old sport."

"Yes. She is," C.J. said, too shocked by the whole scene to say much more.

"I'm practicing here because Mr. Fitzgerald's drinking is becoming a terrible problem," Zelda said, smiling at him. "He can't sleep and talks utter nonsense. My not giving a damn attitude about his drunkenness has ended." Scrutinizing C.J.'s expression, Zelda wagged a finger at him. "Don't worry, I'm not moving in with you."

"You're going to take us both to dinner," Maggie said, standing and planting a quick kiss on his forehead.

"Do you mind if I wear my tutu?" Zelda asked, walking toward him to pat his cheek. "Yes, I suppose you do," she said, pleased with the distress on her friend's face. She skipped into the bedroom to change, not bothering to close the door. "It will disappoint me if you don't peek."

LIX

Chapter Fifty-Nine

The letter from Grace was going to start a fight—and not a minor one.

Mags,

I'm running for congress. I am going to be the first woman elected to the House.

Come home. My campaign needs you. Do so if you must knock your husband unconscious to drag him on the ship. We've history to make.

Grace

A patient woman would bide her time, wait for the right moment. Not Maggie. She tossed the letter in C.J.'s lap. "Read this."

He laughed and held the note up for Maggie to take back. "We'll send her a donation. I doubt she has much chance, but I hope she wins."

"We'll hand her the donation. And I will be an awe-inspiring campaign director."

C.J. chuckled again. "We can't be sailing back and forth to America every time Grace gets a wild notion."

"Of course not. This time, we are going back to stay."

That was unexpected.

"Don't be preposterous," he said. "We're doing no such thing."

"That's where you're wrong, old sport. Start packing."

Most of the time, this would be where Maggie would run her fingers through his hair, bat her eyes, and humorously threaten to withhold her charms. Not this time. This time, she was laying down an ultimatum.

He used Arnold Rothstein as the opening volley in his counterattack.

"That dog won't hunt," Maggie replied, proud of her folksy metaphor.

"You can't prove he ordered your old roommate done in. I doubt killing him had anything to do with us if he did. Rothstein is your excuse to remain in France. You're all caught up in your lost generation writing friends and like Paris. We went home for Grace and Tommy's wedding. Not one thing happened. Not one damn thing."

After a deep breath, Maggie started in earnest. "We've been here three years, and I admit I've had success. I've loved the roles I've had. I acknowledge I've become a star. But I want to go home. I want an opportunity to glow in America."

There it was. The real reason. It wasn't disliking Paris or France. "Elliott," she said with determination in her eyes he hadn't seen since that night in his touring car when she laid the law down about his roommate. "I want to perform again at the Met. I want to play my cello, even if it's in a woman's orchestra. I can't play it at all in France. The discrimination here is worse than in America when it comes to concert musicians. I want to be on the covers of American magazines. After all, I am American, don't you get that?"

"I think you're immature and selfish."

That didn't go over well.

Red-faced, she threw the glass in her hand, missing his head by inches. Grabbing a heavy clay ashtray, her aim improved. She hit her target in the chest, knocking the wind out of him.

"What the hell is wrong with you?" Two long strides and C.J. had her wrapped in his arms while trying to avoid her flying feet. "Quit kicking me."

"Let go of me."

"Stop kicking."

Out of breath, Maggie stopped and went limp in his grasp.

"Are you done?"

"Let go."

"Are you done?"

"Yes."

Maggie stumbled over and collapsed down on the damn red deco couch. "I hate this torcher rack."

"I think you cracked my sternum."

"It serves you right."

She tried to ignore his moaning. But furious as she was, she didn't want him dying from internal bleeding. A quick death would have been acceptable. But not a slow, painful one. Dammit. She did love him.

"Do you need to go to a hospital?"

"Yes. I want to tell them what you did to me."

Mired in repentance, Maggie crept over closer to her husband. Not ready to reveal the depth of her contrition, she gave his shoulder a slight nudge. "You shouldn't make me mad."

"I guess not."

Slipping away, an old thought darted across C.J.'s mind, causing him to mumble to himself. "I was right. Life with you is exciting. But damn, you are a stunner."

"I heard that."

***

The Fitzgeralds, well, Zelda, became distressed when they found out their friends were leaving France. "The exciting times are done here," Zelda said. "There'll be nothing left but boredom."

C.J., still unhappy about going, had been hoping Zelda would be more helpful, maybe have an emotional break over losing her pal, making Maggie so sad she'd decide to stay. If not a nervous breakdown, she could have gone crazy, wild in insanity, insisting the Elliotts remain in France. But that wasn't Zelda's way, at least not yet. She disappointed C.J. by encouraging Maggie to go fight to get a woman elected to Congress.

The visit with the Fitzgeralds turned worse for C.J. when F. Scott Fitzgerald, the turncoat, betrayed him.

"With your novel so recently released, you should be in America helping Scrivner promote it. I'm surprised Max or someone in the promotions department hasn't insisted you get back to New York."

Scott, his supposed friend, kept hammering nails in C.J.'s

coffin. "You should be doing book signings and speaking engagements at Amherst and every large institution that will have you. Not to mention having tea with every snooty ladies' group you can charm yourself into. Publicity is the most important part of selling books." Fitzgerald took a deep drag on his cigarette. "What kind of writer are you? Get on the first ship heading to New York."

* * *

In a letter Maggie sent Grace, she told her former roommate and brother not to meet them in New York. They needed a new automobile and would buy one in New York and drive home. They purchased a wheat-colored Duesenberg Model X, wheat with green trim, the de facto choice for wealthy American actors, industrialists, and crime lords.

Near gale-like wind, clouds, and pounding rain greeted them in Bar Harbor. The harbor waves were heaping up with white foam streaking off breakers.

"That's disconnected," Elliott said when Maggie picked up the telephone to call Grace.

"Well," she said, twisting her mouth, "We'll have to slide over there. Our cupboards are empty, and I'm hungry."

A massive green and yellow campaign sign, almost yelling O'Sullivan for Congress, was waving back and forth at the front of Grace's entry gate. For a moment, O'Sullivan stunned Maggie. Laughing, Maggie said she was still having trouble thinking of Grace as an O'Sullivan, not Brown.

Splashing down the driveway, Grace, clad in unbuckled black galoshes, threw her arms around Maggie before she was out of the car. Elliott scampered around the Duesenberg while opening an umbrella, which the wind turned inside out and blew away.

"Let it go," Grace yelled. "You'll be chasing the thing forever."

C.J. didn't listen. He chased it down the street; there was no reason to lose a new umbrella.

Both women were soaked by the time they made it to the house. "You look like a drowned rat," Tommy said, keeping his sister at arm's length. Maggie wasn't having any teasing. She grabbed her brother's neck, giving him a wet hug, soaking his shirt.

Maggie was comfortable changing into her sister-in-law's clothes. C.J., not so much about wearing Tommy's. Perhaps because the pants were wool and unlined.

Grace grilled lobster and baked potatoes while C.J. scratched his itchy legs. Over their dinner, Grace dropped a bombshell. "In two weeks, I'll deliver my major campaign address. The one in which I'll detail what I intend to accomplish in Congress. In short, the address will make my case for election."

Reaching across the table, she took C.J.'s hand. "This will be the key to my winning or losing." Grace paused, either for effect or to ensure she had his attention. "I want you to compose my speech."

"Don't be so shocked," Maggie said, looking at C.J., her face gleaming.

"I'll give you a list of my positions. I need you to make my goals appealing."

The entire drive home, C.J. expressed doubts. "I'm not qualified. I've never even thought about working on a political speech. I write fiction. I make things up. If people don't like what I created, it doesn't matter. At least not to anyone else. My novels won't affect the welfare of the nation."

"Oh, stop. You're being ridiculous."

"What if Grace doesn't like what I write? She didn't like my first attempt at a novel. She called my vampire a toothless mosquito. What will she say if I pen toothless prattle?"

His nervousness and doubt amused Maggie. She was enjoying the terror he was suffering. "You will create her beautiful oratory perfection," she encouraged him. "Just take everything you despised about that bigot Wilson and take the opposite positions. If you don't craft a moving oration, I'll withhold my charms for a month. Or two."

For four days, C.J. didn't leave his writing room—except to eat his meals and sleep. The task's weight kept him from sleeping more than two or three hours at a time.

When he finished, Grace took the completed treatise and, ignoring his pleas, read his speech aloud.

One week later, without one change, she laid out her campaign with her considerable oratorical skill. She explained her positions point by point as C.J. wrote them.

First, we must consider the economy. Nothing is easier than the expenditure of public money. It does not appear to belong to anybody. The temptation is overwhelming to bestow it on somebody. But the results of extravagance are ruinous. The property of the country, like the freedom of the country, belongs to the people of the country.

Also, we cannot prosper without fair wages. The twelve-hour day is now almost unknown. But there are, unfortunately, a multitude of workers not yet sharing in the general prosperity of the Nation.

We, as a people committed to the fair treatment of all, must also consider the negro, rout race prejudice, and extend all elements of equal opportunity and protection under the laws guaranteed by the Constitution. We can never allow a return to the policies embraced only a few years ago by the Wilson administration.

Finally, let me speak about the importance of our National Defense. Our national defense policy is not one of making war but of ensuring peace.

Our military power must guarantee the execution of the law at home and security for our citizens abroad. No self-respecting nation can...

Grace expressed a desire to leave a legacy of caring commitment. "I want to improve the lives of the people in our district and the state of Maine."

After Grace's address, Maggie, the campaign manager, told the enthusiastic audience, "Maine could not have a more impressive individual to serve as their first woman in Congress."

As soon as she freed herself from the admiring crowd, Grace threw her arms around C.J. "You've gotten me elected to Congress."

* * *

Grace ran opposing an incumbent congressman who did not appreciate running against a woman. Too bad. The newspapers and radio stations loved her.

Much of Grace's charm grew out of her vibrant and witty personality, which made her presence known from the earliest days of her electioneering. When asked how she managed such a successful operation, Grace replied, "Sex appeal!"

An engaging campaign manager didn't hurt her cause. When asked during a live interview to discuss Grace, Maggie quipped, "You always know how Grace Brown O'Sullivan will vote. But only God has the slightest inkling of what she will say."

Maine's Senior Senator said, "Congress better treat her right, fear her, admire her, and listen to her. Otherwise, they'll regret their actions."

When pressed on whether she would back the repeal of prohibition, Grace patted the reporter's face. "I've learned one thing: not to meet the issues until they arise and not to talk too much. So, I am not going to say I will do anything except to represent my constituents the best I can."

Her answer was succinct, leaving no reason to continue. But her manager did.

"Nasty rumors claim if Grace is elected, she'll be assigned to a committee with little value to our district's needs. They tell me she should expect to be relegated to Indian Affairs, a common assignment for the few congresswomen of this era. Let me say this: the only Indians in our district are in front of cigar stores. Grace's future colleagues will be wise to keep that in mind."

By all projections, the election would be close. Everything changed when the Ku Klux Klan opted to place their backing behind Grace's political rival.

With the Klan's help, Grace's opponent attacked, alleging she accepted bribes in return for support. The accusations proved to be unsubstantiated after an independent investigation.

Voters in long-standing Democratic cities and towns crossed party lines to voice their opposition to the Klan and

Klan-backed politicians by voting for the anti-Klan Grace Brown O'Sullivan.

They celebrated her landslide victory at the Elliott home. Gale-force winds ripped across the harbor, and a snow-sleet mixture pounded the windows. Not even the storms damped the merriment of the evening. Tea, lemonade, and Coca-Cola flowed. Maine had sent its first female to the United States House of Representatives.

Two days after her inauguration, a picture of the new Congresswoman, taken by Maggie, graced the front page of countless papers. The Honorable Grace O'Sullivan, the youngest member of Congress, sat in her congressional office —her feet on a table—smoking a cigar.

LX

Chapter Sixty

The Bar Harbor Symphony, such as it was, accepted Maggie. And why wouldn't they? By any honest appraisal, she was the most talented musician in the orchestra, or band, as Maggie called them privately.

"Isn't this the big time?" Sarcasm dripped from her tongue. "How am I going to stand the excitement of performing on the third Saturday of every month. They say sometimes the audience hits fifty. During the summer, we'll play each week. Maybe for over a hundred people. Can you imagine?"

Armed with her natural energy, cunning, and sensuousness, Maggie intended to rise above this low situation.

"Elliott, I want New York and Hollywood. Bar Harbor can provide us a fine place to relax, be at ease, and hide from the fame I plan on achieving. But I want a star's life. I want to be famous—but elusive."

Without telling her husband, she wrote to her pal, Clara Bow. Clara didn't write back, but she did telephone.

"Maggie, Tinseltown is starved for fresh stars. They're crying for actresses with sex appeal and the nerve to flaunt their sexiness. They also need screenwriters. Writers capable of churning out fascinating scripts collect high salaries; better yet, they're hard to find."

To escape from her current life, Maggie would need to overcome objections. C.J. did not love change.

Sitting at his mahogany desk with an early-morning cup of coffee, Elliott learned of Maggie's plans. The political drama of the past few weeks had diminished, so he was again working on his second novel and enjoying the newfound silence. Maggie, still in her silk kimono, slipped up behind him. Her hands gently massaged his neck.

"Let's go to California. To Hollywood."

"When?"

What? No objection? Maggie stopped caressing his shoulders. She stepped around in front of him, bent down to gaze straight into his eyes, breathing in a rhythm identical to his.

"Did you say when?"

"I believe I did."

Maggie sat on the desk and took a deep breath. "No argument?"

"None."

Maggie put her hand on his forehead. "You're not sick, are you?"

He scooted his chair back, smiled, and laughed. "I got a note last week from a buddy of yours. Movie studios are searching for screenwriters. Your friend says they pay well."

"Well," Maggie said, flopping in his lap. "We wouldn't want an opportunity to pass by without taking advantage of it."

"Of course not. And by the way, Miss Bow, I believe Bow was her name, referred to me as Dear J.J. You'll have to do something about her confusion."

"I'll snatch her bald if she calls you J.J. again."

After dressing, Maggie called Tommy. His sister and brother-in-law going to California did not thrill him. In his irritation, Tommy brought up Arnold Rothstein. "Gangsters are growing bolder and more violent."

"I don't care. I don't give a damn." She waved her arm, jabbed her finger in the air, and pounded her fist on the table as if Tommy were standing before her rather than on the phone. "Don't you dare try to scare me with Rothstein. I'm done with worrying about him."

"Well, he might have had Sam taken care of." Sam, the pain in the hindend, was still annoying her. Exasperating her from the grave.

For ten minutes, Maggie reamed her sibling. Until she ran out of breath, Tommy had no chance to respond. The conversation ended with Maggie slamming the phone down.

"I should have shot your roommate while I was still at Holyoke."

"Too late now," C.J. noted.

***

Not wanting to be screamed at for the next hour, C.J. revealed something unknown to Maggie. Sam sent him a long letter before they left Paris for Grace and Tommy's wedding. Sam detailed a plan to make himself rich. He'd met men who were the British equivalents of Arnold Rothstein.

Rather than bootleg alcohol, they dealt in gambling, drugs, and prostitution. Sam had not changed at all. He also admitted Rothstein had no interest in the Elliotts after C.J. declined his proposal. Never had.

Maggie reacted to the news with mixed emotions, not surprising C.J. She was unhappy, although not volatile, about not being told when Elliott received the letter. But she was relieved Rothstein wasn't stalking them.

"I suppose we should celebrate," Maggie said. "Take me to dinner. At a fancy place."

The Duesenberg roared to life before settling into a smooth purr. At the end of the driveway, the wheels spun on the ice. The backend fishtailed in response to C.J. accelerating.

"Are you trying to kill us?" Maggie yelped while pushing both hands against the dash, hoping not to fly forward.

"The road's slick. Hold on. And be quiet," he laughed, easing off the gas pedal. "Only a couple of fools would go out on a night like this."

"Oh, Elliott, we're not fools. We're only borderline fools."

"Who frequently cross the border," C.J. said, taking his eyes off the road to smile at his wife.

"Watch where you're going."

The restaurant they chose sat on a cliff overlooking the harbor. A window wall designed by a modernist architect awarded diners an expansive, beautiful bay view. Tonight, however, was foggy. Even with the glass wall, little was visible through blizzard-like snow.

Two other couples sipped coffee while waiting for their dinners to be served. The rest of the black tablecloth-covered tables remained empty.

"We'll take the railroad to California, won't we?" Maggie asked. "You wouldn't try to drive across the country in winter, would you?"

Instead of the coat and tie, he would typically have worn, C.J. wore a flannel shirt and heavy work pants, a concession to the nasty conditions outside. "Trains have a difficult time plowing through all the slush. I read they are taking all the cow catchers off the front of the locomotives. In this weather, the trains aren't going fast enough to catch any cows. But nothing will keep them from climbing on from the back."

"You stole that from Mr. Twain," Maggie said, her eyes smiling. "We studied his writing at Holyoke. You've been caught, you plagiarist."

The waiter stopped to refill their coffee. "You folks are courageous, venturing out in this storm."

"We're foolish, not brave," Maggie said.

LXI

Chapter Sixty-One

A Street of Dreams

If nothing else could be said about California, the weather was warmer. Hollywood Boulevard slithered with cars, celebrities, want-to-be celebrities, expensive shops, restaurants, hotels, and theaters.

Economic prosperity gave people more time and money to spend on leisure, and Americans fell in love with motion pictures. Movies were a cheap form of entertainment, and making them was a booming industry. America idolized personalities like Rudolph Valentino, Clara Bow, John Barrymore, Mary Astor, Charlie Chaplin, Mary Pickford, Douglas Fairbanks, and Greta Garbo.

Sprawling out under the fifty-foot-high letters of the HOLLYWOODLAND sign was Tinsel Town, a place where dreams are made—and crushed.

Jack Warner claimed Hollywood was "full of fast-buck characters from everywhere, con artists, the real estate chiselers, soda jerks, writers who never wrote, call girls with agents, hoodlums, gamblers, and touts."

Amid scandals and headlines, the pressures of living a Hollywood life were tricky for anyone, let alone the actors and actresses who came to the film industry at a tender age, lacking any experience and often with little talent. Most never got their big break.

Tragedies and slander plagued their private lives. Drinking and drugs led many to early deaths.

Maggie didn't care. She wanted to be idolized. It didn't matter to her how few wanna-be actors and actresses made the screen. Most were lost in menial jobs, some became prostitutes, and others lived waiting for the call from general casting. Maggie didn't worry about such things. She had more talent, more beauty, and much more confidence.

On their second day in Hollywood, Clara Bow picked them up in her open Kissel car accompanied by two red chow dogs matching her hair. She whizzed them down Sunset Boulevard to meet with studio officials. While Clara cut in and out of traffic, dodging cars—and pedestrians, the Elliotts got their first close-up look at the Hollywoodland sign.

"That's kind of a disappointment," C.J. said, pointing at it as if to help Maggie locate the behemoth landscape. I expected some glorious work of art. It's nothing but a big wooden sign. Any journeyman carpenter could have built it. It also needs another coat of whitewash."

"Someday, I'm going to climb up on that thing, on the Y, I believe, throw my arms out wide and scream, 'I'm Clara Bow, and I'm the queen of Hollywood.' Maggie, my dear, do you want to scale it with me? We could holler our names twice as loud."

"Not me. I hate heights."

As Maggie headed into the first meeting, Clara took her by the arm and offered some advice.

"Be yourself. Don't let these imbeciles change you. They yell at me to be dignified. But what are dignified people like? I'll tell you what they are like. They are snobs. Frightful snobs. I'm a curiosity in this town. I'm a big freak because I'm myself. Be yourself."

Maggie nodded. She would be herself. They could take her or leave her.

And take her they would. They'd take her the first time they met her.

Fox had a project for which they wanted Bow. MGM, however, held Clara's contract, and they refused to loan her out. Despite never seeing Maggie as Zazà because she couldn't afford a ticket, Clara bragged about Maggie's brilliance. She told the studio heads Maggie would be perfect as her replacement. "My friend is beautiful, and a good and honest person. She personifies the flapper girl. But I warn you, she is more complex than that. My Maggie will keep you fuddy duddies on your toes."

As soon as she scampered in, the moguls recognized her as incredibly natural and alive, a beauty who could epitomize the darling flappers of the wild and hedonistic Jazz Age. She would bring to screens a sense of fancy-free, flirtatious fun.

A director asked Maggie to cry. Without missing a beat, tears flowed. They asked her to read some lines. She did so for at least thirty minutes while acting out the actual scenes. She swooned, paced the room, and dramatically raised her forearm to her head. Impressed, the man, a vice president, set up a test for the coming Wednesday.

He dug through his desk and pulled out a few script pages. "Go home and work on this," he said in a demanding tone.

As she left, not that she slowed her walk to hear their whispering, Maggie listened to what they were saying.

"The girl has a mysterious quality."

"She is spontaneous and natural."

"Her face is incredibly expressive, which, of course, is essential in a film."

"It is impossible not to feel a connection with her. Audiences certainly will."

C.J.'s meetings went better than he expected. Two studios expressed interest in turning *Life* into a movie, although both desired to wait for "talkies," which would be a reality in the next eighteen months. In the interval, three productions needed screenwriters.

On the way back to her Kissel, when Maggie mentioned the director had been a dash rude when he tossed the script at her, telling her to "work on this," Clara advised Maggie not to pay much attention to the jerk's manner. "They're all arrogant," she said. "You never become used to insolence. But you will learn to ignore them."

On their way back to the Elliotts' suite, Clara asked them to join her the next night at a dinner party.

"Not many people ask me to their parties. They think I'm incorrigible. But Frank Tuttle is one director who likes me.

I'm dining with his family at the Beverly Hills Hotel. It's an exquisite place."

"We can't go. We're not invited," C.J. said.

"Oh, J.J., don't be a silly Billy. I'm inviting you. And we'll stick Frankie with the bill."

"Are you sure?" Maggie asked.

"Of course. You have to be bold out here. Wallflowers end up waiting tables or shining shoes. Waitressing is not for you."

"Well, I hope they don't object," C.J. said.

"They won't."

"I meant to tell you, Clara, my initials are C.J., not J.J."

"Not anymore. Maggie told me what C.J. stands for. It will only be a question of time before some movie boss or reporter asks you what your initials are for. You can't be telling them, Cecil. Cecil is an awful name."

Clara told the Elliotts she'd pick them up at about 7:30 the following evening. They were about to discover first-hand how little fear the hard-partying screen goddess had of breaking rules.

✳✳✳

Divas always got away with racier clothing. But Clara raised a few eyebrows when she showed up wearing nothing but a belted bathing suit and high heels.

Her nerve shocked not just the Elliotts but also Frank Tuttle and his family. Her white swimsuit with a black belt and trim around the shoulder straps, neck, and bottom violated the Beverly Hills Hotel's dress code and Hollywood's rule of formal attire for evening engagements. Yet Clara couldn't fathom the fuss.

"Why should something I wear make someone else uncomfortable? Whatever the reason, I don't care."

Throwing Clara Bow out would make headlines in every newspaper. Ignoring her inappropriateness and letting her stay might go unnoticed. Not unseen by the other diners, but they would avoid coverage in the press. There might not be any bad publicity for stars and starlets, but there could be for fancy hotels.

As Clara left, the staff quietly suggested she never come back. Clara stuck her tongue out at them.

"Let's stop by my house so I can change clothes," Clara said as they got into her Kissel. "When I'm in appropriate apparel, we'll go someplace where we can cut loose the right way."

"My pal, Zelda Fitzgerald, is going to love you," Maggie said.

Clara took them to a club on the outskirts of Los Angeles. A place far enough out that orange groves surrounded it. Thick smoke hung from the ceiling. The jazz was loud, and booze was flowing.

Before partying twenty minutes, a young man wearing a sweater in the University of Southern California's colors and a fox tail hanging on the side of his head whispered in Maggie's ear.

"My, how daring," Maggie said, pinching him on the cheek. "You are awfully tempting. But," Maggie paused and pointed toward C.J., "I'm afraid you'll have to ask permission from the good-looking gentleman standing next to the punch bowl. In the meantime, go eat your Wheaties."

After waving goodbye to the USC boy, Maggie grabbed the elbow of another fella, this one in a bow tie, and led him to the dance floor. When C.J. cut in, she threw her arms around his neck and locked her lips on his.

"I think, old sport, we may have found our place to shine."

***

One screen test. That's all it took for Maggie to be cast in her first movie, a small production with not much of a budget. But the film was only meant to expose her to the public, to be a building block for the production they wanted her for, *The Wind*. Better yet, that role excited Maggie. The story addressed a young woman trapped by circumstances and her gender.

The first movie was completed in three weeks. Maggie immediately started work on *The Wind*. She swooned over the film's theme. Elation overtook her thoughts. On the sound stage, bent and leaning into the gale, she skillfully turned the wind into an issue and a metaphor for other problems.

Even C.J., who still held mixed feelings about Maggie acting in movies, believed the script to be intelligent and worthy of her talent.

She became Letty, a young woman who loses her mother, forcing her to leave her tranquil life in Virginia. Brooding and forlorn, she revealed how she missed her old home, a place of exquisite beauty. How she loathes her new home, a wasteland, a cruel land with no rustling trees, blooming flowers, or singing birds. Her spirit breaks, her shoulders bow.

The wind is ceaseless, constant, continual, unabating, eternal, perpetual, continuous, nonstop, uninterrupted, unbroken, unremitting, persistent, and relentless. Maggie, exposing a stricken character, ill-prepared to live in the harsh environment of the bleak, desolate Texas plains, brings Letty to life in a soul-crushing sense of painful reality. Filled with little but thorny brush and cactus, the land brought her to the brink of prairie fever. The numbing blizzards, the howling sandstorms, and the loneliness of the prairie combine to undo her nerves. But the wind—the wind embodying a demon incarnation of evil eventually drives her into the darkness—into madness.

Rehearsals exhausted Maggie. They began around dawn and lasted past dark. Breaks, except the lunch break, were short or didn't happen. Reading script changes gave her trouble since she refused to wear her glasses at work.

On occasion, she would run into Clara, whom her new director referred to as crisis-a-day-Clara. Those instances most often led to both actresses being late getting back to their sets. That irritated casts and crews.

The Wind started filming after three weeks of rehearsing. Maggie had a dreadful blowup with her male co-star. Not appreciating the depth of an on-screen kiss, she doubled up her fist and blacked his eye, ending the day's shooting.

A female co-star was immensely jealous of Maggie. Maggie was gifted. She was brilliant, seemingly effortless in her elegant movements, but in truth, Maggie was never easy for other cast members to get along with. She could be extraordinarily challenging.

Working in a long wig and shaggy clothes reminiscent of the 1880s, Maggie, with her eyes made up with dark eyeshadow above and below, created a character tired and sad. Still, a face as beautiful as Maggie's—the mesmerizing eyes and the way passion or gentleness or some mysterious pleasure unknit her brows—was penetrating when it filled the screen.

Out on the town with C.J., and most often with her bosom buddy Clara and her current beau, Gilbert Roland, Maggie's appearance and attitude changed. Wearing short skirts, saucily winking, flashing a dazzling smile, throwing kisses from pouty lips, and coyly peeking over a raised shoulder all became part of her fresh personality.

C.J.'s aloof suaveness, coupled with Maggie's what-the-hell carefreeness and readiness to wiggle at the first note of the Charleston or Rhapsody in Blue, made them everything the "Jazz Age" stood for. Without question, an extraordinary sense of excitement raced around the Elliotts.

Yet, for all this, Maggie and C.J. delved deeper into life. They were more adept at maintaining their stability amidst all the partying, at least C.J. was. In their lives, things never spun fully out of control the way they did for the Fitzgeralds or their new pal Clara.

"I don't know about you, old sport, but I'm exhausted."

"It's two in the morning. You should be."

"I have to be on location at six. I guess not having any sleep is helpful. Letty is supposed to be tuckered." She kicked off her shoes, shed her dress, and flopped across the bed in her knickers. "Make sure I get up when the alarm goes off."

C.J. flipped off the bedroom light and drifted over to the desk where he worked on the screenplay they had engaged him to write. The movie was a romantic thriller set in the Kentucky hills about a storekeeper trying to win the love of an innocent schoolteacher. She is so put off by him that she runs away and seeks refuge with a hermit. C.J. expected the film to be a flop.

He supposed *The Wind*, Maggie's film, would likely be a

triumph. The screenwriter of her script had artfully merged the most popular genres. He created a Western, a historical epic, and a melodrama in one. He was a talented writer.

For thirty minutes, he skimmed through what he had written, concluding his script stunk. The premise reeked. C.J. regretted taking the first project they had offered him. He wished he'd come to Hollywood six months earlier. They might have hired him for Scott's The Great Gatsby if he had. Rumors circulated about the screenwriting not going well; worse, the producers had poorly cast the picture.

Weary of the dull Kentucky tale, he closed the folder and put the writing aside. Fixing the mess could wait until tomorrow.

LXII

Chapter Sixty-Two

In telegrams to Grace and Zelda, Maggie proclaimed that *shooting on The Wind wrapped. The movie, as they say in Hollywood, is in the can.*

The producers chose The Rosslyn Hotel for their cast party. The specific location for the bash was room 275, an annex on the other side of 5th Street, accessed by a subterranean corridor. But it wasn't where the real party was.

"Elliott, there's a tunnel running through a hidden basement containing barber shops and shoeshine stands, leading to a speakeasy named the Monterey Room, a high-class place. Let's go."

Reaching the other end, they found a hatcheck room and receptionist greeting visitors. She reminded C.J. of the girl who wore the too-red lipstick back in Maggie's dorm at Holyoke.

She told them, "Remaining covert is of little concern to

the owners or our revelers. Speakeasies are common in Hollywood. They squint down on, or up from, half the sidewalks in Los Angeles. One newspaper estimates we have more than 400 illegal bars operating in our city. Celebrities like Charlie Chaplin, Ana May Wong, W.C. Fields, and American Venus, Esther Ralston, frequent them. You don't need to worry about coppers raiding us."

The crew and stars of *The Wind* celebrated hard and deep into the night, except Maggie.

"Why so unhappy?" the film's director asked as he sat beside her.

"I'm tired, nothing more," Maggie said, lying.

"You should be. I'm sure you didn't understand what you were getting into."

"I guess I didn't. Is making pictures always so rough? I've only done opera."

"A higher creative form," her boss laughed.

The comment gave Maggie pause. "I didn't mean to infer that," she said.

"Of course you did."

Embarrassed, Maggie leaned away. Before responding, she studied his face. Was he being hateful? Was he just making conversation?

"Opera is artistic. Wouldn't you agree creating theatre is more complicated than a movie? There is music, orchestration, singing, and performing in front of an audience. Everything must be perfect as the presentation unfolds. You can't re-shoot a scene."

Milner smiled at her. "Well, I will admit we are producing entertainment. Films may not attain the high virtuosity of the opera, but we reach more people. Our first goal is to entertain them. Still, I hope we sometimes cause them to think."

He took a glass of champagne offered by a passing waitress before explaining how some movies are strictly to amuse or divert, but some are more consequential. "Our tale is reflective. The story delves into the subconscious mind. The depth of the subject made filming hard."

After a deep drink and a long stare at Maggie, the man continued making his point.

"I believe you will appreciate our efforts when you see our work on the screen." He patted Maggie's hand and put his hand on her shoulder. "You did a remarkable job. You fully fleshed out the character and made her intense and addictive. The realism of your interpretation of Letty's growing desperation and the results of her anguish will make the second half of our film harder to watch but crucial for audiences to absorb. We've created a piece of art, an intelligent story, a masterpiece viewers will not forget."

After freeing himself from one of Maggie's co-stars, C.J. came over and asked her director if he'd had the chance to view the finished project.

"It's in the final editing. I'll scrub through the entire thing in four or five days. We'll fix any issues prior to bringing in everyone for a full-cast preview. I anticipate the release in about six weeks."

The Elliotts made one more round through the party-goers before slipping away to meet Clara Bow and a few others at the Coconut Grove. They'd promised to arrive ahead of midnight.

The Coconut Grove, inside the Ambassador Hotel, was

decorated with fake palm trees used in Rudolph Valentino's The Sheik. When the Elliotts arrived, the place was in mayhem.

That was because, in a drunken moment, Lionel Barrymore released a cage of live monkeys, terrifying many guests. Less than a minute after their arrival, a squirrel monkey, at least according to Clara, jumped on Maggie's shoulder and then her head. Maggie took her misfortune well. Until the little beast stood and peed on her nose.

LXIII

Chapter Sixty-Three

Twice, three times, Maggie woke up, never finding C.J. in bed. The third time, she couldn't go back to sleep. Still in her dressing gown, she opened the bedroom door.

C.J. sat at the breakfast nook. In front of him lay his screenplay. He was scribbling notes when Maggie wrapped her arm around him.

"You scared me."

"I didn't intend to." Maggie plopped down on the stool next to him. "How long have you been up?"

"All night."

"Being up all night is unhealthy," Maggie said before asking him what was wrong.

He took a drink of his coffee and winced. Standing, he wandered to the small sink and poured the stuff out.

She scrutinized her husband but didn't speak. His face was pale and drawn, his shoulders drooped, his breathing was sporadic. He looked not only unhappy, he seemed very sick. The question wasn't one she would ever ask him, but she fretted over whatever happened to the thrilling young optimist who courted her. The one she fell in love with.

The hero of his screenplay took a beating from life. Sometimes, Maggie feared C.J. saw himself in the character. She hoped not.

He turned to her. "I don't feel like a success. More like a failure."

Where did that come from? At times, Maggie struggled to comprehend the man's mind. "Don't be silly. You wrote a best-seller."

"With Fitzgerald's guidance."

Maggie's jaw dropped. Her eyes widened. "What are you talking about? Every writer has someone review their work. Make suggestions and offer a little editing. For heaven's sake, Zelda may do half of Scott's writing." Maggie's face flushed. "And don't get me started on Hemingway. You and Scott fixed everything he scribbled out."

"Not true. Hemingway is a fine storyteller. You just don't like him."

No one could argue with that. She didn't like him.

"Being born wealthy has been a curse. I've never needed to achieve anything. It never mattered whether I succeeded. Everything's been given to me. I'm a leach."

"Oh, stop."

"Why? I'm telling the truth. I doubt I could have written a novel if our livelihood depended on the book selling. If I'd failed, what would the consequences have been? Nothing. We'd have kept dancing through life with everything earned by someone else. I'm like a ballplayer who walks a lot but never gets a hit."

He was just getting warmed up. "Anyone who has been a failure can tell you nothing is pleasing, literary, or noble about failing. It's like a weight you can't escape. It mortifies you, making the slightest things like washing your face or leaving your house as difficult as scaling a cliff."

Fine. Failure can be fatal. But C.J. was accomplished, and Maggie wasn't going to put up with his self-pity. In that respect, she differed from other wives. Most would express sympathy for their discouraged husbands. Not Maggie. She didn't dwell on setbacks in her life, at least she wouldn't admit such, and she wasn't going to accept such behavior from her husband.

Maggie suffered down days, of course, usually because what she wanted didn't come fast enough to suit her. When adversities came along, she did not let them deter her, or more accurately, she pretended not to. When what she desired came too slow, she set out to speed the process up.

She already had a huge following. Her first movie, the one that only took three weeks and was meant to be a throwaway little piece of hokum, turned out to be a hit. Reviewers said there was a primal sexuality dripping from the new starlet. They blathered on and on about how this new star blazing across the screen had dazzled at The Met in New York and the Paris Opera House—in Paris—they always added. Along with her opera triumphs, they extolled how she had sung jazz with Cole Porter and George Gershwin.

It didn't bother her that she had a growing reputation as a party girl or that a few false scandals were whispered around.

She was wholly exposed to the public eye, and that was who she was.

Maggie knew how to live, and she made every second count. She was mixing it up with the biggest stars of the day. And best of all, she was wanted.

Laid bare, her natural sensuality turned her into one of the most erotic figures on the screen. She was unafraid. She was becoming legendary. She had everything she desired.

Maggie was not one to give up. Still, this lifestyle painted a target on her back. Being so popular could lead to complications. Admiration was not easy to hold on to. Sometimes, the lust for life and a person's energy could start to ebb away without notice. But, if that demon was lurking, seeking to devour her, she didn't know it, or wouldn't acknowledge it, not yet.

She didn't wallow in misery, at least not since Paris, and wouldn't have C.J. groveling in his.

"You're not a failure. Stop pitying yourself. You graduated from Amherst Summa Cum Laude, you sign off on or veto every decision at your grandfather's businesses, penned a best-seller, and in case you've forgotten, you captured my affection and my hand. Not something to be taken lightly," she said, winking.

He sighed. "I didn't tell you yesterday, but they scrapped the project I was working on."

If he was expecting compassion, C.J. would get none from her.

"So what? You said the whole idea stunk. Now you're free to find something else. Wouldn't you rather work on something worthwhile than something terrible?"

No one trapped a person like Maggie. He was out of a job, and she was turning his unemployment into a benefit. The production being down wasn't a bad thing. It was an opportunity. He couldn't disagree. Something excellent did beat something awful.

She'd taken the set, the game, and was now going to finish the match. "Clara told you Famous Players Studio wants *Life*. Who would be more qualified to write the screenplay than the author?"

"Or to play the female lead than the author's wife," C.J. said, with a lot of sarcasm.

Maggie thought his comment over. Why so sarcastic? Why wouldn't he want her in a movie of his book? Not wanting her was stupid. His tone peeved her.

"I'm perfect for the part. Am I not your muse?"

He glanced at a clock hanging in the living area. "Four-thirty. I didn't think it was so late."

"It isn't late. It's early," Maggie said.

"Whatever it is, let's try to rest."

In bed, Maggie inched close to C.J. and cuddled. Sleep eluded her. Not C.J., he fell almost immediately into a deep slumber. He slept so soundly that her fitful movements never changed his breathing. Unlike Maggie, he didn't flop around or roll all over. She was jealous of his capacity to sleep.

Sunlight peeked through the window curtains, destroying any chance of Maggie drifting off. It didn't matter. Weeks of shooting made her used to rising at dawn. She leaned over and kissed C.J. No response. He didn't stir. She shook him harder.

"Stop it," he finally mumbled.

"I thought you were dead."

"Well, I'm not. Now leave me alone."

He went right back to sleep. A little aggravated, Maggie was still careful to be quiet while she dressed. After patting his shoulder, she slipped out of their suite and walked down the stairs to the ornate lobby. Traveling businessmen were checking out or sitting around downing coffee and smoking cigarettes.

The hotel cafe bustled with people, forcing Maggie to wait almost twenty minutes for a table. "Eggs Benedict and English tea," she told the waitress, smiling. The morning newspaper said Bobby Jones won the U.S. Open, becoming the first to win the British and U.S. in the same year. "Jordan Baker would beat you," she whispered to herself. "Without cheating."

On page two, she read about lightning striking Picatinny Arsenal in New Jersey. The resulting fire caused several million pounds of explosives to blow up. Maggie wondered why a golfer made page one instead of an explosion. Not that she cared.

C.J.'s cynical remark about her being in a film version of his novel still irritated Maggie. Kaye was, for the most part, based on her. Why shouldn't she portray her?

"Your Benedict looks yummy," the young waitress said as she served Maggie.

"They smell delicious." Maggie unfolded her napkin and placed the green cloth over her lap.

When a man at the next table started talking with the server, she bubbled about how she wanted to be an actress. Her work in the restaurant was temporary. Maggie chuckled to herself.

"Would you like anything else, Ma'am?"

"Yes," Maggie said, "another order of Eggs Benedict. My husband turned into a sleepyhead this morning. I don't want him to starve."

C.J., awake and reading when Maggie returned, asked about her meal.

"I brought you Eggs Benedict. They're scrumptious."

"I have a question for you," C.J. said about halfway through his breakfast. "Does it upset you we wasted about three years running from an imaginary villain?"

"What are you talking about?"

"Arnold Rothstein. We fled the country and spent all that time in France because he scared us. As it turned out, there was nothing to it. We ran for no reason."

Well, fine. Now, the argument over being in the *Life* movie needed to wait; first things first.

In her mind, Maggie always denied fleeing. She tried to convince herself they went to seek new opportunities. Not true. But she always told herself it was.

"I thought we went to dodge melancholy," she said. "And families we were sick of."

He finished his eggs, grinning at Maggie.

"Besides, I thought you liked Paris," Maggie said, hoping to end the conversation.

"I did. But we wanted to avoid danger." He stopped chuckling, and the joy left his face. "A non-existent threat. Does that upset you? Running instead of facing our fears."

"No. Even if that's true, I'm not bothered. I didn't want to be murdered. Did you?" She let her question sink in. "I was ready to come home before you were. I won't deny longing to come back to America. But—I'll also admit we had fun. We flourished." Maggie started laughing—hard. "We made fine friends and did guzzle too much gin. We were even murder suspects. That's not something you accomplish every day."

"We should send Arnie a thank you note," he said, picking up a pen.

"An invitation to lunch."

LXIV

Chapter Sixty-Four

The studio released *The Wind* the first week of August. The public flocked to watch Maggie, trapped by circumstances, gender, and occupation, succumb to madness overcoming her thoughts and being. Filmgoers wept watching the tragic heroine driven to insanity and murder.

Audiences enticed by her pragmatic persona adored Maggie. Off screen, with her messy bobbed hair and exciting eyes, she made the flapper style more popular, and American females, at least the young ones, craved her way of life.

Smitten critics raved over Maggie's portrayal of a character ensnared by conditions beyond her control, evils she could not defeat. Some reviewers called *The Wind* gothic. Others said brilliant.

The Los Angeles Times said it captures the power of the sun, sand, and wind on the physical appearance of both men and women. Their critic proclaimed the picture an anti-romantic vision of the nineteenth-century Southwest.

Those who didn't like the film, especially critics in Dallas and Houston, claimed it was tedious. The images of the harsh Texas climate, land, and its toll on the citizens, expressly females, angered many Texans.

Everywhere else, newspapers and magazines called her a remarkable actress, much more natural than most. But soon, Maggie fell victim to a dangerous drug. Maggie became a huge star.

Her reputation as a wild child and reveler blazed hotter. Her friendship with Clara Bow and Louise Brooks fanned the flames of speculation. Like Clara, she didn't 'play nice' the way other actresses did. Like her party pals, she refused to dull herself down to blend in.

While Maggie partied, C.J. worried. He grew anxious about her notoriety. How vulnerable would she be to fame's addictive qualities and its consuming greed for more? How perilous was the blinding light of stardom? The answer was —very.

Despite the boundless energy she reflected, C.J. feared fame had put Maggie on the dead-end cycle of a merry-go-round with no way to climb off.

Within two weeks of *The Wind's* release, studios offered Maggie three more movies. She accepted all three, starting work on two for Metro-Golden-Meyer simultaneously.

While making three films for Paramount Famous Players, faithful to her word, Clara wrangled C.J. a meeting with the studio to discuss his novel.

He instantly knew the company heads expected to make

a favorable deal with the debut author, an arrangement advantageous to their business. He flatly told them they were mistaken.

Sixteen days later, he took Maggie and Clara out on the town to celebrate when the studio ended up with an agreement giving the novelist's wife top billing, though the novel's true protagonist was the male, Reid Johns. Better still, C.J. negotiated for the movie to be made as a talkie. With *The Jazz Singer and Lights of New York* nearing production, *Life* would still be one of the first ten talking pictures.

LXV

Chapter Sixty-Five

Tommy telephoned before daylight. "I need to talk to Mags."

"Do you know what time it is out here?" Elliott asked, irritated by the hour.

"Yes. But I have to speak to her."

"I'll have her call you when she wakes up."

"C.J., I need to talk to her now."

Aggravated, he told Tommy to hold on. He touched Maggie's shoulder and gave her a slight shake.

Half-slapping at his hand, she ordered him to leave her alone.

He jiggled her again. "Tommy's on the phone. He wants you."

Rolling halfway over, she asked what time it was.

"Four in the morning."

"Tell my moron brother I'll get back to him. Or hang up on him."

"I tried to tell him you'd call back. He says he has to talk to you now."

Maggie rolled out of the sheet she was sleeping under. She headed across the room in a rather tiny nightie.

"This better be important," she snapped into the phone.

Two or three seconds went by before Tommy spoke. "Our parents are dead." He didn't say another word.

"What did you say?" she asked. Her brother was breathing in shallow bursts, not saying anything. "Are you there?"

"Maggie, it's Grace. Your folks are gone. I'm sorry." Grace drew and released a deep breath. "We got a call about an hour ago from the Tulsa police. Patrol officers found them around one this morning." It was the same time Maggie had struggled with sleep.

Maggie sat next to the table where the telephone was. Any chance for a resolution with her parents disappeared. Love, anger, regret, none of those feelings would ever be expressed. Grace kept talking, being deliberate about what she was saying, but Maggie battled to concentrate on what she was revealing.

"My mom and dad are dead," she said, turning to C.J., her normally copper-hued skin fading to a pasty gray.

Taking the phone, C.J. asked Grace what happened.

"I'll let Tommy tell you."

Maggie glanced at her husband. Despite disowning and abhorring them, their sudden deaths still struck a blow of a magnitude she didn't expect. A storm cloud hovered over her head, casting a shadow over everything in her life; she moved toward the bathroom. Without speaking, she closed the door and turned on the shower. Alone, she slipped into a low state of energy. The showering required a deep strength from within that she didn't have. She shut the shower off, leaned against the shower wall, and slid to the floor. There, she curled into a fetal position and quietly wept. It would be the only tears she would shed for them.

"Early this morning," Tommy said, "the Tulsa police found the folks' car in front of one of Tulsa's funeral homes." After a brief pause, Tommy, sounding disorientated, said leaving them at a mortuary must have been some kind of joke. "They were both shot. Twice in the chest, once in the head. Investigators called the murders an execution."

C.J. sat on the couch, collapsed, really. Questions raced through his mind, not one he dared ask out loud.

"You might not want to tell Mags how they died." Neither said anything for some time, resulting in awkward silence. "Let me call you back when I can tell you more," Tommy said. Without saying anymore, they hung up.

For several minutes, he stared out the window. Not adept at deception, he struggled to decide what to tell Maggie. For some reason, he tapped on the bedroom door before opening it. Curled in a ball, Maggie was pallid.

"You look ill," C.J. said.

Sitting up, she put her feet on the floor. "I'm not going to any wake. I'm not a hypocrite." A deep breath, in and out. Standing, she went over to the bureau, picked up her hair-brush, and sat on the delicate metal chair, sliding under the boudoir table to brush her hair.

"Are you alright?"

"How did they die? A car wreck?"

"They found them in their car. But it wasn't an accident."

She stopped brushing and turned toward him. "Executed? Or was it murder, suicide?"

"They were gunned down."

"By who? Do they have any idea?"

"No."

"I'm not surprised. Are you?"

"Yes." Putting his hands on her shoulders, he said he was sorry.

"Don't trouble yourself being unhappy. Pop was no saint." Maggie kept fiddling with her dark red locks. "You reap what you sow. Isn't that what they say?"

"No, I believe it is sew the wind, reap the whirlwind."

Maggie started dressing, acting disinterested.

"Tommy said he'd call back when he learns more."

"He needn't bother. Doesn't he remember? We're estranged from our parents. The whole family."

"When you want to talk, I'll be in the other room," C.J. said, pointing at the suite's living area.

"Don't hold your breath."

***

The absence of emotion, a reflex born from years of trying to lock ancestral wretchedness out, flooded through her. Strange how the lack of something could overpower her. But shutting out feelings was her method of self-defense. Or her reaction to guilt.

She sighed and went into the room with C.J., where she dropped on the blue Italian provincial sofa, the enormity of her repressed trauma on her face. She leaned back into the couch, her eyes half-closed. Hotel guests scurrying around the hallway made more noise than was courteous in the wee hours of the morning.

"I wish those people would quiet down. Don't they care what time it is?"

"Well," he said, "I could stick my head out the door and tell them to shut up."

"No, don't. People in Los Angeles delight in being rude. We don't need to spoil their amusement."

"Do you want me to stop the clocks, close the curtains, and cover the mirrors?" he asked.

Maggie laughed at his question. "I'm not that Irish anymore." She hesitated, "With Paddy dead, there may not be anybody left to hold a wake at their house. If they do, I hope they remove the coffins feet first. I don't want them finding their way back."

If honest—and brave—C.J. would have told Maggie she was too heartless regarding her parents. He was not so honest. Or brave.

Maggie dragged out her cello and began to play what sounded like a dirge. Without skipping a beat, she switched to jazz. Instead of insisting on Maggie making plans to attend their burials, he went to the small corner desk and worked on his new novel.

***

Right after noon, the phone rang. "I'll answer it," Maggie said. "It's going to be Tommy."

She remained silent and stiff as Tommy detailed the way their parents perished. He provided more specifics than she cared about, including how he didn't think they suffered before dying.

When C.J. sat next to her, she held the receiver out so they could both listen to her brother. With significant frustration in his voice, Tommy asked her if she was going to say anything. If she was going to ask if the police were investigating anyone.

"What difference does it make? They brought everything on themselves."

Tommy did not take his sister's cold response well. "How can you say such a thing? They were our parents."

"Oh, don't climb on your high horse. You didn't invite them to your wedding."

Tommy fell silent. He hung up.

"Jackass," Maggie said as she slammed down the phone. She turned toward C.J. "Don't you start on me."

He didn't. Instead, he called Tommy back, something she reacted to by disappearing into the bedroom.

Grace answered. "Well, that didn't go well. After Tommy cools off, I'll make him call her back. Why don't you try to calm Maggie down?"

"I'm afraid there'll be another fight the next time they talk," C.J. said. "She says she's not going to the funeral."

He knew few things Maggie said or did, dazed Grace. Refusing to go to her parents' service did. Grace gasped. "Do you think she'll change her mind?"

After a moment's hesitation, C.J. said he didn't think so. Trying to ease the tension, he asked if Tommy had any idea who committed the killings. If they had any suspects.

"Are you asking about Arnold Rothstein?"

"I suppose so," C.J. said.

"Tommy may think so. But I can tell you the Bureau of Investigation doesn't. They refer to Rothstein as 'the brain.' Tommy's looking for an easy explanation. None of the authorities think Rothstein takes part in violence. But he has associates who do."

Grace paused the conversation to respond to Tommy when he asked where to find their candy. She waited to say anything more until he left the room.

"One of Rothstein's protégés is a fella named Luciano. I believe you popped him in the mouth once," Grace said, laughing a bit. "From what I hear about him, he's capable of killing. Luciano and a couple of Italian gangsters have started bootlegging operations with Rothstein financing. At least, that's what Tommy's pals at work say. I eavesdropped on Tommy talking with his boss one night about the possibility of Rothstein setting those Italians up to do business in Tulsa. My guess is Tommy's dad crossed them."

Sensing C.J. was concerned Rothstein might want to hurt him or him and Maggie, Grace tried to reassure him. "I'm on a new House Committee on Crime. I can check on those guys if you want me to. But I'm all but positive you have nothing to worry about. Tommy thinks Rothstein had something to do with Sam Taylor's murder, but no one else in his office does. Tommy is a little paranoid. But don't you ever tell him what I said."

C.J. and Grace agreed to let the riff between their sibling spouses cool before trying to convince them to talk again. They believed both would come to their senses, although Maggie might not attend the funeral.

After Elliott hung up, Maggie acted like nothing had happened. She didn't utter a word about her parents or Tommy. Unfortunately, within minutes, fatigue sat in. An overwhelming low mood grew into a lack of motivation, lasting days and making it impossible to complete daily tasks.

***

Three mornings later, someone started pounding on the door. In France, it would have been Scott and Zelda. In Hollywood, it was going to be Clara Bow.

"Read what's in the L.A. Times, here in the entertainment section. The entertainment pages are where all the important stuff is." Clara tossed the paper at Maggie. "Read the top story. You've been named a WAMPAS Baby. The WAMPAS Baby Stars are a yearly selection of the thirteen most promising starlets made by The Western Association of Motion Picture Advertisers. I was one two years ago. They'll formally introduce you at the Frolic, a coming-out party covered by the press. Being a WAMPAS is a monstrous honor."

Maggie read the article with Elliott looking over her shoulder.

"You're included with Mary Astor, Dolores Costello, Joan Crawford, Dolores Del Rio, Janet Gaynor, and Fay Wray. You're better than any of them," Clara squealed, throwing her arms around Maggie. "This is something to celebrate. Let's revel tonight until we all pass out."

"We'll make a night for Hollywood to remember," Maggie laughed for the first time since Tommy's call about her folks. Dancing all over the room with Clara, she caught C.J. staring at her. She flashed him a scowl to clarify he wasn't to mention her parents.

"I have to run," Clara said. "I'm supposed to be on set. I need to hurry back before they miss me."

"Do you think they will?" C.J. asked.

"They better," Clara answered. "I'm in every scene they're shooting this afternoon."

After Clara left, Maggie reread the story about her being a WAMPAS Baby. Each budding actress on the list was young, beautiful, and poised on the brink of movie stardom. They were picked to reign as symbols of new life waiting to be breathed into the Hollywood community.

To justify their selection, and in some part, the title of "Baby," the girls were young, typically under twenty-five. Maggie was ancient, almost twenty-eight. A WAMPAS girl nearly always had four film credits under her belt. Maggie had two, albeit as the star, not a supporting actress. It couldn't be denied Maggie was an unusual choice.

Being a curious pick didn't matter to Maggie. Many starlets received nominations every year, but only a lucky thirteen made the final list. A committee within WAMPAS handled the elections and ballot counting. They chose Maggie.

Given the clout of the award, those elected met with excitement and anticipation from the entire industry. The impact and buzz crescendoed in the Frolic ceremony that followed.

"Take me to Coconut Grove. I want to perform someplace exciting."

C.J. agreed. If he hadn't, she would go on her own.

After considerable persuasion and crossing his hand with cash, Maggie convinced a desk clerk with a lousy attitude to take her to the Grove's general manager. "I starred at the

Metropolitan Opera and the Paris Opera. I sang twice every week at the most famous jazz clubs in New York and Paris. I've been accompanied by Cole Porter and George Gershwin. I'd like to be on stage here."

Starring in a silent picture didn't impress the man. However, being the lead in two operas at major venues got her an audition, a tryout, not an engagement. Singing opera doesn't mean you can entertain a nightclub audience.

"When do you want me to sing for you?"

"Now."

"Do you have any musicians here?"

"I don't need to try out my instrumentalists. Each one of them can play. I want to find out if you can sing."

Less than halfway through 'Makin' Whoopee,' he hired Maggie. She'd perform every Thursday night and every other Saturday night.

***

Clara returned at seven-thirty with her new beau, Gilbert Rowland, and fellow bad girl, Louise Brooks, in tow. "We're going to Pickfair if they'll let me in," Clara said.

"Of course, they will," Brooks said. "You have a rare quality. You have flesh appeal." Brooks threw an arm around Clara. "Flesh, all the boys want to have sex with." Turning toward Maggie, right after patting C.J. on the cheek, Brooks laughed. "You can learn a lot about being a star from Clara. Every girl wants to be her. Every boy wants to date her. And old people think she's a sign of the apocalypse."

Clara rushed over to Maggie, pressed her body against her, and kissed her eyebrows. "You are devastatingly beautiful. You can be the beguiling newbie. The one who threatens the integrity of the old guard. They're going to hate you. They'll try to exclude you. They always want to exile me. And they would, too, except I rake in forty thousand fan letters a month."

The new young heartthrob, Gilbert Roland, with whom Clara had recently filmed a spicy dance scene in their film The Plastic Age, smooched Clara's cheek. "Clarita," Roland always called her 'Clarita,' "Clarita, you are the most gorgeous woman in the world. Everyone loves you."

Every male Hollywood star loved Clara. Gary Cooper adored her. But Cooper was a mamma's boy, and Clara was not the sort of dame any mamma wants around. Director Victor Fleming had strong paternal feelings for her. Clara drove them all away with her vacillation, infidelities, and wavering. Of course, she didn't know if any of them loved her, or just loved escorting a red-hot mamma.

On the drive to Pickfair, Brooks talked about hoping for a glimpse of the ghost.

"What ghost?" C.J. asked.

"Pickfair is haunted. The spirit of a female servant spooks the whole place. Mary and Doug have seen her on several occasions. The specter always dresses in a long, white gown."

"No one else ever sees the woman," Clara said. "I think they make the entire thing up."

"I hope so," C.J. said. "I don't care to meet an apparition."

"What would be grander than to meet a departed soul?" Maggie asked before jabbing C.J. in the ribs and pulling his head down to her face by his ear. She whispered to him. "As long as the ghoul is not one of my parents."

Elliott shook his head. Dumbfounded.

Going to Pickfair fulfilled the dream of everyone in Hollywood—and everywhere else. An invitation meant you were someone. Many said socializing at Pickfair was as prestigious as being asked to the White House—some said it was better.

As they turned into the driveway, the idea of intruding on Mary Pickford and Douglas Fairbanks unnerved Maggie. They had not invited her. She and C.J. were invading as guests of Clara. Being Clara's guest might be like being the companion of Scott and Zelda, interlopers tagging along with someone whose own invitation was, in all probability, offered with reluctance.

The first person they saw was Charlie Chaplin, who lived next door. Clara swerved her car right at him. What a wonderful beginning.

"I knew you were behind the wheel as soon as the car veered toward me," Chaplin said, cuddling Clara and giving her lips a peck. "Louise, you should keep better company," he said, hugging Brooks, with whom he was rumored to be having an affair.

As Maggie stepped out of the back seat, Chaplin extended his hand. "I recognize you, Mrs. Elliott. You were outstanding in *The Wind*. You invade the audience's subconscious more than any actress I have ever seen."

Maggie was flabbergasted. Flattered but flabbergasted.

Pickfair was impressive. Marion Davies and Colleen Moore, a rival of Clara, were paddling a canoe around a crescent-shaped swimming pool surrounded by a sand beach.

Clara told Maggie it was the first outdoor private pool in the Los Angeles area. Celebrities were playing badminton and croquet on the sweeping lawns. Dorothy and Lillian Gish were waiting for horses to be saddled up at the stables. They'd be able to ride to the ocean.

Reclining in a chase lounge away from everyone, one person grabbed Maggie's eye like no one else. The woman with a cigarette tucked between her fingers sat glaring into the distance, her face impassive, almost like a mask, but eloquent.

Wearing slacks, men's Oxford shoes, and a shapeless, ill-fitting sweater, she came across as practical, sensible, and undemonstrative—or unkempt.

"Who is she?" Maggie asked, yanking Clara over close to whisper to her.

"Oh, that's Greta Garbo. Her first picture came out a couple of weeks ago. She's like me, temperamentally unsuited for Hollywood. Rumors are she only cares about herself. They say she's a perfectionist about her work so much as to be a pain in the ass. They also say she doesn't give a tinker's damn what anyone else thinks."

"I'm going to talk to her," Maggie said. "I think I might like her."

"Be careful. She bites."

Maggie stopped for two glasses of wine. Pickfair ignored prohibition. Fairbanks would simply point out to any invading law enforcement that it was not illegal to drink spirits, only to purchase them.

Maggie held a glass out to the woman she wanted to meet. "I'm Maggie."

"Whoopee for you."

"Thank you."

"I'm Garbo. Thanks for the Cabernet."

Maggie sat in the chase next to her, putting her feet up.

"That's some voice. Its smoky depth suits your pale blue eyes. I must say I admire your style."

"You mean the way I dress? My agent forbids me to go in public in an outfit like this. I ignore him."

"You should find another agency."

After taking a long drag on her cigarette and exhaling through her nose, Garbo smiled at Maggie. "I recognize you. The poor unfortunate waif in *The Wind*."

Maggie sipped the wine. "Yes, it was a torturous picture to make."

"I finished my first. Well, my first in America, a trashy thing titled *Torrent*. I played a Spanish peasant girl. The dippy audiences swooned. I hated the whole clumsy production." Puffing again, Garbo gave Maggie a mysterious half-smile. "Irving Thalberg, you surely know Irving, MGM's wonder boy. Anyway, he wants me to play young, but worldly-wise, women. I said to him, Mr. Thalberg, I am just a young gur-rl. I don't like playing the exotic, the sophisticated, the woman of the world. He says he knows best."

"Men always think they're smarter. They seldom are," Maggie said.

"I suppose Irving does know something about making pictures. But I want to play somber personas and tragic characters. I prefer being a naïve innocent, not experienced near adultress woman not far from a whore. In the end, they mean more to the audience. I believe they will be longer in people's memories."

"I heard you are going to be cast with John Gilbert," Maggie said.

"They say we will have 'chemistry' together," Garbo said

in reply. "I'm not dumb. They're saying we will have a sexual appeal on the screen. I don't know how anyone knows that. I'm not sure I like the man." Garbo's mysterious eyes locked on Maggie. "If it is sex appeal they want, they should cast you. You would ooze seductiveness standing next to Louis Mayer.

LXVI

Chapter Sixty-Six

"No," Maggie said, "I will not go to their funeral. Stop goading me."

The squabbling lasted another ten minutes—until Tommy surrendered. By the time they hung up, with Grace's assistance, Maggie convinced Tommy he and Grace should come visit her after the burying. In Tulsa, they were halfway to Los Angeles.

Since filming *The Wind*, Maggie had found resting at night difficult. After her parents' murder, it became harder. Nightmares were now a nightly companion. They were so real she was afraid to go to sleep. Before going to bed, she checked to ensure the door and the windows were locked. If she woke, she tried the locks again.

When awake, she was endlessly lonely, confused by her emotions, and plagued by sadness and anxiety. She built walls between herself and everyone else, including C.J. Strange feelings of not having any life of her own overwhelmed her. She misplaced her soul.

With tears running down her cheeks, she shook her sleeping husband. "Elliott, I need you to hold me."

"What's wrong?"

"Wrap your arms around me. Squeeze me tight."

For minutes he held her. Rocked her in his arms. No one spoke. No one let go.

"Elliott, I'm miserable. Who am I? I'm so adrift."

For Maggie, what was once challenging was now devastating. What was sad was insufferable. What was pleasurable was pleasureless—or, at best, a flitting drop of enjoyment in a sea of pain.

Even if nothing was amiss, a moment later, everything seemed hurtful. Suddenly, no one could be trusted. No one loved her. Elliott's tenderest touch felt painful. No one cared or understood.

Everything was meaningless, including her accomplishments and what had given life significance. As much as she wanted to receive Elliott's help, it was difficult to describe the turmoil she was living in.

"I'm numb. I can't overcome my apathy about everything. The fight to exist takes up all my energy, emotional and physical. The devil is sitting on my shoulder, whispering that I'm rubbish, worthless."

What she said shocked him. She'd always been the positive one. When C.J. told her he felt like a failure, she took him to the woodshed. Criticized him for doubting himself. Now, she was the one doubting herself. The one defeated.

Sometimes, a person takes a long time to lose themselves.

Other times, it happens in a hurry, almost like an explosion. However, they lose their way, they need someone to help them back. Maggie needed help. No one can recover alone.

Two appearances on the screen and Maggie Elliott became a beloved star, rushing toward becoming a pure Hollywood legend. MGM determined to cash in on Maggie's adoring audience.

After *The Wind's* release, a gossip rag asked through a rather lurid title: 'What is this quivering—pulsating—throbbing—beating—burning across our screens?'

Maggie was an absolute marvel on-screen; no film would ever showcase that more than *Wind*. She wore her temperaments so close to the surface she could call on them at any instant, emoting with an earnestness few other stars achieved.

On giant screens, her dark, mysterious eyes danced when joyful, melted when sad, and sparkled with naughtiness afoot. She also had curves that magnetized men.

Maggie shined, combining a happy, open-mouthed purity with candid adult themes. Being so easy-going and exuberant, she pulled off stunts others, except Clara, dared not try.

That was because underneath the shell lay a woman who honestly did not believe dancing through life or showing a little leg hurt anyone. Maggie didn't act naïve about these things. She simply considered her actions harmless and nobody's business. Unfortunately, this would soon make her a bad girl of the screen. Something that might destroy her.

"I don't know when I got this way, but being lost is terrible," Maggie said.

C.J. took his arms off her and stroked her cheek. "You've been astray for a long time. Life had wrecked you before we went to Paris. That's why I took you. I was hoping for you to find yourself. The truth is, for me, Rothstein was an excuse. I wanted you to get a fresh start."

Walking over to the window, Maggie pulled the curtains back and gazed off at the city. "All I ever wanted to be was a cellist. Just to play."

"Oh, Maggie," C.J. said, "you coveted fame. It didn't matter how it came."

Those words hurt. She didn't understand why, but they broke her heart. They weren't true. At least, she didn't want them to be. She wanted recognition. Yes, recognition, not fame.

Wasn't being recognized different from fame? Wasn't recognition more reverenced than fame? Maggie pursued recognition. To be esteemed as a female. She longed for women to be acknowledged for their talent. Her goal wasn't about personal admiration. Everything she wanted, she wanted for her gender. She always told herself as much.

Females deserved to be successful. They merited the same appreciation for their accomplishments as men did. That was why she fought so hard for Grace's election. Why she respected Zelda, Clara, and every woman making headlines. It didn't matter if they had to be scandalous to get them.

Her face was ashen when she turned back toward Elliott. "No. I wasn't seeking fame."

"What then?"

What a foolish thing to ask. Wasn't it obvious? It should have been apparent to anyone—except a fool.

"I wanted to be a success."

"You could have taught music. Or school. You might have

opened a business or worked as a secretary. Being a nurse was an option. You'd have succeeded at a lot of occupations."

Of all the damn things for him to say. Maybe recognition wasn't anything different. But it sounded more refined.

"Tell me this, smart boy," Maggie said, not yet ready to surrender. "I'm a WAMPAS Baby. My name is on a movie marquee right down the street. I've starred in operas, and I sing in jazz clubs in front of picky crowds. Starting next week, I'll be singing at The Coconut Grove. Everybody knows me."

"They know your name, not you."

Sadness again flooded over her face. "If fame is what I want, why do I feel lost? And so heartbroken?"

"Because fame is a deceiver. Acclaim is untrustworthy. And fickle." Elliott paused. "At its worst, fame is built on a lie. In most cases, actors are nothing but imposters, playing someone they're not. They aren't skilled. They're no more than pretenders."

"So, Clara has no talent? Fairbanks and Barrymore are talentless?"

He waited to answer, thinking over his response.

"Clara is different," he said. "She doesn't pretend to be anyone else. She bursts on the screen as who she is. She is the same on-screen or having dinner. She is genuine. Because she is, other actors don't like her. Their success is phony. They're dependent on a director telling them what to do. She's not."

"Am I talented? Or am I one of those phonies?"

He almost went to her, nearly wrapped his arms around her. But he didn't. He stayed on the other side of the room, unreadable emotions playing across his face before he spoke.

"You have enormous musical ability...as a cellist and a

vocalist. Why music doesn't satisfy you is something I don't understand. Why isn't being a musician enough? Why are you jealous of others? I don't understand your envy of actors. Their careers don't last long. Worse, half of them are scandal-ridden. They backstab their friends and care about no one but themselves."

Maggie didn't respond. More lost than ever, she wandered into the kitchenette and retrieved a bottle of wine she brought home from the Pickfair party.

Coming up from behind, C.J. put his hands on her shoulders. "Why can't you be satisfied with your success?"

She couldn't answer.

For several days, he hoped Maggie would stop acting. Drop out of the two movies she was shooting. She didn't. Instead, she signed the contract to star in the movie adaptation of his novel *Life*.

LXVII

Chapter Sixty-Seven

The train bringing Grace and Tommy pulled in two hours late. Grace glowed. Being a congresswoman agreed with her. A tuckered-out Tommy dragged along behind.

"If you're interested," Tommy said, after hugging Maggie, "the Tulsa police apprehended a petty thief for our parents' murders. He claims Pop cheated him in a deal fencing stolen jewelry."

Maggie hurried her brother away from the others, the same way she had when she arrived in Tulsa for Christmas vacation six years earlier. "I'm glad they arrested someone." Pausing, she put her arm through his and squeezed. "I'm sorry I didn't come to the funeral. I couldn't. Some things happened you don't know about. Things I don't want you to know about. Not ever."

Before Tommy responded, Maggie spun around and, running, pulled him back to Grace and C.J.

"Aren't you famished?" She asked, grabbing Grace by the hand. "You must be. Train food is horrible. I'll bet you haven't eaten anything all day."

Grace denied being hungry, but Maggie paid no attention. She had made the decision. They needed to feed Grace and Tommy.

Insisting on Café Montmartre because it reminded the Elliotts of France, Maggie went so far as to order for Grace and Tommy. Roast duck for Grace. Lamb for Tommy. The eighty-cent meals included a salad, French fried potatoes, chocolate cake, and coffee.

"We'll come back here Friday night," Maggie said. "The place will be crawling with stars. We'll be swatting them off like flies."

After Grace and Tommy checked into a cottage on the grounds of the Ambassador Hotel, Maggie insisted on a shopping spree with Grace. The boys could do whatever pleased them. As long as they didn't accompany Grace and Maggie.

Shopping wasn't really on Maggie's mind. She wanted to be with Grace alone.

The coffee shop Maggie chose for the clandestine discussion she longed for was not fancy. Bessie's Bistro was a dark little secret tucked in a basement far from Hollywood Boulevard. The entrance opened off a narrow path wandering between brick buildings, a romantic way to describe an alley.

Maggie didn't enjoy hedging. So, she didn't. "I don't like who I am. I don't like the color of my life."

"Life has a color? What color?"

It was a silly declaration. Yet, somehow, Maggie felt the senseless statement held the answer to her future.

With her elbows on the oilcloth-covered table, Grace leaned toward her friend. "What the hell are you talking about? Since when does life have a color?"

Maggie laughed. She should have anticipated Grace wouldn't put up with such an absurdity. Laughing harder, Maggie said, "Since now—I guess. I think mine is dark purple."

"Dark purple," Grace said, mocking Maggie. "I think my life is orange. Yes, I'm sure of it."

"Orange is better than my dark purple. My stormy dark purple."

"I think you should consult an alienist."

"A head doc?" Maggie said, feigning astonishment.

"They'll inject you with malaria. That's the newest treatment. It will give you a brutal fever. The fever will fix your brain. If you don't die." Grace finished her coffee and asked for another cup. "I don't understand you, Maggie O. Most people would give anything for your life. You're rich. You live wherever you want to. You headlined at the Metropolitan Opera, lived in Paris, and starred in a motion picture. How can you not be happy?"

"A lot of help you are."

"What makes you so unhappy?"

There was no answer. That was the problem. If honest with herself, Maggie wasn't that discontent, certainly not miserable. But she wasn't content. Her life didn't satisfy her.

Sometimes, she watched Elliott write. He'd sit drinking cups of French coffee while tapping on his typewriter. He wrote slowly, with lots of crossing sentences out. He seldom ripped pages out, wadding them up like he did when writing his vampire novel. The one he tossed in the Bar Harbor Bay.

Watching him reminded her of observing a painter throwing out bold brushstrokes. His eyes, those intense blue eyes, sparkled when he was satisfied with the words.

Maggie's creative life was different. She experienced confusing and painful circumstances so invasive they didn't leave any room for contentment or self-recognition. Instead of joy, her talent brought pain, tension, and angst.

A swallow of black tea and a deep breath helped a little—not much. "At Holyoke, I was happy. Life thrilled me. What happened?"

"In those days, you dreamed about the future. You pictured what you wanted and eliminated everything else. Unfortunately, life isn't a dream."

What life is...is a disappointment, Maggie thought.

Unlike Maggie, Grace viewed life in pragmatic terms, not giving any substance to celebrity. For Grace, more pressing matters needed attention.

Grace concentrated on more weighty concerns than Greta Garbo making her American film debut or Rudolph Valentino's dying, regardless of Pola Negri continually fainting.

"I'm rather dismayed about you losing sight of what's important and letting such frivolity as celebrity take you over," Grace said.

Maggie didn't answer. Not at first. She took a minute or two to decide on a response. Her reply should be terse and brusque. The question was, how brusque?

"I'll leave all those big worries to people like you, Congresswoman."

Grace switched her empty cup with Maggie's still half-full one.

"I miss you, Grace. You kept me balanced."

"Balancing you was exhausting," Grace said, patting her old friend's hand and giggling a little. "I could never keep up with you, although I never wanted you to know that. You bounded between profuse bursts of joy and abrupt periods of somberness." Grace had always thought Maggie's appreciation of happiness, even life, could disappear at the slightest hint of disappointment. But Maggie was too determined not to go after it.

"The thing I dislike about my life," Maggie said, sounding sad, "is that achieving what I want is temporary. They offer no one any promise of lasting fame. Operas come to the end of their run, and movies leave theaters and are never seen again. Being popular today doesn't mean you'll be wanted tomorrow." If loss could be found in someone's eyes, it was moving into Maggie's.

"It has nothing to do with what we're talking about," Maggie said as she poured tea from the small white ceramic teapot the waitress had left, "but Elliott drinks too much coffee. He pours it down by the quart."

"Be glad it's not alcohol," Grace said.

"I told him the other day that everyone knows me. He said, they know your name, I don't know what he was driving at. What do you think?"

At eight that evening, Maggie bounced on stage at The Coconut Grove. No one, not a friend or a stranger, would have thought she wasn't happy. Her red bob, curly and long enough to dance wildly from her head, almost had a life of its own. She broke into 'Let's Do It," a brand-new ditty Cole Porter cabled her to open with a bang. She'd be the first to ever perform the song.

***

Revitalized, all Maggie talked about Friday was going to the party at the oh-so-swanky Café Montmartre. "The festivities start around nine and go until the last person passes out. The Montmartre is owned by a Frenchman who instinctively understands anything French is considered classy. So, he fancied up French cuisine with a menu to outshine the fare at every other Los Angeles restaurant."

Hollywood's first nightclub was on the second floor of a building on Hollywood Boulevard. They found a table on the left side of the room, a good spot because they weren't too close to the band.

"I hope no one recognizes you," Maggie said to Grace. "The queen of the gossip columnists, Louella Parsons, shows up on a regular basis to table-hop in search of spice and scandal. You wouldn't want to be the subject of a scandal, would you, Congresswoman?"

The Montmartre had a vast dance floor and a decent orchestra. Not that the masses needed much inspiration to Charleston or Black Bottom.

"This place has legendary dance contests," Maggie said. "The winners are often attention-hungry newcomers. Last Friday night, however, Clara Bow won the contest. An upcoming starlet, Joan Crawford, danced the Charleston on a tabletop. No one is more attention-hungry than Crawford. Of course, at this point in her career, she may be plain hungry. A girl has to eat."

LXVIII

Chapter Sixty-Eight

Grace and Tommy were leaving mid-morning on Monday. Maggie wanted Grace alone one more time before she left.

"Don't ever tell Elliott what I'm going to tell you," Maggie said. "Promise me."

Grace did.

"My next movie starts shooting on Thursday. It's a western about a hero trying to recover his stolen horses from rustlers. He saves me from the outlaw gang and a raging river. Can you imagine? In the one after, I play a flapper. At least I have a little experience with flapping."

Maggie rambled about the long hours required when filming. At last, she got to the part Grace was supposed to keep secret.

Almost as if someone else was talking, she detailed how you forget your lines and miss your cues when you get too tired. Since time is money, and they love money, they offer you cocaine. After you get too keyed up, they give you heroin to help you calm down.

"Are you using that stuff?"

"Not yet." Maggie leaned away. "Not heroin, anyway." But she admitted getting an occasional boost from cocaine.

"Maggie, you have to stop."

The warning was unnecessary. Maggie knew the horror stories. The chaotic lives and self-destructive lifestyle of starlets under too much pressure often paved the way to a bad end. It didn't take long for many to become hopelessly addicted. Innuendo and unsubstantiated accusations fed scandals. Scandals led to more desperate behavior.

Some eased the pain with a cocktail—or ten. Others, like Barbara LaMarr, whose notorious wild romantic encounters and delicious bordering on salacious wit endeared her to an entire generation of flappers, lost their battles, dying young.

Maggie was well aware of the necessity to stop. But the need for fame was like being on a treadmill with no way off. Sometimes, you had to ride to the end.

Before Tommy and Grace left, Maggie promised her old friend she would stay clean. She wasn't convincing.

LXIX

Chapter Sixty-Nine

C.J.'s novel was a work of psychological complexity. It found praise and success as a portrait of obsession. MGM's wonder boy, Irving Thalberg, was enthralled, so anxious to sign a deal for production rights he let himself be bamboozled in negotiations with the novelist. Elliott outfoxed him in navigating what he'd be paid for the narrative and again in negotiating Maggie's salary.

"What I like about your book," Thalberg said, "is how complicated your characters Reid and Kaye are."

Aren't all literary heroes complex? They were in C.J.'s mind. At least, they should be.

"Reid is focused, strong-minded. If he faces setbacks, he plods ahead. He stays his course. I like his determination," Thalberg said. "Though Reid loves Kaye, she is a thorn in his side. Her temperamental, unpredictable moods enrich the story. When success is slow in coming, unlike Reid, she alters her direction. She wants immediate fulfillment. Kaye is the perfect foil to the conservative and thinking Reid. They will make a wonderful film."

The movie opens with Reid sitting at a desk writing. The camera closes in on the sheet of paper and the phrase he has scribbled: *Life passes in seasons.*

After enough time for the line to be read, the scene fades to a young woman, Maggie, as Kaye is tending to roses in a garden and playing with three puppies. Her content moment is disturbed by a fine-looking but awkward Reid, whom she met and danced with at a party the week before.

Though struggling with his shyness, he asks her for a date. She declines. The man is contrite, apologizes, and turns to leave. Seeing this, Kaye's manner, even her posture, alters. She puts a reassuring hand on his arm and changes her mind.

In classic romantic narrative, Reid and Kaye marry. A new season of life begins.

The Great War soon interrupts their marriage, but they continue to share an almost spiritual connection throughout their separation. This beautifully sincere film presents love through troubling circumstances and continuous ups and downs.

Since C.J. was the screenwriter and novel's author, they allowed him on set while shooting the movie. Watching Maggie act was not something he always enjoyed.

The production was incredibly lavish but, like the novel, also a little seedy. A growing appetite for spicier fare led to movies being more open about sex and marriage. More mature films from Germany and France created a challenge for Hollywood studios. New attitudes influenced the filming of *Life*.

Rhythmic edits and poetic shots of the actors looking straight at the lens resulted in a more sophisticated, emotionally raw love—a more sensual film. The shooting captured intimate details between the pair, minor touches, Maggie reclining entangled with her on-screen lover, running her hand through the male actor's wavy black hair. At times, his hand brushed over Maggie's body.

After the war, when the marriage hits a rough time, brought on by Kaye's eye being caught by a single man sitting at the next table in a restaurant, Reid becomes disenchanted and sails for Venice, where an Italian vamp had tempted him during his days as a soldier.

With Reid away, Kaye flirts with other men. Meaning Maggie kisses more actors. With the director demanding passion, the scenes became more sensuous. As the sensuality on the set increased, life at home changed. C.J. grew distant. He moved away when Maggie approached him. He refused to talk even when Maggie asked what he wanted or how he felt. Affection almost disappeared.

Nervous over Maggie's mounting on-screen intimacy, he questioned Clara Bow about how genuine movie embraces were. Clara loved kissing her co-stars. Often, she would suggest they should rehearse away from the cameras. More than one rumor was bouncing around town regarding Clara's dating habits.

But, while Clara was perhaps careless about her own life, she was protective of her friends. She lied to C.J.—J.J., as she insisted on calling him—claiming screen kisses were always repulsive. She said no one would do them if the directors didn't demand them. According to the red-hot mamma, J.J. had nothing to worry over.

Nevertheless, he became ecstatic over Reid returning from Europe. Reid's and Kaye's hands touch. Both are still wearing their wedding rings. They are reunited in an embrace, and the film ends.

A memorable highlight of the movie was a comic bit, where Maggie donned a flannel shirt and baggy trousers for a flamboyant rendition of *California Here I Come*. The scene was from the novel, but not the song.

C.J. hoped Maggie would be tired of motion pictures. Why shouldn't she be? The shooting schedules kept her exhausted and in a sour mood. Or at least they kept her drained and brooding.

But her role in *Life* and fierce determination to succeed made her so popular that hundreds lined the streets outside movie theatres to see her perform onscreen. With a snap of her fingers, MGM, just like that, offered her top billing in five proposed film projects. Her life was never to be the same again.

Maggie's pictures were also huge across Europe, especially France. She was grateful for the European support but vowed never to return there.

LXX

Chapter Seventy

The cable came early on Tuesday morning. The Fitzgeralds had returned to America, and Scott had been offered a job in Hollywood writing a movie script, a fine modern college story for actress Constance Talmadge. He had accepted, and they were on their way to California. Zelda said they couldn't wait to frolic with their best friends.

A second cable said their arrival would be delayed by two days because Scott got a terrible stomachache on the train. He hurt so much he thought he had appendicitis. They had to deboard in a place called El Paso. "By the time we got to the hotel," Zelda wrote in her telegram, "Goofo was all well. I could shoot him."

As she'd done for Grace and Tommy, Maggie booked the Fitzgeralds one of the cottages on the grounds of The Ambassador, a luxurious setting Zelda would love. For neighbors, they would have some major stars, such as Pola Negri. Something else that would please Zelda.

"The weather here reminds me of Paris," Zelda said on their second day in California.

"It's better here," Maggie said. "There's no Hemingway."

It surprised Maggie when Zelda told her she missed Paris. She claimed to be homesick for the pink lights and gay streets.

"Friday night, we'll introduce you to Clara Bow. She'll show you how exciting Los Angeles can be."

"How does C.J. like California?" Zelda asked.

The question was difficult to answer. How much her husband liked Hollywood was hard to determine. He wasn't thrilled over his wife being in movies. She was sure of that.

"We party a lot," Maggie said. "But unlike Paris, we limit our partying to Friday and Saturday nights. Everyone out here works too many hours to play during the week. Hollywood is rather dull from Monday through Thursday. We compensate for our boredom starting on Friday nights. Weekends are when the booze and cocaine come out."

"Cocaine?" Zelda asked. "I've never done narcotics. Is coke your candy now?"

Straightaway, Maggie wished she hadn't mentioned drugs. Drinking, even if it was illegal, didn't have much of a stigma. Drugs, however, drugs were wicked. Admitting to drug use, at least admitting it out loud to another person, made her feel depraved. Neither heroine nor cocaine were socially acceptable, not even at the wildest parties. "Only when I have to work twenty-hour days. But don't you tell Elliott."

Zelda laughed—a lot. She threw an arm around Maggie and said, "I'm no snitch."

Maggie asked Zelda if she had seen *Life*.

"No."

"You need to see it. Right now."

Grauman's Chinese Theatre was ornate—and packed when Maggie and Zelda sat down in the thirtieth row. To avoid being noticed, Maggie pulled a scarf down, hiding much of her face. A trick she learned from Clara.

LXXI

Chapter Seventy-One

Despite everything Maggie faced, 1927 and 1928 remained stellar years. Audiences loved her. The masses adored her so much ruthless studio heads had to be cautious of not alienating her to the point she would walk away.

In November 1928, gangsters dealt with Arnold Rothstein. When the police asked him who shot him, he refused to say, telling the coppers, "You stick to your trade. I'll stick to mine." When they asked him again, he said, "My mudder did."

C.J. tossed the newspaper on the mahogany end table as Maggie swept across the living room. "Rothstein got plugged. He's dead."

"Good," Maggie said, shoving eyeliner and lipstick into her purse. "I've got to get to the set. I'm going to be late. That'll tic my good old director off."

"What's the rush? They haven't finished the casting?"

"I'm testing with the men being considered for the male lead."

"Fabulous."

Not long after she arrived at the studio, she was shuffled into a room to begin the screen tests. All that was present was a chaise lounge.

"Go recline on the couch and follow my instructions."

Prone and growing indignant, actors sprawled on top of her to play out a love scene by passionately kissing her. She began to fume. The producer, director, and crew looked on. In Maggie's mind, drooled on.

"Get off me." Maggie shoved the foul-smelling oaf off, sending him hard to the floor. Flying off the couch, she kicked the actor, charged the director, slapping him violently—over and over again.

Two of the crew pulled her away. But not before she landed a clenched fist, splitting the boss's lip. An actress, not a star, but a frequently cast actress waiting to audition for a secondary role said to her, "Don't worry, we've all had to do it."

"Then you're all idiots. I'm a woman, not a mattress."

By the time she objected, eight men had lain down on top of her and played out the scene. She stomped out of the auditions, screaming at the studio executives to cast whoever they wanted as the male lead. "Whoever the hell you want. But I won't be pawed one more time. If you don't like it, find another actress."

***

"They won't hire anyone else," C.J. said. You're too popular. And you make them too much money. They can't lose you. You're the real jazz baby."

"I don't feel like a baby. I feel old." Maggie hesitated, turned to C.J. Do I look old?"

He shook his head. He didn't bother to answer.

"I should quit. These movies have brought me more sadness and scandal than joy. They treat me just like they treat Clara. They call us birdbrains and dumbbells. They refer to Clara as crisis-a-day Clara. Or worse."

"You should quit," C.J. said.

"Do you know what I resent the most? Those damn studio executives manipulating me while I make them masses of money at the box office."

In truth, C.J. knew she would not quit. She was too enamored with fame and celebrity. The only way she would give those things up, those demons, would be for her physical and mental health issues to be so exacerbated by the stresses of her notoriety, particularly the fallout from what the press made up, that she would suffer a total collapse.

***

On Black Tuesday, October 29, the stock market crashed. The Great Depression wrecked the country. Despite all the rumors, floods of people did not leap from windows. There was no epidemic of suicides.

Still, The Depression devastated countries, rich and poor. Personal income, tax revenue, profits, and prices dropped, while international trade plunged by more than 50%. Unemployment in the U.S. rose to 25% and, in some countries, as high as 33%.

Despite the economic hard times, the full transition to talkies in 1929 made Maggie more popular, as producers now highlighted her beautiful voice. But, instead of protecting their golden goose, they worked her harder.

When Maggie balked at her treatment, her bosses called her crazy, hurting her to the core. She considered the insult a gendered trope. Something Maggie hated.

Friends started to worry over changes in Maggie. They described her affect as always changing. Before C.J. realized how sick she was, he recognized she saw a strange significance in everything.

"Have you noticed, Elliott, how colors are getting brighter, or darker? The air has a taste. I've never discerned that in the past. Have you?" She alleged music beat behind her forehead and other times fell into her stomach.

Obsessions began to manifest. Maggie played her cello for hours, often in the middle of the night. She insisted C.J. spend specific periods each day writing. She fixated on calling Grace every day.

Maggie started to blame C.J. for her sorrow and feelings of being lost. "You have to stop leaving me alone. You don't love me anymore." Twice, she screamed at him for not wanting her in his bed. Constantly, she complained he turned her into a perpetual migrant, robbing her of her sources of emotional support.

Stardom wore psychologically on Maggie. Now perhaps America's most popular actress, she became movie magazine fodder.

She cried to C.J. about how studio heads ran her career as though she were a machine, pushing her until she broke. When she balked at their treatment, they made movies loosely based on her life. Always emphasizing something hurtful.

Maggie now lived in anger, lost in torment and misery. Her pain showed first in her eyes, then in her hallow face. An inability to reason followed.

Watching her overcome by those demons, C.J. cautioned of her anger being born of pain and sadness. Embracing her, he whispered, "Quiet yourself—hold tight to my love and protection."

Audiences also picked up on her anguish. When it beset her on stage or the screen, there wouldn't be a dry eye in the house.

One afternoon, she collapsed while walking along the beach with C.J. She came to speeding down Sunset Boulevard strapped to a stretcher in the back of an ambulance. She became hysterical, screaming about directors praising her in interviews but crucifying her on the sets.

Shaking and sobbing, she begged C.J. not to let her be discarded. "Don't abandon me. I can't be alone.".

Except for Clara Bow and Louise Brooks, Hollywood friends betrayed her. Bow and Brooks, going through the same treatment, stayed loyal. Once she was released from the hospital, Clara visited her every day.

Some days, Maggie's conversations made no sense. "Please, Clara, give me your frank opinion. Do my pants clash with the color of the carpet? Is that why I am so nostalgic for Paris?"

She quarreled with C.J. over everything. She told Clara, "Elliott has met a pretty actress who charms him."

Maggie did not take the imaginary crush lightly. In public, each young woman they came in contact with was the tramp stealing her husband.

She declared to Clara, "I'm always polite to the girl, even warm."

In private, she burned C.J.'s clothes in the bathtub.

One day, in a phone call, she shocked Zelda Fitzgerald after the Fitzgeralds left California. "I know if you were not so close to me, you'd do anything to bed C.J. Thankfully, such an awkward situation will never occur. Both you and C.J. are far too fond of me."

She went on massive spending sprees. Intense social relationships with men increased in public, although they didn't appear to slide into her private life to the point of affairs. Her responses to disappointment grew melancholic. She was not one to give up, but her lust for life and her vitality ebbed away each new day.

Clara told C.J. Maggie had hallucinations about what was appearing on screen when she watched a movie with her. It was not the only incident Clara had observed.

"I was on the beach with her when Maggie, poor dear, went loopy. She had gone into the water and suddenly screamed that the ocean was boiling."

In 1932, a newspaper article unnerved C.J. A 24-year-old actress, Peg Entwistle, ended her life by jumping from the 'H' of the Hollywood sign. RKO Pictures had not renewed her contract. When her body was discovered, a note in her purse read: "I am afraid I am a coward. I am sorry for everything. If I had done this long ago, it would have saved a lot of pain."

The Entwistle story tormented C.J. Could this be the path Maggie was on? Sleepless night followed sleepless night. Without Maggie's knowledge, he reached out to Grace and Tommy.

Then, on Grace's advice, he made an appointment with a psychiatrist. A meeting he would not tell Maggie about.

The doctor, a USC graduate with, according to himself, a list of luminary patients, including Hollywood stars, recommended not pushing Maggie. "It's best not to pressure high achievers. Success, in all likelihood, is what is most important to your wife. If you fight her, I think you will lose her."

***

It takes a lot of vulnerability to tell someone you're struggling. Maggie struggled with depression and anxiety for a long time. In 1933, Maggie built up her courage. She opened up about her demons. "Elliott, I need help."

The critical emotional event of Maggie's life was about to unfold. In a moment of recognition, she wrapped her arms around her husband.

"My brain is playing pranks on me. You don't know about treachery until your own mind betrays you. I am dependent on you. Hold me. Get me assistance. I'm sick. I want to be cured."

They chose to seek professional care. C.J. interviewed several doctors, not including the USC graduate. Maggie refused to see them until Elliott had made a decision. She said she was too ill to be involved.

"Most modern theories about the link between creativity and mental illness suggest both spring from a genetic disposition limiting a process called latent inhibition," one physician said.

Another claimed, "Some kind of filters control the amount and type of information brains take in from the world and enable them to order the information in an orderly manner."

Another said some people are too creative, making them crazy.

Freudian doctors wanted to probe the dark nature of Maggie's subconscious mind. Jung followers wanted to probe her collective unconscious. C.J. didn't understand the difference. He questioned if the doctors did.

Based solely on what C.J. told them, most doctors diagnosed Maggie with Schizophrenia. He was told schizophrenia is a thought disorder rather than a mood disorder. Schizophrenics gradually lose their sense of self, growing increasingly unorganized in thought and incoherent in speech.

Realizing it was being indiscriminately diagnosed for virtually anyone who showed signs of psychosis, C.J. was skeptical. None of those symptoms fit Maggie, who was, most of the time, lucid and even eloquent. Frustrated with his search, he finally convinced Maggie to see doctors with him.

Rockhaven Sanitarium, a facility taking a radically different approach from the other institutions, was a shaded, solitary place in a quiet residential enclave in the La Crescenta Valley, sitting among a collection of Spanish Colonial cottages. It was a facility for females only. They were called the ladies—never patients.

Maggie arrived at Rockhaven late on a January afternoon. She showed no sign of resistance. But not long after the beginning of her stay, Maggie decided she was fully recovered. "I am ready to go home. All I needed was rest."

No one, not the staff, not C.J., none of her friends, agreed.

"How much of Maggie's downfall is her fault and how much is the product of her environment is irrelevant," her calm and attractive female physician told C.J. in a private session. "I can tell you that between stardom, depression, and alcohol, Maggie's life could end tragically. What makes it worse is that she has a rebellious streak. The kind that often leads to self-destruction."

At first, C.J.'s visits were times of heated arguments, usually provoked by C.J.'s attempts to keep her calm.

Her eruptions were similar to each other. "I'm losing precious time. The treasures of life are passing me by. You don't want me happy. Do you want me trapped in this slammer? I think you're sleeping with my head doc."

Early sessions with her doctor were also volatile. She disagreed with her observations, argued about her treatment plans, and being forbidden to have her cello sent her into a rage.

As time passed, so did Maggie's angry outbursts. She began to enjoy the sessions with her counselor. "My dark times don't come as often, and they aren't as black," she said one rainy afternoon.

"So the times are gray, not black," her therapist asked. "Can you tell me how you feel in those times? And what do you do when those periods creep up on you?"

Maggie tried to relax, sinking deeper into her overstuffed leather chair. She looked out the window and rubbed her hand across her thigh. A slight smile slipped across her mouth, although she didn't know why she wanted to grin.

"It's like I have a weight on my chest, but it's not as heavy as it used to be. During those periods, I feel I am a failure as a person, wife, and friend. When I was acting, and people praised my work, I still felt worthless."

Maggie reached for the pitcher next to her and poured

herself some water. "When I came here, I was suffocating in my emotions. Now, I can breathe. I was so mad when you people wouldn't let me have my cello, but now I realize I didn't have enough energy to play it. I think Elliott was happier for me to get it than I was. He must have been so tired of having me scream at him about not having it."

As the weather improved, so did Maggie's demeanor. She grew calmer, smiled, and began to laugh. "I think I'm getting better. Don't you?" She loved to be outside. She and Elliott would sit in the flower beds for hours while she played classical music, not jazz.

When her doctor told her she believed she was ready to go home, she asked, "Are you sure?" And then she cried.

In C.J., she found what she needed. He did not oversimplify or invalidate her struggles. Never did he make Maggie, still occasionally depressed and woeful about herself, sink lower. To support her, he listened. He asked questions about her feelings, allowing her space for deep thoughts and emotions. An awkward silence was a frequent companion. His most critical role was offering trust and being an open place for hope to dwell.

Walking along a peaceful ocean one evening, he asked her if she wanted to go home.

"More than anything," Maggie said, embracing the man she loved.

As for Hollywood, one day, suddenly, she vanished. Photoplay Magazine ran the headline, What happened to Maggie Elliott?

The LA Times wrote about the bright lights of Hollywood blinding many of those who made it to the pinnacle. Maybe

Elliott was one of those. A national news magazine made a point of informing its readers Maggie had to be accompanied by attendants when she left the asylum where she was reportedly being held.

Whatever was printed, the public knew Maggie Elliott was unafraid. Her triumphs were legendary, her failures and tribulations were easily forgiven. When attacked in the press, her reputation was restored in an instant. Everyone outside the media loved The Magnificent Maggie: the critics, the movie fans, everyone was spellbound by Hollywood's missing starlet.

What happened to her? How could this happen? Look at her! She's brilliant! What the hell happened?

The truth was Maggie had been given a second chance, hope for change, and a quieter future, which she was not going to turn down.

LXXII

Chapter Seventy-Two

On a Thursday evening in May 1936, Maggie and C.J. drifted into their living room. Congress was in session, so Grace, now Senator O'Sullivan, was in Washington. Tommy was in Canada, negotiating the return of a crook who robbed a Bangor Bank. Their absence didn't matter. The Elliotts were home.

Memories filled every room. *Maggie laughing in the sitting room while C.J. made fun of the way she played chess. The smell of brownies baking in the oven.*

Both stared a moment at the spot where he promised to dig her a fishpond for some kind of fancy Japanese fish she read about in a catalog.

"I hope you know where your shovel is. You've got some digging to do."

They could hear the old rocking chair, Maggie's first

purchase after their wedding, creaking in the breeze drifting through an abandoned corner of the back porch.

Neither C.J. nor Maggie were sentimental. But ambling through the spacious home, she slipped her arm around his waist.

"Do you ever think about what our life might have been if we'd stayed in Bar Harbor instead of living like gypsies? No nervous breakdown. No being treated like we weren't human, mere hostages in someone else's recital. And best of all, no Hemingway."

With that, she got a chuckle and a hug from CJ.

The afternoon passed in a relaxing fashion. By the time the sun dropped into the bay, a deep sense of satisfaction washed over them.

"We should have never left here," he said.

"Maybe not. We don't need to talk about all the things we should or shouldn't have done." She leaned closer, slipping an arm around his waist. They spent the rest of the evening poking along the harbor.

There it was. An ugly black and gray striped devil slithering by the water's edge—right at Maggie's feet. Life was no longer normal. Her flesh crawled; her stomach coiled. The five-foot fiend attacked. Her heart raced, but her body refused to move. Her life was going to end.

Heroically, C.J. bent down. Without fear for his own welfare, he picked the serpent up.

Maggie screamed in terror as it wrapped around his arm. "Wanna hold it?"

***

The rising sun cast an orange and lavender hue across the

horizon, as if it had missed the bay and sleepy streets during the dark night. A flurry of early-morning activity accompanied C.J. as he ran into town for food.

When he returned, he found Maggie cheerful and bright. But when she replied to questions about how she wanted to spend their first week home, her answers became long and disjointed.

"I think Curls should come visit. Grace should run for President. You and I should open a bookstore. Since we missed breakfast, I suppose we should eat two lunches."

Although her thoughts bounced about without order and made almost no sense, they had meaning to C.J. Her notions weren't rational, but he understood her emotions. At least as much as anyone could understand Maggie's emotions.

Physicians, all of them, had offered assurances her anxieties would quiet down as she eased into a stable routine. They told him she would, over time, be able to relax into normal life.

Soon, Maggie settled into a schedule. C.J. stopped worrying, at least some.

"I'm sleeping well, playing my cello, and I want you to write at minimum two hours daily."

She did, however, refuse to discuss anything troubling her. There was a noticeable difference in how she behaved. With C.J., she was loving and touchy. With others, she was taciturn and aloof.

Bar Harbor was sweltering hot their second week back. Maggie abandoned the wide-legged and high-waisted trousers she wore most of the time. She switched to baggier, casual lounge pants around the house and when in town.

"I've decided I'm not going to ever wear a skirt or a dress. On the beach, I'm going to live in shorts, scandalously short ones."

When Grace came home during Congress's spring break, she kept commenting on Maggie's eyes. Those sparkling green eyes. Except for C.J., Grace was the only one who saw any light in Maggie's eyes. Everyone else seemed to see gloom.

***

Stealing Maggie away for lunch, Grace asked about her life. "Still dark purple?"

"You were right. Life doesn't have a color. Our lives are just life." After a deep breath, Maggie admitted she feared she had lost her zest for living. But she did say she would like to find it.

"How's your marriage?"

"My marriage...?" Maggie smiled and chuckled. "That's the one solid thing I have. How's yours?"

"Mine is," Grace paused, "We spend too much time away from each other, but ours is good, too. I love Tom. I wish we didn't have so many weeks apart."

"And how do you like being a Senator?"

Grace lit up. "I bask in being 'The Honorable' Grace O'Sullivan. If I win another term, hell, Mags, I may be President someday. What would you think of that? You can sleep in the Lincoln bedroom. You'll be able to tell everybody you made love in Abe's bed."

***

Later, Maggie fell asleep on the couch, giving Grace a much-wanted chance to talk to C.J.

"How's Maggie doing?"

C.J. said he wasn't sure. "She's complicated."

"She always has been," Grace said.

"I don't know what she wants. I don't think she does. I do know she never gets it. Whatever it is."

"She wants to impact the world." Grace laughed, then turned grim-faced. "She can't figure out how she wants to impact it. Do you want me to tell you why?"

Before telling him, Grace led C.J. out on the back veranda. Never one to mince her words, Grace went right to the point. "Her father was an s.o.b. Until Holyoke, Maggie's life was inconceivably heinous. When she was twelve, a neighbor tried to sexually abuse her. He failed, but it was still traumatizing. And it wouldn't be the last time she suffered. She suffered immense physical and psychological trauma at home. All that hurt shaped her adult life and her career choices.

Grace became reluctant. C.J. wanted her to spill all.

"Maggie will tell you her father was strict and remote. He was much worse. Think about how gifted Maggie is with beauty, grace, and high spirits. I'm sure you appreciate her expert flirtation skills. Her father hated every one of those strong points. He abused her. Did everything possible to discourage her, including horrifying beatings. What's most heartbreaking, her mother did nothing to help. She suffered a miserable childhood and youth."

Grace went on a rant about how Maggie's father demanded she conform to near slave-like conditions. She emphasized how he believed females' only role was taking a man's name, assuming his entire identity, including his career and social standing. To her old man, a girl was worth nothing on her own.

"His never-ending abuse wrecked any trust she had in herself. I think that's why she leaps from one thing to another. She's afraid success will be stolen from her, so she always wants an alternative to fall back on."

Grace said only two more things. "You are the only constant Maggie's ever had. If you ever tell Mags I've told you this, she'll never speak to me again."

He disagreed. A little. "You've been a dear and solid friend to Maggie. Maggie has been lucky to have you." C.J. hesitated. He had to. His emotions were overwhelming him. He took his handkerchief and wiped his eyes. "Tommy is an exceptional brother and someone Maggie trusts. Zelda and Clara Bow are good friends. I appreciate them. They've been through so much themselves, yet they are so wonderful to Maggie."

"What are you two up to?" Maggie startled both Grace and C.J.

"We're talking about you," Grace said.

C.J.'s breath caught.

"What about me?"

"About how worried we are about you," Grace said.

Maggie sagged into a wicker chair. One she disliked because Elliott painted a fine natural-colored chair a sickening green. "Why are you worried about me? Do you think I'm crazy?"

C.J. responded, perhaps too swiftly. "We think you're sad. I think you're afraid to be happy."

"Who's not sad?"

Always blunt, Grace replied without hesitating. "I'm not. I don't think C.J. is. Except about you."

Maggie reached out to touch them both. The winsomeness

of her gesture moved him. She was wearing a pink blouse, a color C.J. didn't care for on her.

Watching her as she started to speak, he hated how her face grew strained every once in a while, and her mouth dropped, getting lost in a hundred deep lines and shadows. In a strange manner, she squinched up her eyes into many wrinkles as she stared out into space.

Maggie's conversation strayed from one topic to another. "I appreciate your concern. I'm fine. I'm gaining control of all my problems, learning to separate things, the important from the unimportant." She patted Grace's hand. The issue was settled.

C.J. got up to fix a pitcher of lemonade. Grace and Maggie could hear him sigh from the other room.

"I've been listening to a preacher on the radio," Maggie said when C.J. returned. "He loves talking about redemption. He calls God a God of grace. He says you must be born again. Being re-born is something I want to learn more about."

Maggie stayed abstract. She asked Grace if she believed people could change or if they were stuck on some pre-determined path. Herself, she was unsure.

After saying she was unsure about the ability to change, Maggie appeared shaken. C.J. decided they had talked long enough.

For something to do, they walked to Bar Harbor. The streets burst with tourists and summer residents.

Maggie insisted on taking in a movie matinee featuring Garbo as a Budapest bar entertainer. "Greta plays a discontented alcoholic pursued by many men. She lives with a novelist until a strange man shows up, claiming Garbo is another woman, the wife of his close friend. Everyone is searching for the truth when a mentally ill woman arrives, saying she is the real wife."

"I wonder if they based that movie on us?" C.J. asked, grabbing Maggie by the arm. "A novelist and a crazy woman who both drank too much."

***

Later in the summer, a letter came from Zelda.

Aching to do something on my own, I wrote a novel, Save Me the Waltz. Scott is irate. He's been working on his new book for several years, and I turned mine out in a few months. I've created the fiercest territorial struggle. Too bad for Goofo.

Zelda hinted at fearing going utterly insane. She revealed having another breakdown and entering Phipps Psychiatric Clinic in Baltimore, where she penned the novel.

The letter distressed Maggie. She sat staring at it for a long time.

"Elliott, I need to be alone. I'm going to take the sailboat out into the harbor."

On the water, she felt the siren's song of the open ocean, the beguiling music of the half-bird, half-woman. An alluring melody, seductive, deceptive, she must resist.

Maggie saw them in the mist. Riding seaward on the waves, calling to her. They promised gifts of wisdom and knowledge of the future.

"Broaden your sails and sail on," their sweet voices lured her. *"Come save us from our deaths."*

She must resist them. But could she?

Epilogue

In the 1920s, the Elliotts and other icons breezed through the Jazz Age. In many ways, it was a perfect time. Exuberance, contagious energy, and stimulating rhythms helped the masses out of the darkness of war.

Maggie and C.J. often reflected on those long-ago days. In many ways, Maggie's life was tragic, but for a brief moment, her star shone as brightly as any other. Then she was forgotten. When she talked about those times, the old light would return to Maggie's eyes. "I loved spinning giddily through the revolving hotel doors and jumping into the fountain at Union Square fully clothed."

"I adored Paris," C.J. confessed. "The friends and the music, the cathedrals and cottages, burning our candles at both ends."

"But, how terribly strange the decade ended," Maggie would often add, her spirit sinking, "It all stopped. The parties didn't last."

When Maggie's mood darkened, C.J. reminded her of the good times.

"Maybe the parties stopped, but during those roaring times, my sweet Maggie, your fashion, makeup, and hairstyles defined the flapper look. You were free, wild, and unshackled."

"And laden with a rebellious streak that sometimes led to self-destruction," Maggie added.

"Yes, but your attitude onscreen and off became synonymous with flapperdom."

Maggie would laugh. "That's not true. Flapperdom was synonymous with me."

Despite the memories, according to Maggie, Paris and Hollywood almost ruined them. "Bar Harbor was our real home—or at least it should have been."

Maggie stopped trying to break into a major symphony. "A harpist might do it one day," Maggie said. "But not a cellist. They deem a female playing the cello indecorous because it's placed between a player's legs."

After Hollywood, Maggie occasionally sang at the Metropolitan Opera. She recorded six records, all hits to some degree. Before deciding she hated the movie industry, she'd made nine movies, including the one based on C.J.'s novel.

In a reflective mood, Maggie tried to explain to Elliott what might have gone wrong. "Hollywood wasn't ready to deal with non-conformists like Clara Bow, Louise Brooks, or the two of us."

After 1939, Maggie starred two more times at the Metropolitan Opera. Then she told C.J.— "I'm done."

In 1953, The Boston and New York Symphonies offered Maggie a chair. She sent each a two-word response—"Stick it."

"Perhaps," C.J. once said, in the twilight of their lives, "Perhaps we were ultimately tragic figures." A broad, wickedly sarcastic smile burst across his face. "Beautiful, brilliant people whose artistic ambitions were suffocated by your being a female and my devastating battles with self-doubt."

Maggie dropped her head on her husband's shoulder. She

touched his stubbly cheek. "Do you ever miss my copper hair? Or the magic times we had?"

C.J. kissed the top of her head. "We've been lucky to have each other. We've sailed the seas, felt the summer breeze, and skipped through the fall leaves. We knew Scott and Zelda at their zenith. When Scott was productive, Zelda was beautiful, before her status faded. It broke my heart how, after the decade ended, she spent the rest of her life battling for her sanity. "

"I judge history as too unkind to Scott," Maggie said. "When he heard of the death of Gerald and Sara Murphy's son, he wrote to them, I still remember his words: "Dearest Sara and Gerald, The telegram came today, and the whole afternoon was so sad with thoughts of you and the past and the happy times we once had." The letter ended: "The golden bowl is broken indeed, but it was golden...""

"He was right, it was golden," C.J. said, rubbing Maggie's arm. "We've gazed at the stars and watched Halley fly twice. Not many can say that."

"Well, my dear Elliott, in every life, there are a few ideal chapters. Only a few."

Before being confined to a hospital bed, Maggie had been rediscovered. Overnight, a Maggie Elliott Film Festival had, once more, catapulted her into the bright light of celebrity. Americans loved her movies. She was a star again.

One afternoon rolled in front of their massive window overlooking the bay, Maggie reached out to touch her husband's hand. "Elliott, my perfect Elliott," the hint of a smile crossed her lips. "All along, it was just you and I, old sport.

My only love and me. You better head home before this snow starts to stick."

Stick? Even after seventy-three years, arguing with this girl was still pointless. A kiss on the cheek remained the best response.